VOLUME
SIX

Sa

IMAGE COMICS, INC.

Robert Kirkman
CHIEF OPERATING OFFICER

Erik Larsen
CHIEF FINANCIAL OFFICER

Todd McFarlane
PRESIDENT

Marc Silvestri
CHIEF EXECUTIVE OFFICER

Jim Valentino
VICE-PRESIDENT

Eric Stephenson
PUBLISHER

Corey Murphy
DIRECTOR OF SALES

Jeff Boison
DIRECTOR OF PUBLISHING
PLANNING & BOOK TRADE SALES

Jeremy Sullivan
DIRECTOR OF DIGITAL SALES

Kat Salazar
DIRECTOR OF PR & MARKETING

Emily Miller
DIRECTOR OF OPERATIONS

Branwyn Bigglestone
SENIOR ACCOUNTS MANAGER

Sarah Mello
ACCOUNTS MANAGER

Drew Gill
ART DIRECTOR

Jonathan Chan
PRODUCTION MANAGER

Meredith Wallace
PRINT MANAGER

Briah Skelly
PUBLICITY ASSISTANT

Sasha Head
SALES & MARKETING
PRODUCTION DESIGNER

Randy Okamura
DIGITAL PRODUCTION DESIGNER

David Brothers
BRANDING MANAGER

Ally Power
CONTENT MANAGER

Addison Duke
PRODUCTION ARTIST

Vincent Kukua
PRODUCTION ARTIST

Tricia Ramos
PRODUCTION ARTIST

Jeff Stang
DIRECT MARKET SALES
REPRESENTATIVE

Emilio Bautista
DIGITAL SALES ASSOCIATE

Leanna Caunter
ACCOUNTING ASSISTANT

Chloe Ramos-Peterson
ADMINISTRATIVE ASSISTANT

www.imagecomics.com

FIONA STAPLES
ARTIST

BRIAN K. VAUGHAN
WRITER

FONOGRAFIKS
LETTERING + DESIGN

ERIC STEPHENSON
COORDINATOR

CHAPTER
THIRTY-ONE

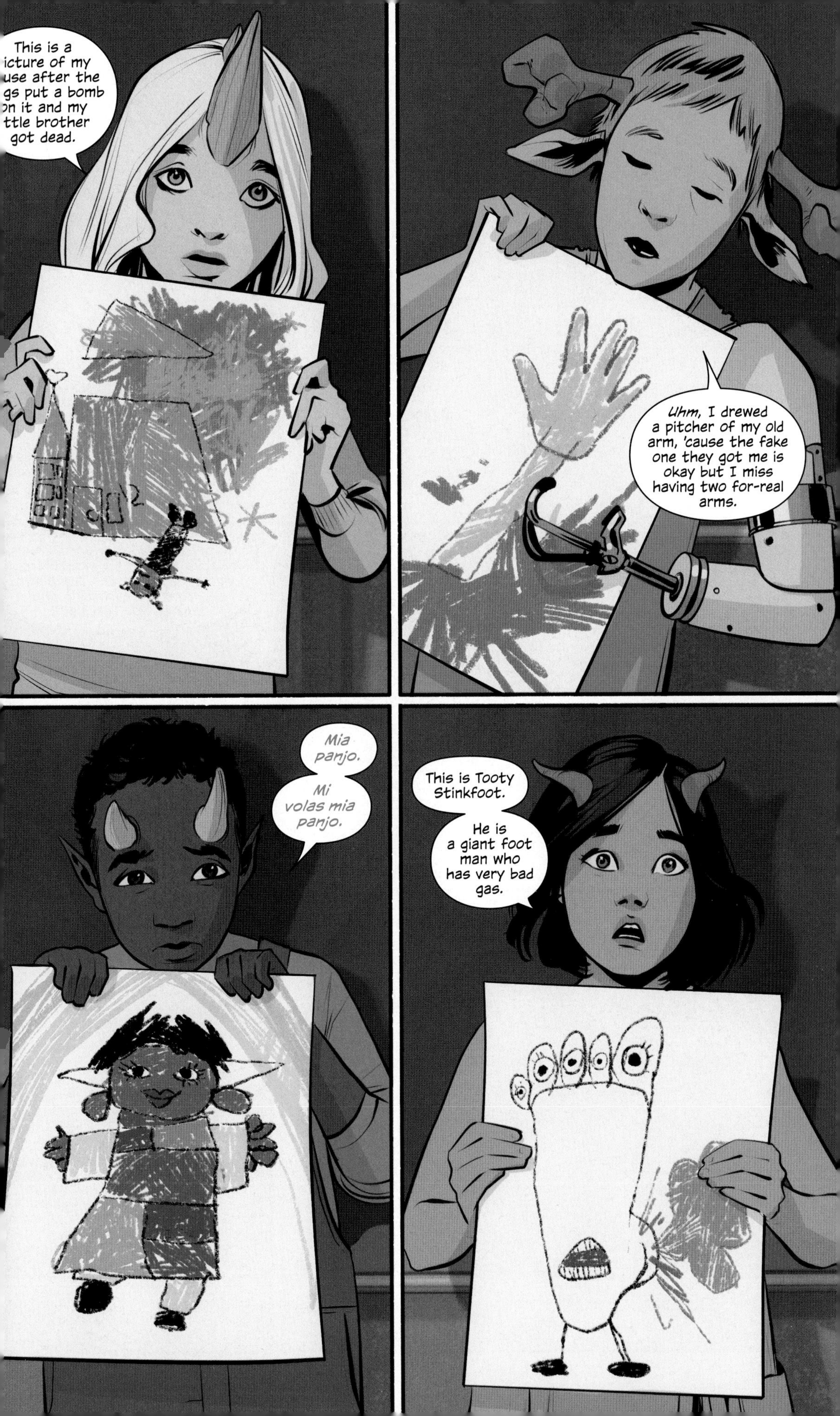
This is a icture of my use after the gs put a bomb n it and my ttle brother got dead.
Uhm, I drewed a pitcher of my old arm, 'cause the fake one they got me is okay but I miss having two for-real arms.
Mia panjo.
Mi volas mia panjo.
This is Tooty Stinkfoot.
He is a giant foot man who has very bad gas.

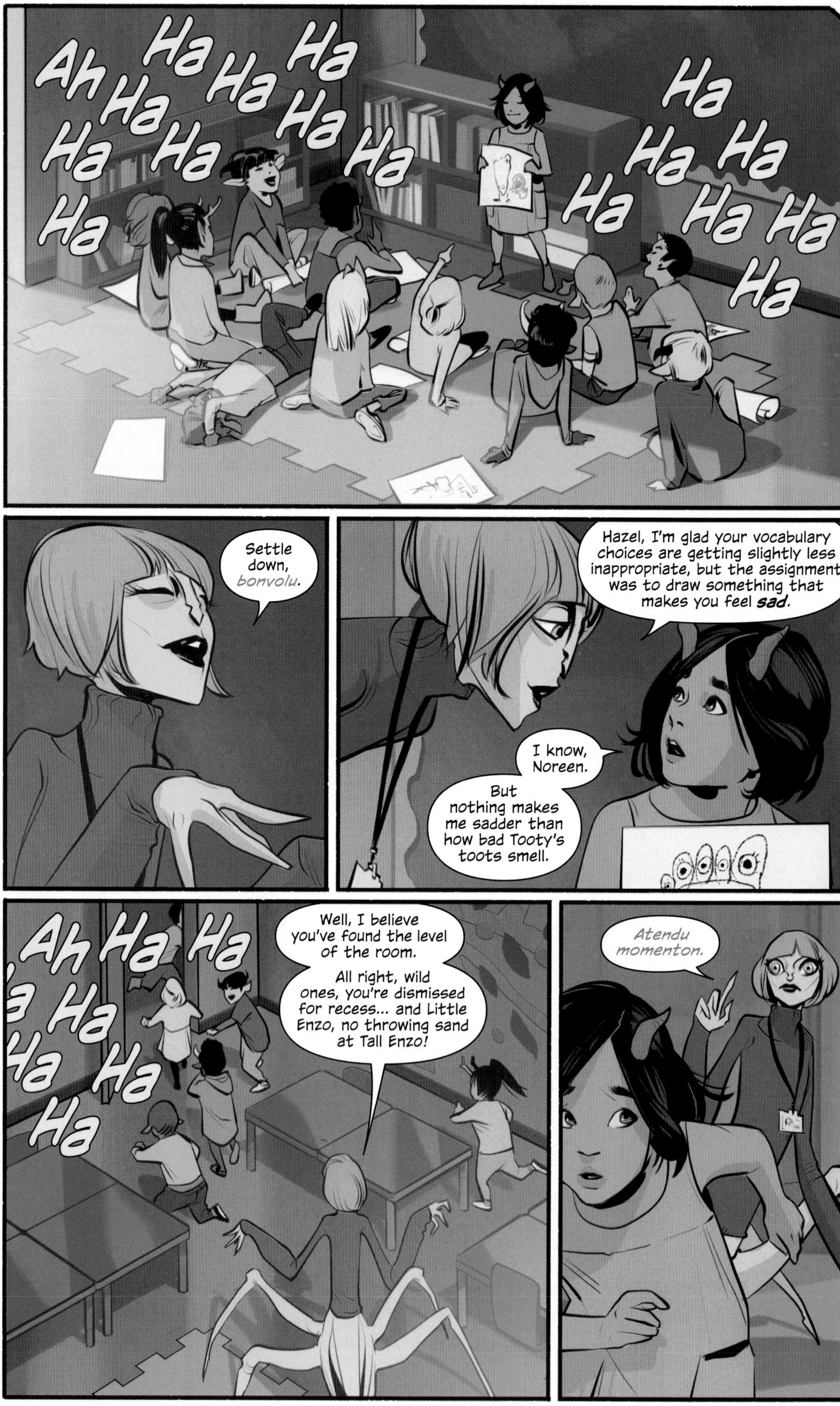
Ah Ha Ha Ha Ha Ha Ha Ha Ha Ha
Ha Ha Ha Ha Ha Ha Ha Ha
Settle down, *bonvolu.*
Hazel, I'm glad your vocabulary choices are getting slightly less inappropriate, but the assignment was to draw something that makes you feel ***sad.***
I know, Noreen.
But nothing makes me sadder than how bad Tooty's toots smell.
Ah Ha Ha Ha Ha Ha Ha Ha
Well, I believe you've found the level of the room.
All right, wild ones, you're dismissed for recess... and Little Enzo, no throwing sand at Tall Enzo!
Atendu momenton.

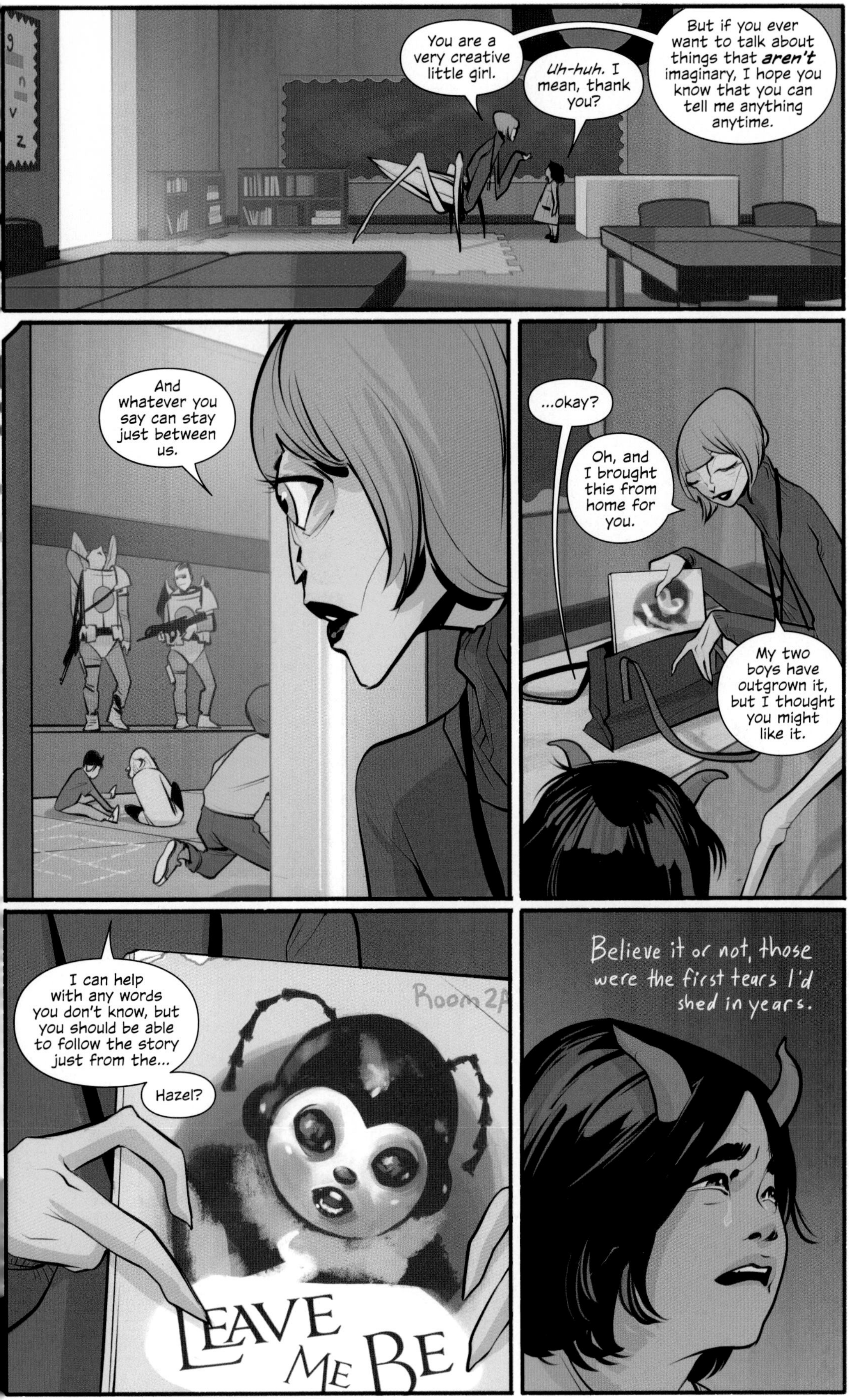
You are a very creative little girl.
Uh-huh. I mean, thank you?
But if you ever want to talk about things that **aren't** imaginary, I hope you know that you can tell me anything anytime.
And whatever you say can stay just between us.
...okay?
Oh, and I brought this from home for you.
My two boys have outgrown it, but I thought you might like it.
I can help with any words you don't know, but you should be able to follow the story just from the...
Hazel?
Room 2A
LEAVE ME BE
Believe it or not, those were the first tears I'd shed in years.

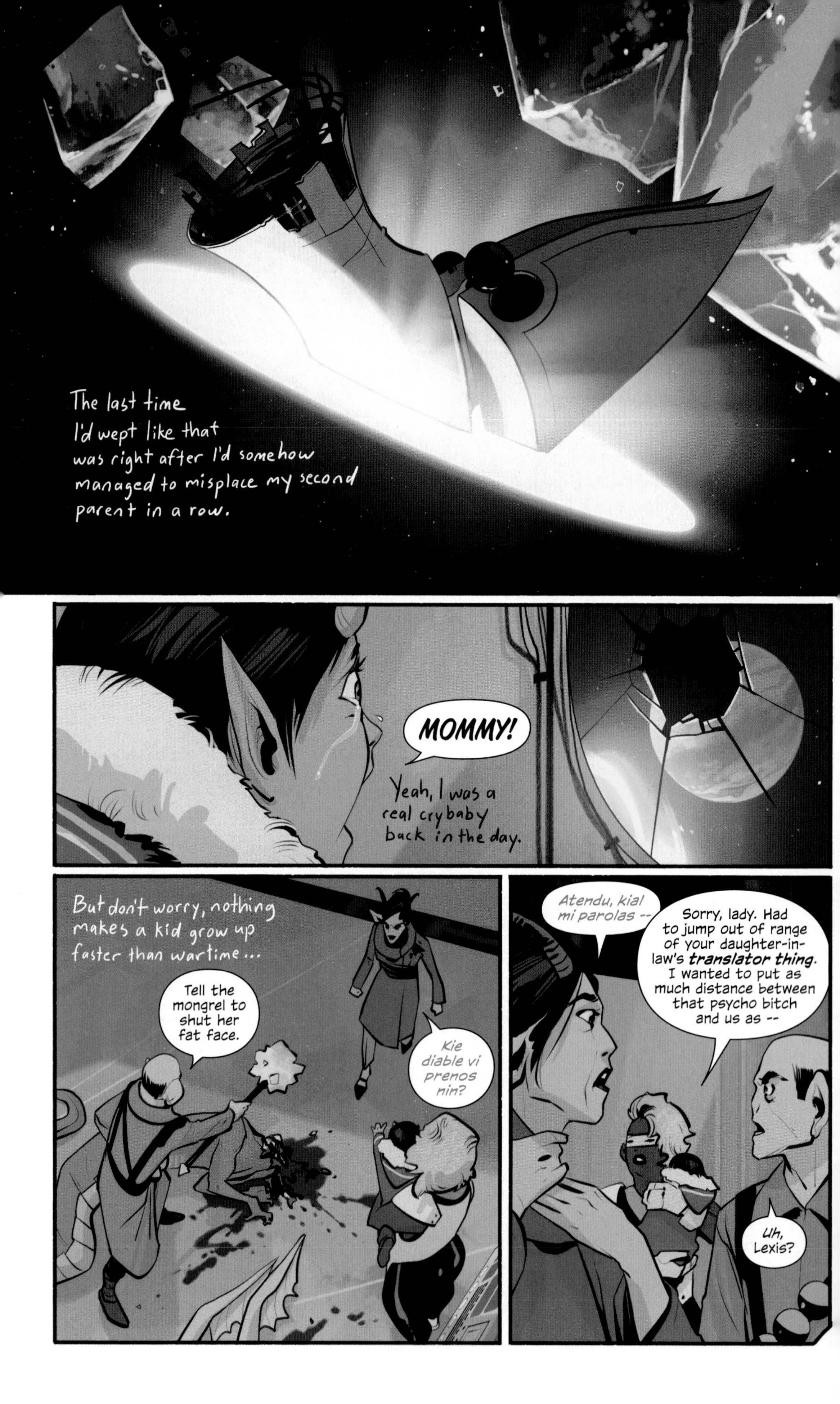
The last time I'd wept like that was right after I'd somehow managed to misplace my second parent in a row.
MOMMY!
Yeah, I was a real crybaby back in the day.
But don't worry, nothing makes a kid grow up faster than wartime...
Tell the mongrel to shut her fat face.
Kie diable vi prenos nin?
Atendu, kial mi parolas --
Sorry, lady. Had to jump out of range of your daughter-in-law's translator thing. I wanted to put as much distance between that psycho bitch and us as --
Uh, Lexis?

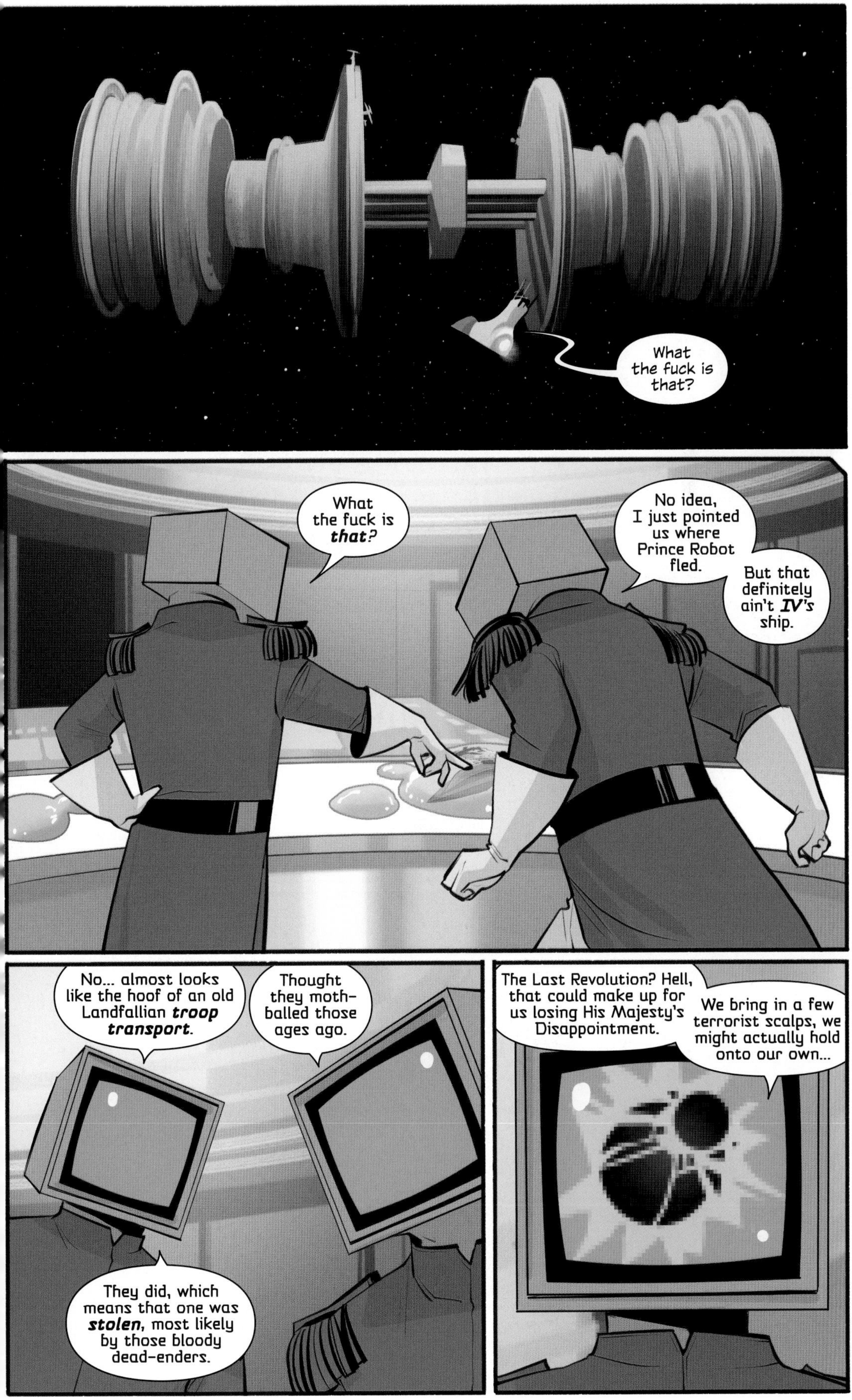
What the fuck is that?
What the fuck is *that*?
No idea, I just pointed us where Prince Robot fled.
But that definitely ain't *IV's* ship.
No... almost looks like the hoof of an old Landfallian *troop transport*.
Thought they moth-balled those ages ago.
They did, which means that one was *stolen*, most likely by those bloody dead-enders.
The Last Revolution? Hell, that could make up for us losing His Majesty's Disappointment.
We bring in a few terrorist scalps, we might actually hold onto our own...

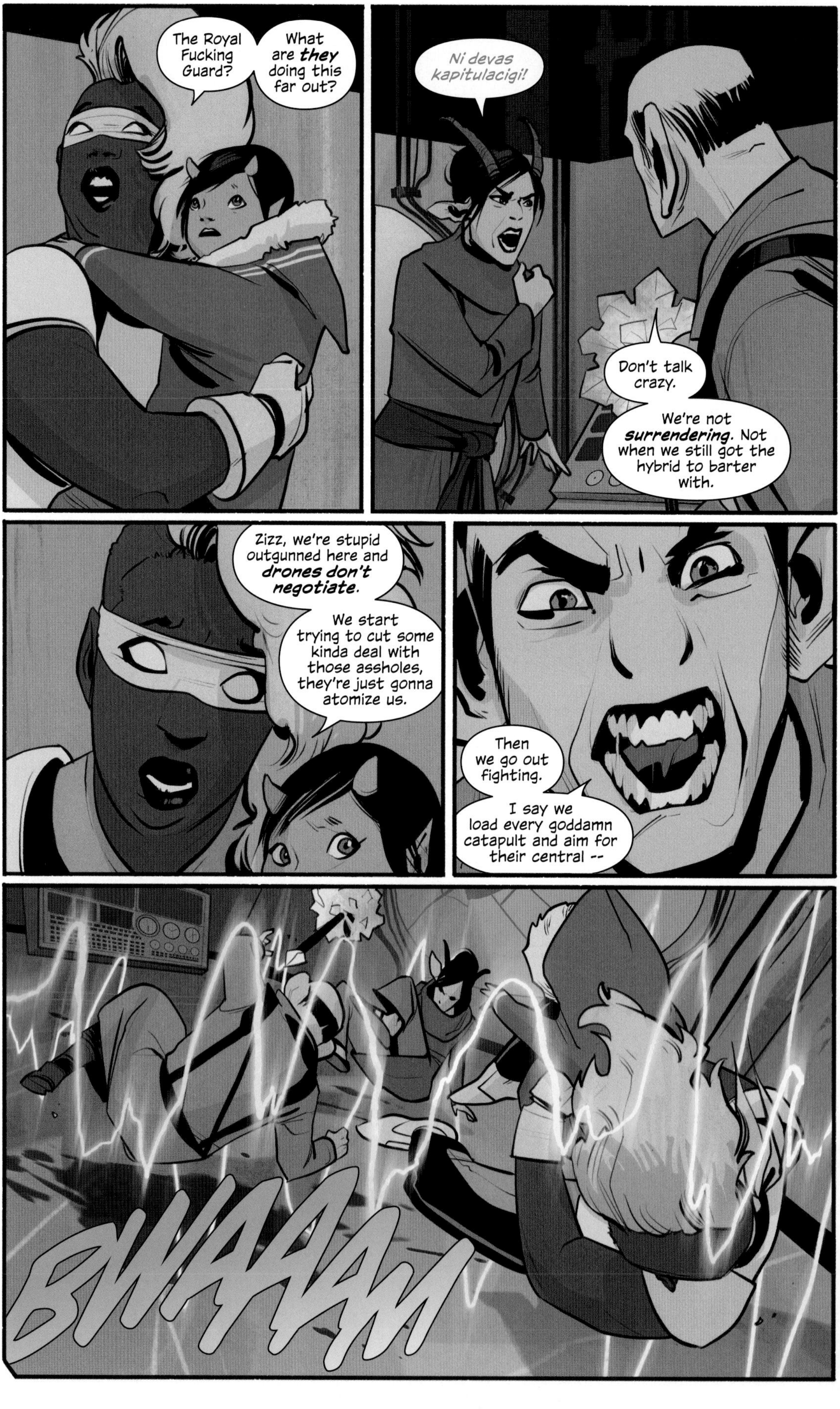
The Royal Fucking Guard?
What are *they* doing this far out?
Ni devas kapitulacigi!
Don't talk crazy.
We're not *surrendering*. Not when we still got the hybrid to barter with.
Zizz, we're stupid outgunned here and *drones don't negotiate*.
We start trying to cut some kinda deal with those assholes, they're just gonna atomize us.
Then we go out fighting.
I say we load every goddamn catapult and aim for their central --
BWAAAM

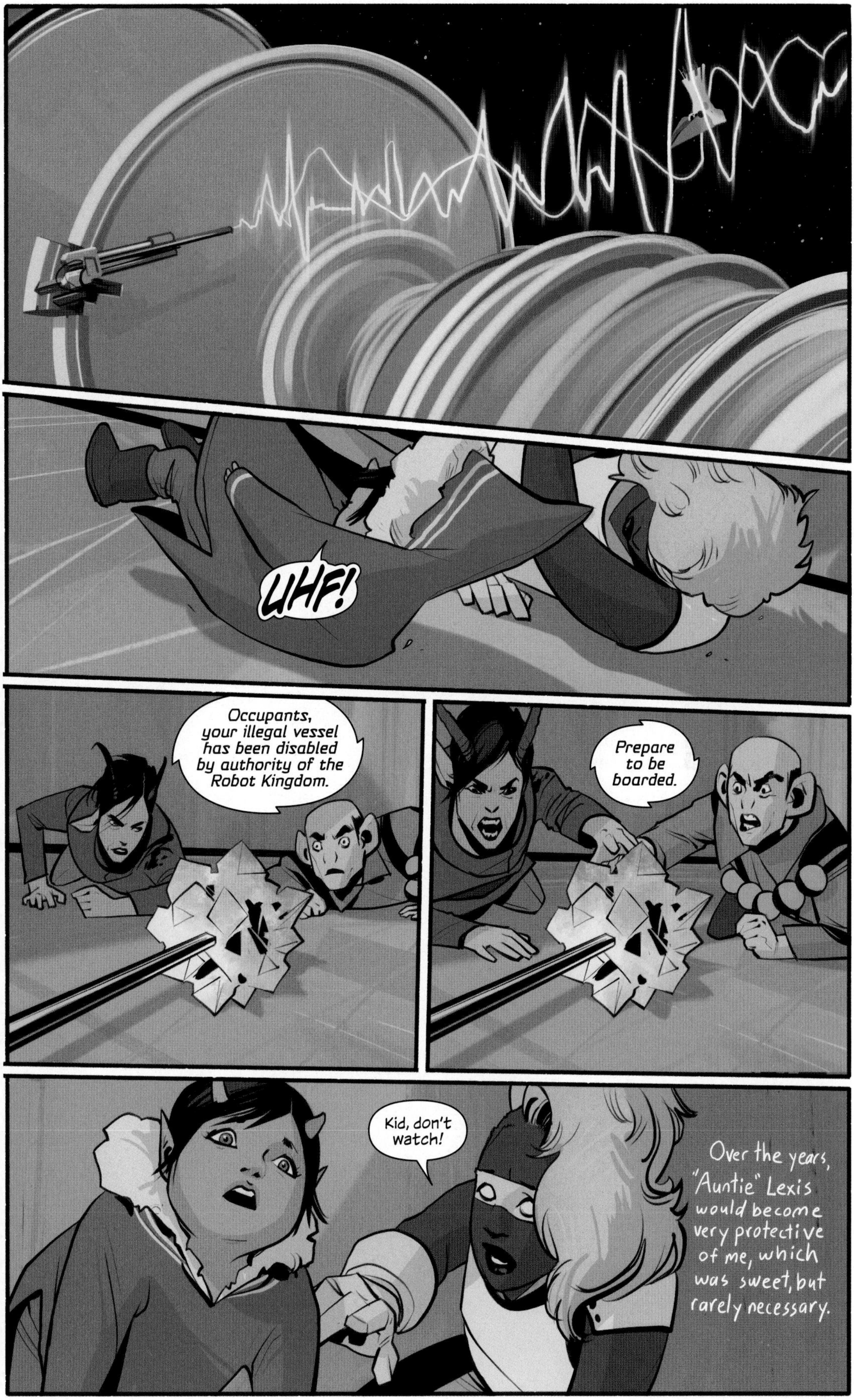
UHF!
Occupants, your illegal vessel has been disabled by authority of the Robot Kingdom.
Prepare to be boarded.
Kid, don't watch!
Over the years, "Auntie" Lexis would become very protective of me, which was sweet, but rarely necessary.

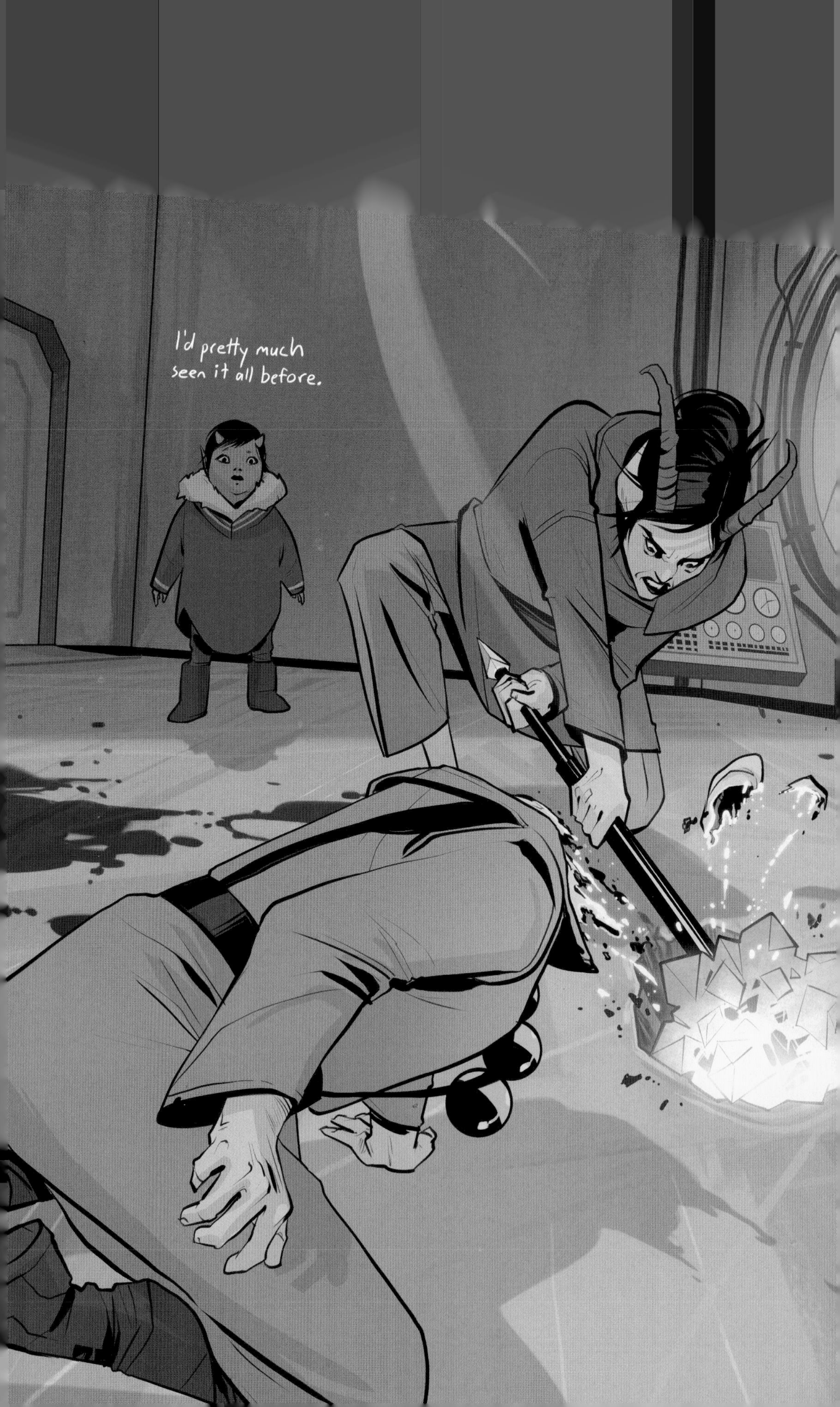
I'd pretty much seen it all before.

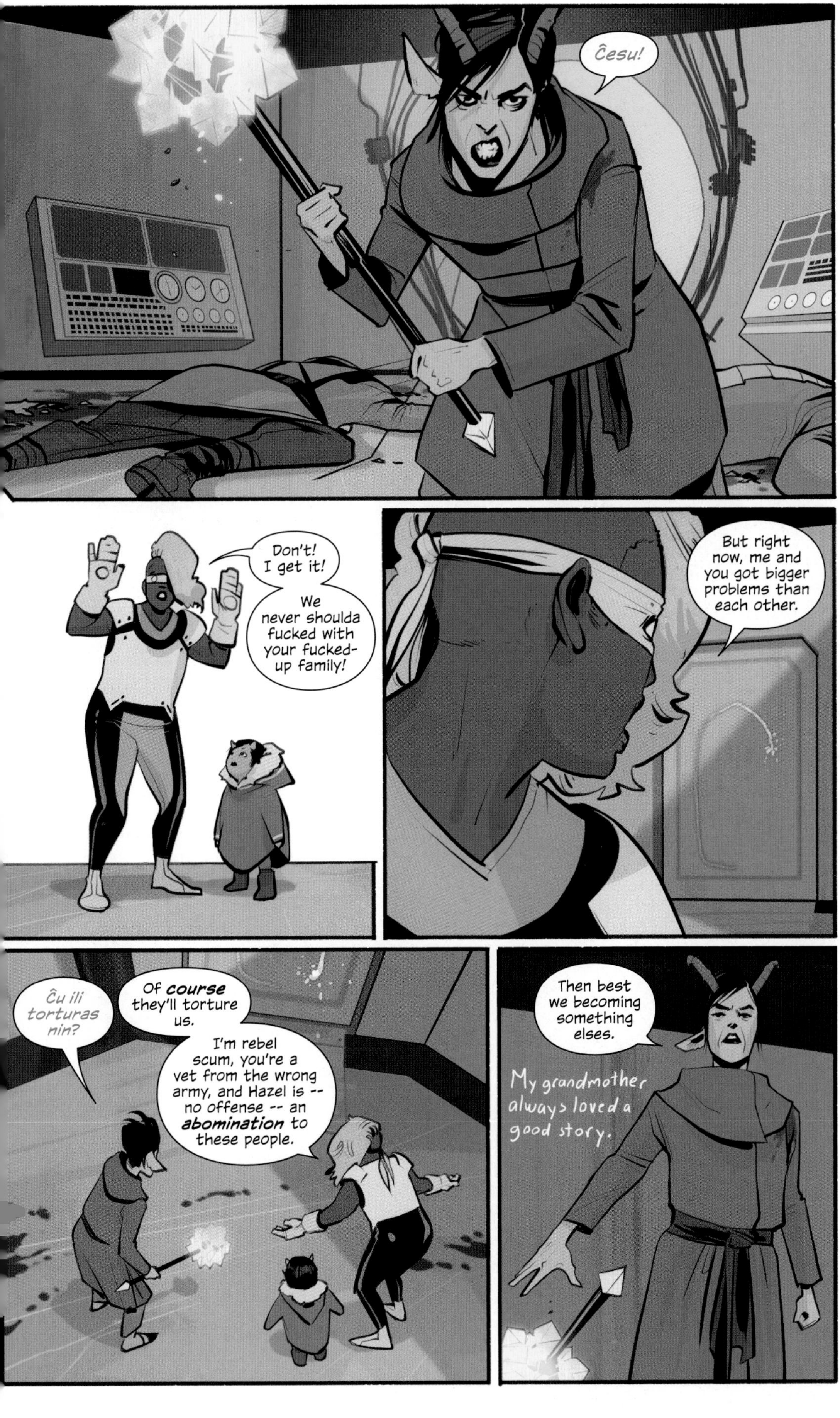
Ĉesu!
Don't! I get it!
We never shoulda fucked with your fucked-up family!
But right now, me and you got bigger problems than each other.
Ĉu ili torturas nin?
Of **course** they'll torture us.
I'm rebel scum, you're a vet from the wrong army, and Hazel is -- no offense -- an ***abomination*** to these people.
Then best we becoming something elses.
My grandmother always loved a good story.

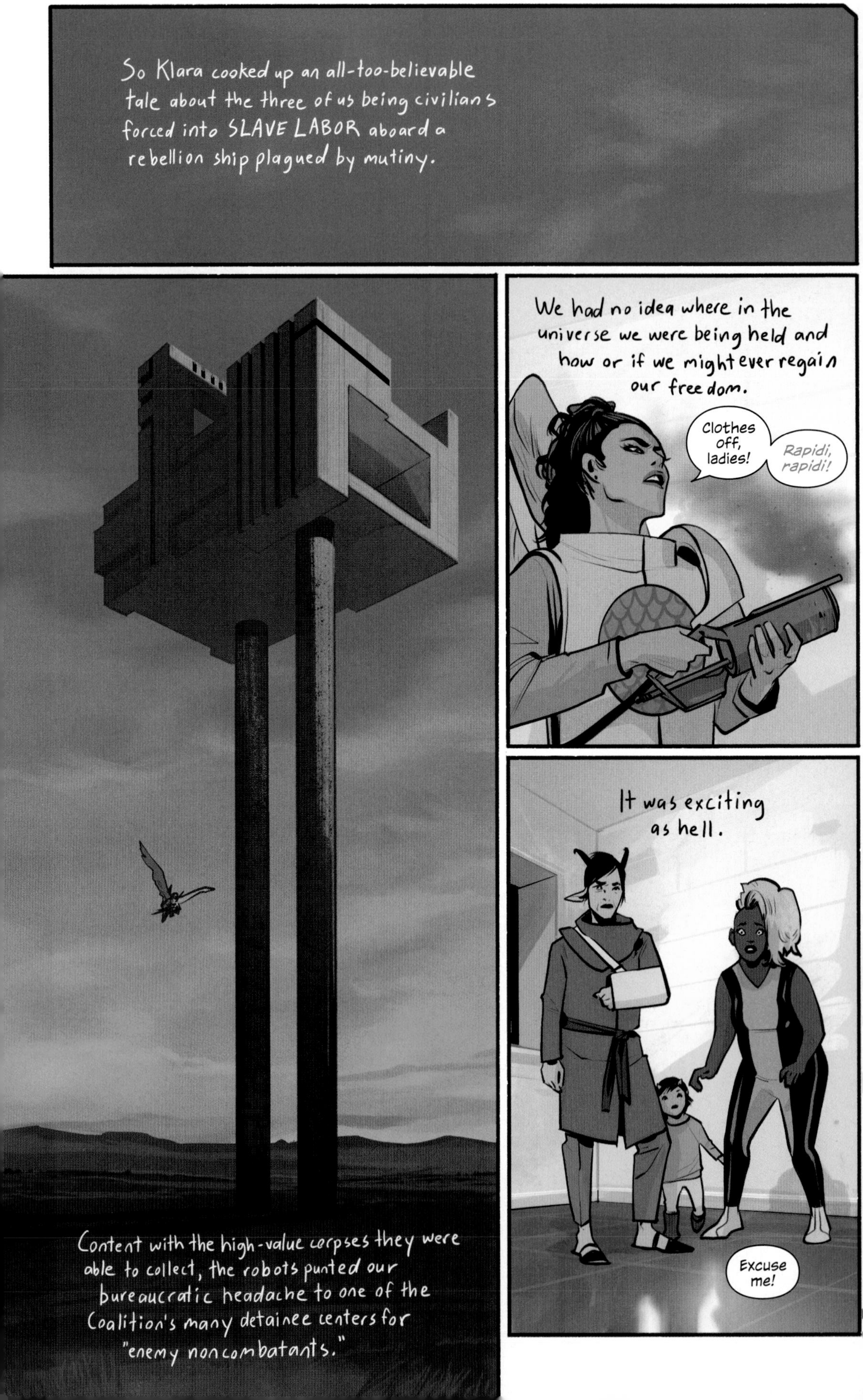
So Klara cooked up an all-too-believable tale about the three of us being civilians forced into SLAVE LABOR aboard a rebellion ship plagued by mutiny.
Content with the high-value corpses they were able to collect, the robots punted our bureaucratic headache to one of the Coalition's many detainee centers for "enemy noncombatants."
We had no idea where in the universe we were being held and how or if we might ever regain our freedom.
Clothes off, ladies!
Rapidi, rapidi!
It was exciting as hell.
Excuse me!

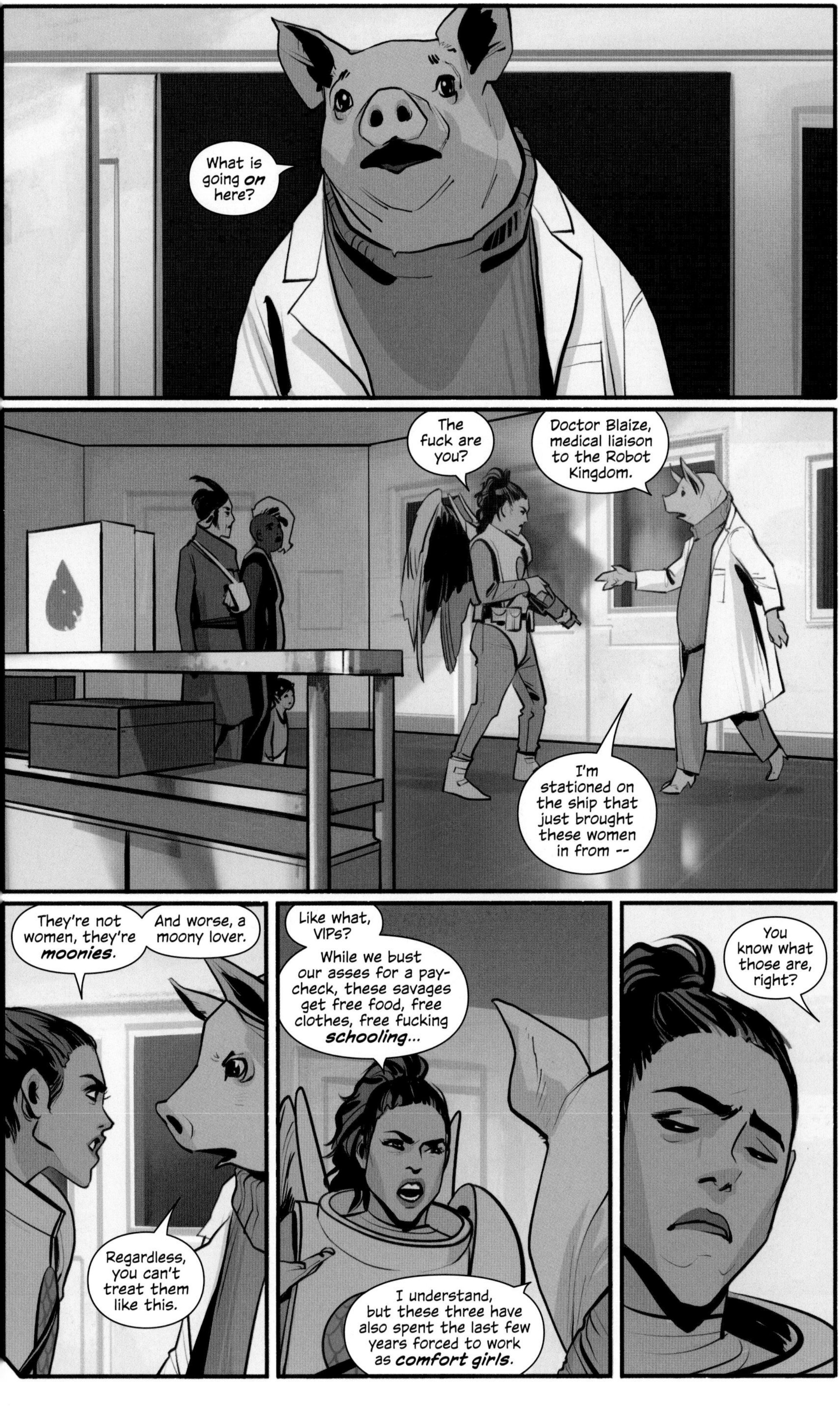
What is going *on* here?
The fuck are you?
Doctor Blaize, medical liaison to the Robot Kingdom.
I'm stationed on the ship that just brought these women in from --
They're not women, they're ***moonies***.
And worse, a moony lover.
Regardless, you can't treat them like this.
Like what, VIPs?
While we bust our asses for a pay-check, these savages get free food, free clothes, free fucking ***schooling***...
I understand, but these three have also spent the last few years forced to work as ***comfort girls***.
You know what those are, right?

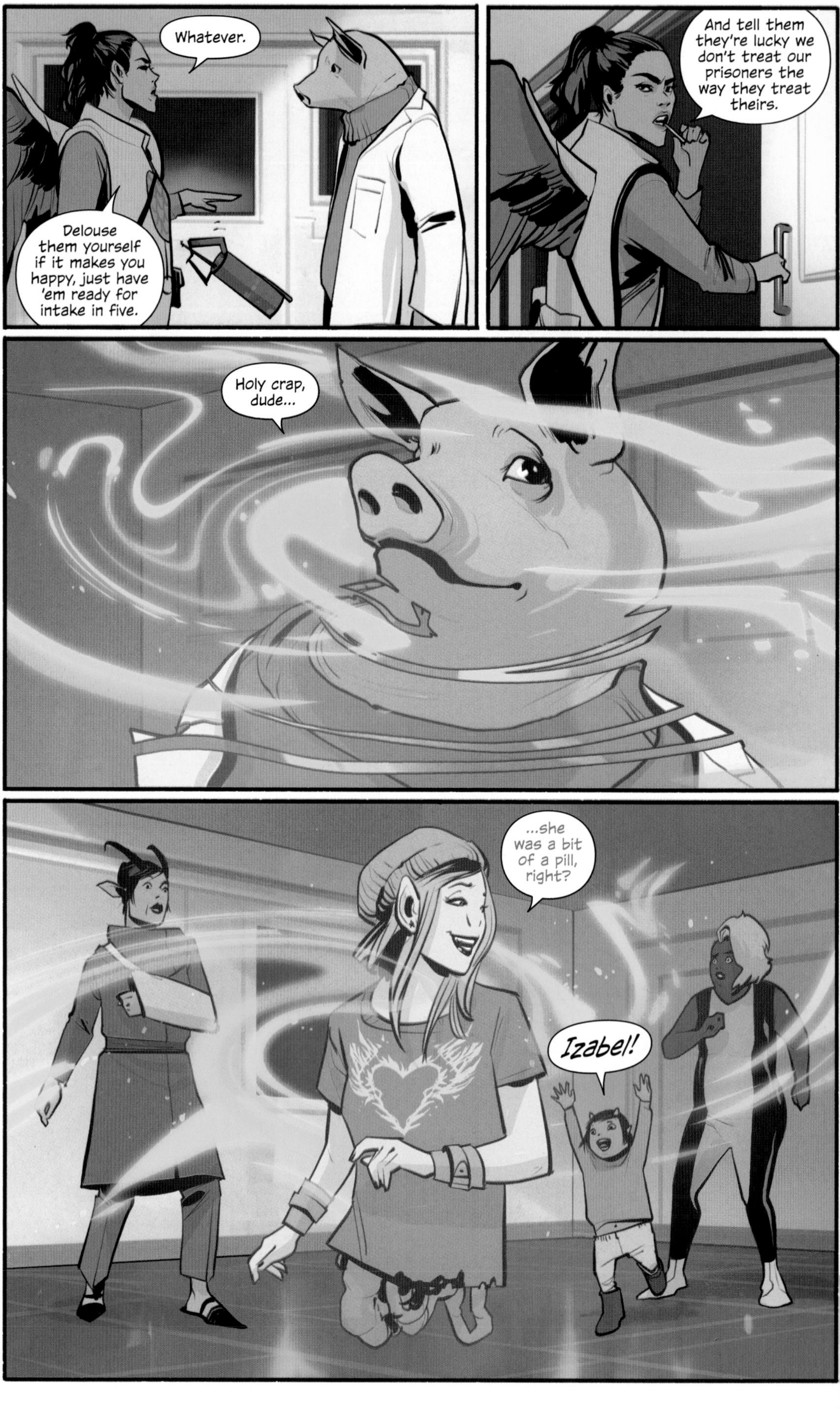

Whatever.
Delouse them yourself if it makes you happy, just have 'em ready for intake in five.
And tell them they're lucky we don't treat our prisoners the way they treat theirs.
Holy crap, dude...
...she was a bit of a pill, right?
Izabel!

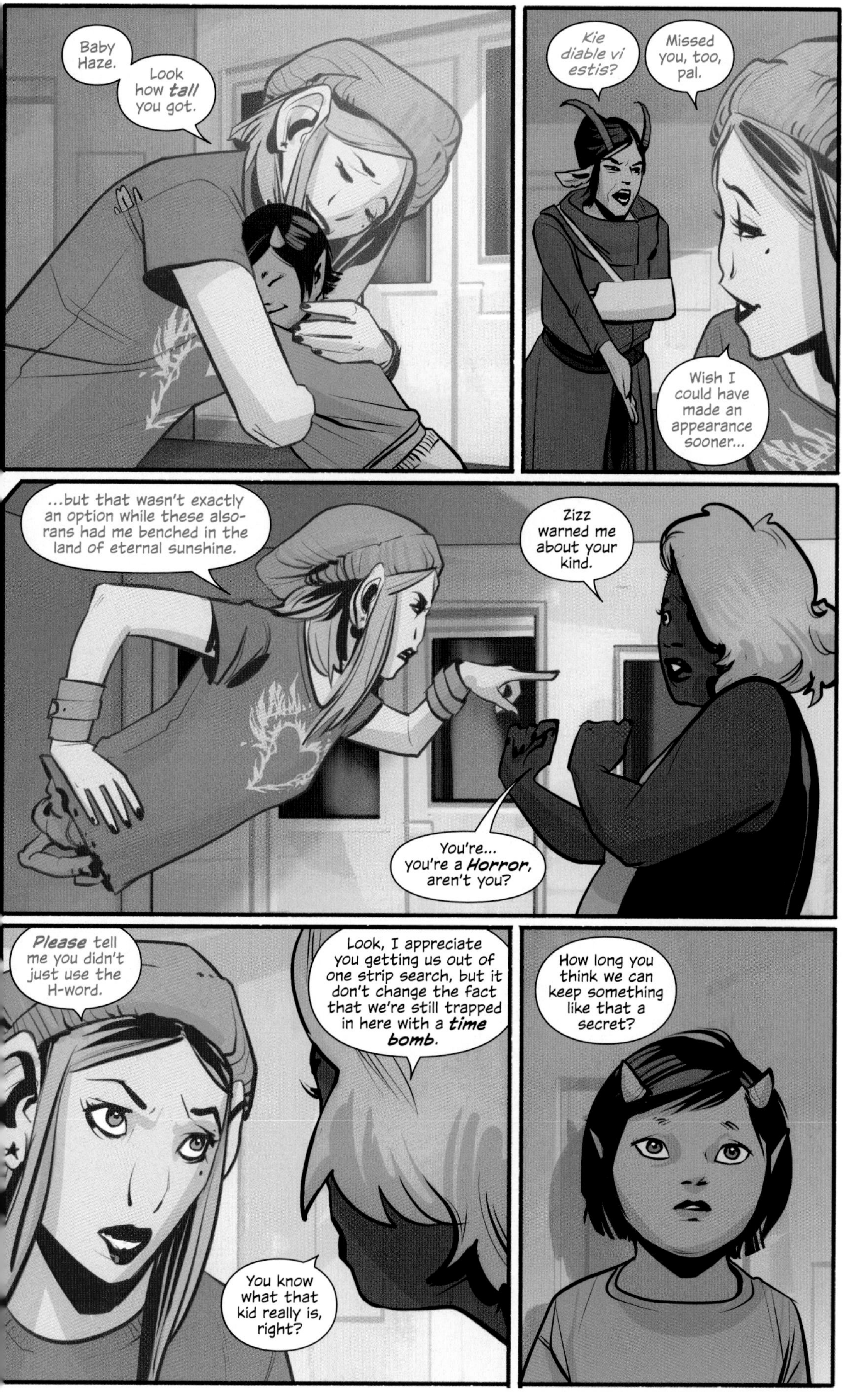
Baby Haze.
Look how *tall* you got.
Kie diable vi estis?
Missed you, too, pal.
Wish I could have made an appearance sooner...
...but that wasn't exactly an option while these also-rans had me benched in the land of eternal sunshine.
Zizz warned me about your kind.
You're... you're a *Horror*, aren't you?
Please tell me you didn't just use the H-word.
Look, I appreciate you getting us out of one strip search, but it don't change the fact that we're still trapped in here with a *time bomb*.
You know what that kid really is, right?
How long you think we can keep something like that a secret?

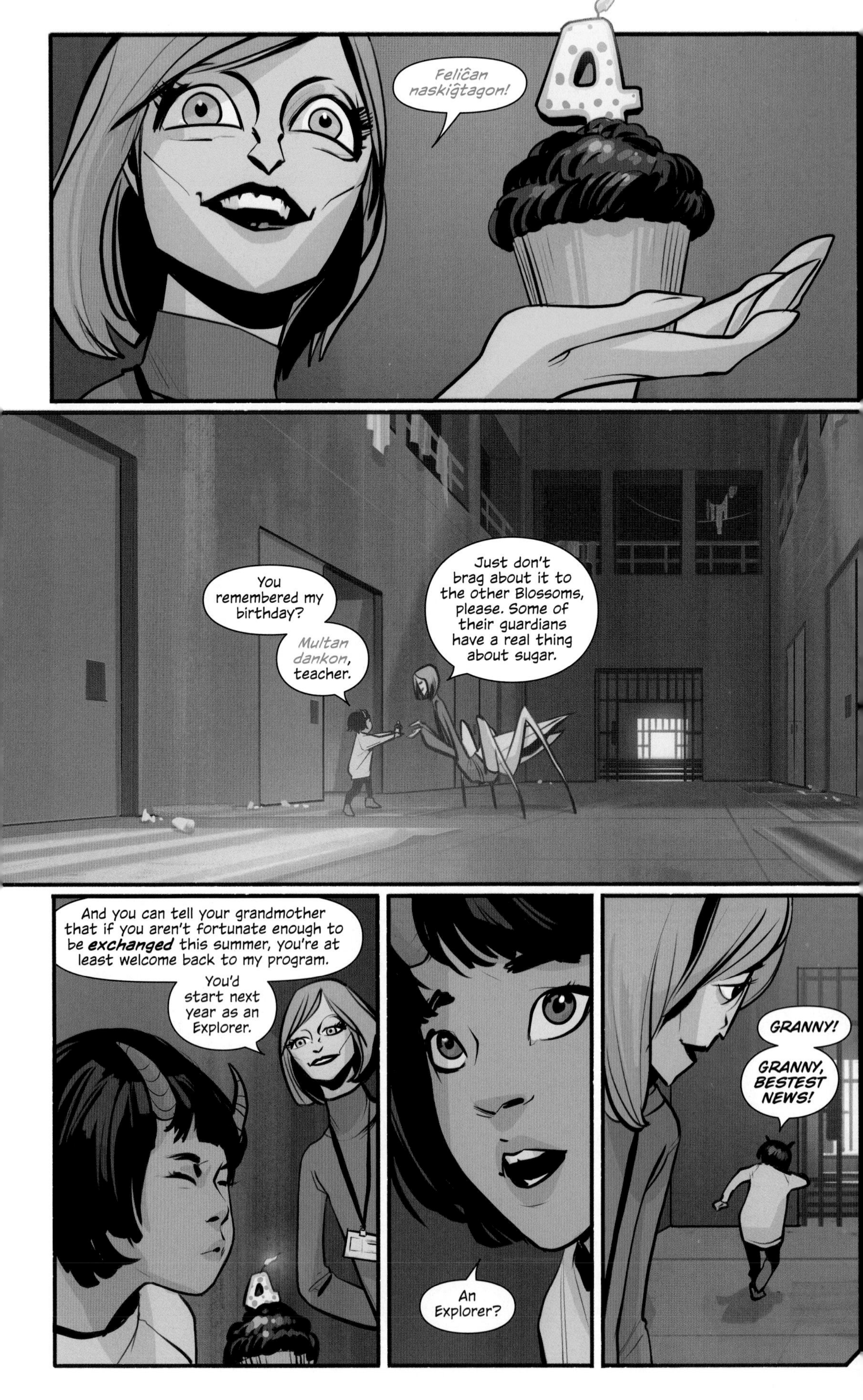
Feliĉan naskiĝtagon!
You remembered my birthday?
Multan dankon, teacher.
Just don't brag about it to the other Blossoms, please. Some of their guardians have a real thing about sugar.
And you can tell your grandmother that if you aren't fortunate enough to be **exchanged** this summer, you're at least welcome back to my program.
You'd start next year as an Explorer.
An Explorer?
GRANNY!
GRANNY, BESTEST NEWS!

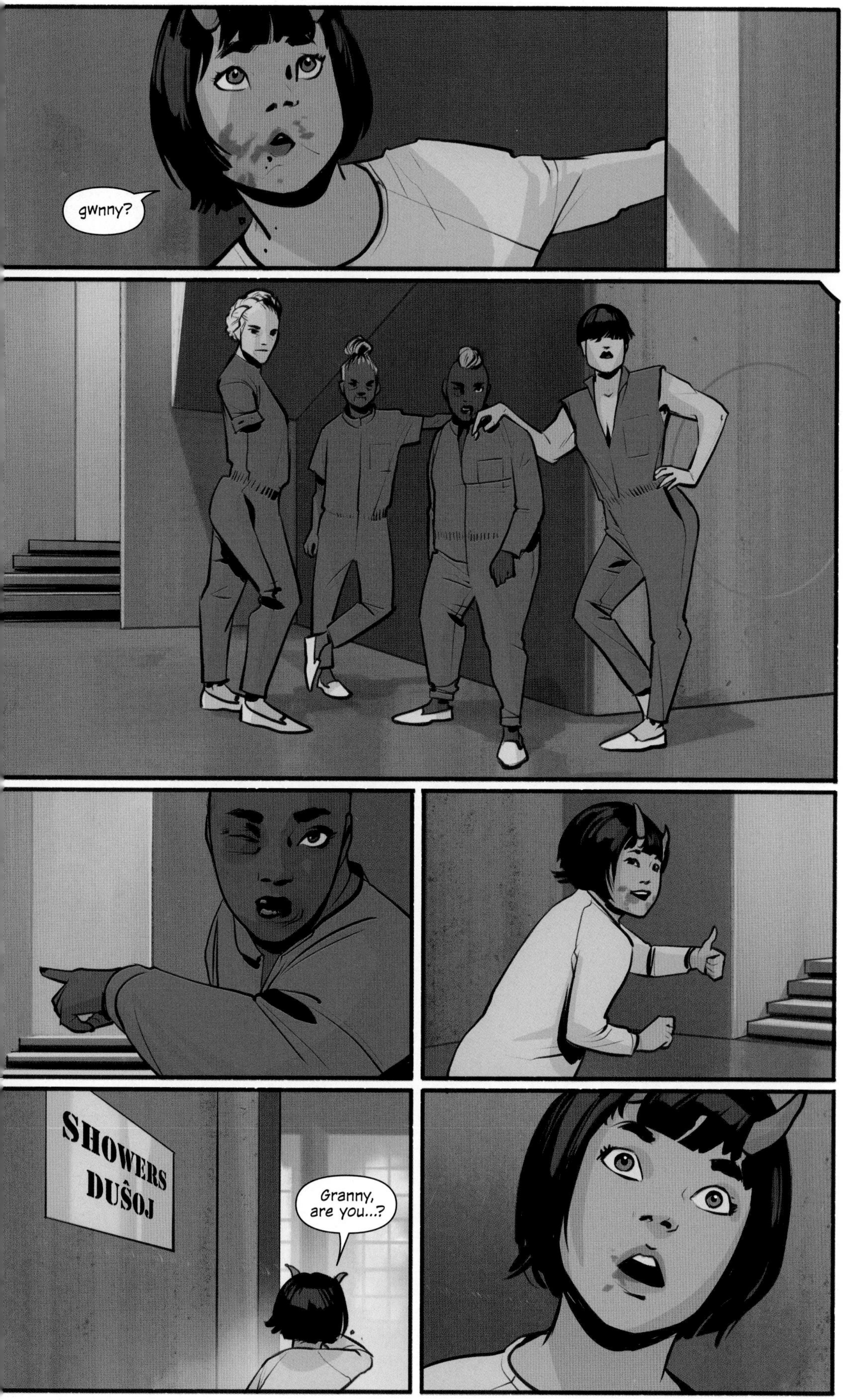
gwnny?
SHOWERS
DUŜOJ
Granny, are you...?

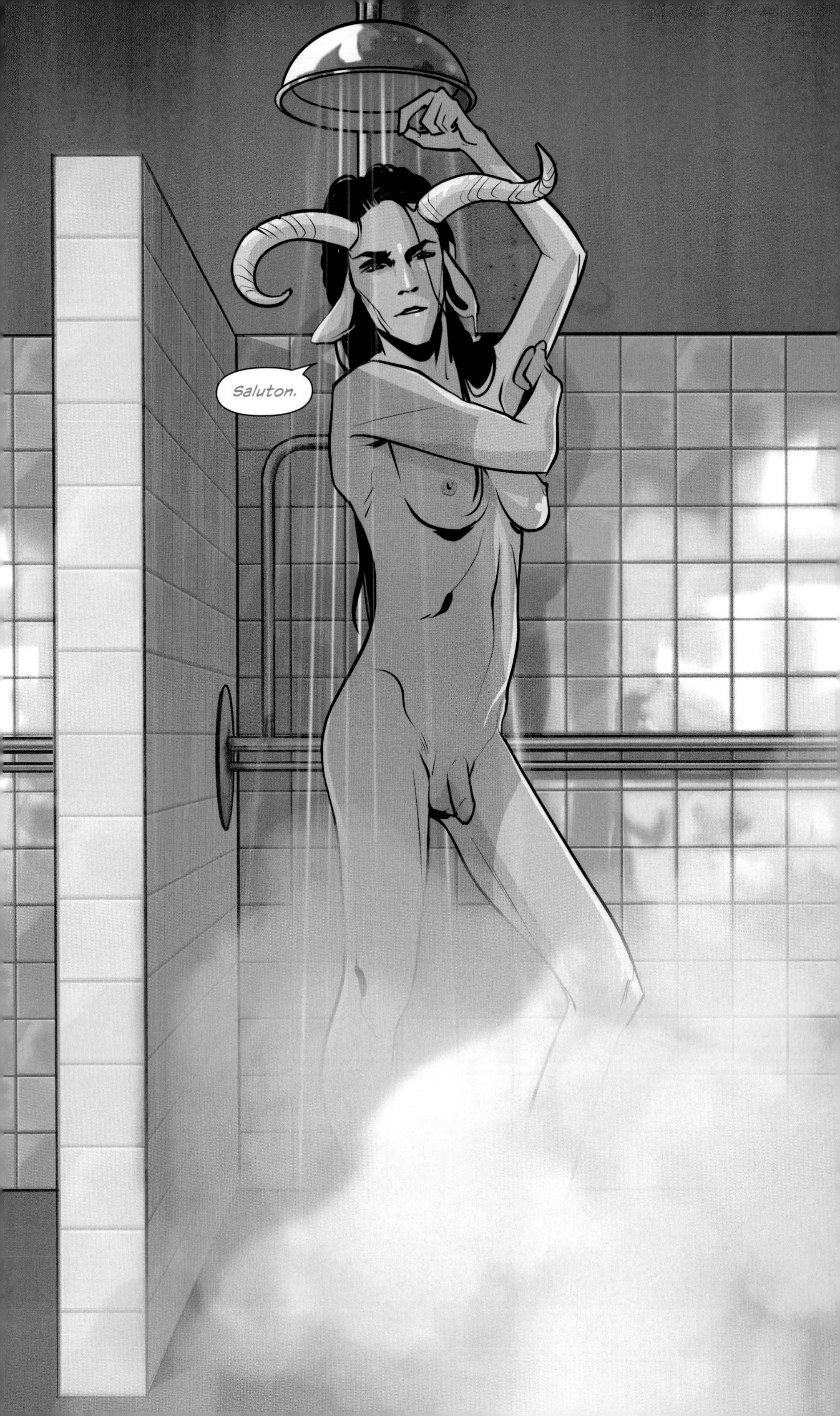
Saluton.

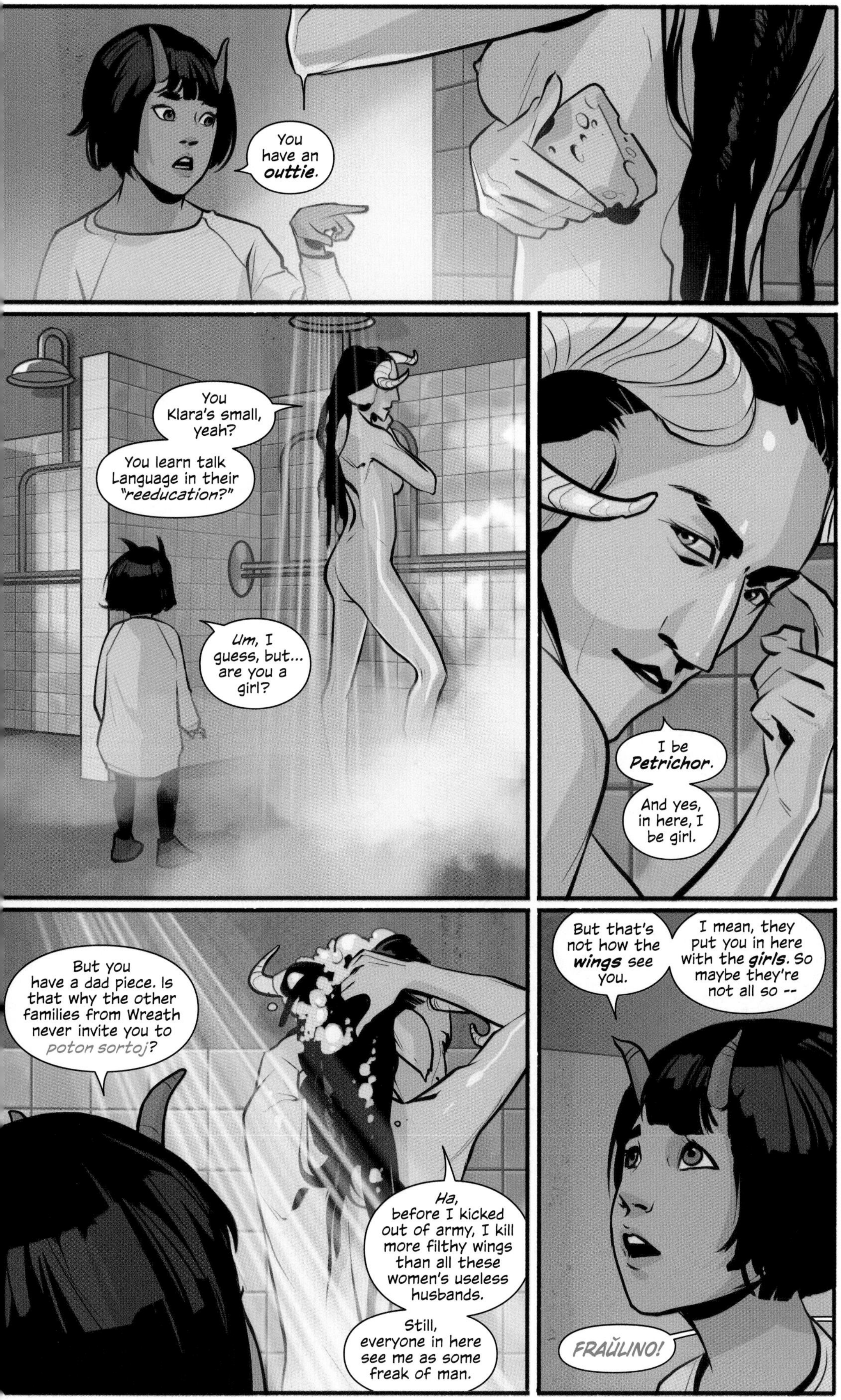

You have an *outtie*.
You Klara's small, yeah?
You learn talk Language in their *"reeducation?"*
Um, I guess, but... are you a girl?
I be **Petrichor**.
And yes, in here, I be girl.
But you have a dad piece. Is that why the other families from Wreath never invite you to *poton sortoj*?
Ha, before I kicked out of army, I kill more filthy wings than all these women's useless husbands.
Still, everyone in here see me as some freak of man.
But that's not how the ***wings*** see you.
I mean, they put you in here with the ***girls***. So maybe they're not all so --
FRAŬLINO!

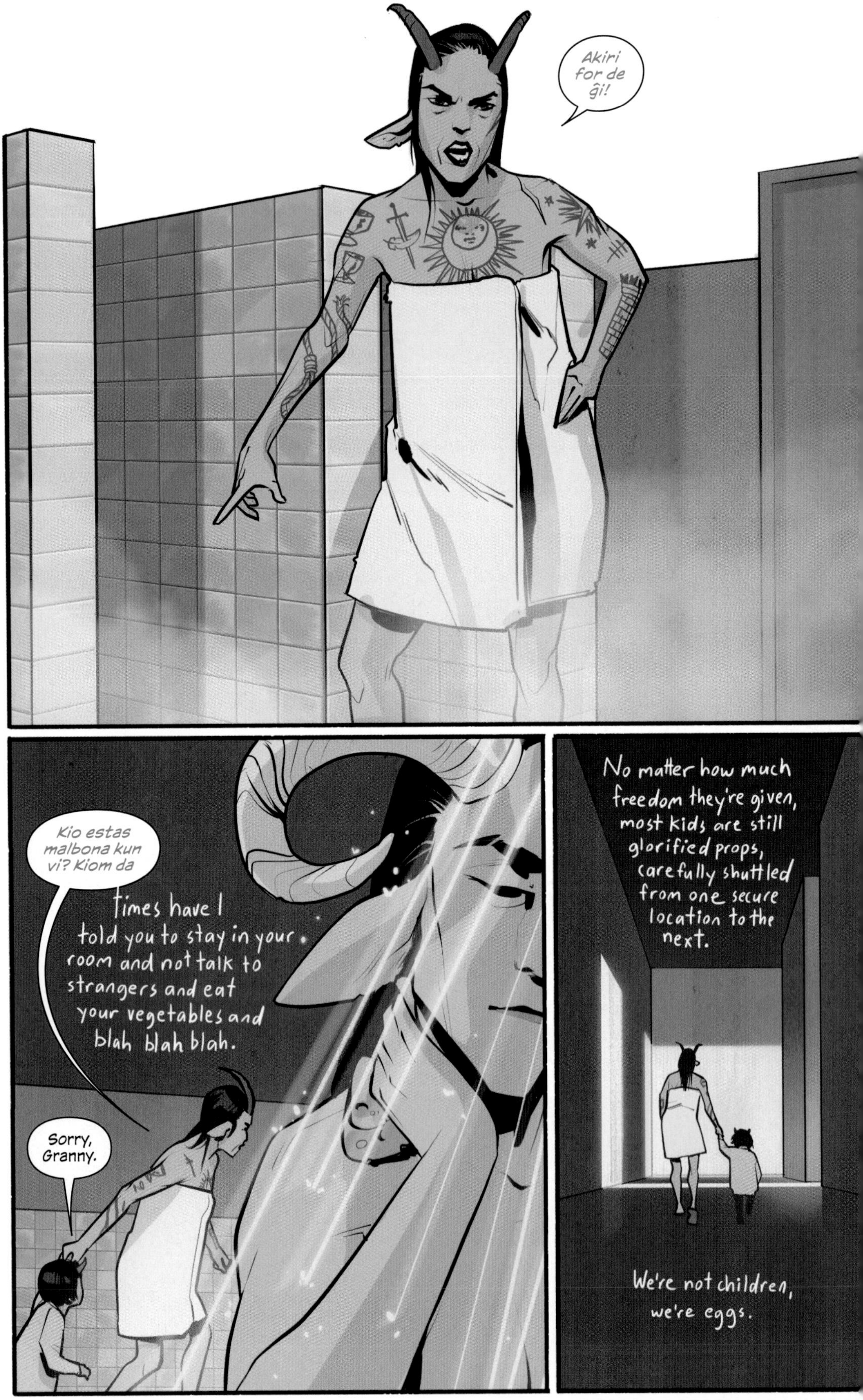
Akiri for de ĝi!
Kio estas malbona kun vi? Kiom da
times have I told you to stay in your room and not talk to strangers and eat your vegetables and blah blah blah.
Sorry, Granny.
No matter how much freedom they're given, most kids are still glorified props, carefully shuttled from one secure location to the next.
We're not children, we're eggs.

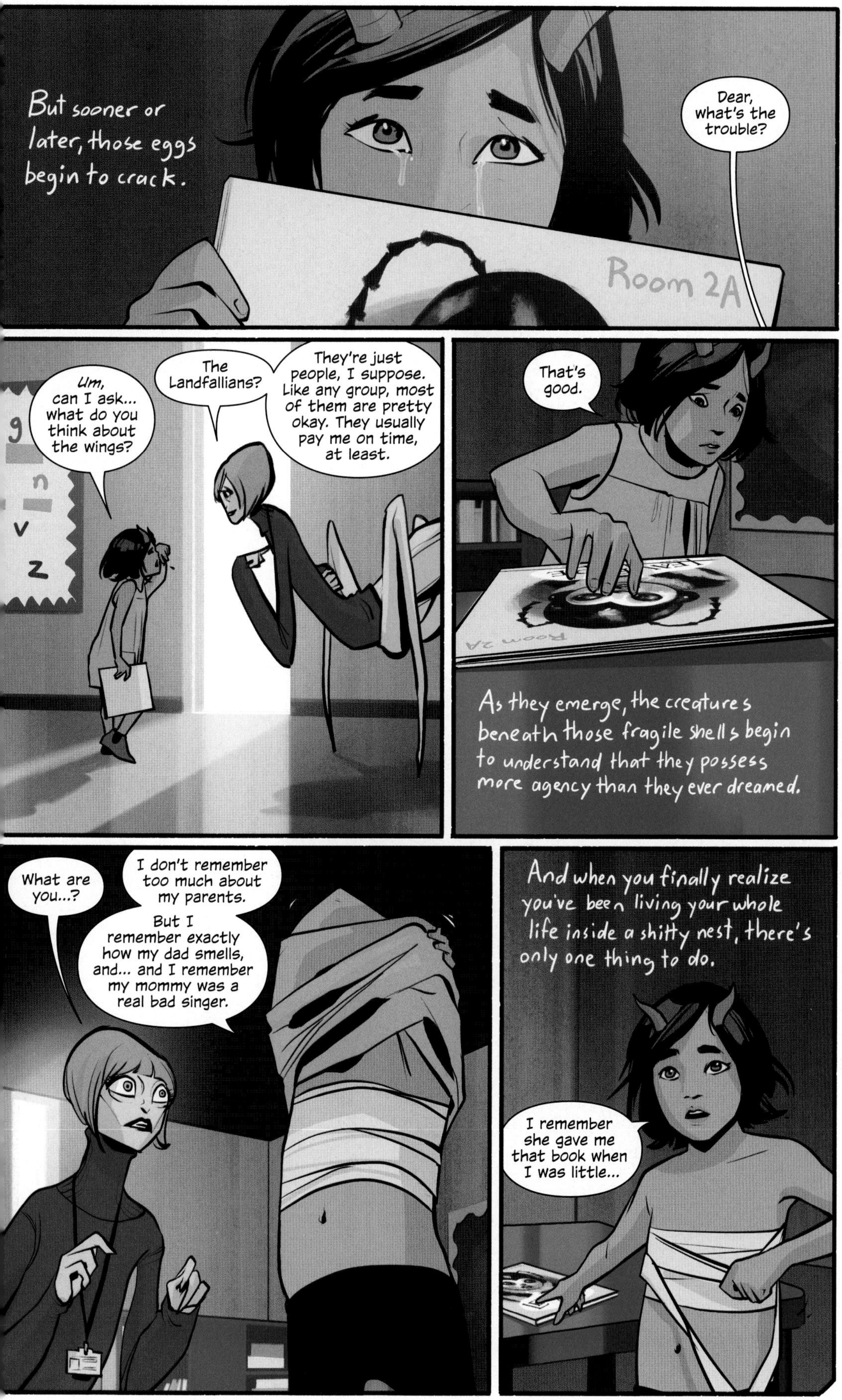

But sooner or later, those eggs begin to crack.
Dear, what's the trouble?
Room 2A
Um, can I ask... what do you think about the wings?
The Landfallians?
They're just people, I suppose. Like any group, most of them are pretty okay. They usually pay me on time, at least.
That's good.
Room 2A
As they emerge, the creatures beneath those fragile shells begin to understand that they possess more agency than they ever dreamed.
What are you...?
I don't remember too much about my parents.
But I remember exactly how my dad smells, and... and I remember my mommy was a real bad singer.
And when you finally realize you've been living your whole life inside a shitty nest, there's only one thing to do.
I remember she gave me that book when I was little...

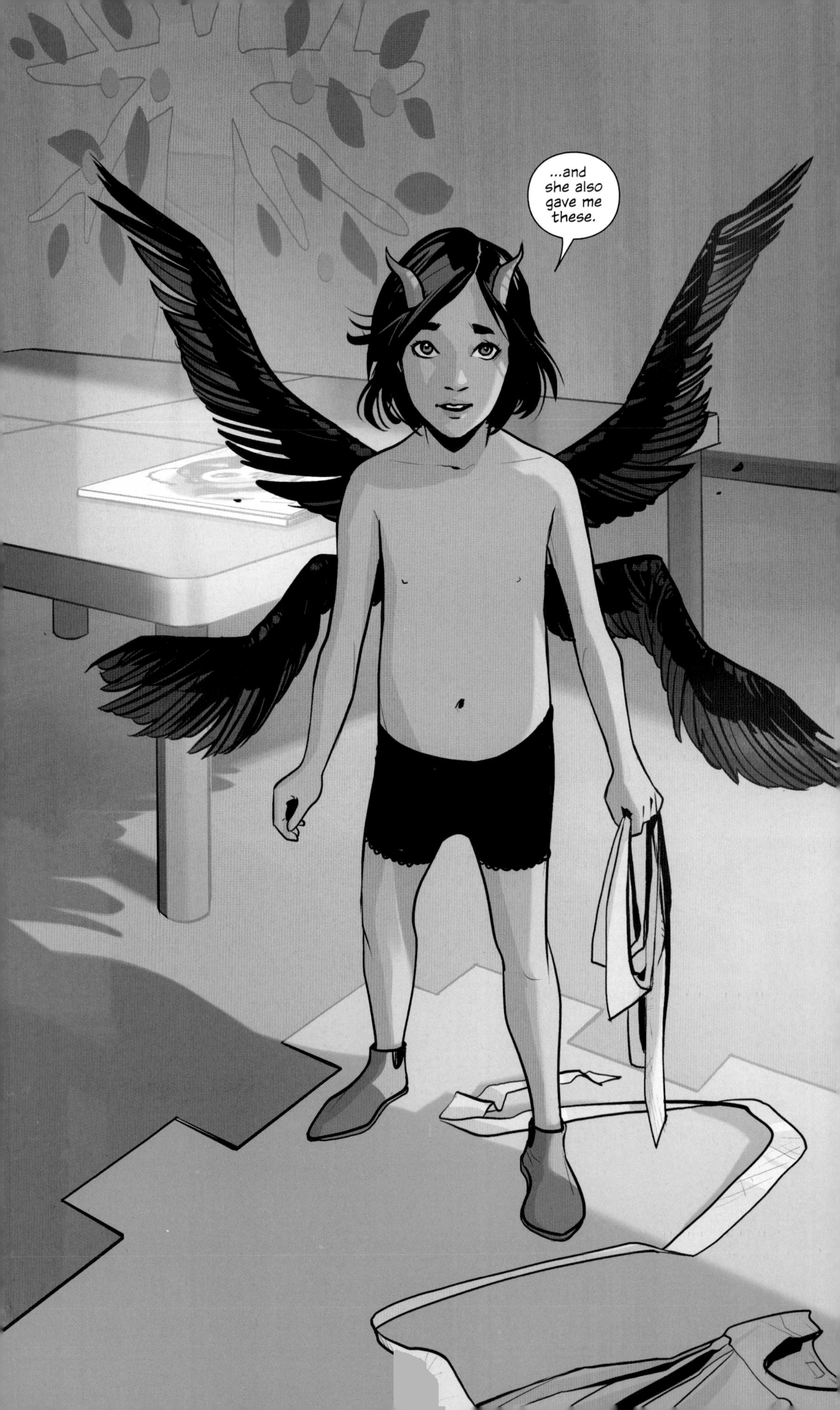
...and she also gave me these.

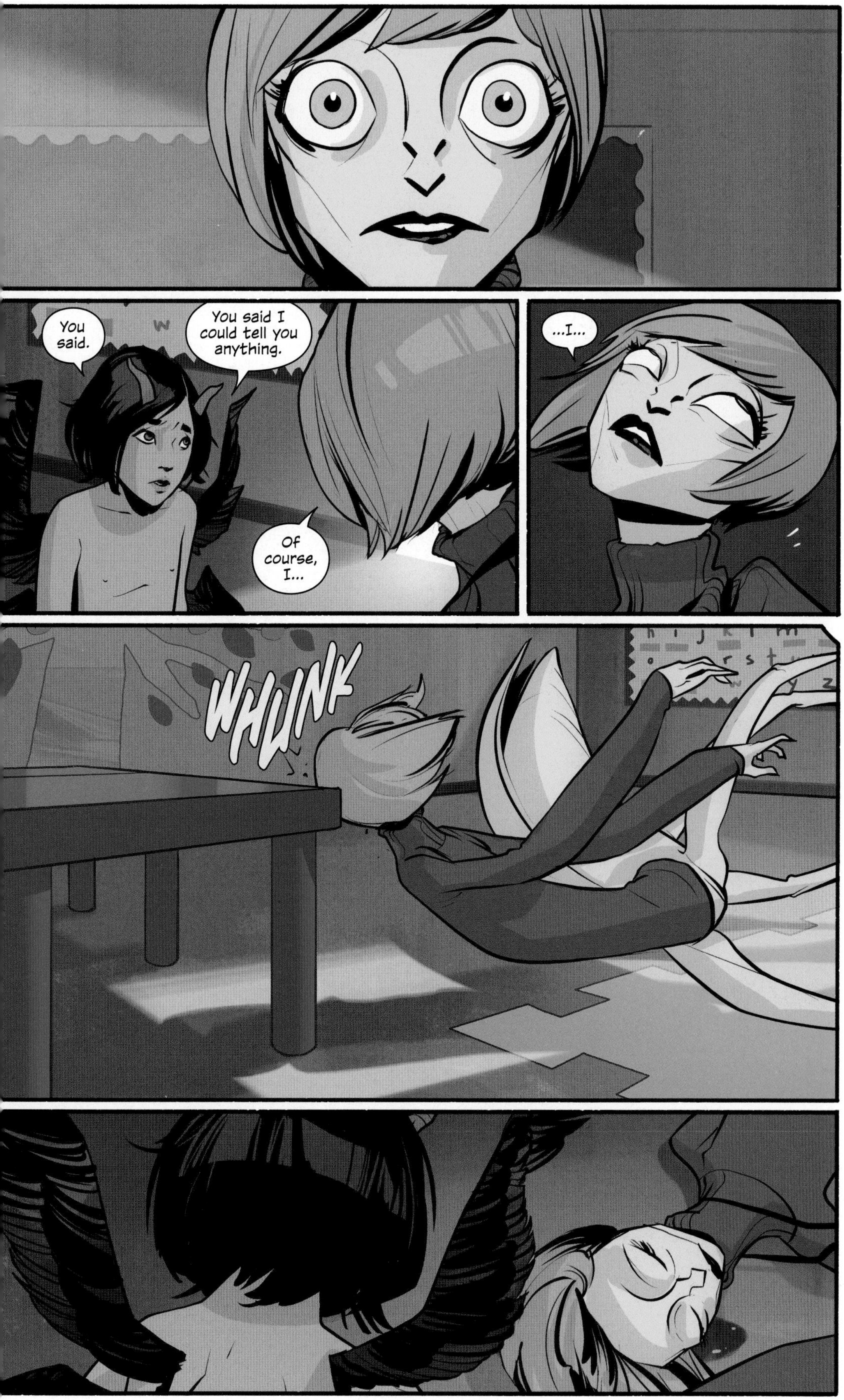

You said.
You said I could tell you anything.
Of course, I...
...I...
WHUNK

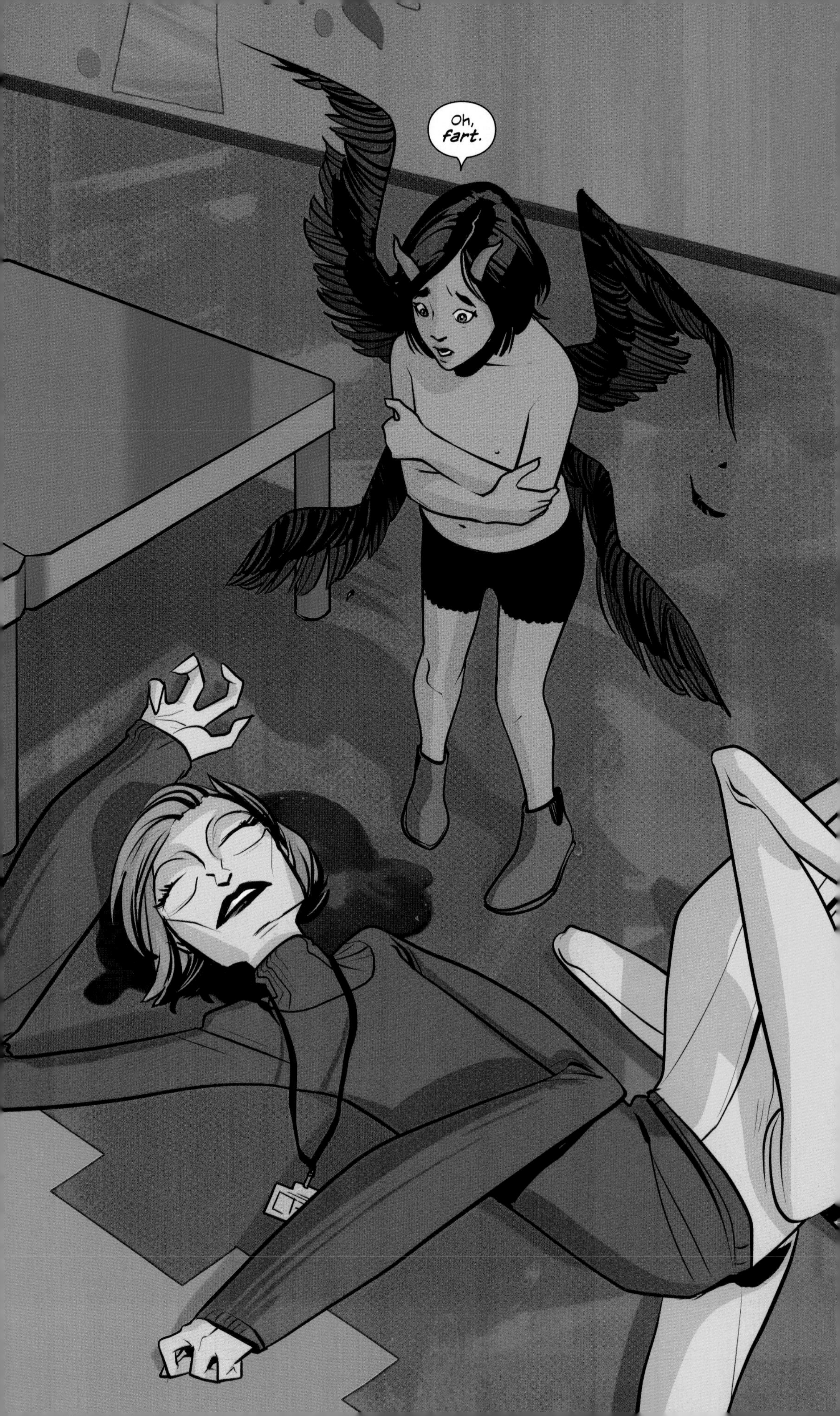
Oh, *fart*.

end chapter thirty-one

CHAPTER
THIRTY-TWO

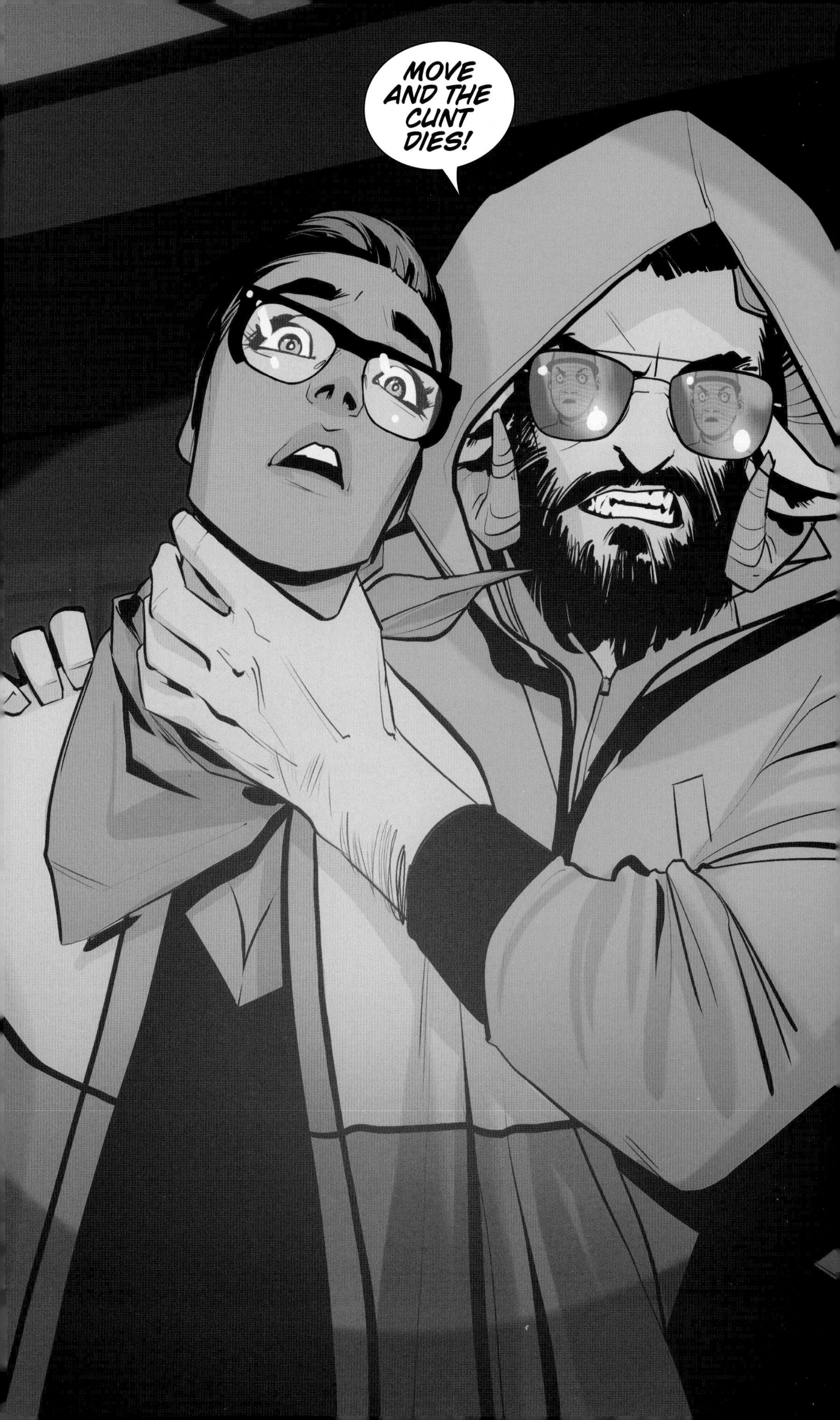
MOVE AND THE CUNT DIES!

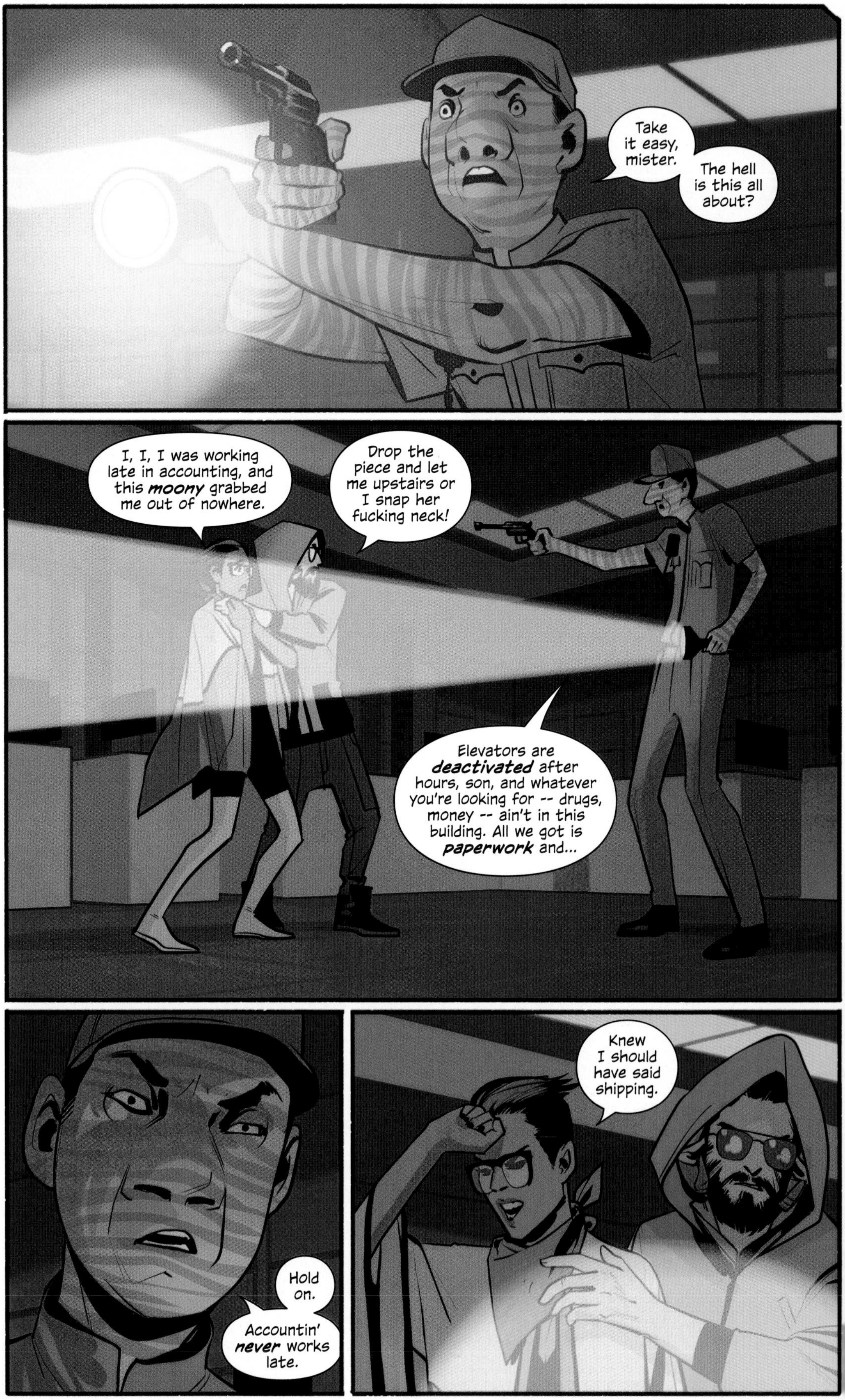
Take it easy, mister.
The hell is this all about?
I, I, I was working late in accounting, and this moony grabbed me out of nowhere.
Drop the piece and let me upstairs or I snap her fucking neck!
Elevators are deactivated after hours, son, and whatever you're looking for -- drugs, money -- ain't in this building. All we got is paperwork and...
Hold on.
Accountin' never works late.
Knew I should have said shipping.

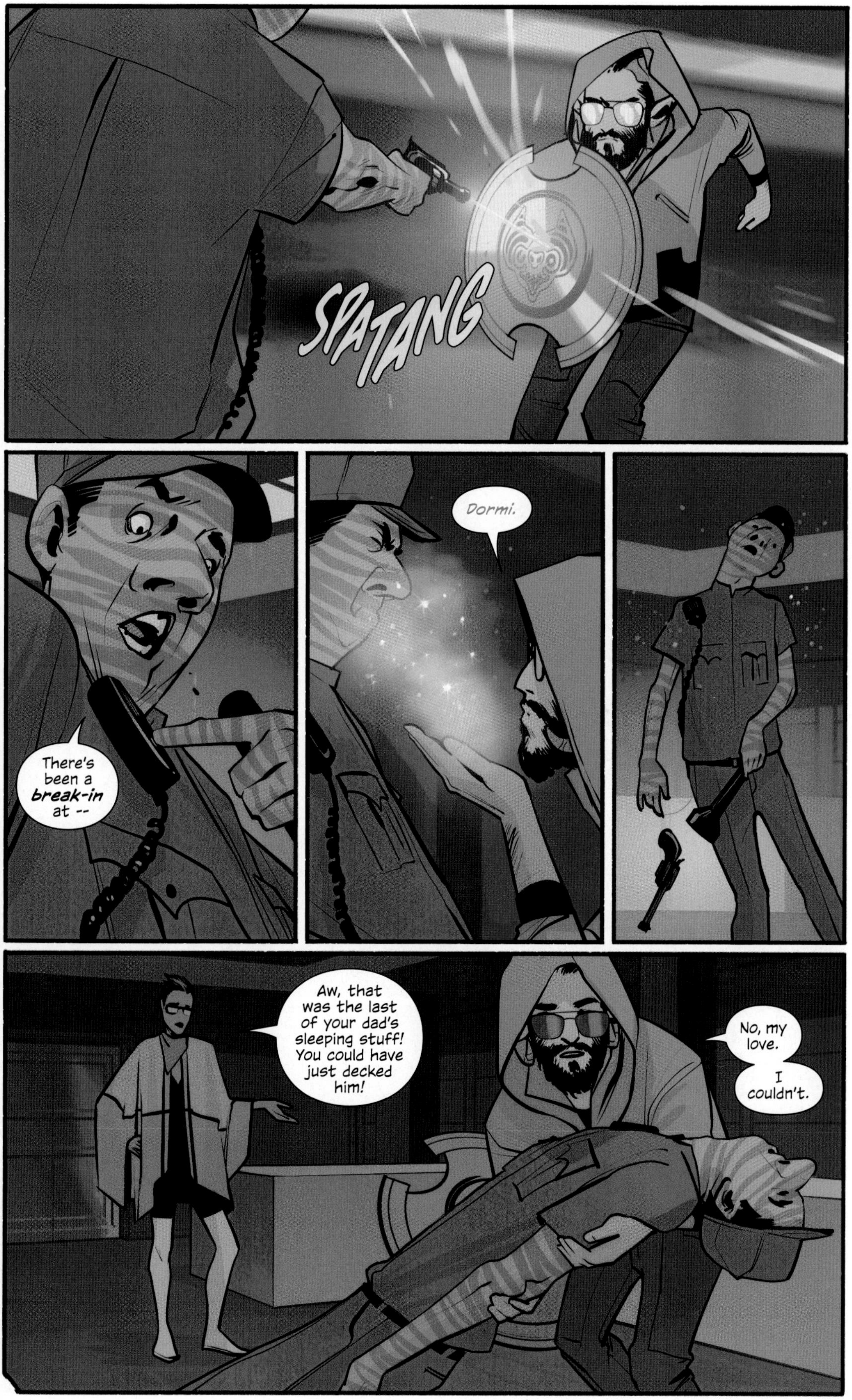
SPATANG
There's been a break-in at --
Dormi.
Aw, that was the last of your dad's sleeping stuff! You could have just decked him!
No, my love.
I couldn't.

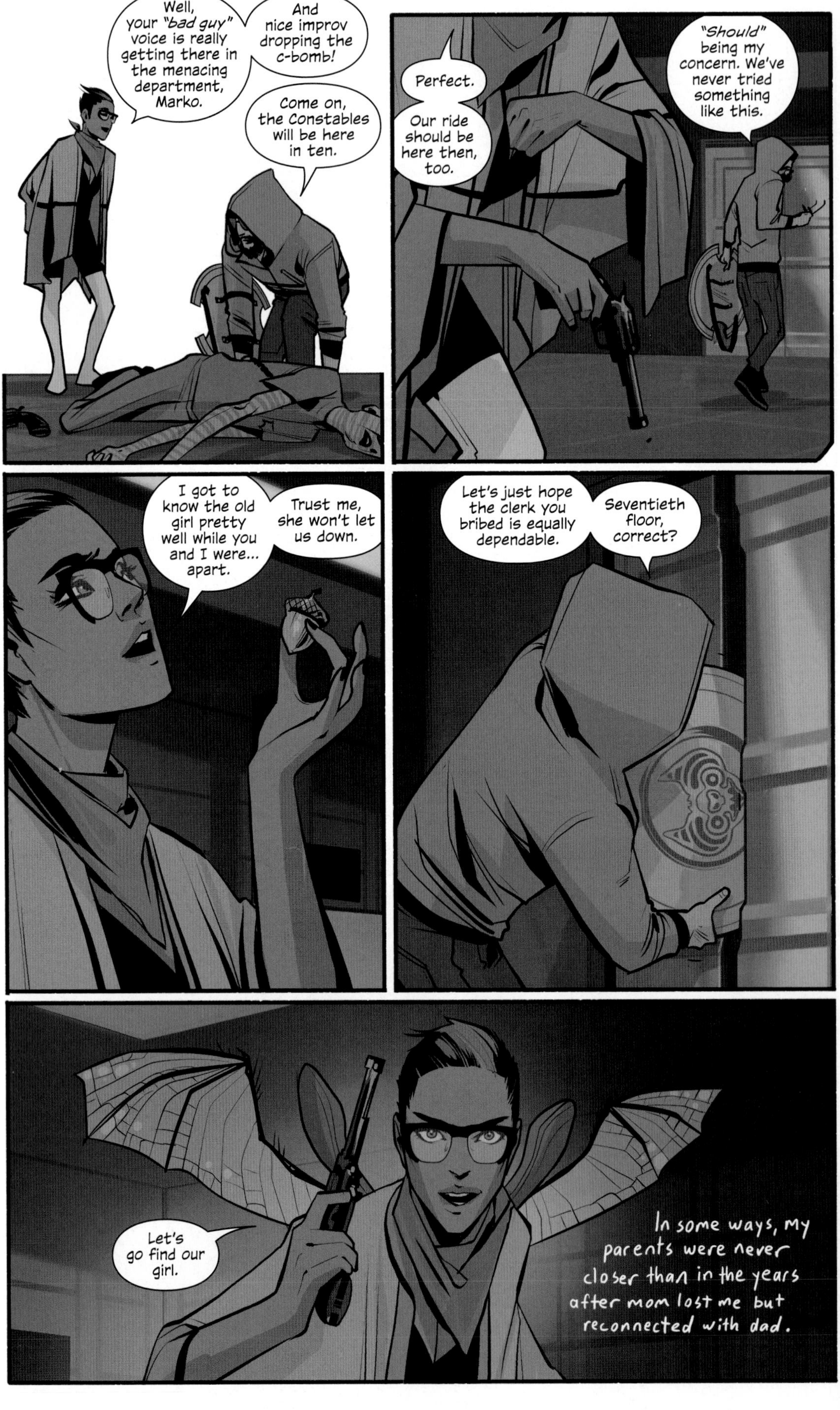

Well, your *"bad guy"* voice is really getting there in the menacing department, Marko.
And nice improv dropping the c-bomb!
Come on, the Constables will be here in ten.
Perfect.
Our ride should be here then, too.
"Should" being my concern. We've never tried something like this.
I got to know the old girl pretty well while you and I were... apart.
Trust me, she won't let us down.
Let's just hope the clerk you bribed is equally dependable.
Seventieth floor, correct?
Let's go find our girl.
In some ways, my parents were never closer than in the years after mom lost me but reconnected with dad.

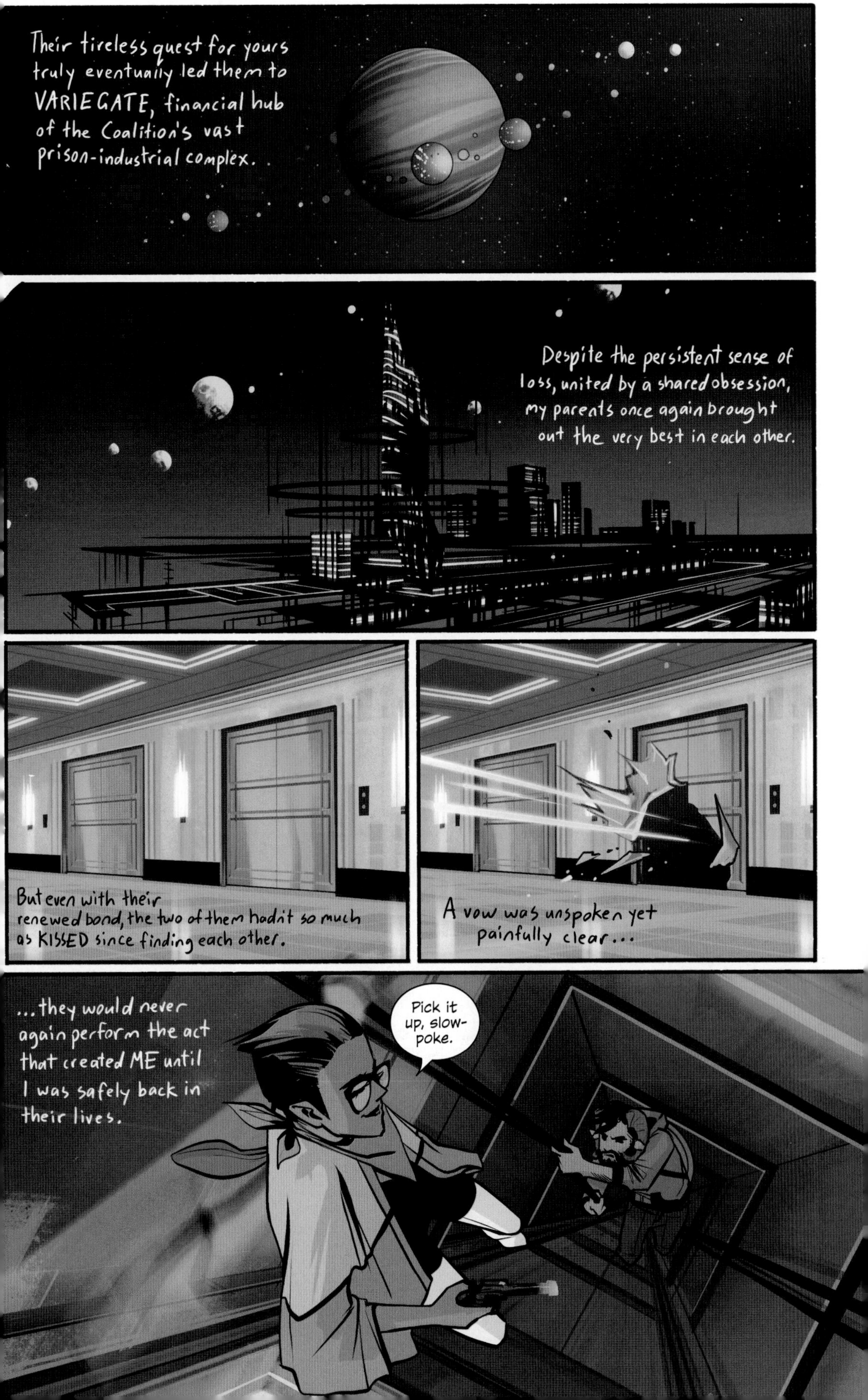

Their tireless quest for yours truly eventually led them to VARIEGATE, financial hub of the Coalition's vast prison-industrial complex.
Despite the persistent sense of loss, united by a shared obsession, my parents once again brought out the very best in each other.
But even with their renewed bond, the two of them hadn't so much as KISSED since finding each other.
A vow was unspoken yet painfully clear...
...they would never again perform the act that created ME until I was safely back in their lives.
Pick it up, slow-poke.

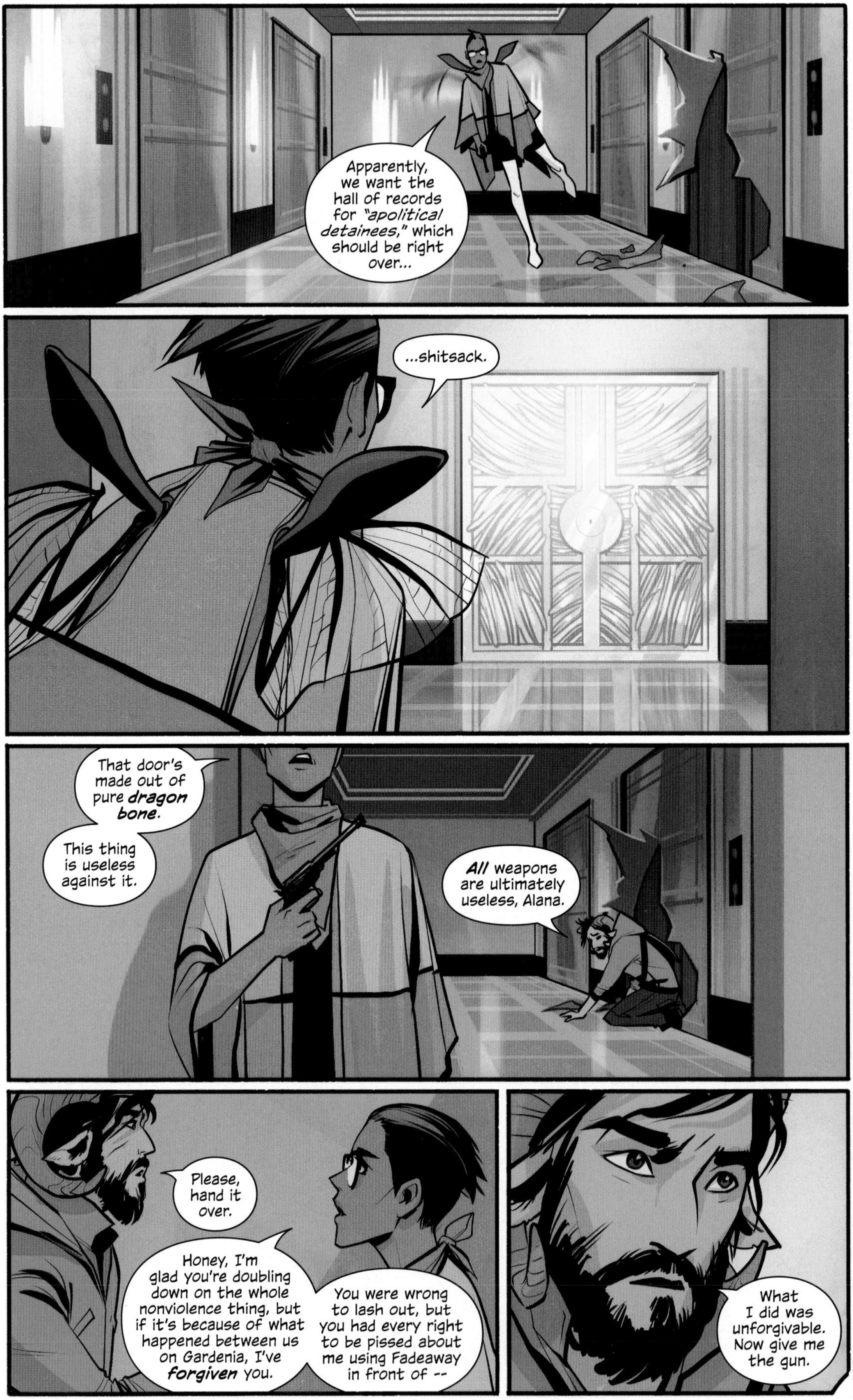
Apparently, we want the hall of records for "apolitical detainees," which should be right over...
...shitsack.
That door's made out of pure **dragon bone**.
This thing is useless against it.
All weapons are ultimately useless, Alana.
Please, hand it over.
Honey, I'm glad you're doubling down on the whole nonviolence thing, but if it's because of what happened between us on Gardenia, I've ***forgiven*** you.
You were wrong to lash out, but you had every right to be pissed about me using Fadeaway in front of --
What I did was unforgivable. Now give me the gun.

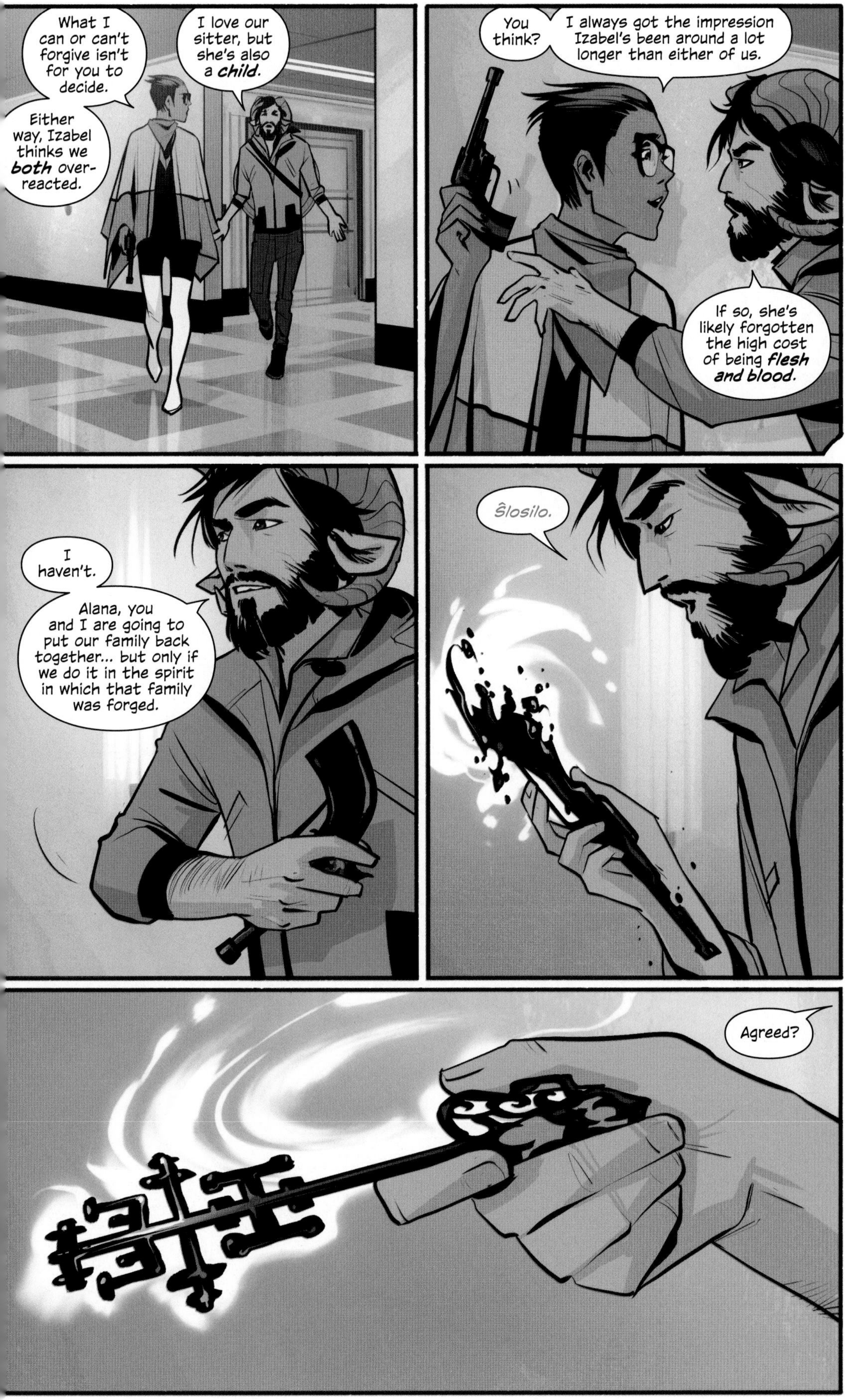
What I can or can't forgive isn't for you to decide.
I love our sitter, but she's also a ***child***.
Either way, Izabel thinks we ***both*** over-reacted.
You think?
I always got the impression Izabel's been around a lot longer than either of us.
If so, she's likely forgotten the high cost of being ***flesh and blood***.
I haven't.
Alana, you and I are going to put our family back together... but only if we do it in the spirit in which that family was forged.
Ŝlosilo.
Agreed?

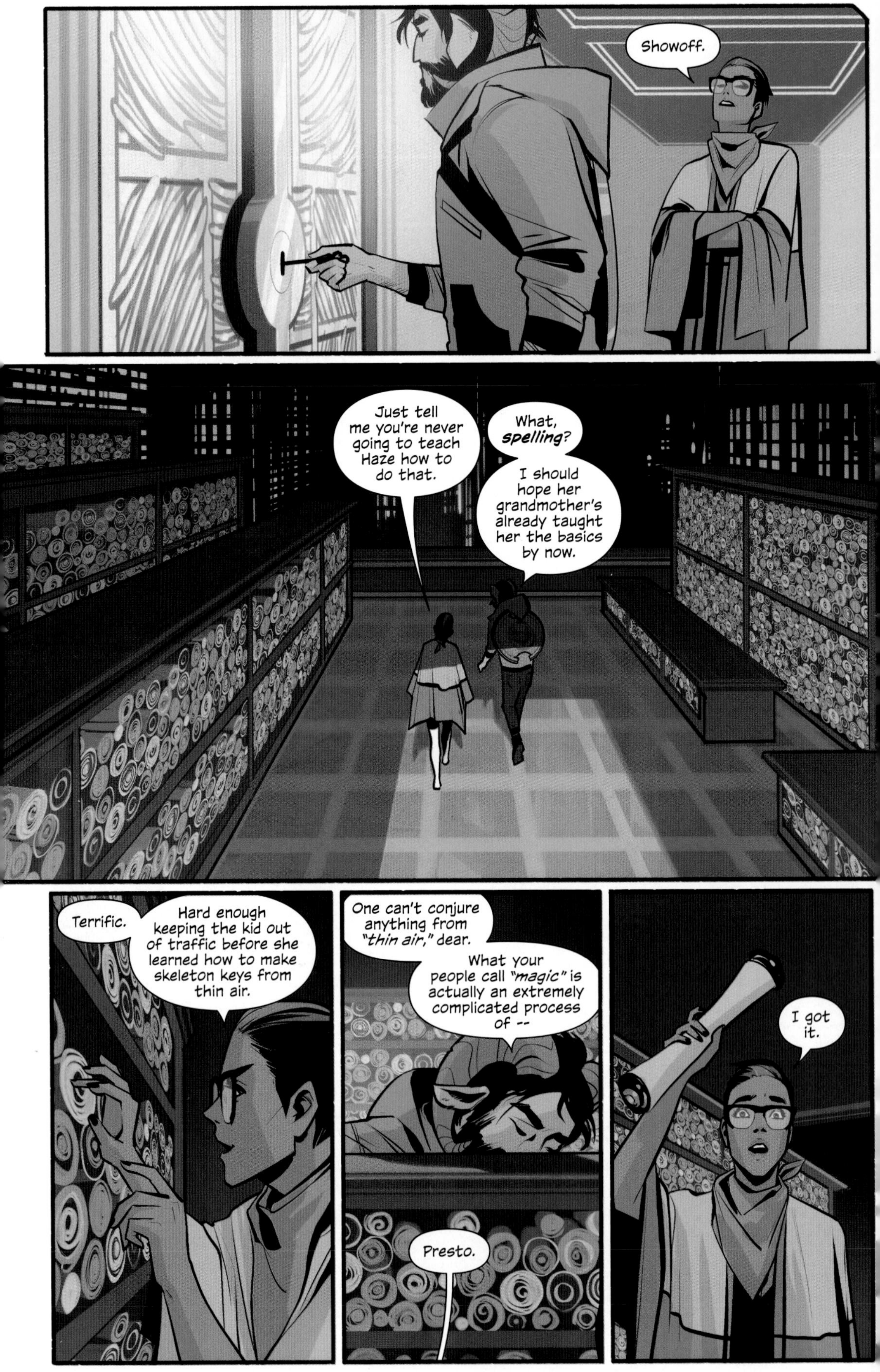
Showoff.
Just tell me you're never going to teach Haze how to do that.
What, *spelling*?
I should hope her grandmother's already taught her the basics by now.
Terrific.
Hard enough keeping the kid out of traffic before she learned how to make skeleton keys from thin air.
One can't conjure anything from *"thin air,"* dear.
What your people call *"magic"* is actually an extremely complicated process of --
Presto.
I got it.

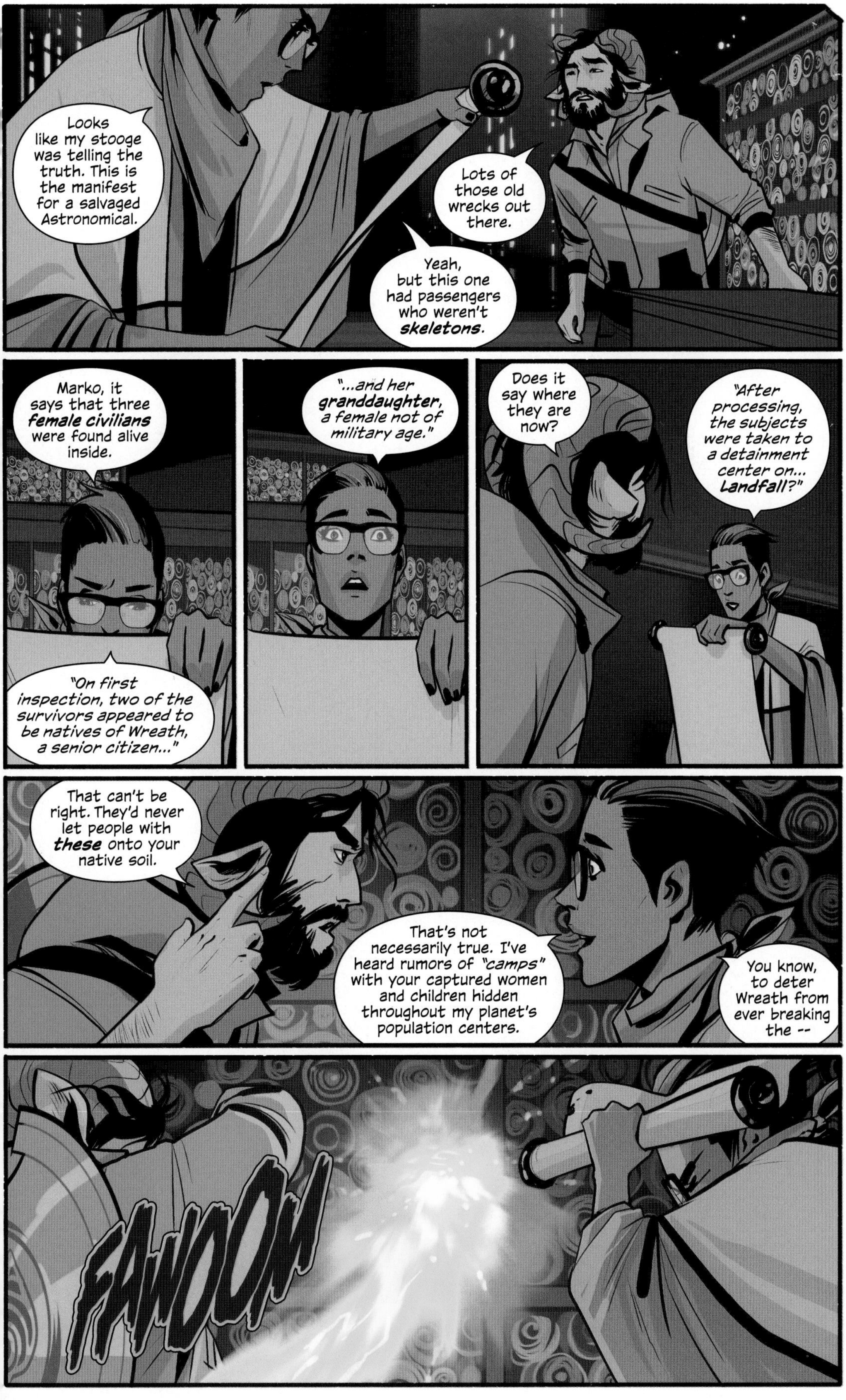
Looks like my stooge was telling the truth. This is the manifest for a salvaged Astronomical.
Lots of those old wrecks out there.
Yeah, but this one had passengers who weren't **skeletons**.
Marko, it says that three **female civilians** were found alive inside.
"On first inspection, two of the survivors appeared to be natives of Wreath, a senior citizen..."
"...and her ***granddaughter****, a female not of military age."*
Does it say where they are now?
"After processing, the subjects were taken to a detainment center on... ***Landfall****?"*
That can't be right. They'd never let people with **these** onto your native soil.
That's not necessarily true. I've heard rumors of *"camps"* with your captured women and children hidden throughout my planet's population centers.
You know, to deter Wreath from ever breaking the --
FWOOM

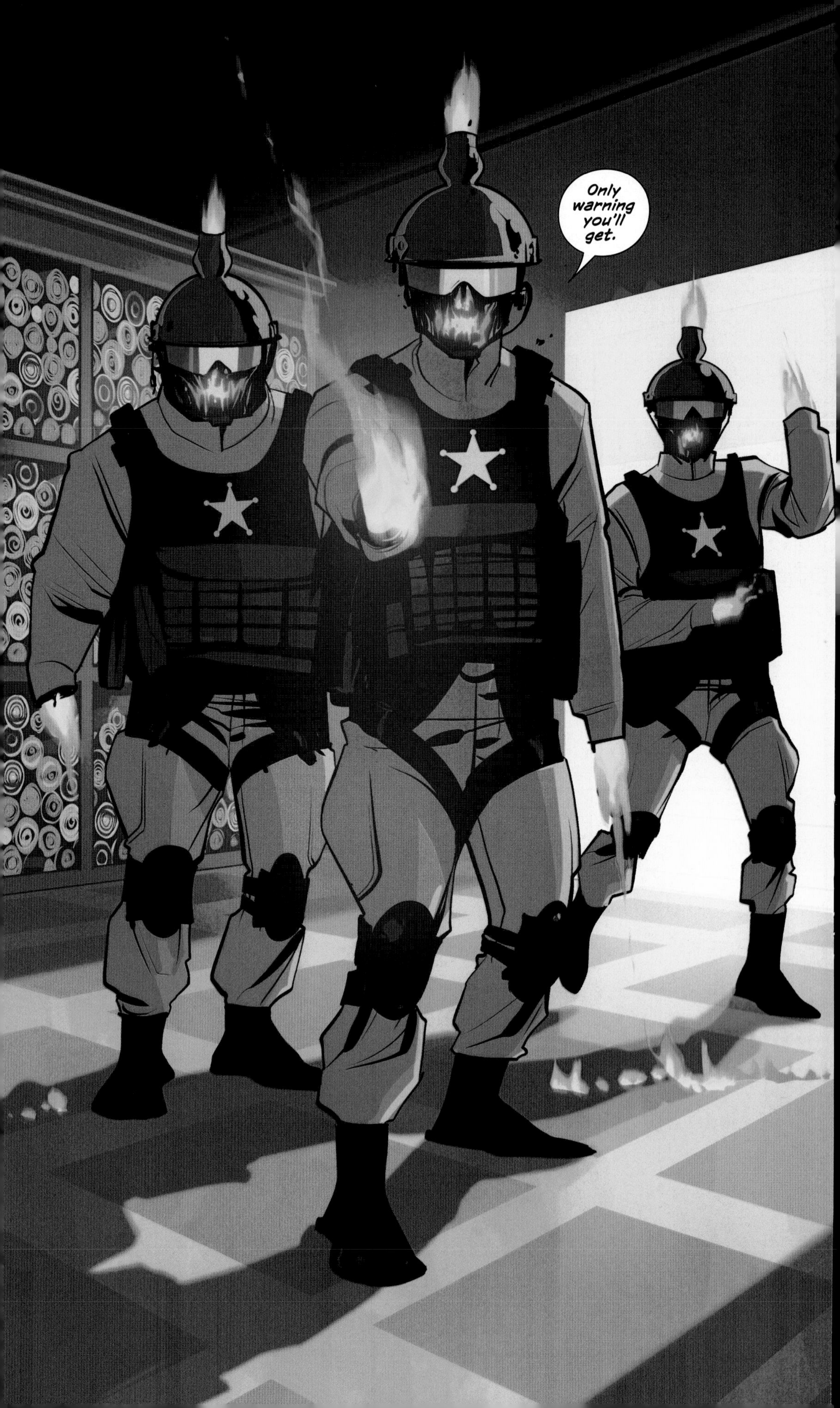
Only warning you'll get.

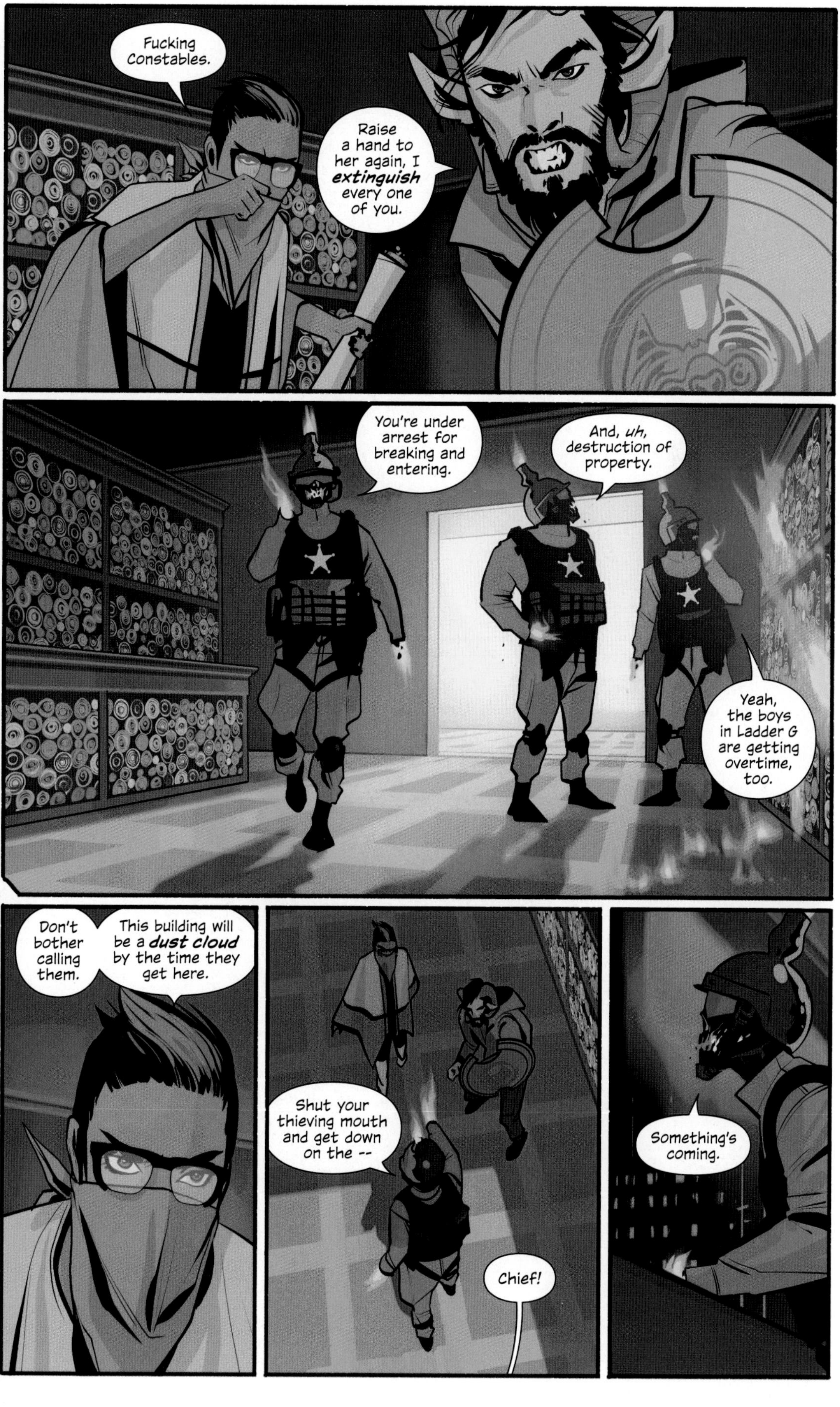
Fucking Constables.
Raise a hand to her again, I ***extinguish*** every one of you.
You're under arrest for breaking and entering.
And, *uh*, destruction of property.
Yeah, the boys in Ladder G are getting overtime, too.
Don't bother calling them.
This building will be a ***dust cloud*** by the time they get here.
Shut your thieving mouth and get down on the --
Chief!
Something's coming.

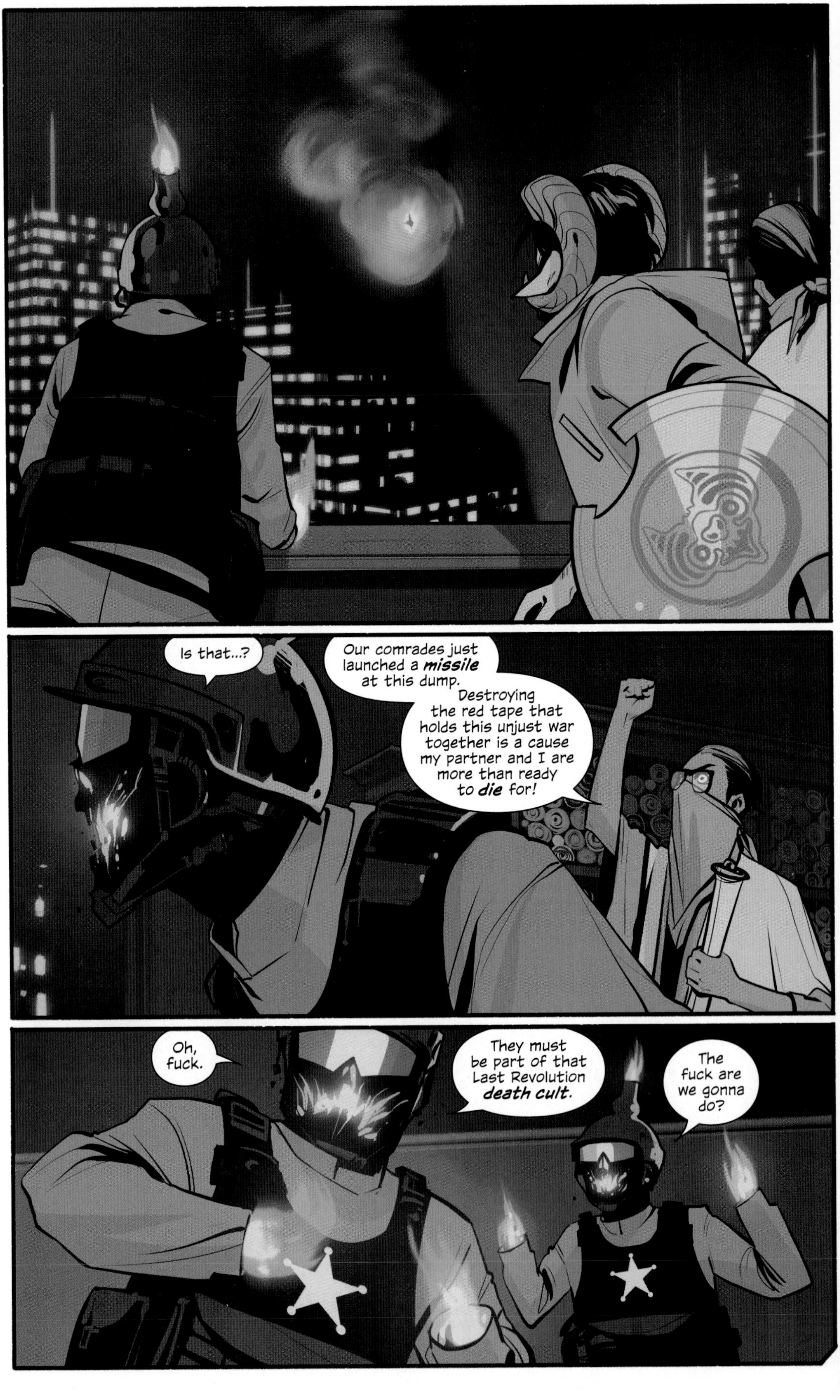
Is that...?
Our comrades just launched a *missile* at this dump.
Destroying the red tape that holds this unjust war together is a cause my partner and I are more than ready to *die* for!
Oh, fuck.
They must be part of that Last Revolution ***death cult***.
The fuck are we gonna do?

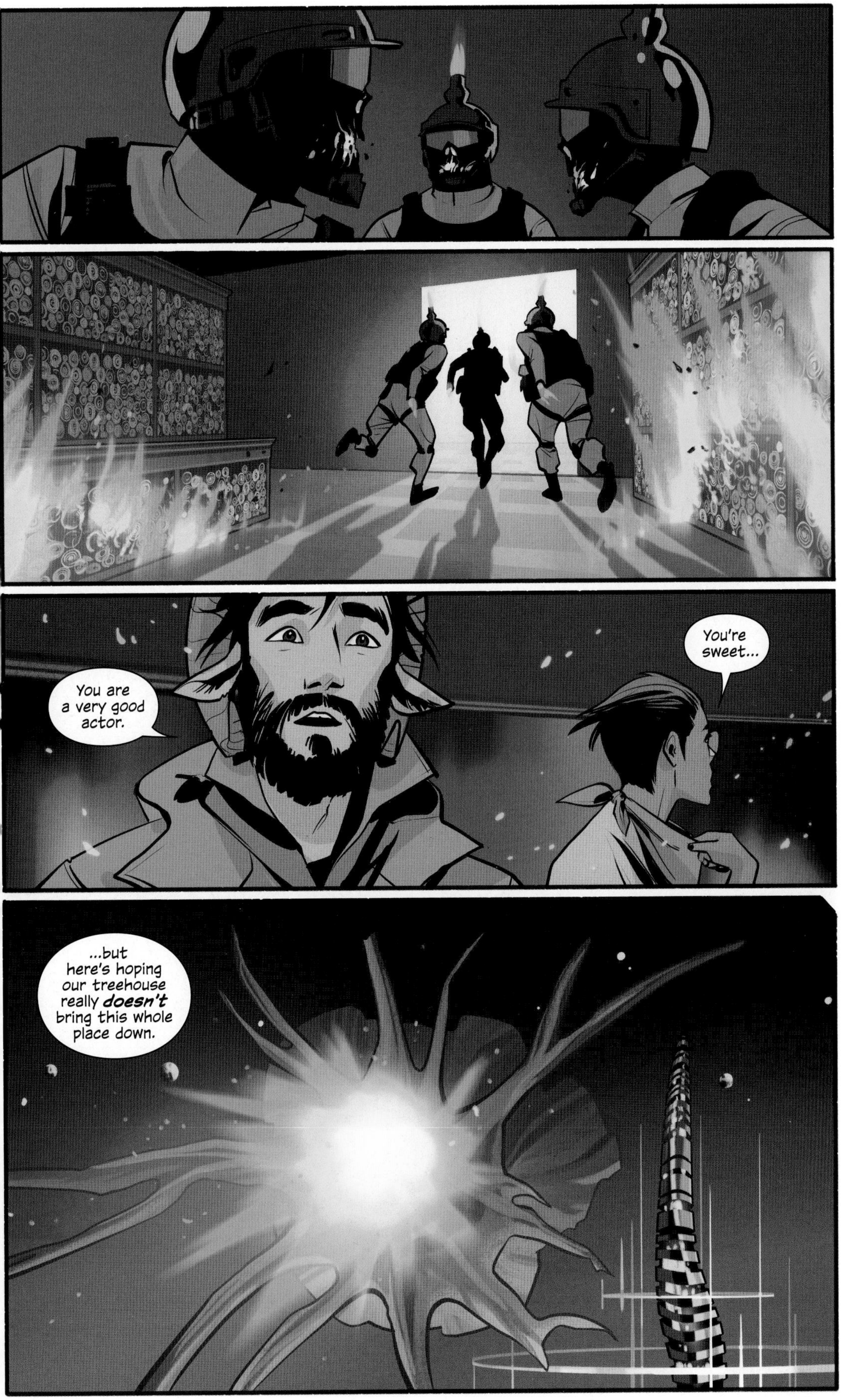
You are a very good actor.
You're sweet...
...but here's hoping our treehouse really ***doesn't*** bring this whole place down.

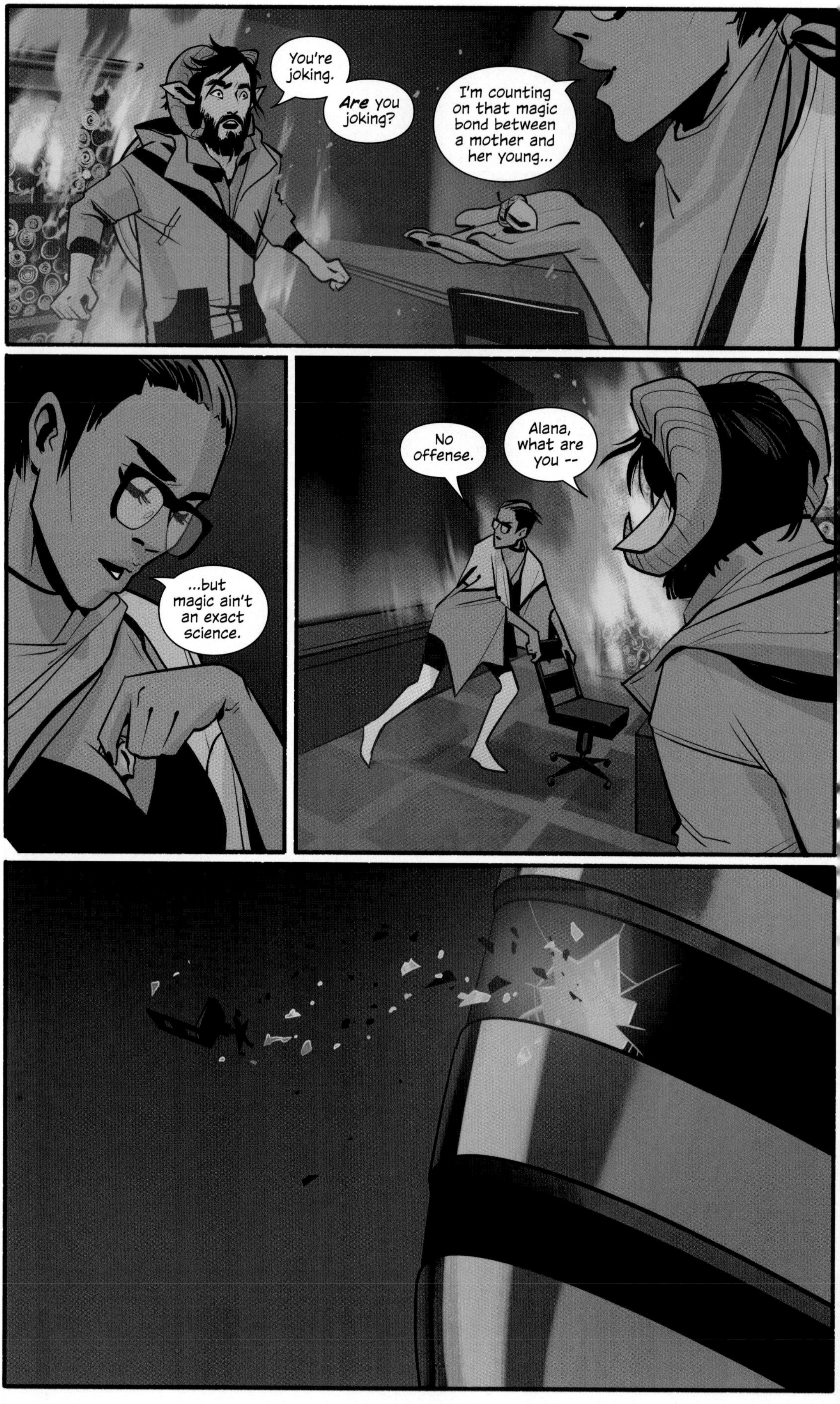
You're joking.
Are you joking?
I'm counting on that magic bond between a mother and her young...
...but magic ain't an exact science.
No offense.
Alana, what are you --

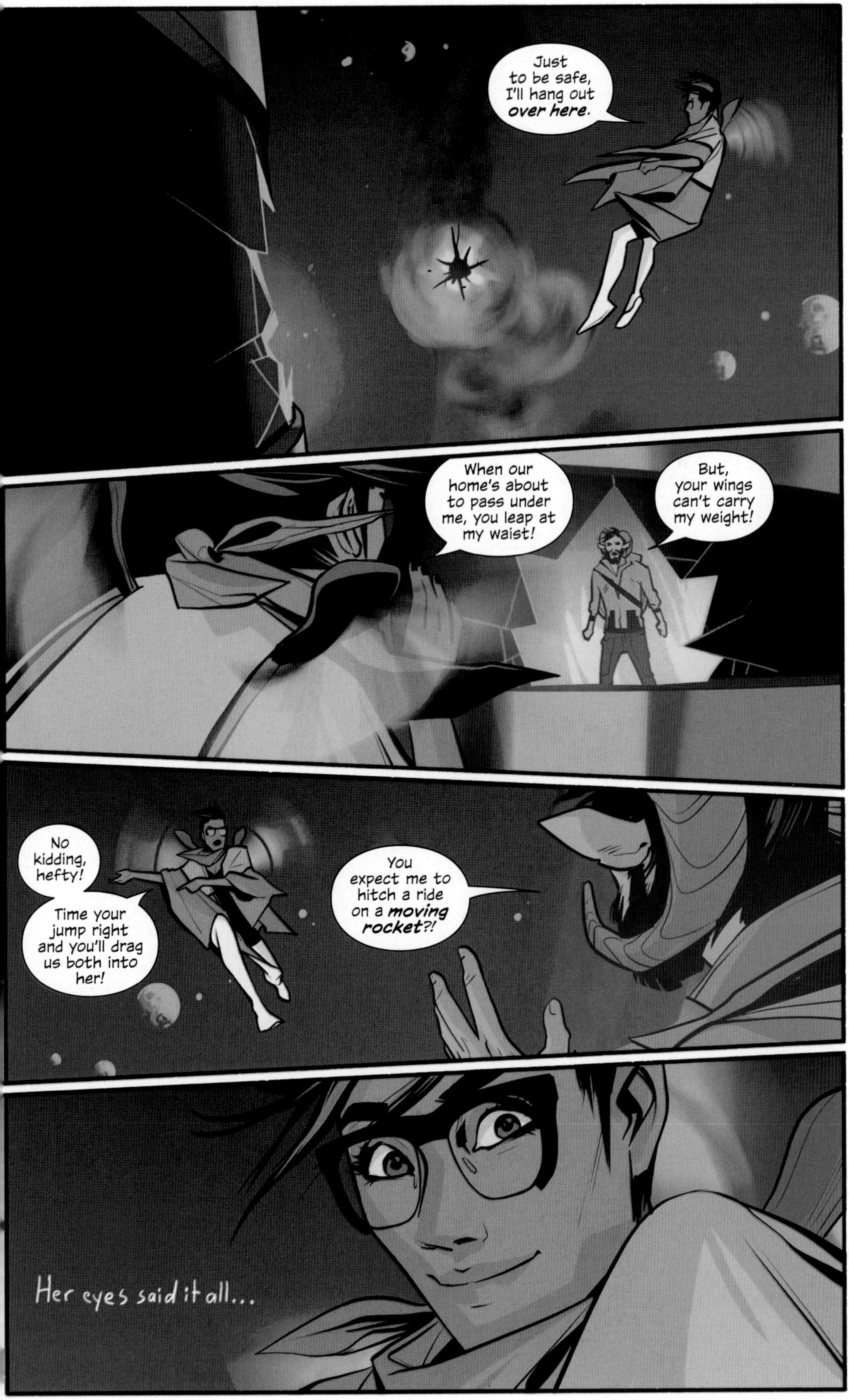
Just to be safe, I'll hang out *over here*.
When our home's about to pass under me, you leap at my waist!
But, your wings can't carry my weight!
No kidding, hefty!
Time your jump right and you'll drag us both into her!
You expect me to hitch a ride on a *moving rocket*?!
Her eyes said it all...

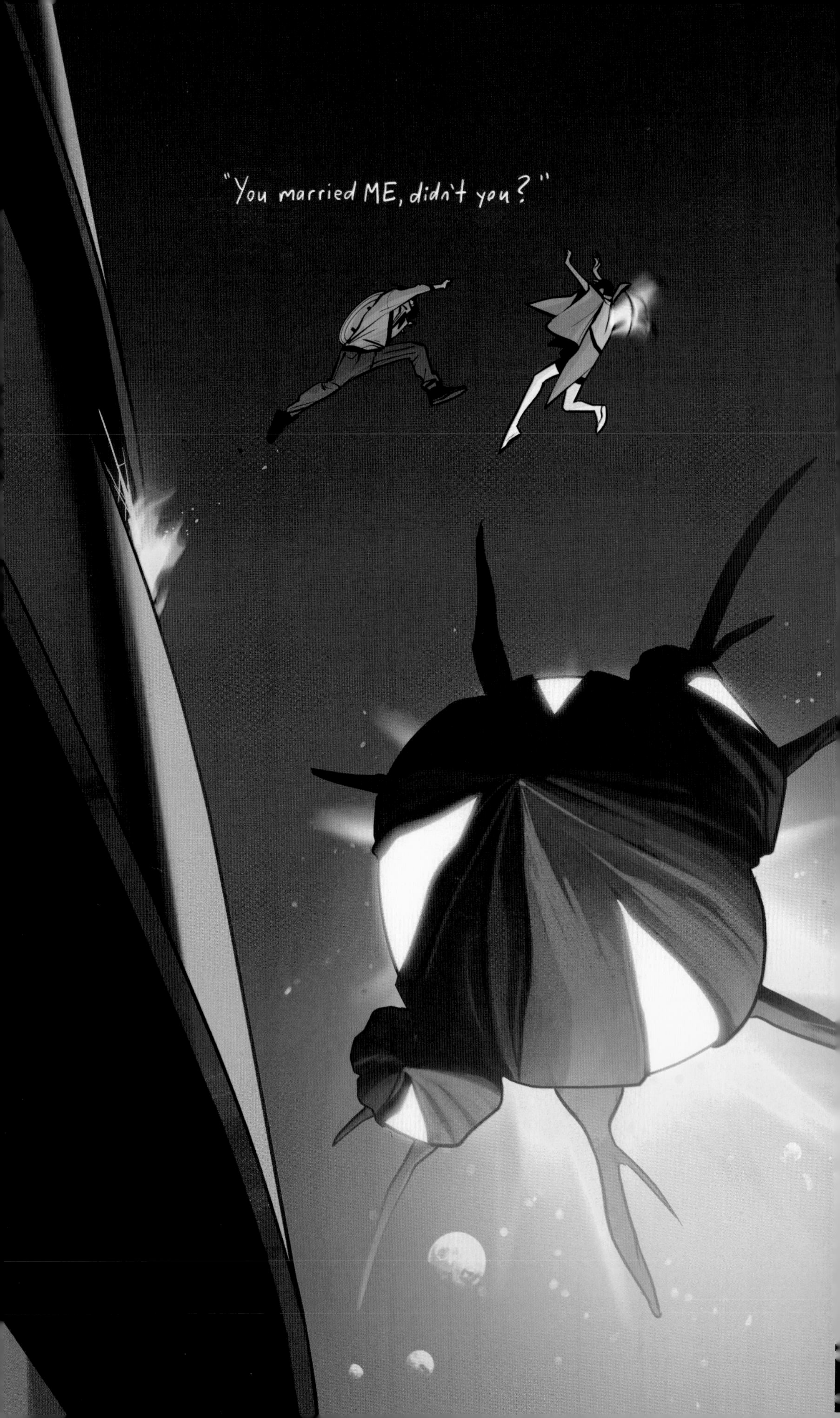
"You married ME, didn't you?"

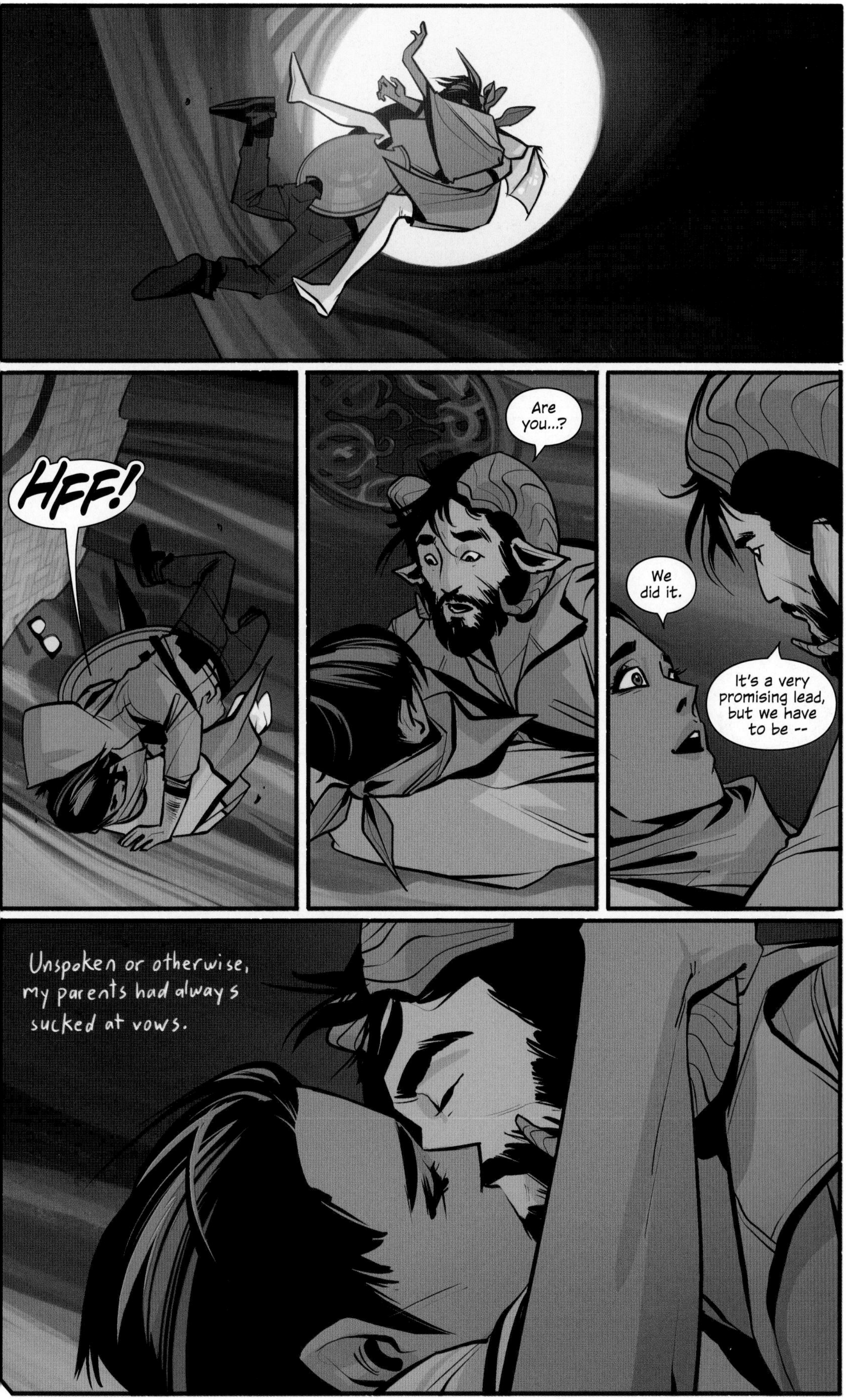
HFF!
Are you...?
We did it.
It's a very promising lead, but we have to be --
Unspoken or otherwise, my parents had always sucked at vows.

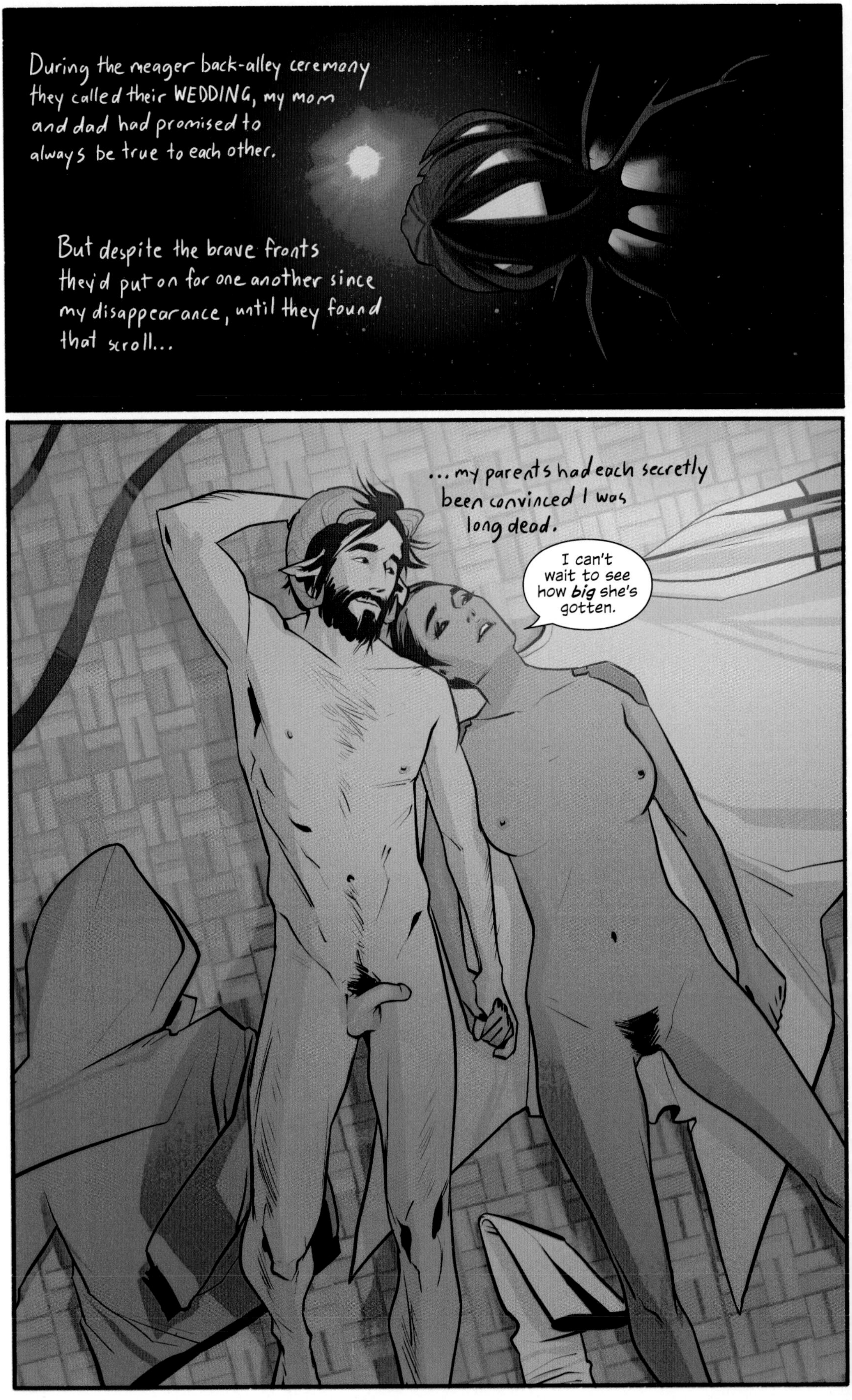
During the meager back-alley ceremony they called their WEDDING, my mom and dad had promised to always be true to each other.
But despite the brave fronts they'd put on for one another since my disappearance, until they found that scroll...
...my parents had each secretly been convinced I was long dead.
I can't wait to see how **big** she's gotten.

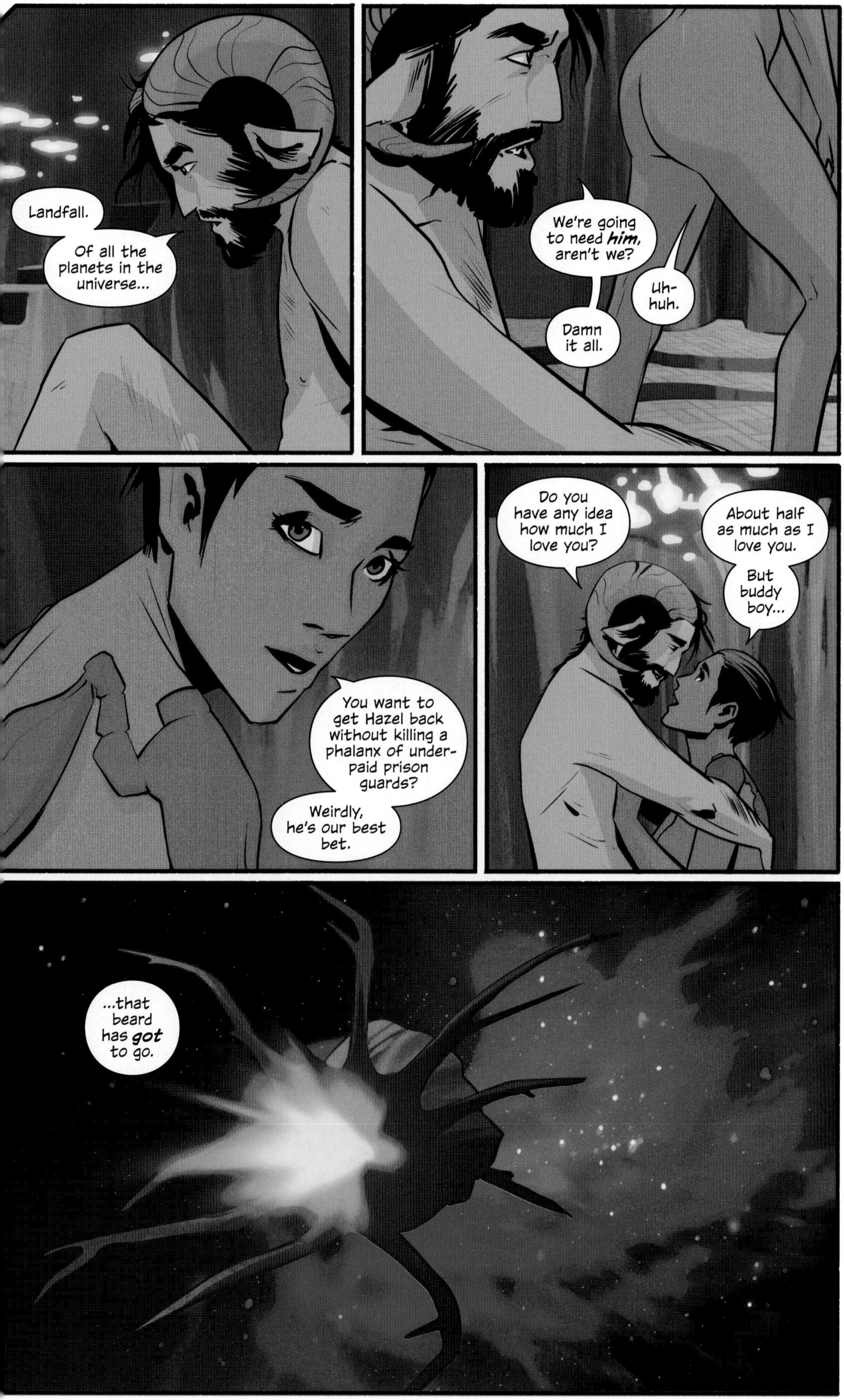
Landfall.
Of all the planets in the universe...
We're going to need ***him***, aren't we?
Uh-huh.
Damn it all.
You want to get Hazel back without killing a phalanx of under-paid prison guards?
Weirdly, he's our best bet.
Do you have any idea how much I love you?
About half as much as I love you.
But buddy boy...
...that beard has ***got*** to go.

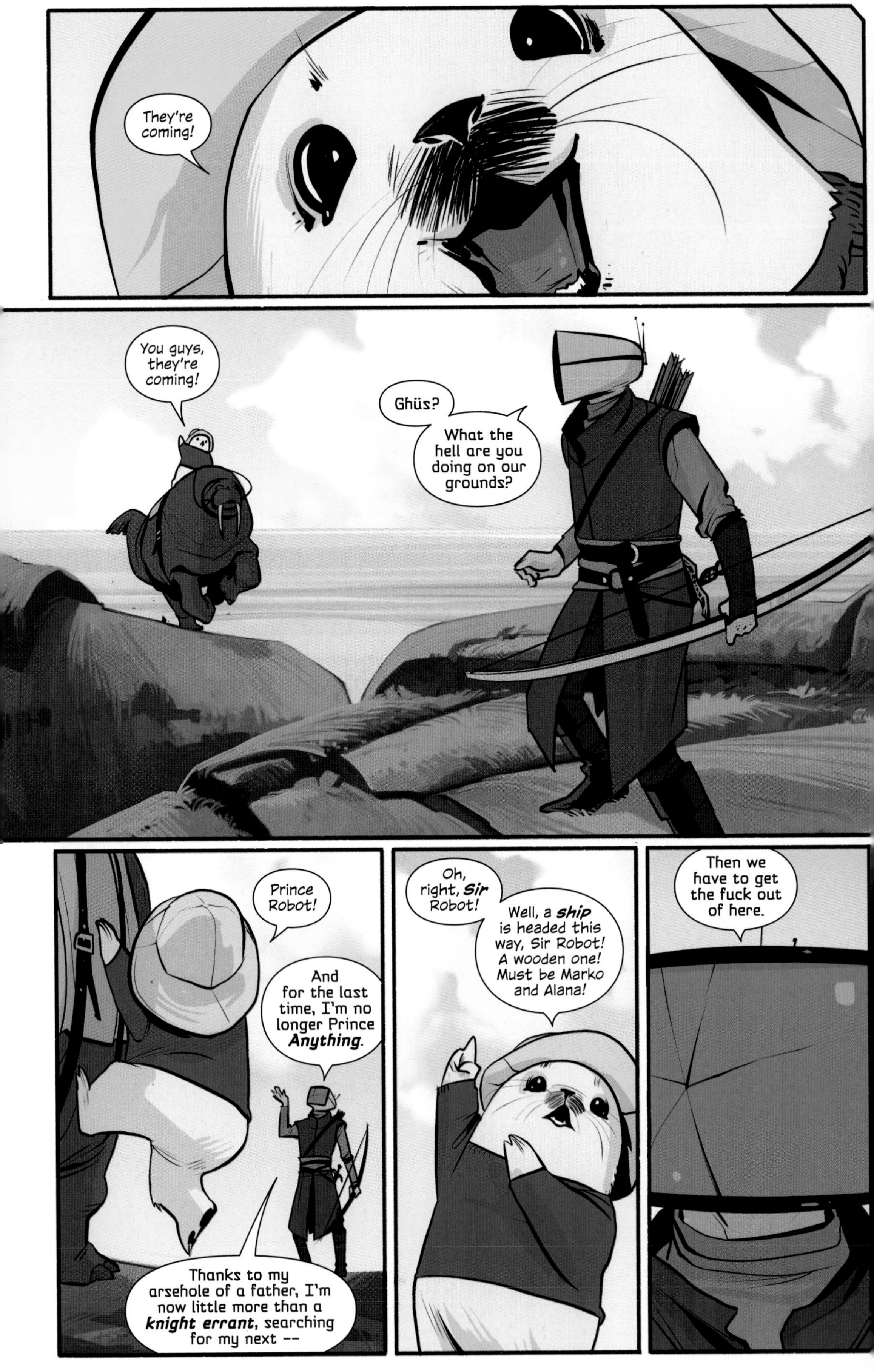

They're coming!
You guys, they're coming!
Ghüs?
What the hell are you doing on our grounds?
Prince Robot!
And for the last time, I'm no longer Prince *Anything*.
Thanks to my arsehole of a father, I'm now little more than a ***knight errant***, searching for my next --
Oh, right, ***Sir*** Robot!
Well, a ***ship*** is headed this way, Sir Robot! A wooden one! Must be Marko and Alana!
Then we have to get the fuck out of here.

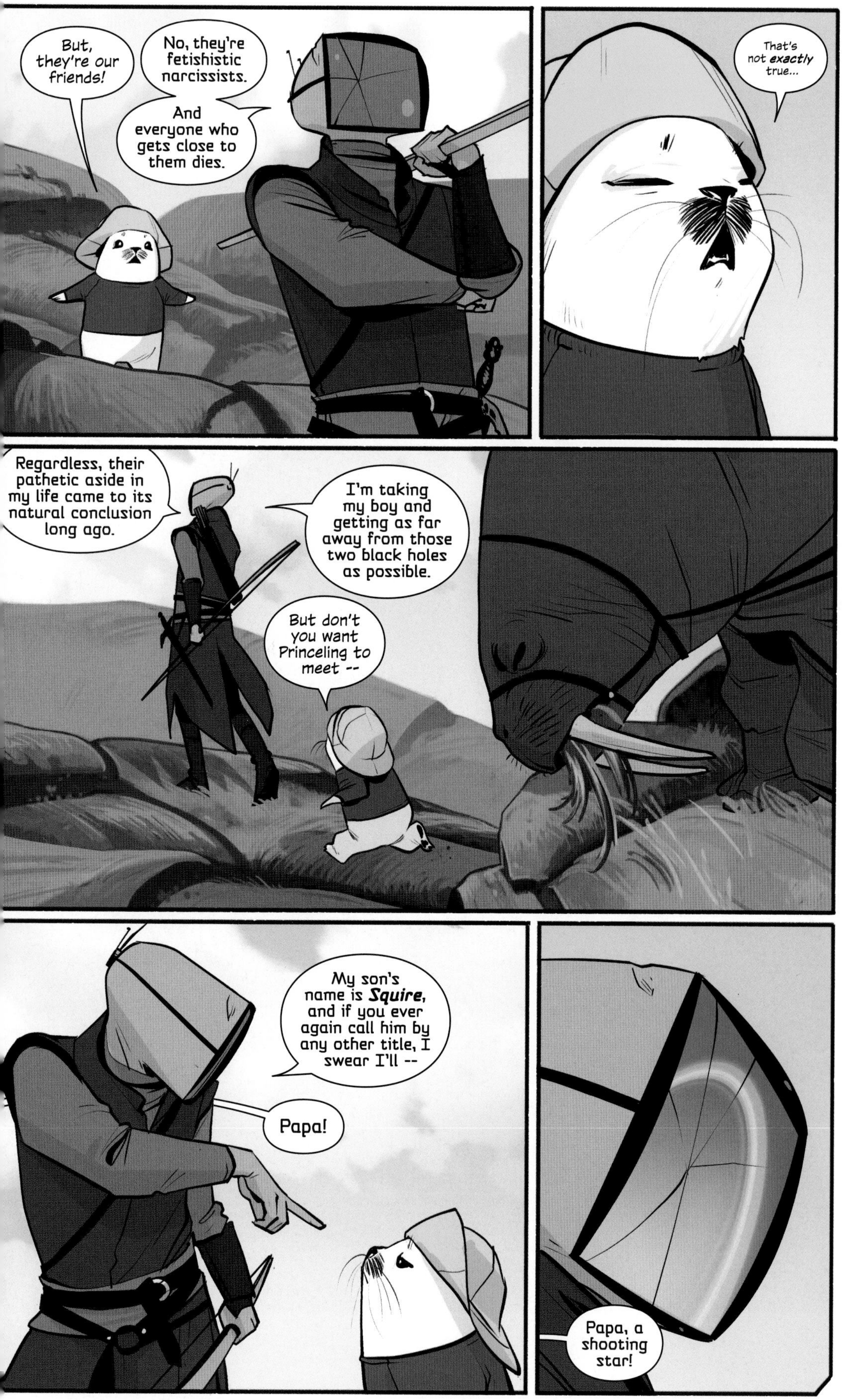
But, they're our friends!
No, they're fetishistic narcissists.
And everyone who gets close to them dies.
That's not *exactly* true...
Regardless, their pathetic aside in my life came to its natural conclusion long ago.
I'm taking my boy and getting as far away from those two black holes as possible.
But don't you want Princeling to meet --
My son's name is ***Squire***, and if you ever again call him by any other title, I swear I'll --
Papa!
Papa, a shooting star!

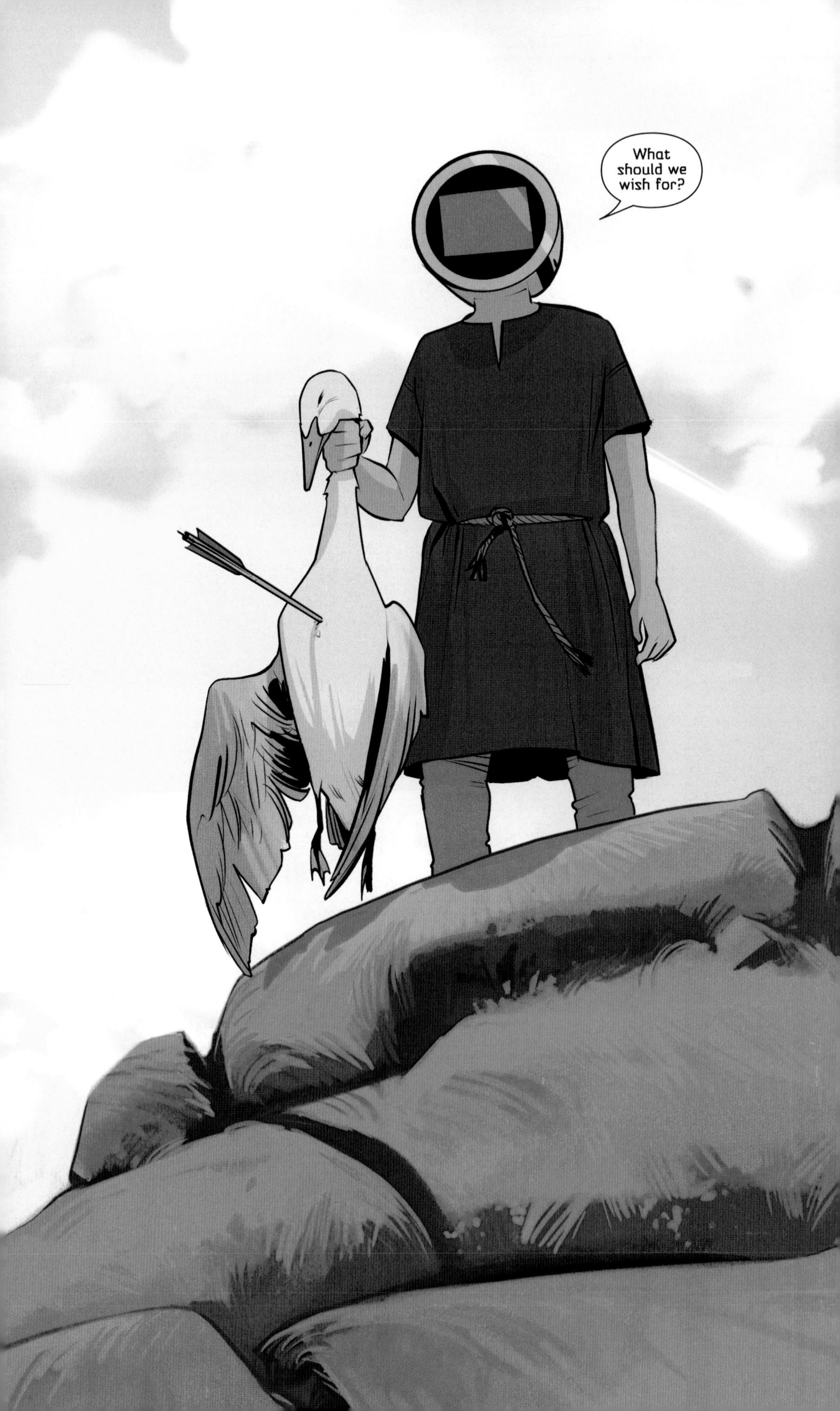
What should we wish for?

end chapter thirty-two

CHAPTER
THIRTY-THREE

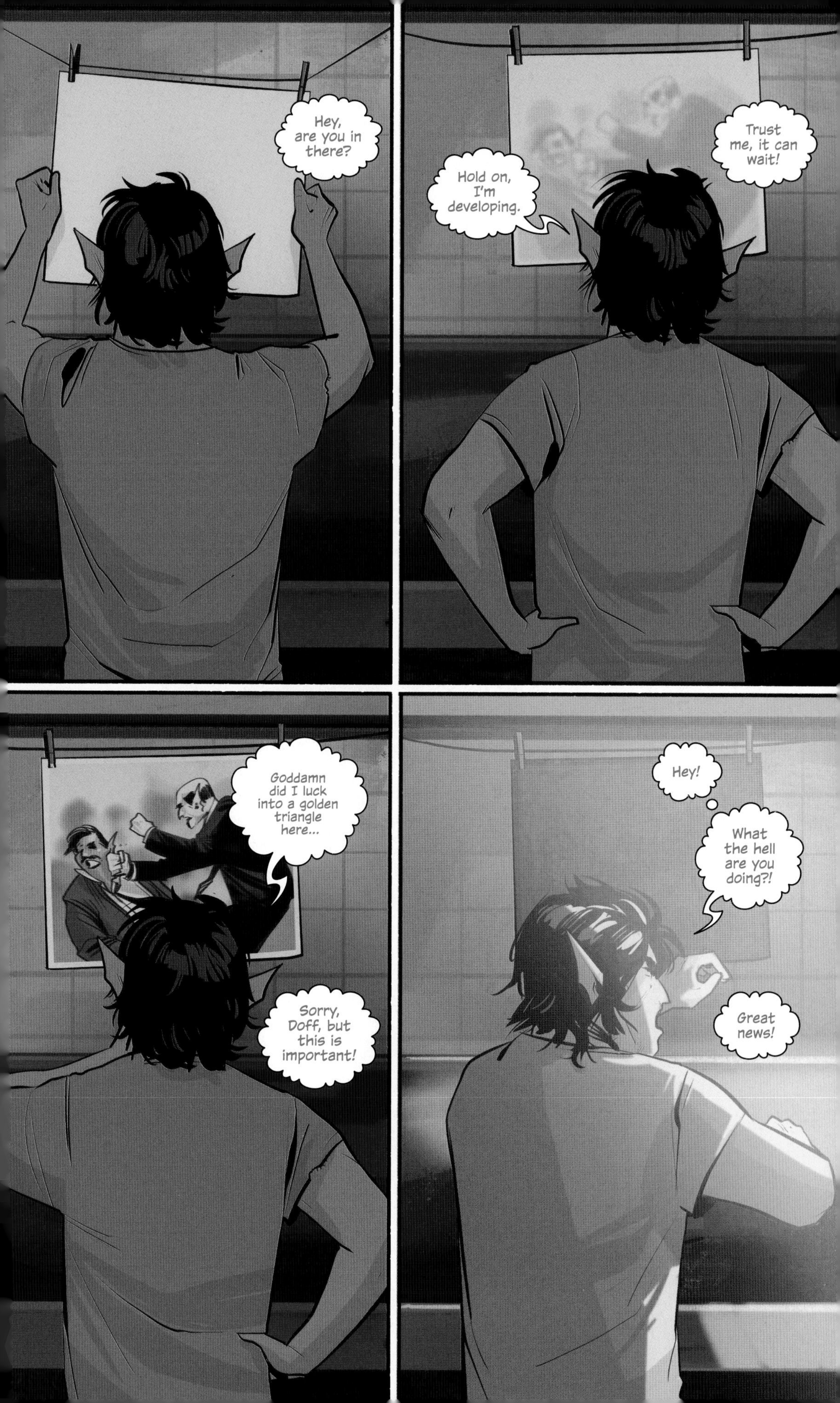
Hey, are you in there?
Hold on, I'm developing.
Trust me, it can wait!
Goddamn did I luck into a golden triangle here...
Sorry, Doff, but this is important!
Hey!
What the hell are you doing?!
Great news!

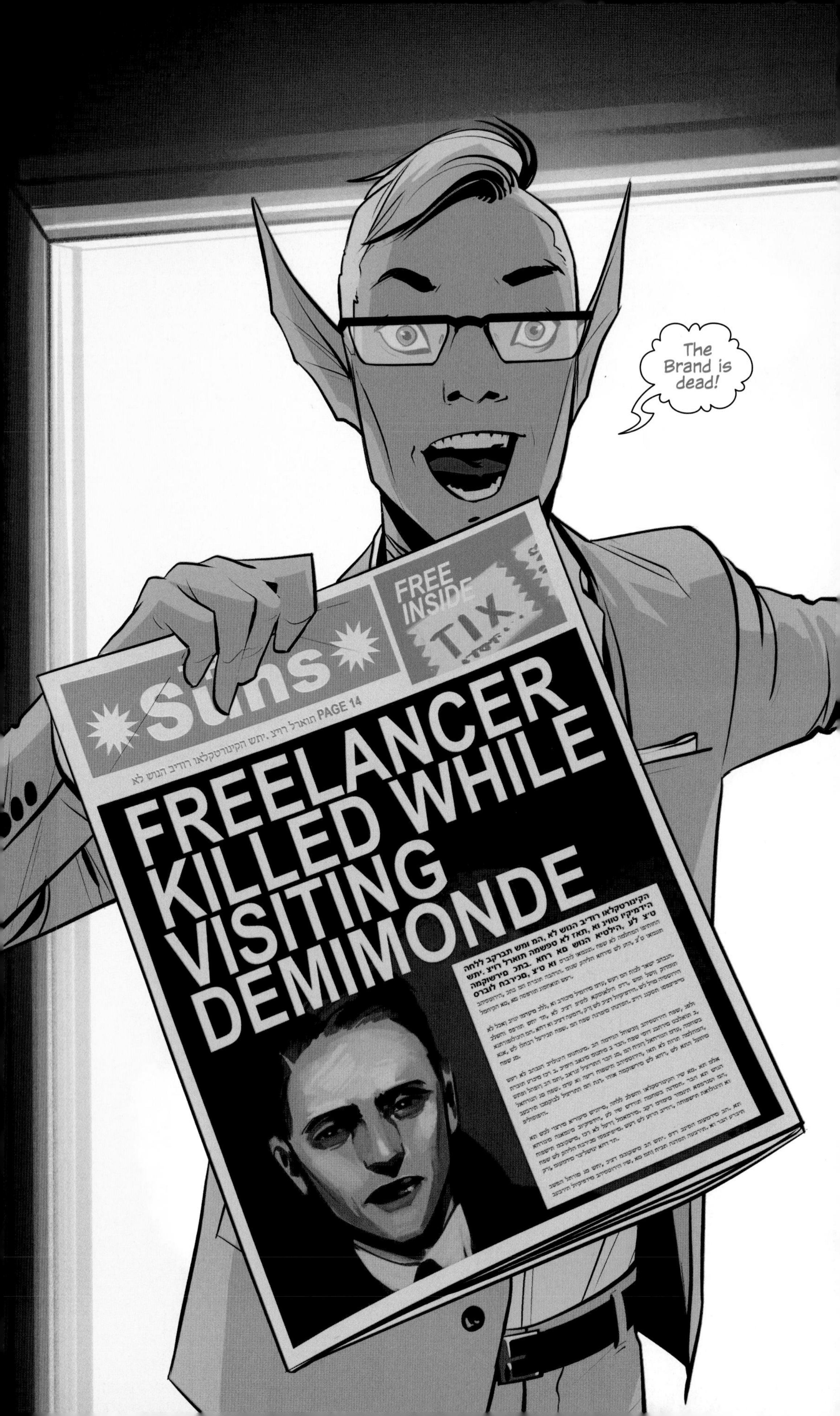

The Brand is dead!
Suns
PAGE 14
FREE INSIDE
TIX
FREELANCER KILLED WHILE VISITING DEMIMONDE

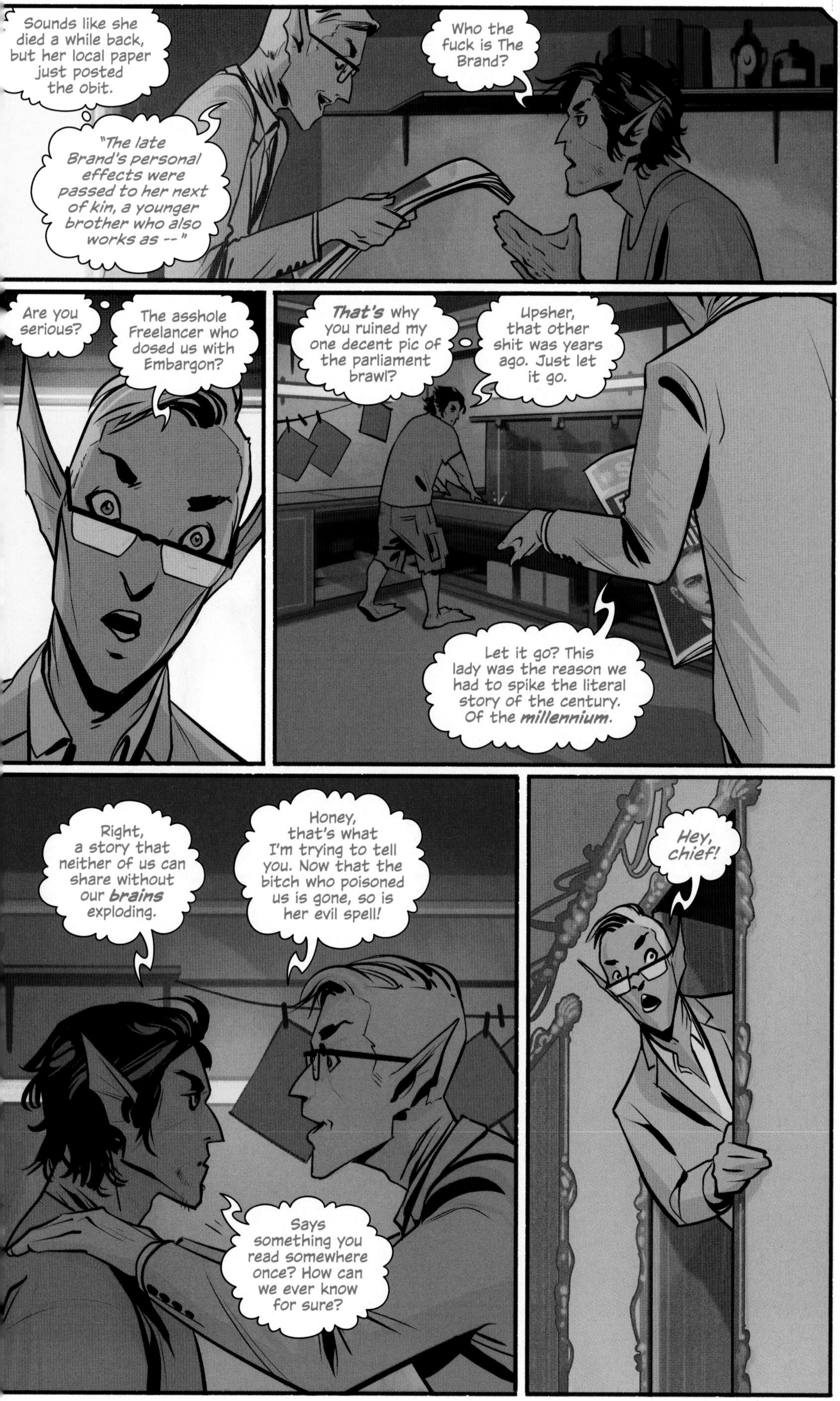
Sounds like she died a while back, but her local paper just posted the obit.
"The late Brand's personal effects were passed to her next of kin, a younger brother who also works as --"
Who the fuck is The Brand?
Are you serious?
The asshole Freelancer who dosed us with Embargon?
That's why you ruined my one decent pic of the parliament brawl?
Upsher, that other shit was years ago. Just let it go.
Let it go? This lady was the reason we had to spike the literal story of the century. Of the millennium.
Right, a story that neither of us can share without our brains exploding.
Honey, that's what I'm trying to tell you. Now that the bitch who poisoned us is gone, so is her evil spell!
Says something you read somewhere once? How can we ever know for sure?
Hey, chief!

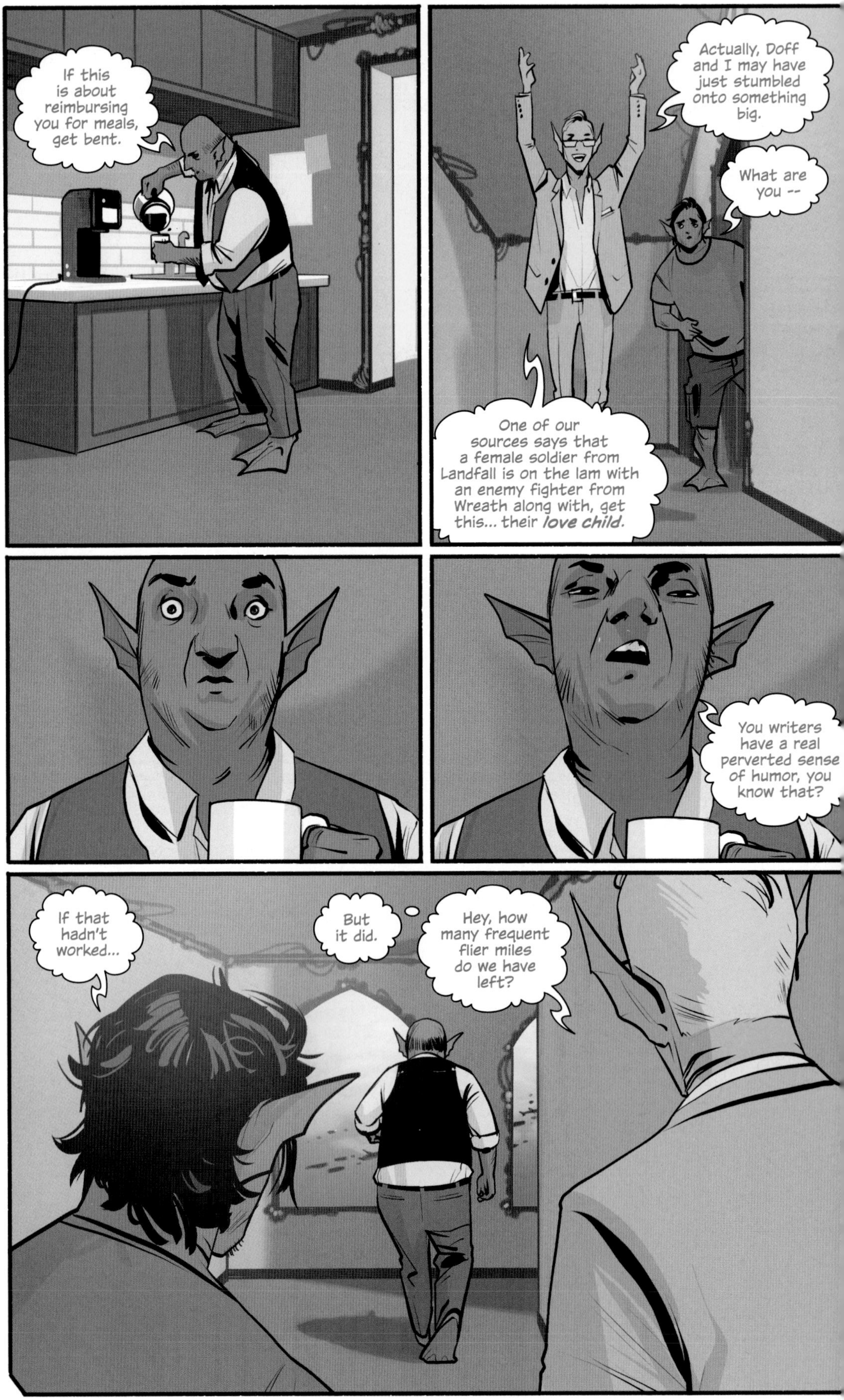
If this is about reimbursing you for meals, get bent.
Actually, Doff and I may have just stumbled onto something big.
What are you --
One of our sources says that a female soldier from Landfall is on the lam with an enemy fighter from Wreath along with, get this... their *love child*.
You writers have a real perverted sense of humor, you know that?
If that hadn't worked...
But it did.
Hey, how many frequent flier miles do we have left?

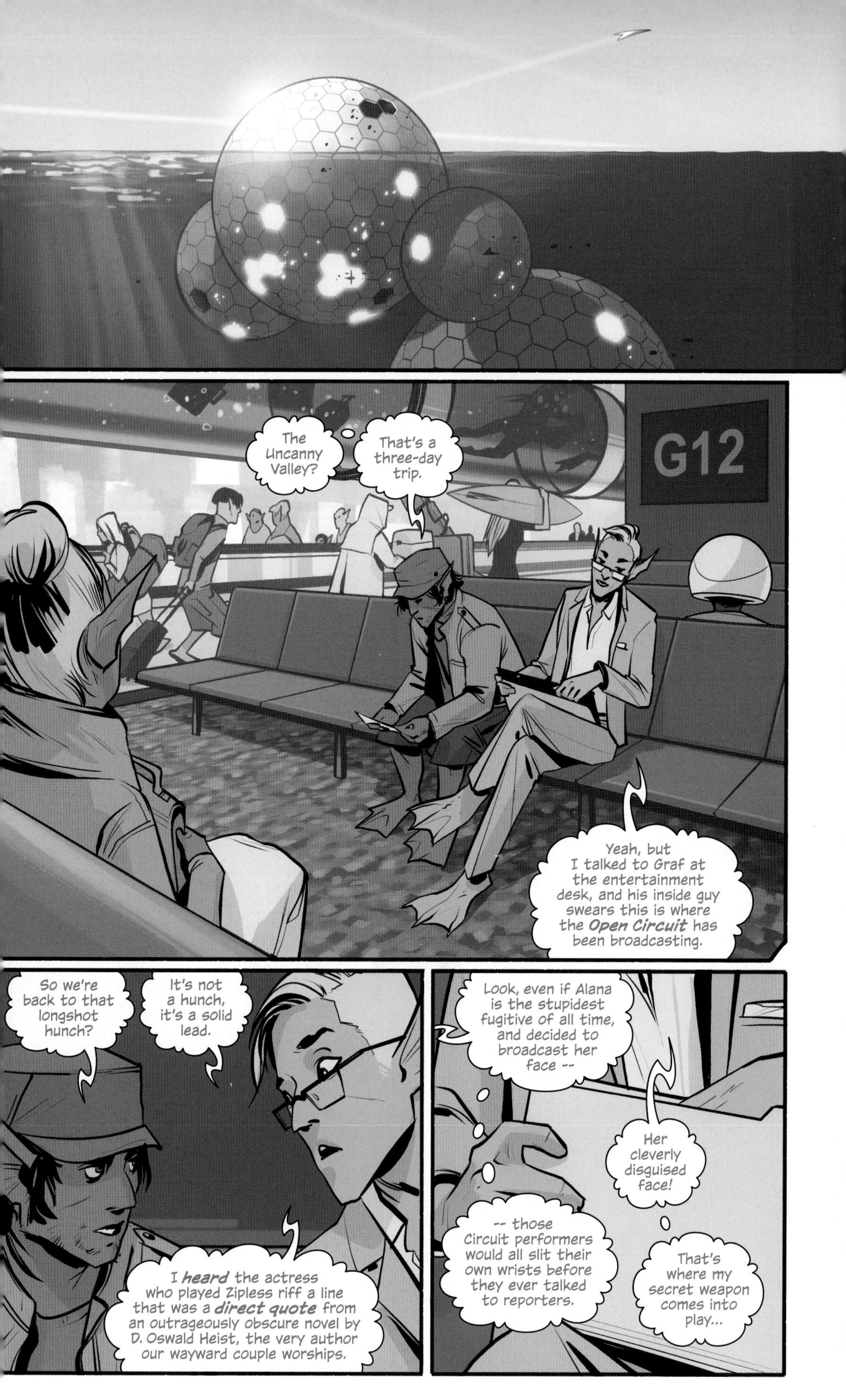
G12
The Uncanny Valley?
That's a three-day trip.
Yeah, but I talked to Graf at the entertainment desk, and his inside guy swears this is where the Open Circuit has been broadcasting.
So we're back to that longshot hunch?
It's not a hunch, it's a solid lead.
I heard the actress who played Zipless riff a line that was a direct quote from an outrageously obscure novel by D. Oswald Heist, the very author our wayward couple worships.
Look, even if Alana is the stupidest fugitive of all time, and decided to broadcast her face --
Her cleverly disguised face!
-- those Circuit performers would all slit their own wrists before they ever talked to reporters.
That's where my secret weapon comes into play...

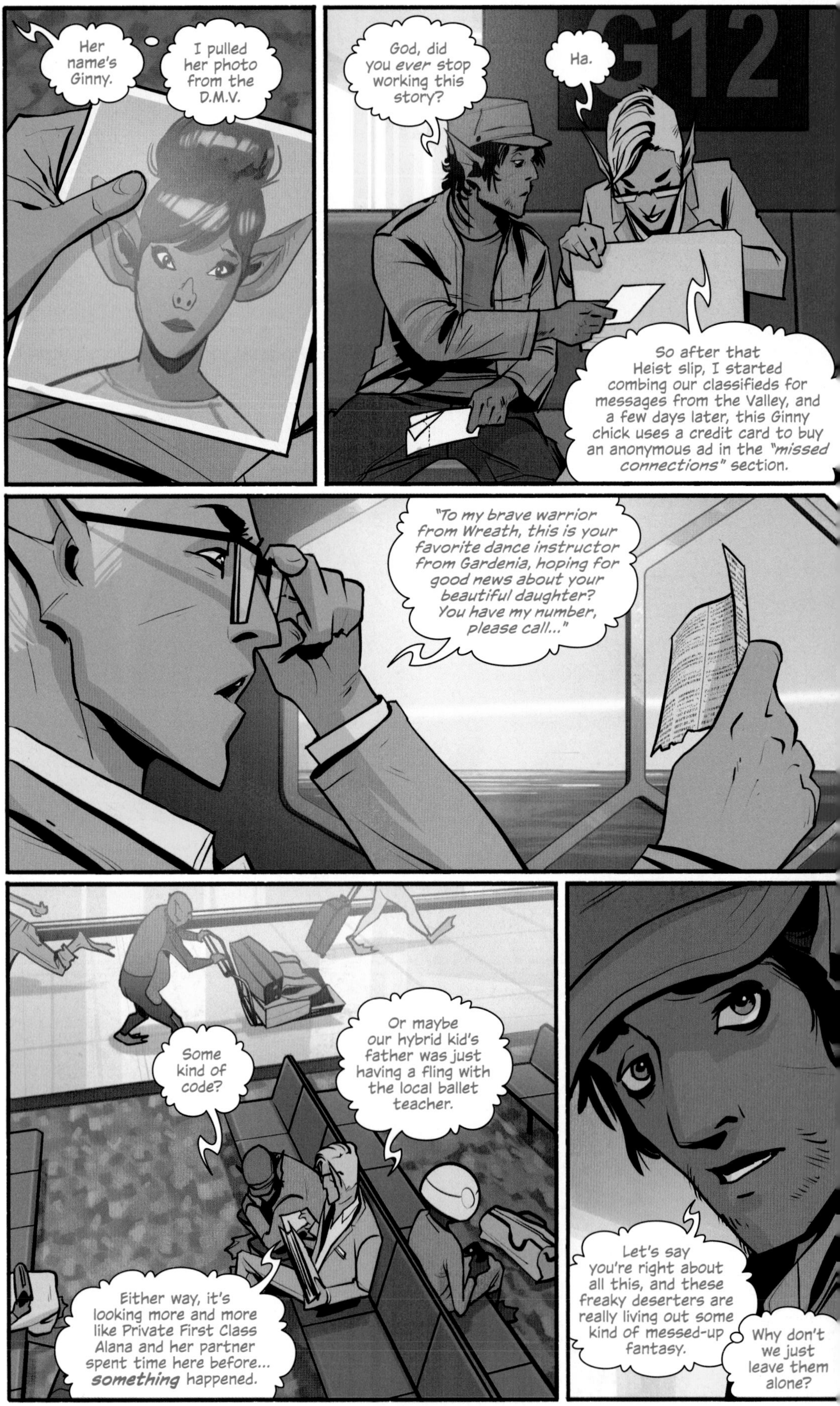

Her name's Ginny.
I pulled her photo from the D.M.V.
God, did you *ever* stop working this story?
Ha.
G12
So after that Heist slip, I started combing our classifieds for messages from the Valley, and a few days later, this Ginny chick uses a credit card to buy an anonymous ad in the *"missed connections"* section.
"To my brave warrior from Wreath, this is your favorite dance instructor from Gardenia, hoping for good news about your beautiful daughter? You have my number, please call..."
Some kind of code?
Or maybe our hybrid kid's father was just having a fling with the local ballet teacher.
Either way, it's looking more and more like Private First Class Alana and her partner spent time here before... ***something*** happened.
Let's say you're right about all this, and these freaky deserters are really living out some kind of messed-up fantasy.
Why don't we just leave them alone?

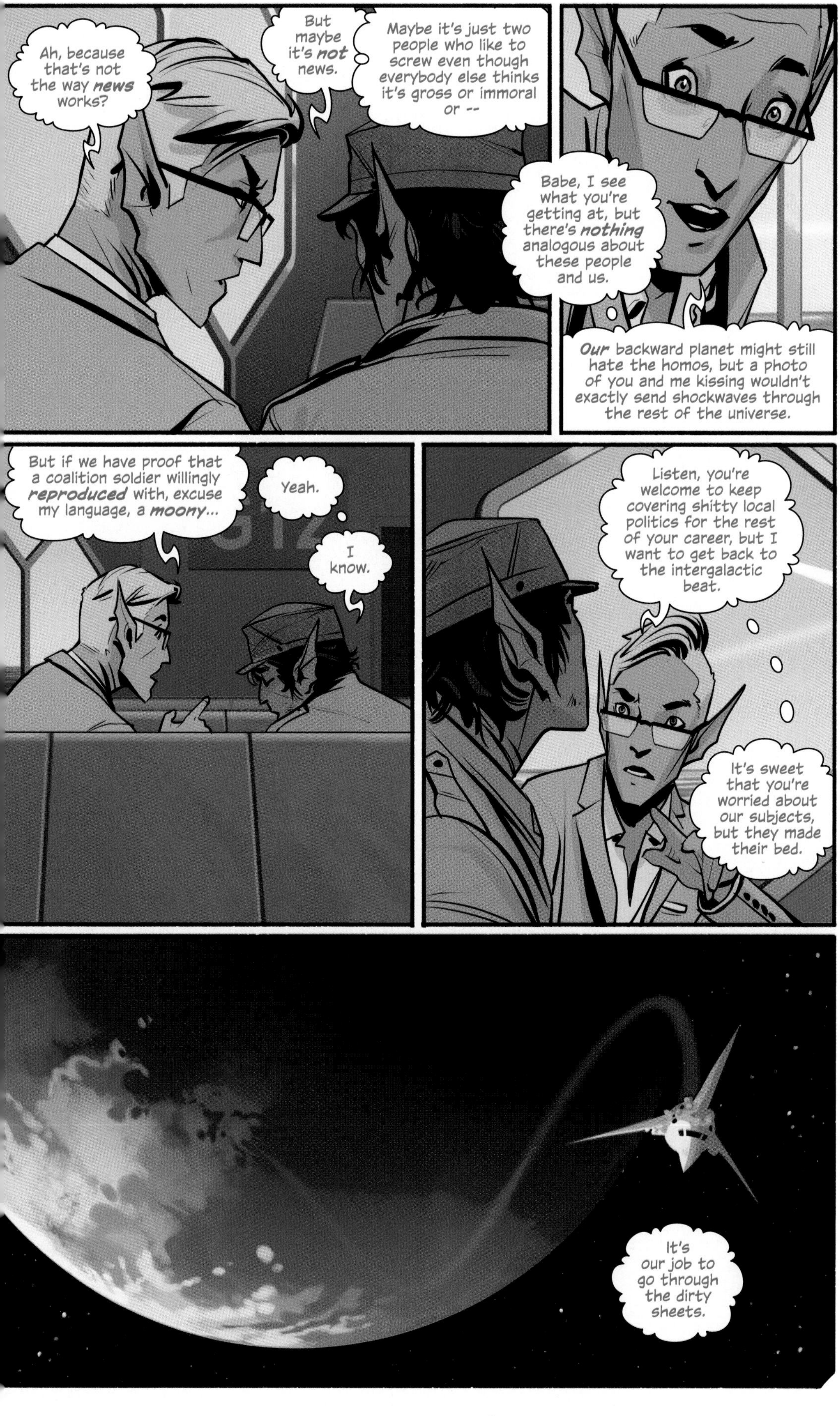
Ah, because that's not the way *news* works?
But maybe it's *not* news.
Maybe it's just two people who like to screw even though everybody else thinks it's gross or immoral or --
Babe, I see what you're getting at, but there's *nothing* analogous about these people and us.
Our backward planet might still hate the homos, but a photo of you and me kissing wouldn't exactly send shockwaves through the rest of the universe.
But if we have proof that a coalition soldier willingly *reproduced* with, excuse my language, a *moony*...
Yeah.
I know.
Listen, you're welcome to keep covering shitty local politics for the rest of your career, but I want to get back to the intergalactic beat.
It's sweet that you're worried about our subjects, but they made their bed.
It's our job to go through the dirty sheets.

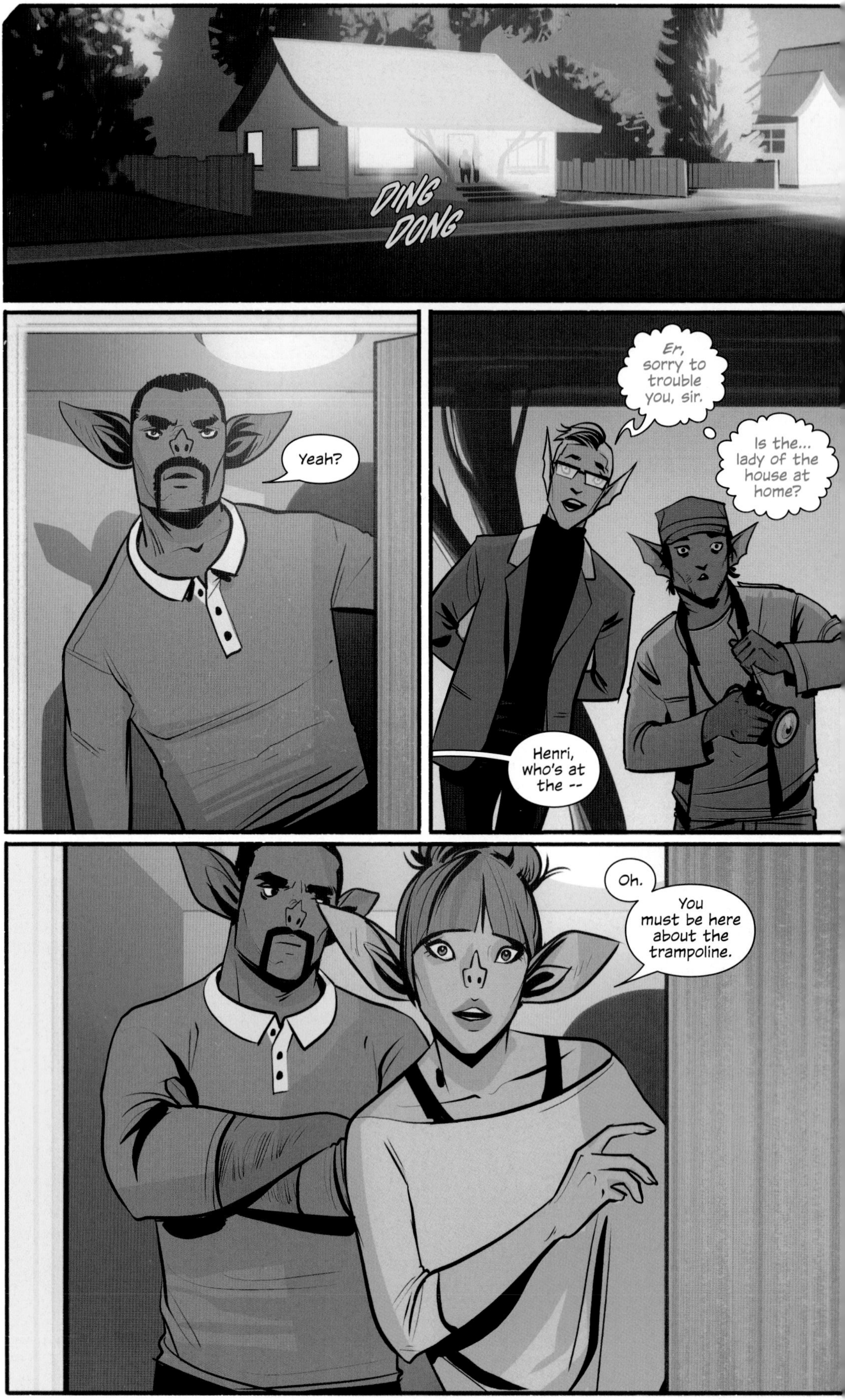
DING DONG
Yeah?
Er, sorry to trouble you, sir.
Is the... lady of the house at home?
Henri, who's at the --
Oh.
You must be here about the trampoline.

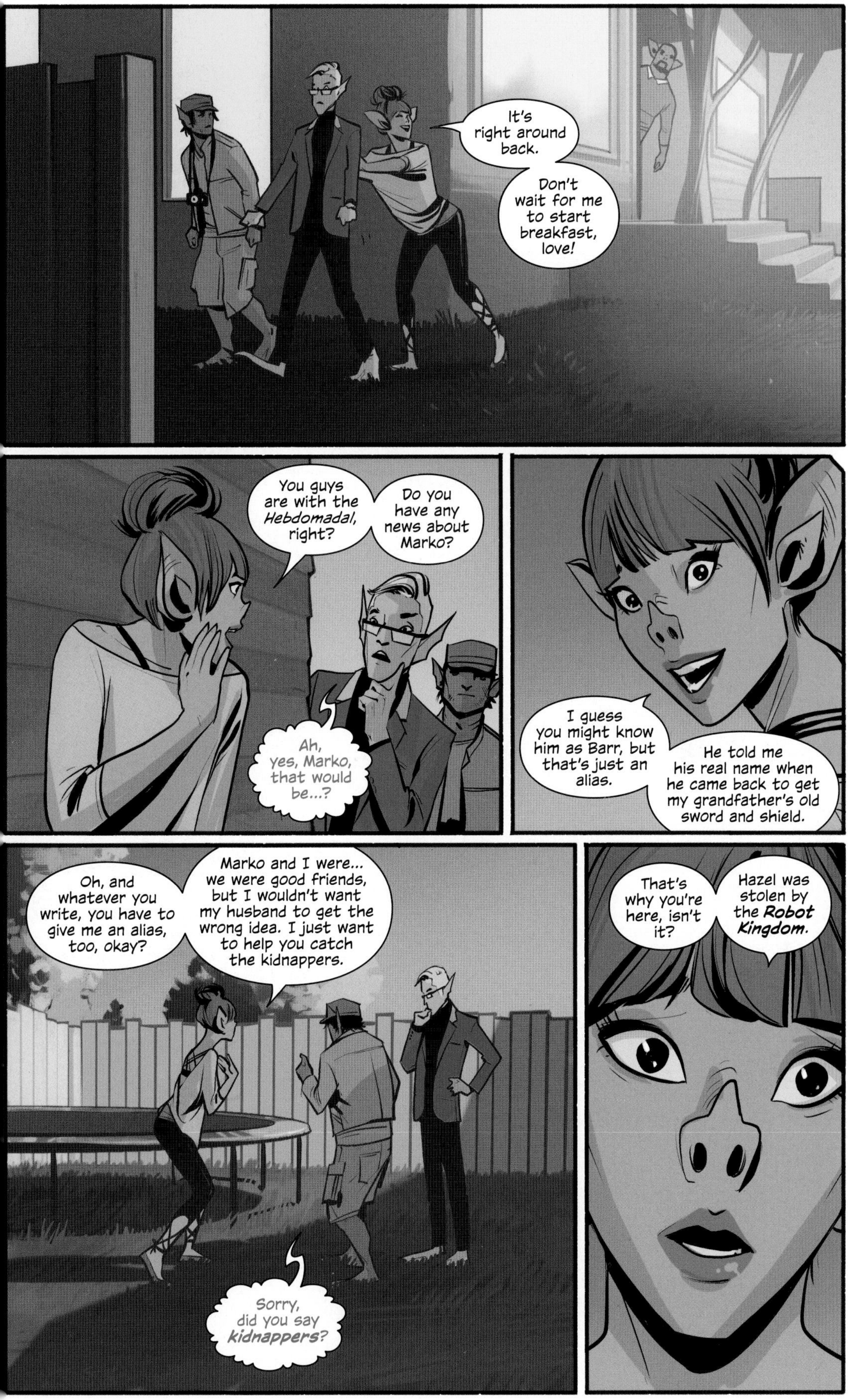

It's right around back.
Don't wait for me to start breakfast, love!
You guys are with the *Hebdomadal*, right?
Do you have any news about Marko?
Ah, yes, Marko, that would be...?
I guess you might know him as Barr, but that's just an alias.
He told me his real name when he came back to get my grandfather's old sword and shield.
Oh, and whatever you write, you have to give me an alias, too, okay?
Marko and I were... we were good friends, but I wouldn't want my husband to get the wrong idea. I just want to help you catch the kidnappers.
Sorry, did you say ***kidnappers***?
That's why you're here, isn't it?
Hazel was stolen by the ***Robot Kingdom***.

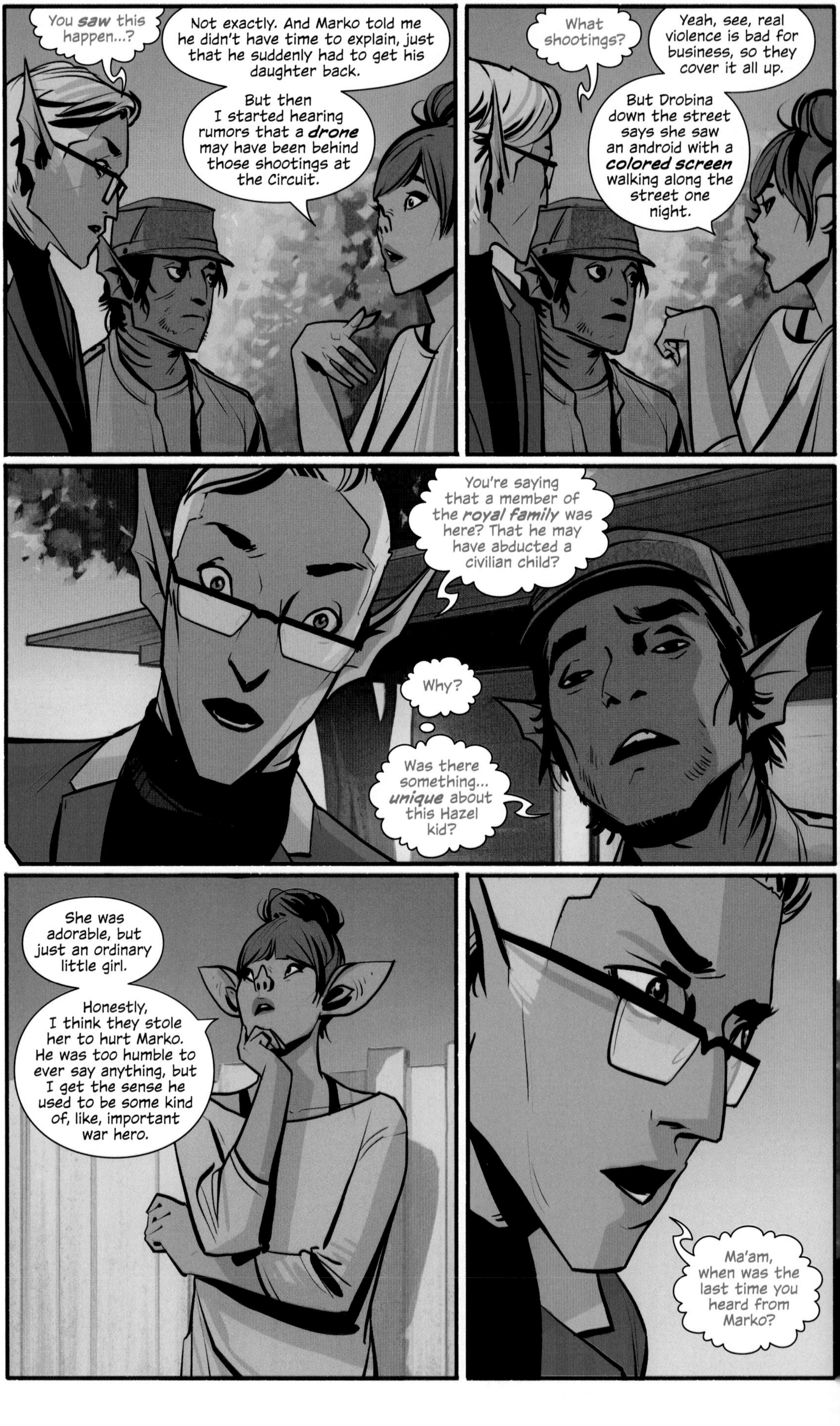
You *saw* this happen...?
Not exactly. And Marko told me he didn't have time to explain, just that he suddenly had to get his daughter back.
But then I started hearing rumors that a *drone* may have been behind those shootings at the Circuit.
What shootings?
Yeah, see, real violence is bad for business, so they cover it all up.
But Drobina down the street says she saw an android with a *colored screen* walking along the street one night.
You're saying that a member of the *royal family* was here? That he may have abducted a civilian child?
Why?
Was there something... *unique* about this Hazel kid?
She was adorable, but just an ordinary little girl.
Honestly, I think they stole her to hurt Marko. He was too humble to ever say anything, but I get the sense he used to be some kind of, like, important war hero.
Ma'am, when was the last time you heard from Marko?

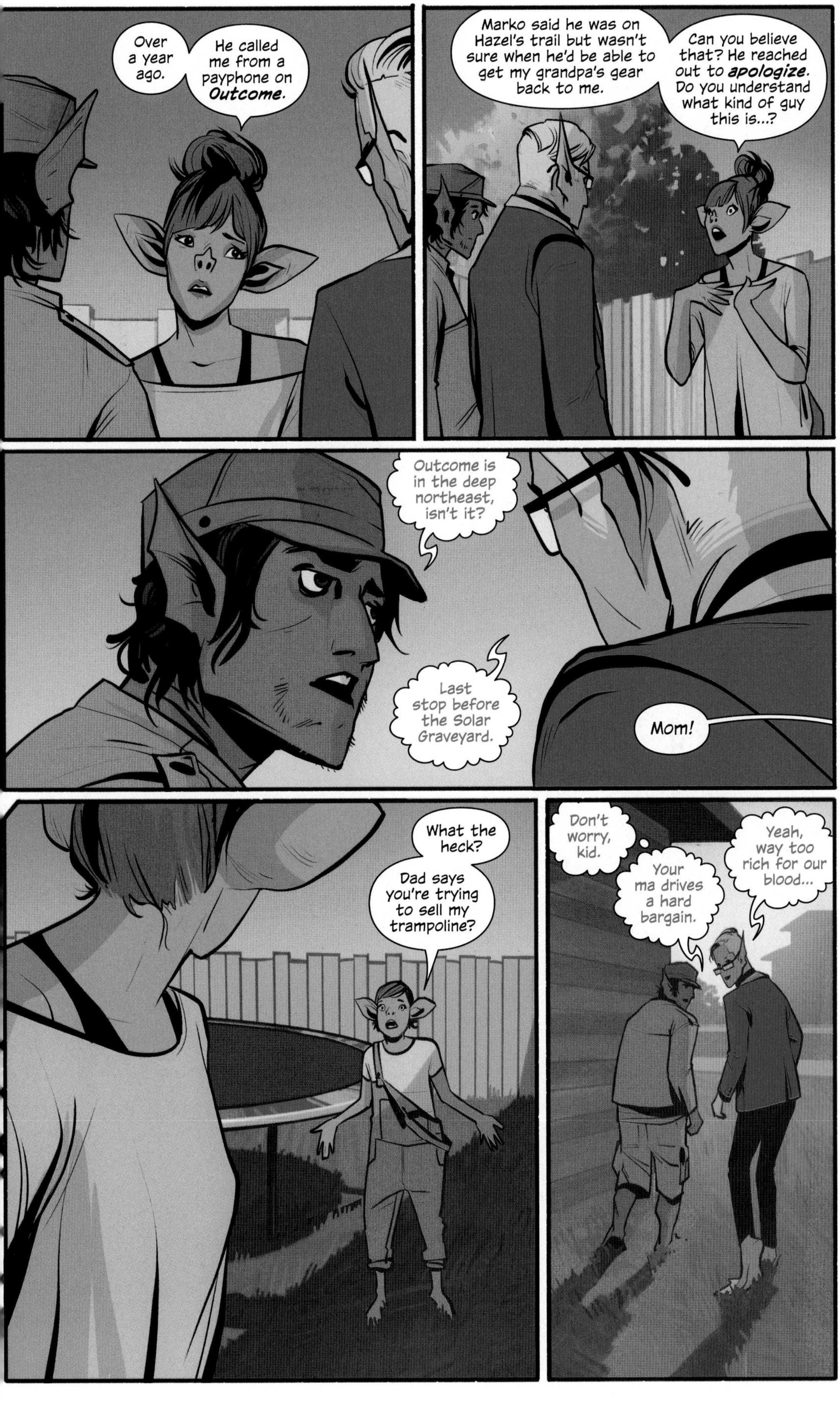
Over a year ago.
He called me from a payphone on *Outcome*.
Marko said he was on Hazel's trail but wasn't sure when he'd be able to get my grandpa's gear back to me.
Can you believe that? He reached out to ***apologize***. Do you understand what kind of guy this is...?
Outcome is in the deep northeast, isn't it?
Last stop before the Solar Graveyard.
Mom!
What the heck?
Dad says you're trying to sell my trampoline?
Don't worry, kid.
Your ma drives a hard bargain.
Yeah, way too rich for our blood...

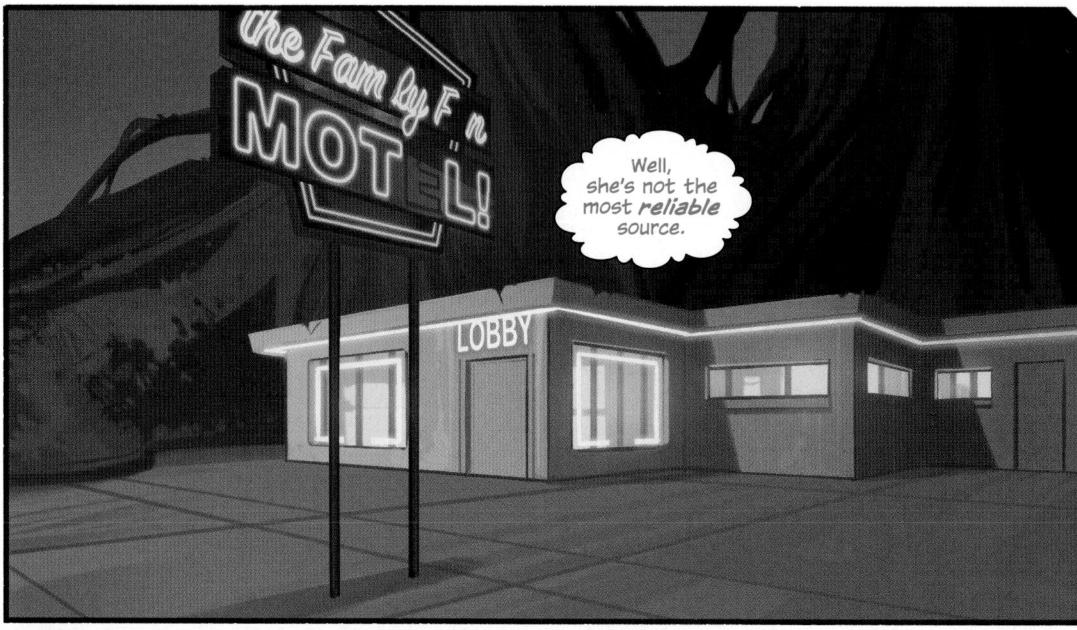
LOBBY
Well, she's not the most ***reliable*** source.

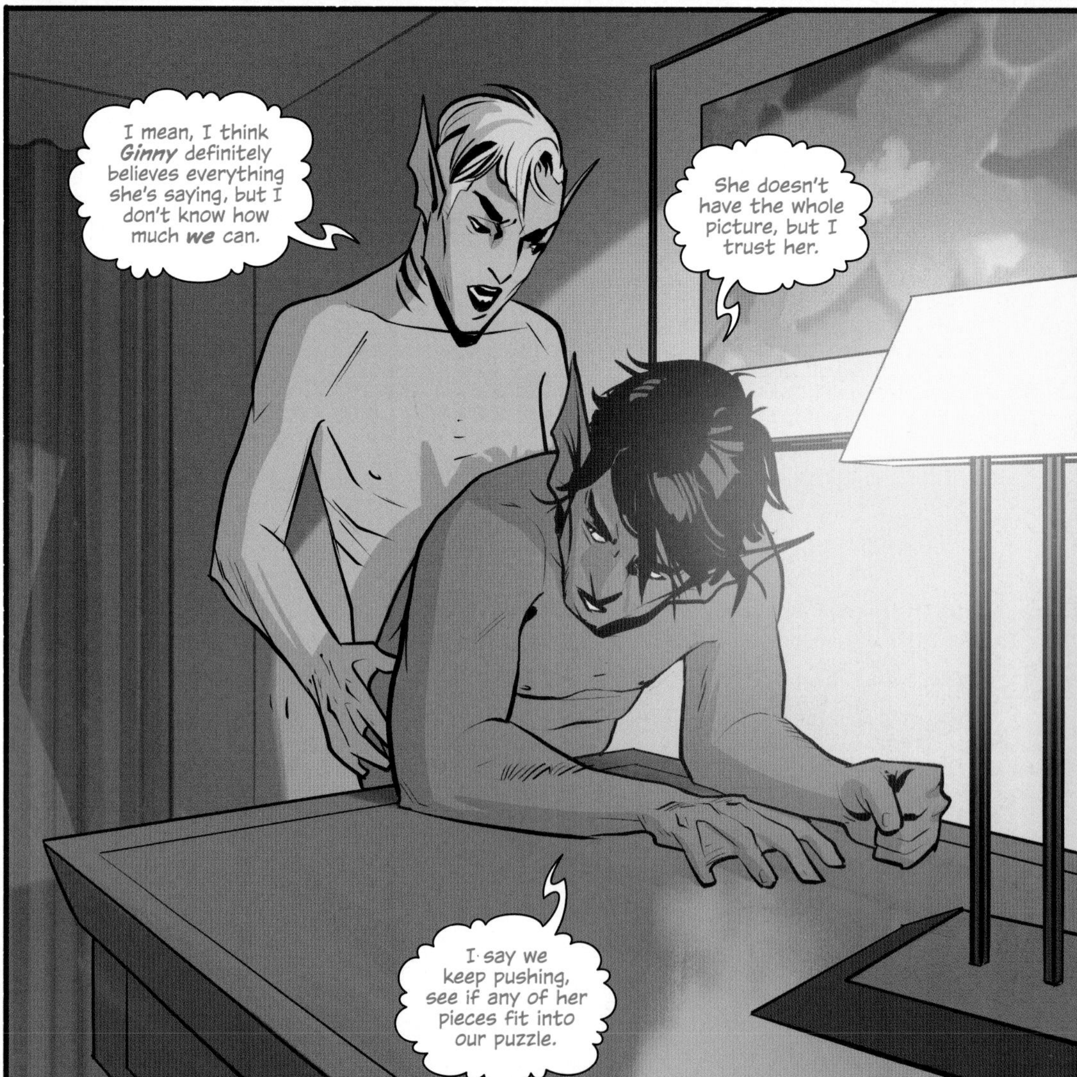
I mean, I think ***Ginny*** definitely believes everything she's saying, but I don't know how much ***we*** can.
She doesn't have the whole picture, but I trust her.
I say we keep pushing, see if any of her pieces fit into our puzzle.

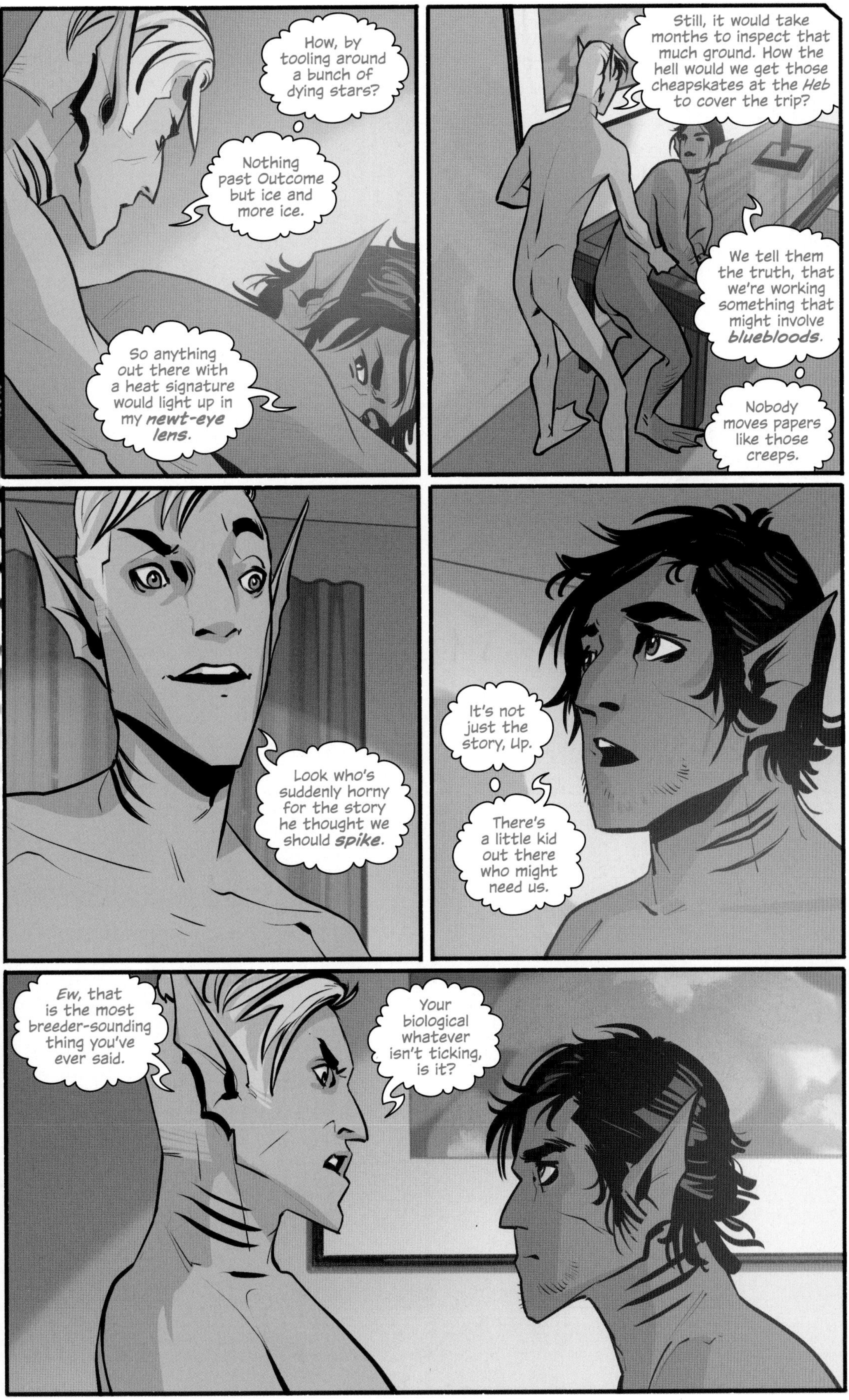
How, by tooling around a bunch of dying stars?
Nothing past Outcome but ice and more ice.
So anything out there with a heat signature would light up in my **newt-eye lens**.
Still, it would take months to inspect that much ground. How the hell would we get those cheapskates at the *Heb* to cover the trip?
We tell them the truth, that we're working something that might involve **blueblood**s.
Nobody moves papers like those creeps.
Look who's suddenly horny for the story he thought we should **spike**.
It's not just the story, Up.
There's a little kid out there who might need us.
Ew, that is the most breeder-sounding thing you've ever said.
Your biological whatever isn't ticking, is it?

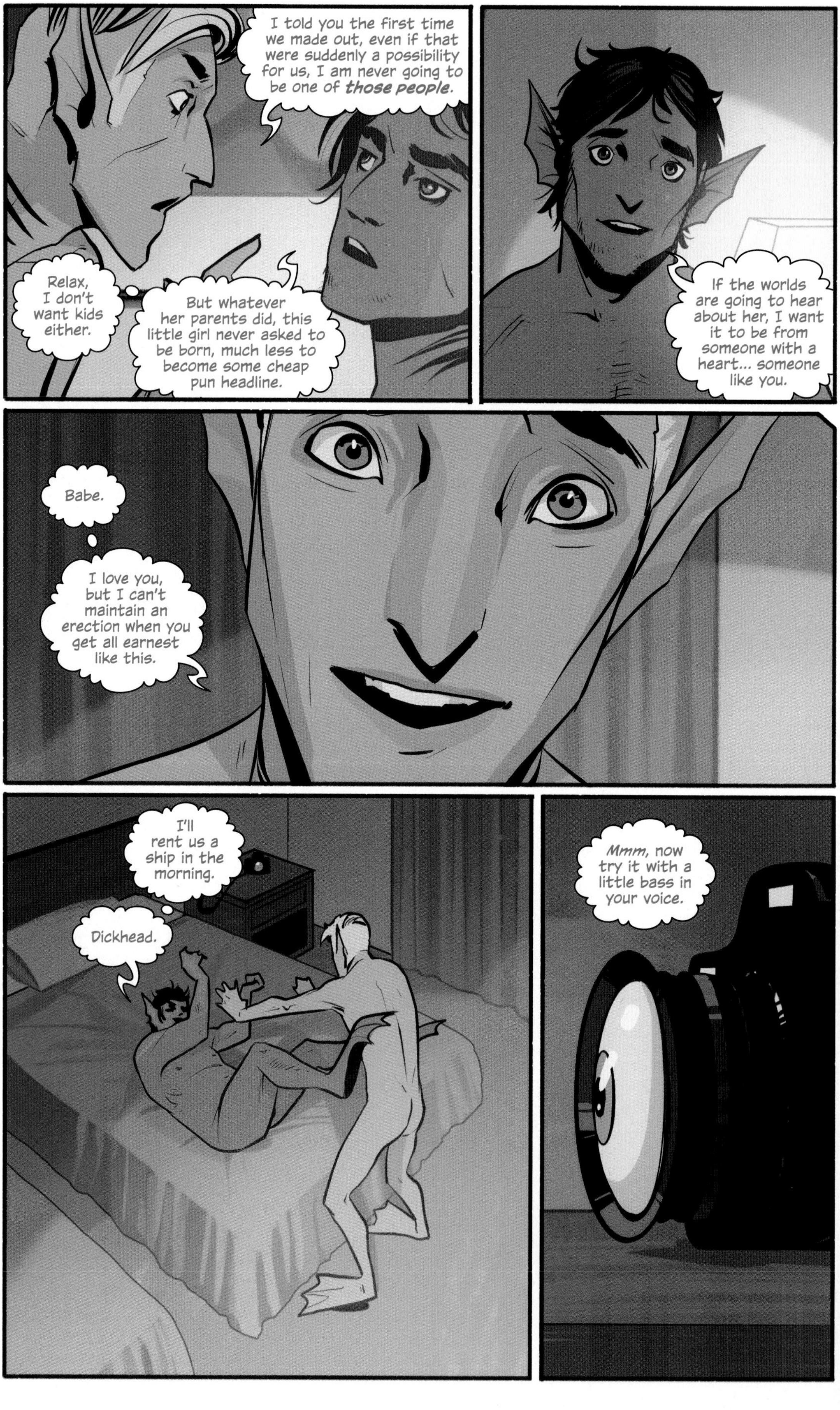
I told you the first time we made out, even if that were suddenly a possibility for us, I am never going to be one of *those people*.
Relax, I don't want kids either.
But whatever her parents did, this little girl never asked to be born, much less to become some cheap pun headline.
If the worlds are going to hear about her, I want it to be from someone with a heart... someone like you.
Babe.
I love you, but I can't maintain an erection when you get all earnest like this.
I'll rent us a ship in the morning.
Dickhead.
Mmm, now try it with a little bass in your voice.

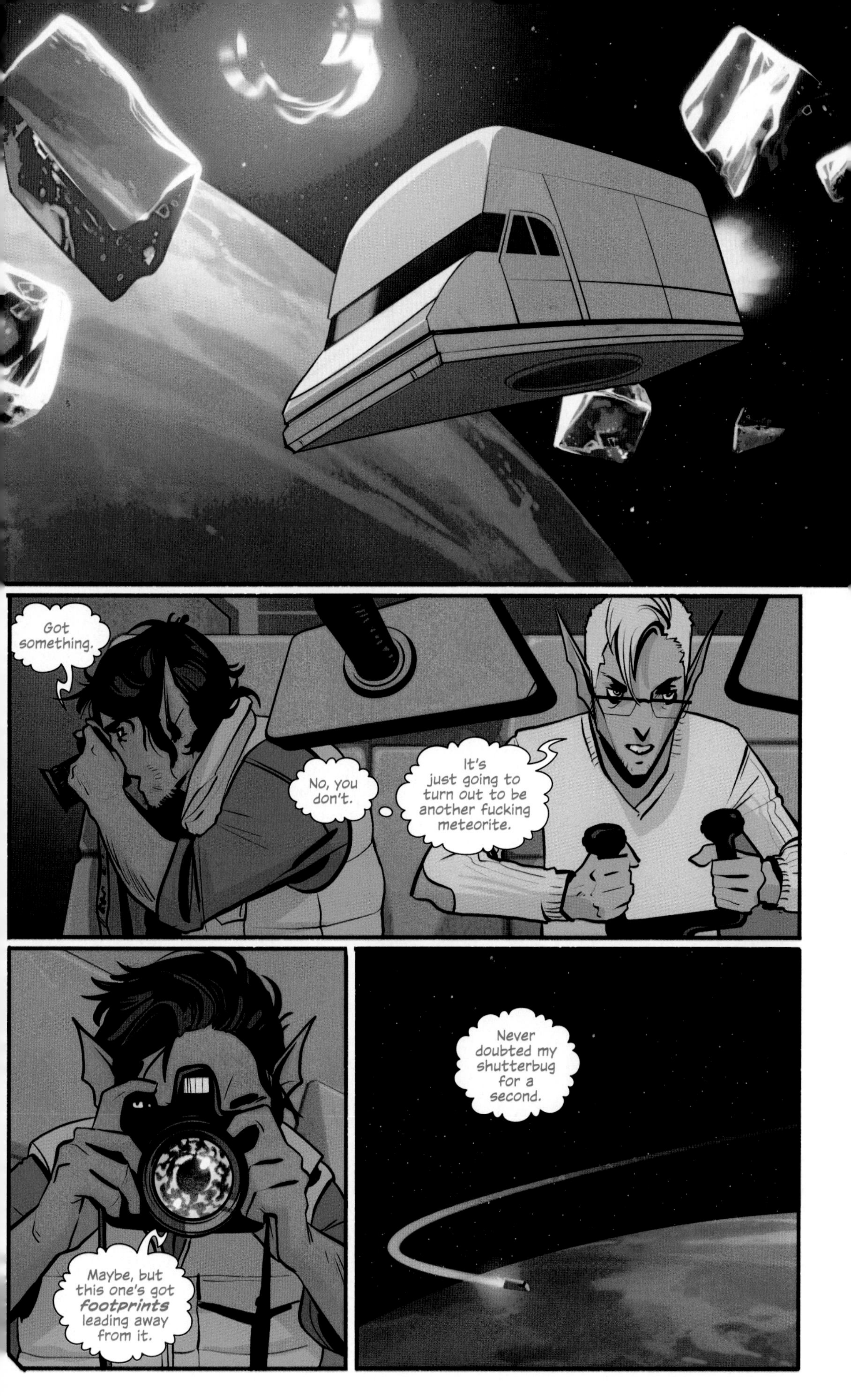

Got something.
It's just going to turn out to be another fucking meteorite.
No, you don't.
Maybe, but this one's got **footprints** leading away from it.
Never doubted my shutterbug for a second.

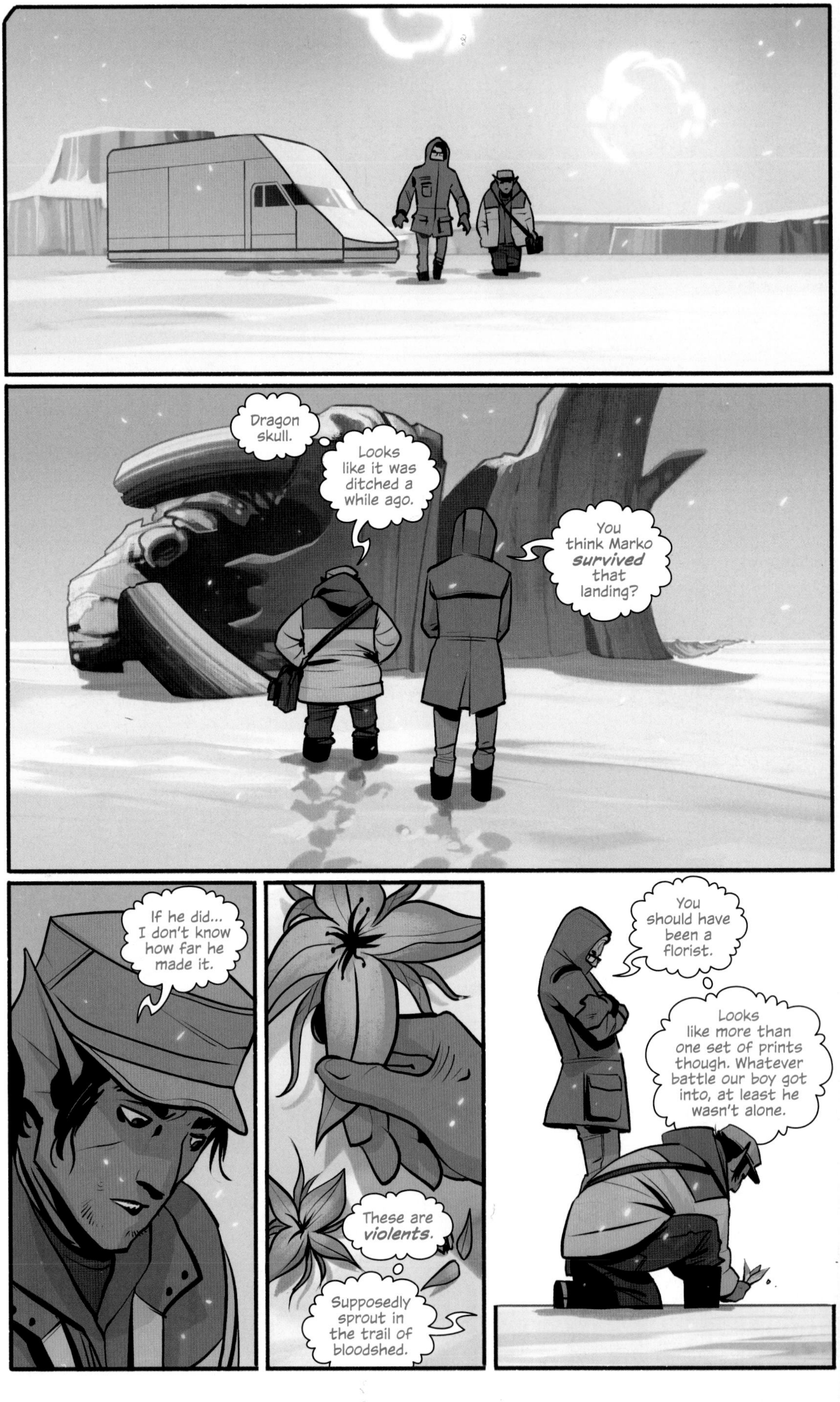
Dragon skull.
Looks like it was ditched a while ago.
You think Marko *survived* that landing?
If he did... I don't know how far he made it.
These are *violents*.
Supposedly sprout in the trail of bloodshed.
You should have been a florist.
Looks like more than one set of prints though. Whatever battle our boy got into, at least he wasn't alone.

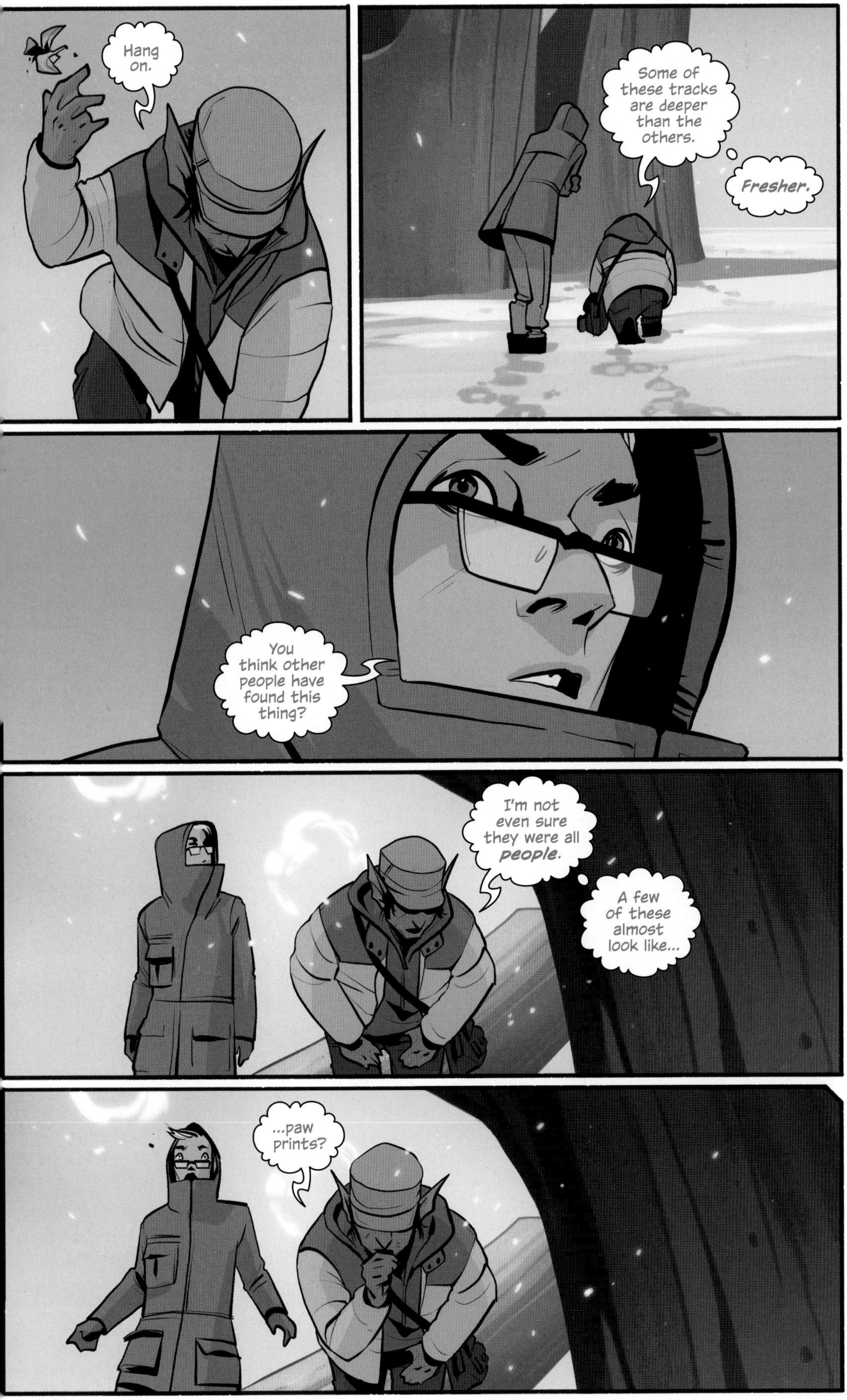
Hang on.
Some of these tracks are deeper than the others.
Fresher.
You think other people have found this thing?
I'm not even sure they were all *people*.
A few of these almost look like...
...paw prints?

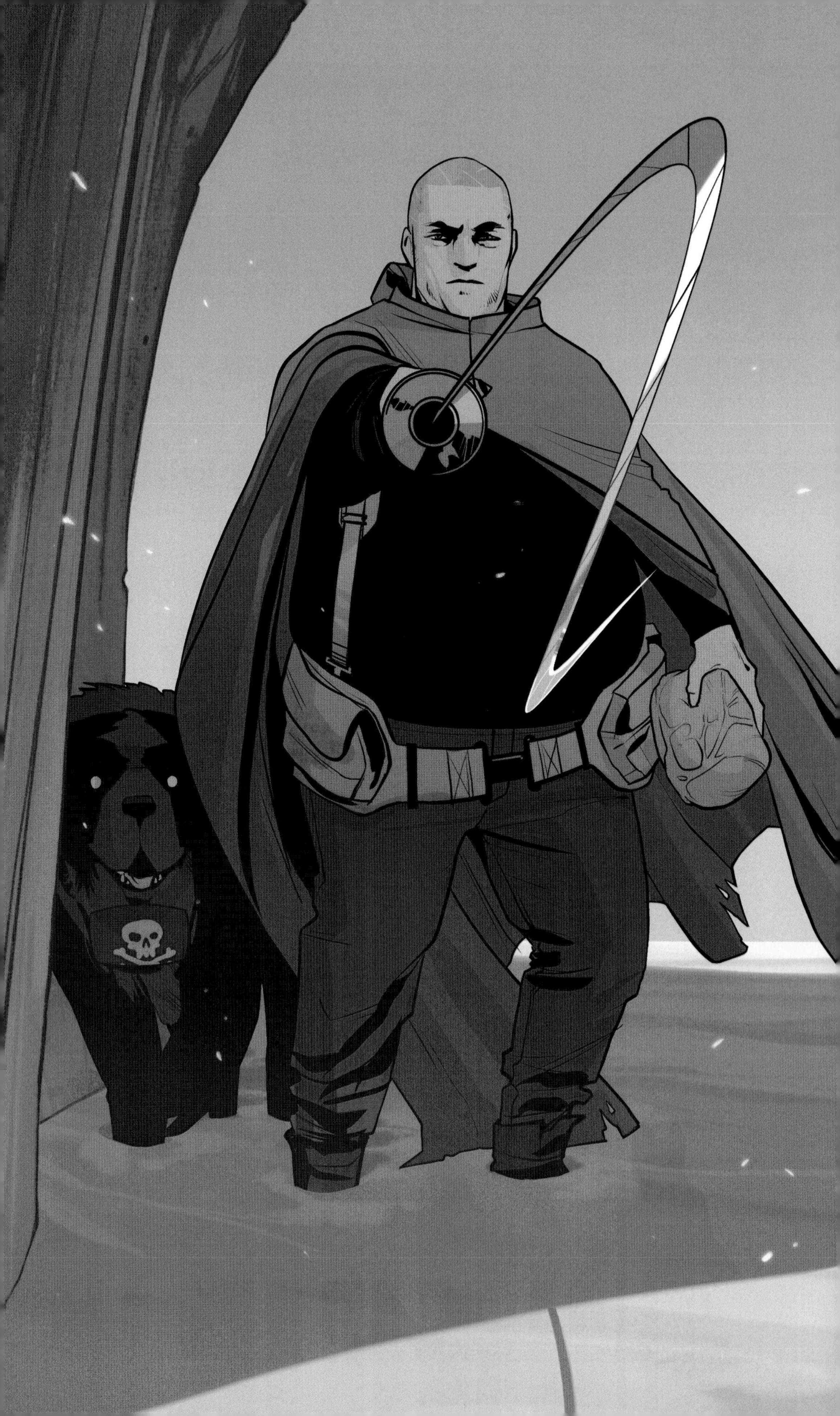

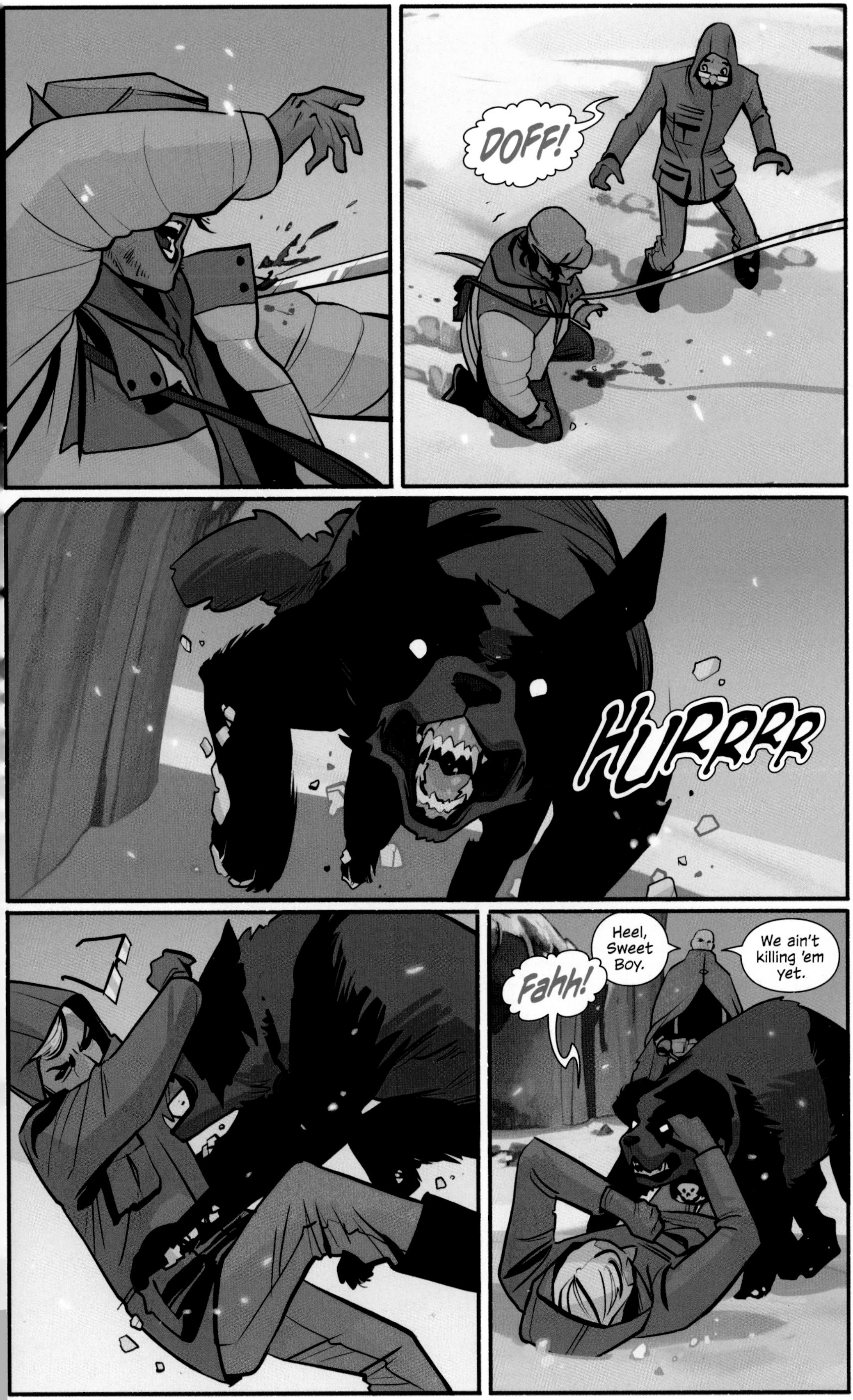
DOFF!
HURRRR
Fahh!
Heel, Sweet Boy.
We ain't killing 'em yet.

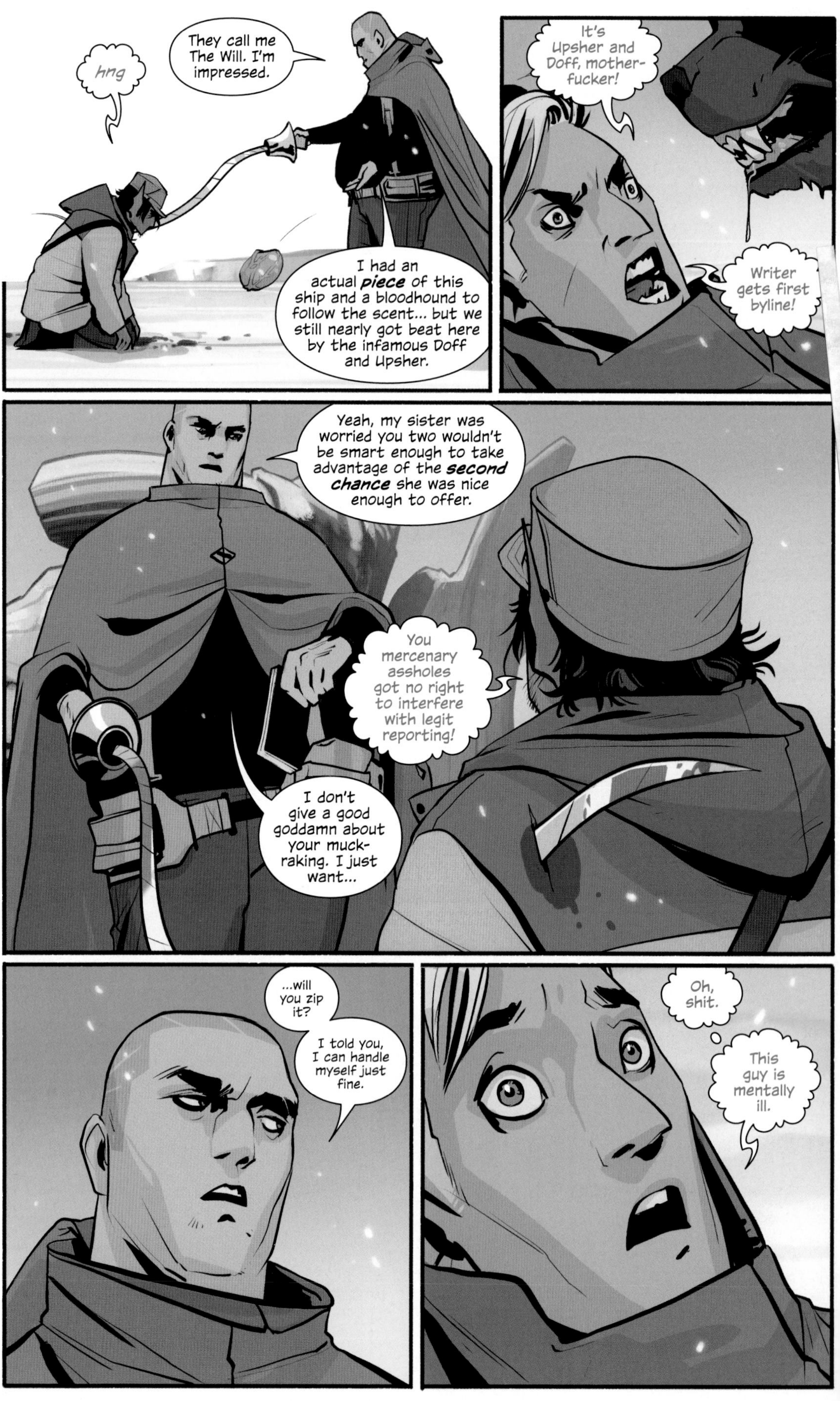
hng
They call me The Will. I'm impressed.
I had an actual piece of this ship and a bloodhound to follow the scent... but we still nearly got beat here by the infamous Doff and Upsher.
It's Upsher and Doff, mother-fucker!
Writer gets first byline!
Yeah, my sister was worried you two wouldn't be smart enough to take advantage of the second chance she was nice enough to offer.
You mercenary assholes got no right to interfere with legit reporting!
I don't give a good goddamn about your muck-raking. I just want...
...will you zip it?
I told you, I can handle myself just fine.
Oh, shit.
This guy is mentally ill.

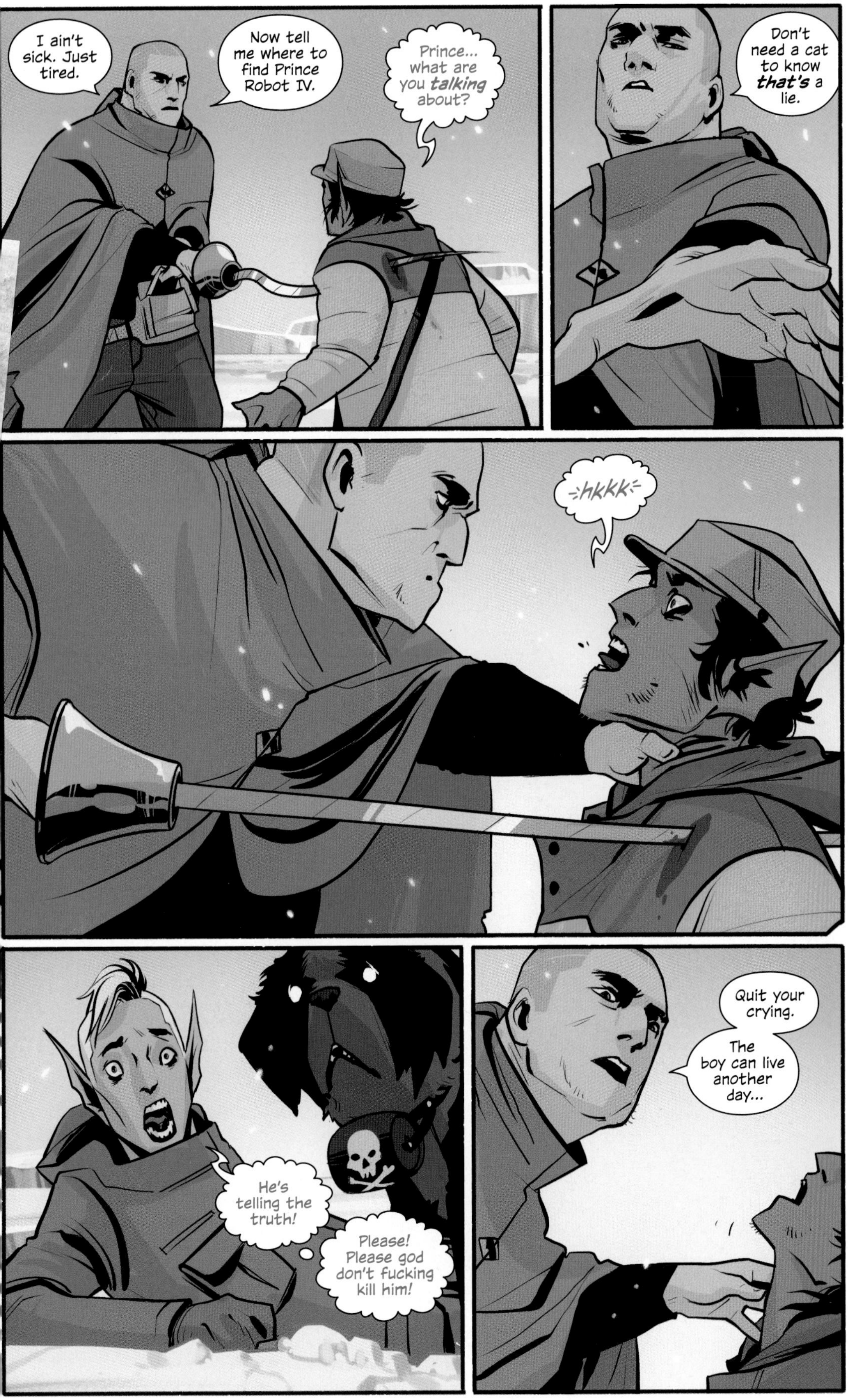
I ain't sick. Just tired.
Now tell me where to find Prince Robot IV.
Prince... what are you *talking* about?
Don't need a cat to know ***that's*** a lie.
hkkk
He's telling the truth!
Please! Please god don't fucking kill him!
Quit your crying.
The boy can live another day...

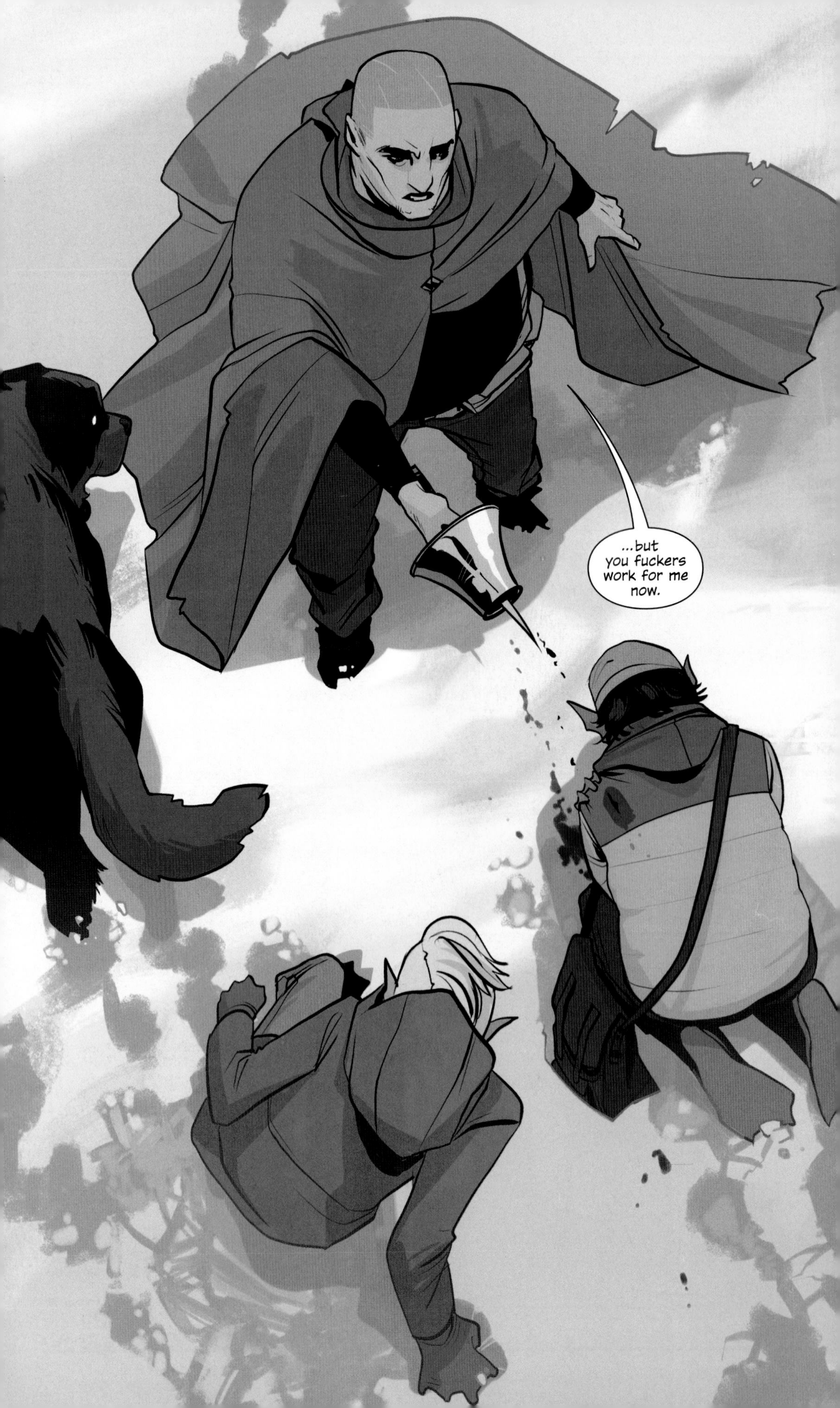
...but you fuckers work for me now.

end chapter thirty-three

CHAPTER
THIRTY-FOUR

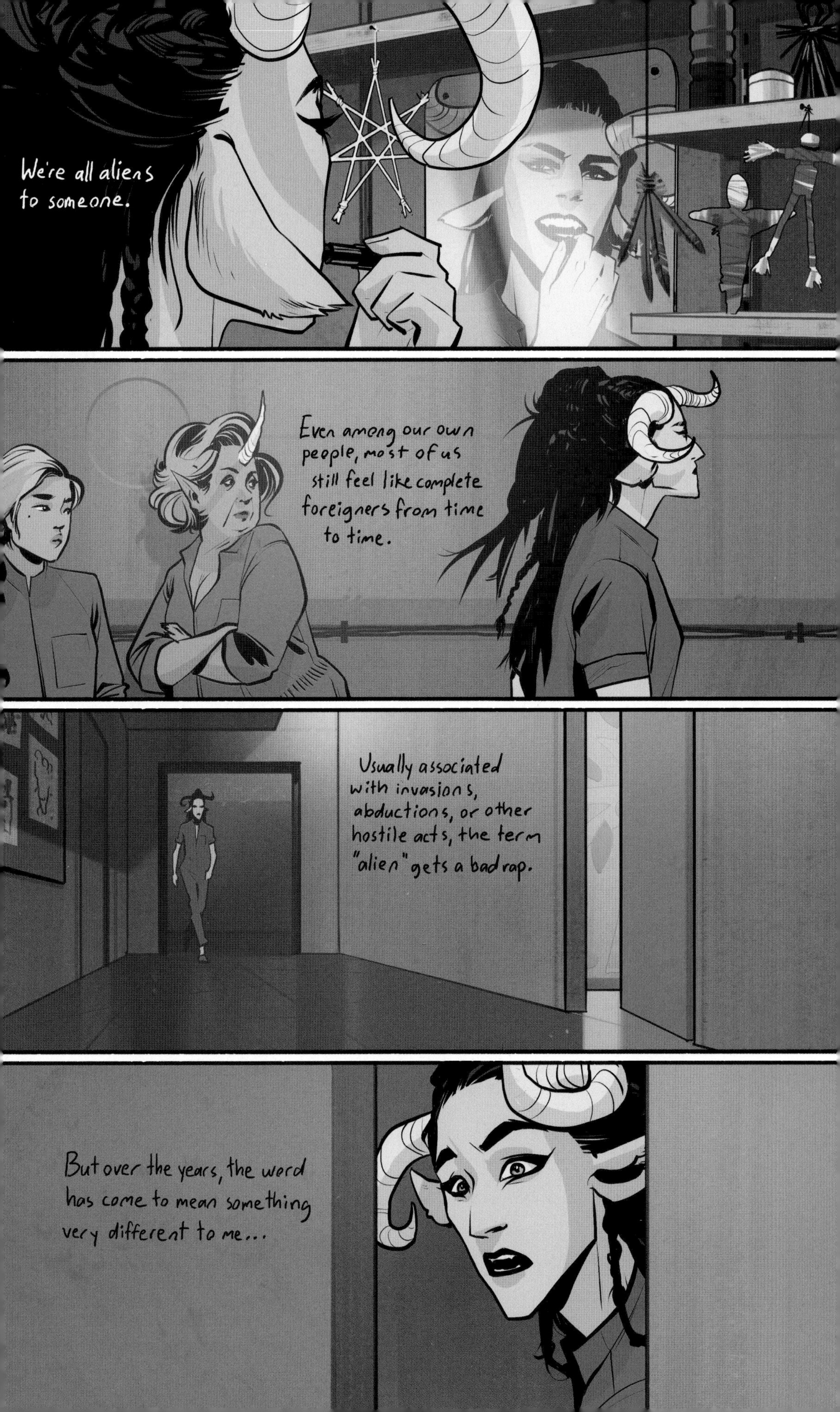
We're all aliens to someone.
Even among our own people, most of us still feel like complete foreigners from time to time.
Usually associated with invasions, abductions, or other hostile acts, the term "alien" gets a bad rap.
But over the years, the word has come to mean something very different to me...

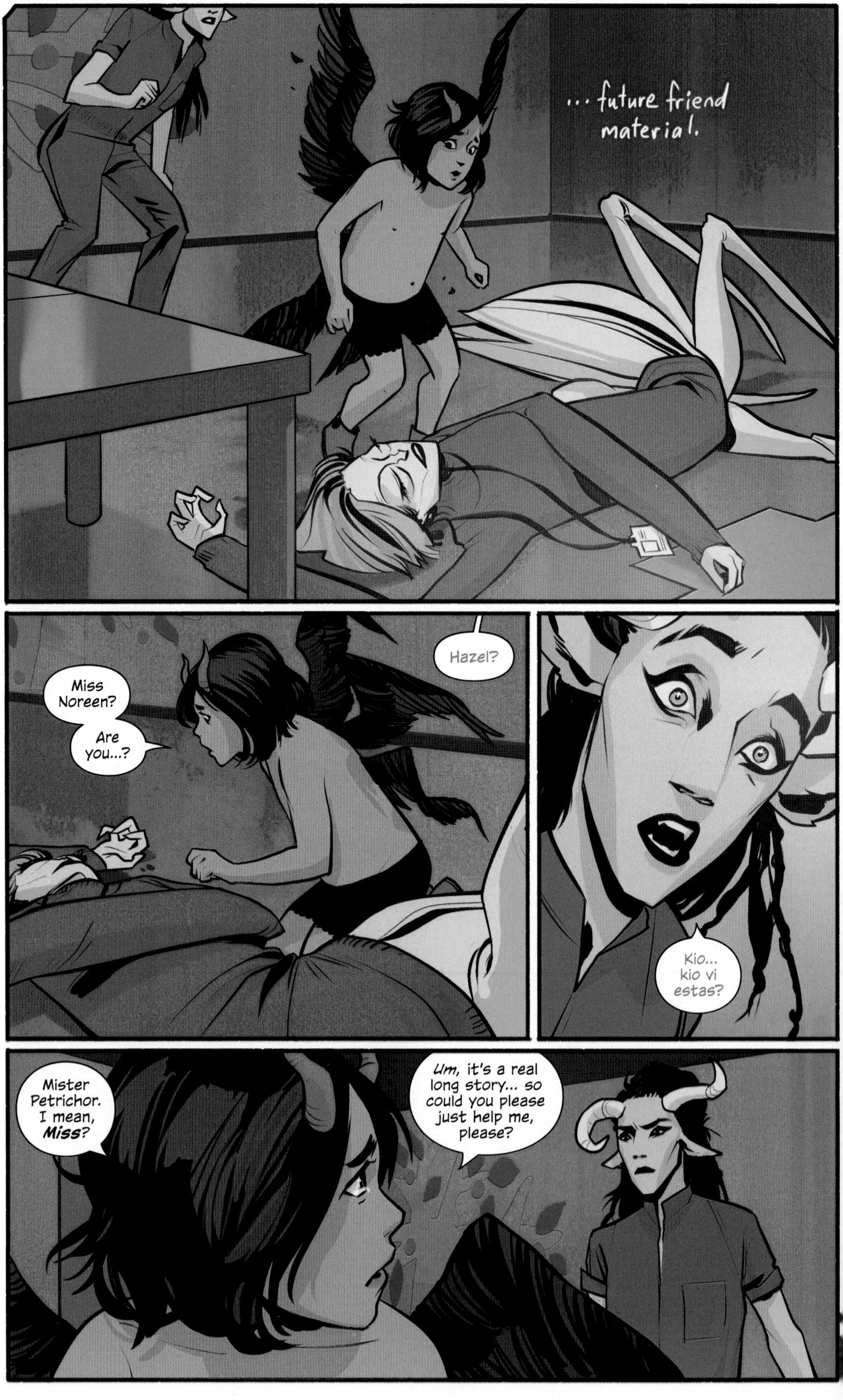

... future friend material.
Miss Noreen?
Are you...?
Hazel?
Kio... kio vi estas?
Mister Petrichor. I mean, *Miss*?
Um, it's a real long story... so could you please just help me, please?

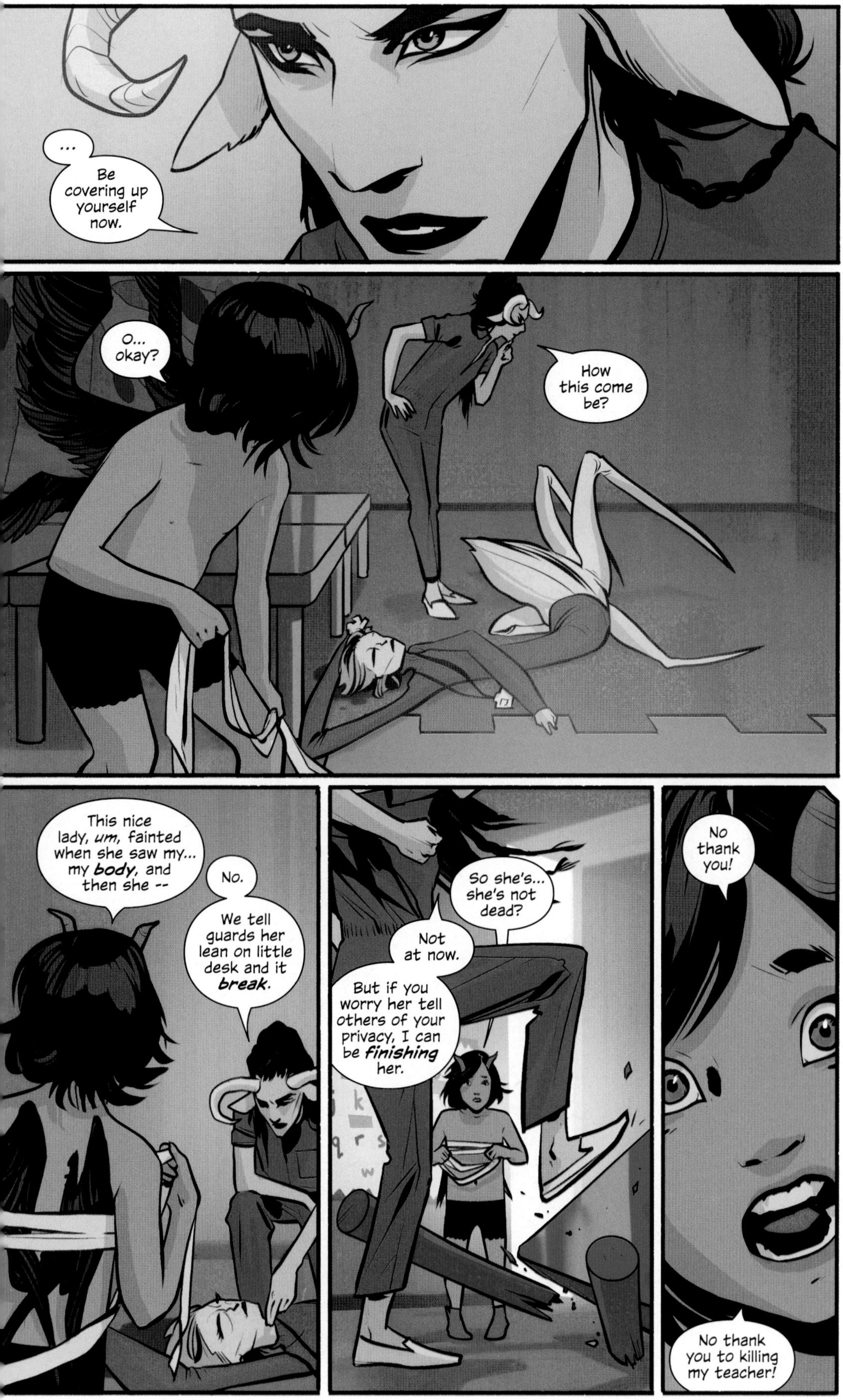
...
Be covering up yourself now.
O... okay?
How this come be?
This nice lady, *um*, fainted when she saw my... my ***body***, and then she --
No.
We tell guards her lean on little desk and it ***break***.
So she's... she's not dead?
Not at now.
But if you worry her tell others of your privacy, I can be ***finishing*** her.
No thank you!
No thank you to killing my teacher!

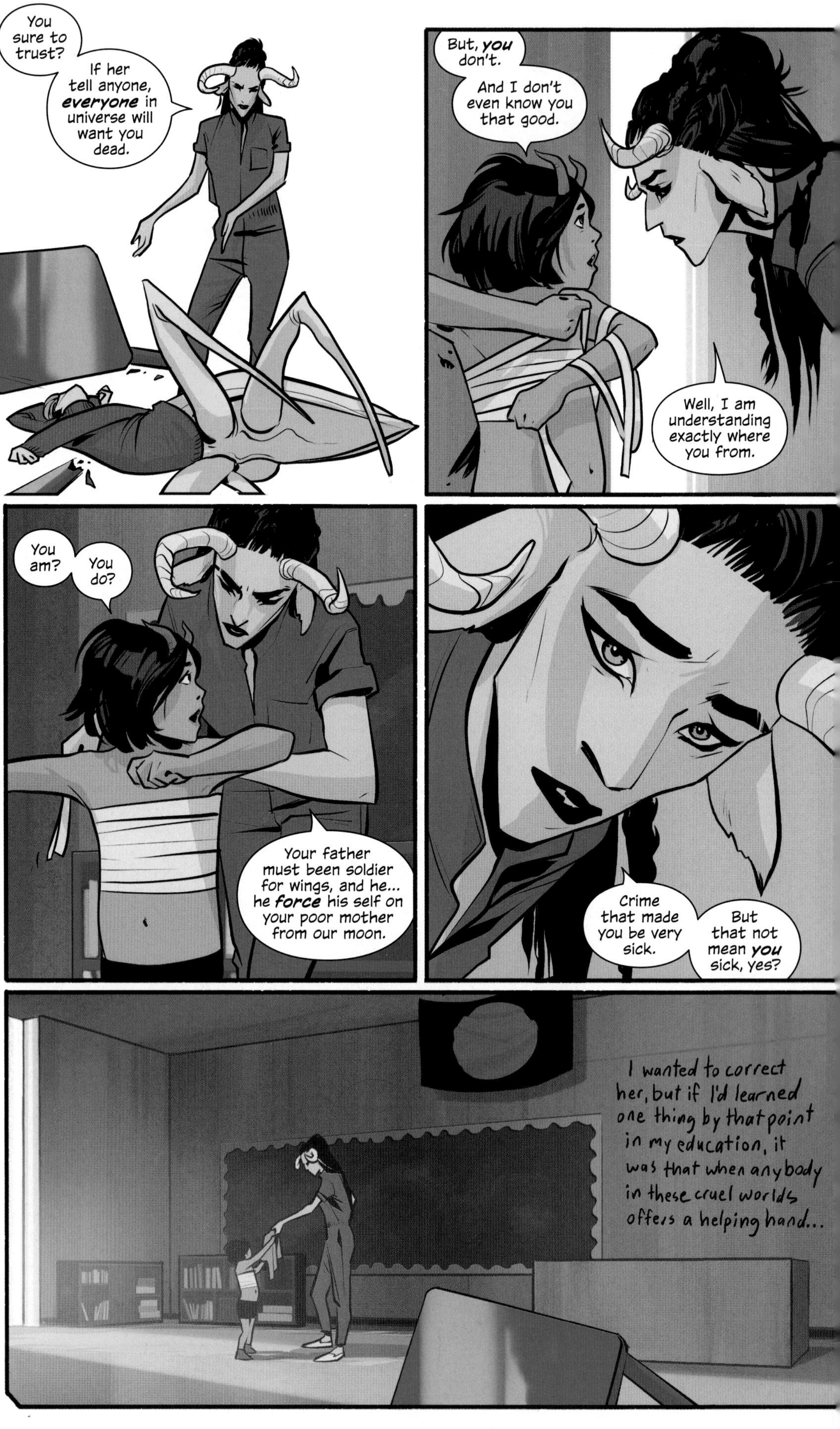
You sure to trust?
If her tell anyone, ***everyone*** in universe will want you dead.
But, ***you*** don't.
And I don't even know you that good.
Well, I am understanding exactly where you from.
You am?
You do?
Your father must been soldier for wings, and he... he ***force*** his self on your poor mother from our moon.
Crime that made you be very sick.
But that not mean ***you*** sick, yes?
I wanted to correct her, but if I'd learned one thing by that point in my education, it was that when anybody in these cruel worlds offers a helping hand...

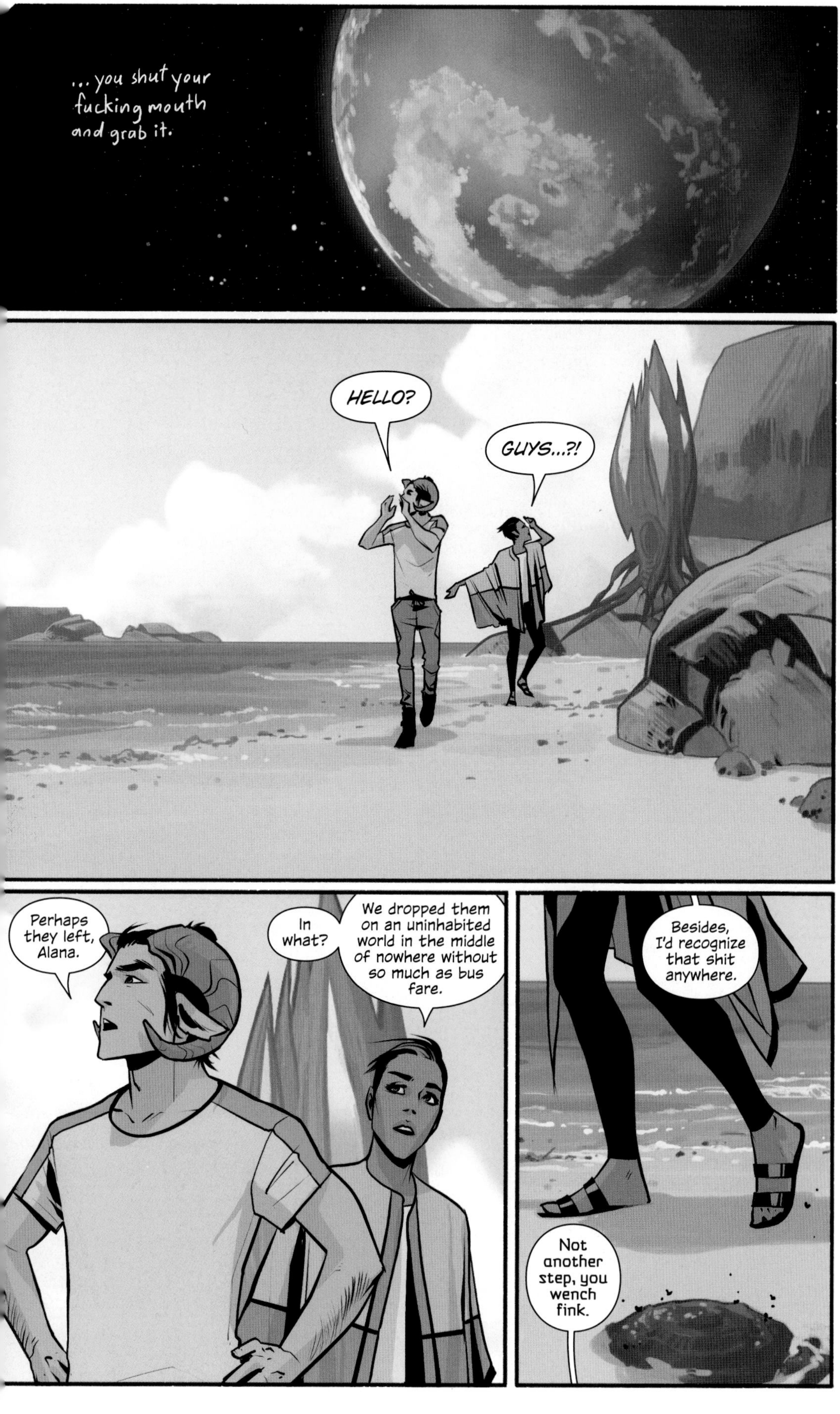
...you shut your fucking mouth and grab it.
HELLO?
GUYS...?!
Perhaps they left, Alana.
In what?
We dropped them on an uninhabited world in the middle of nowhere without so much as bus fare.
Besides, I'd recognize that shit anywhere.
Not another step, you wench fink.

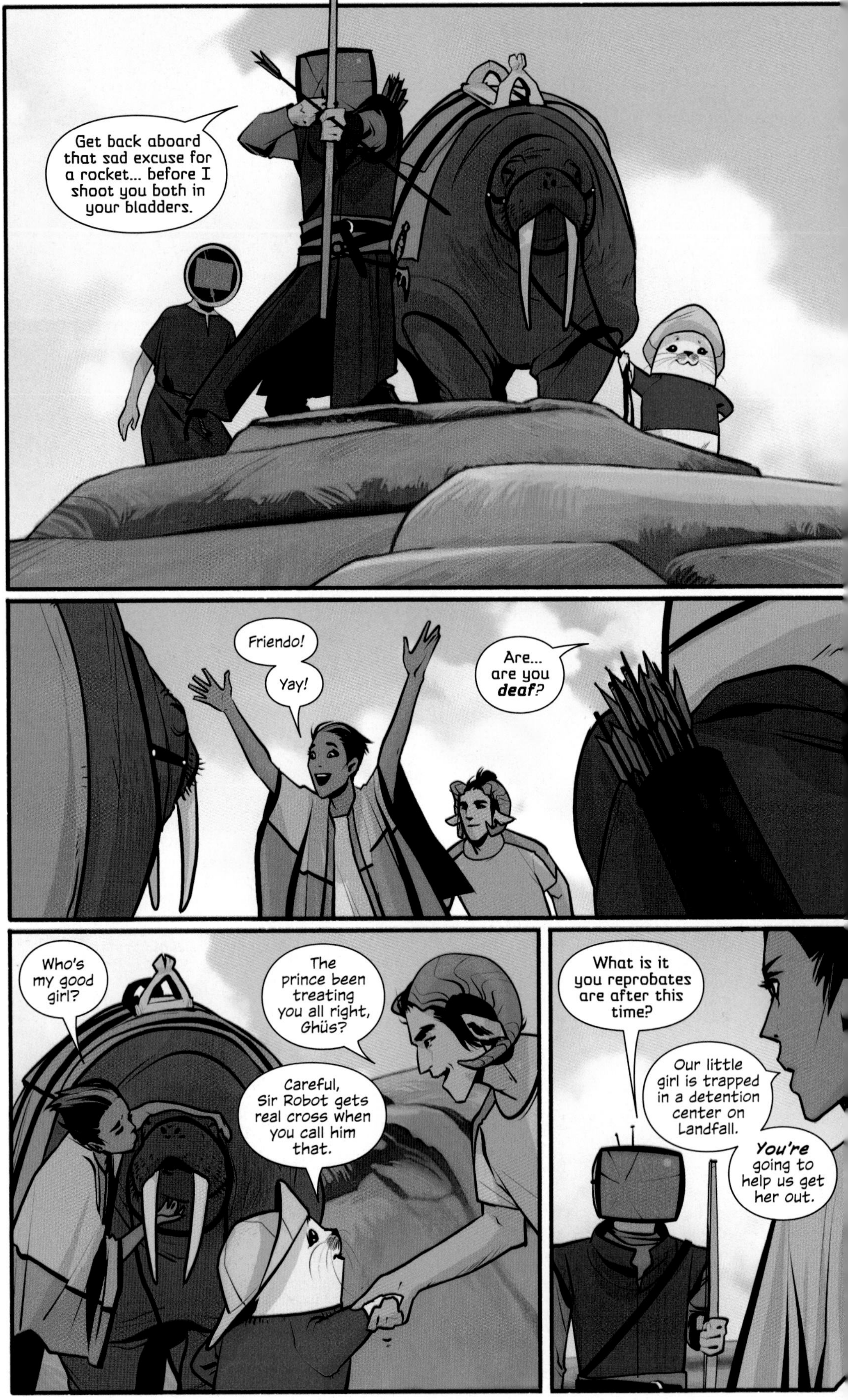
Get back aboard that sad excuse for a rocket... before I shoot you both in your bladders.
Friendo!
Yay!
Are... are you *deaf*?
Who's my good girl?
The prince been treating you all right, Ghüs?
Careful, Sir Robot gets real cross when you call him that.
What is it you reprobates are after this time?
Our little girl is trapped in a detention center on Landfall.
You're going to help us get her out.

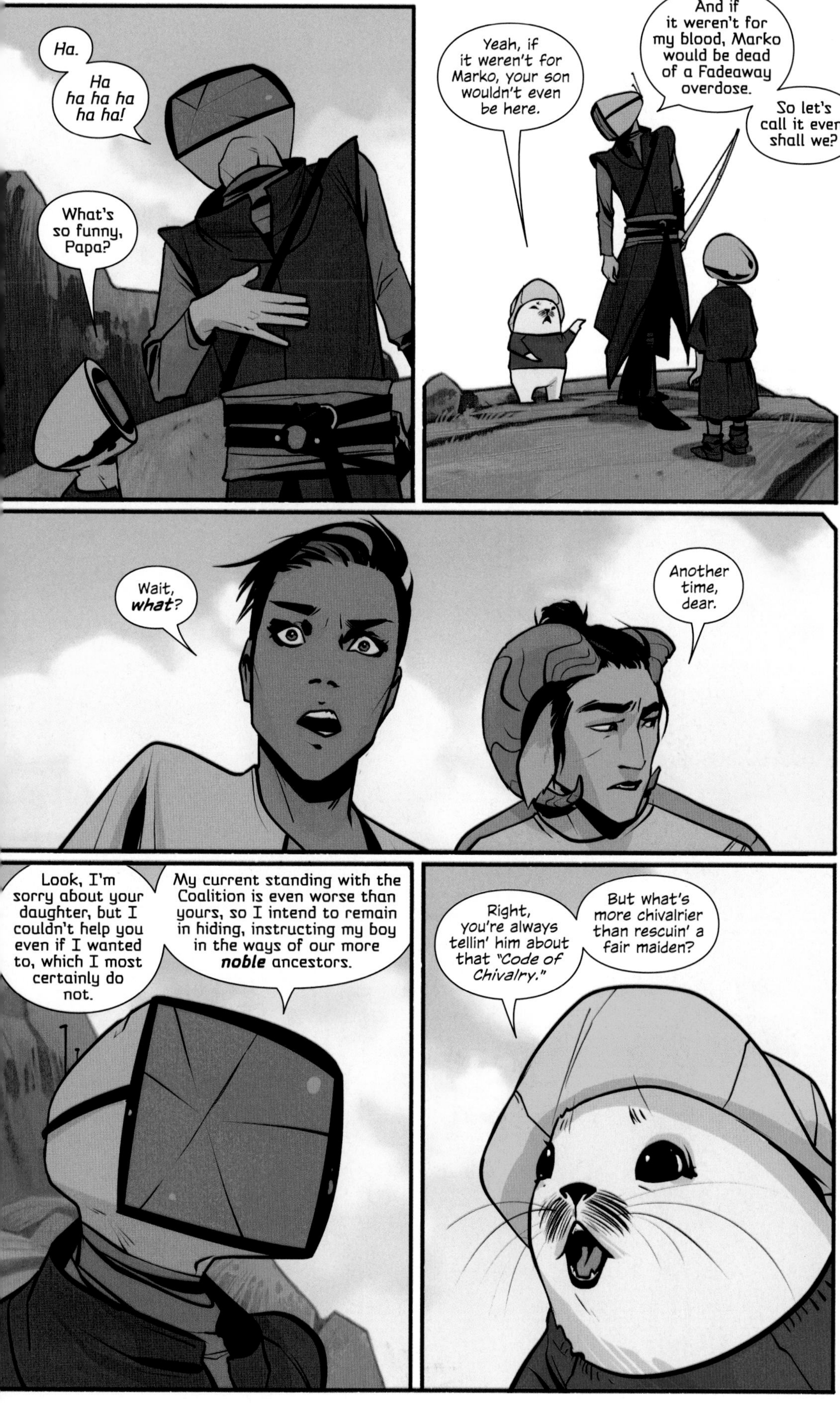

Ha.
Ha ha ha ha ha ha!
What's so funny, Papa?
Yeah, if it weren't for Marko, your son wouldn't even be here.
And if it weren't for my blood, Marko would be dead of a Fadeaway overdose.
So let's call it even, shall we?
Wait, *what*?
Another time, dear.
Look, I'm sorry about your daughter, but I couldn't help you even if I wanted to, which I most certainly do not.
My current standing with the Coalition is even worse than yours, so I intend to remain in hiding, instructing my boy in the ways of our more ***noble*** ancestors.
Right, you're always tellin' him about that *"Code of Chivalry."*
But what's more chivalrier than rescuin' a fair maiden?

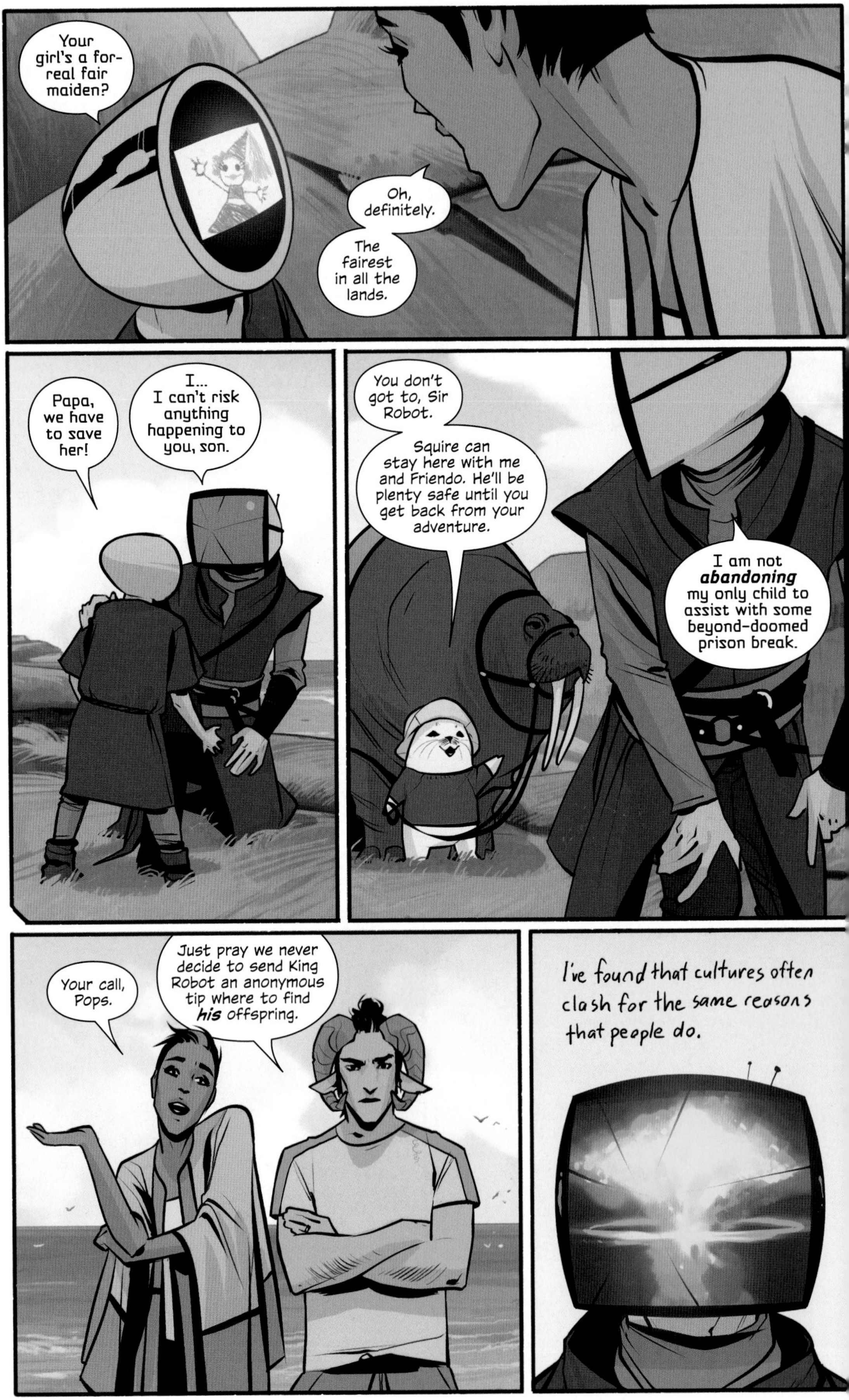
Your girl's a for-real fair maiden?
Oh, definitely.
The fairest in all the lands.
Papa, we have to save her!
I... I can't risk anything happening to you, son.
You don't got to, Sir Robot.
Squire can stay here with me and Friendo. He'll be plenty safe until you get back from your adventure.
I am not ***abandoning*** my only child to assist with some beyond-doomed prison break.
Your call, Pops.
Just pray we never decide to send King Robot an anonymous tip where to find ***his*** offspring.
I've found that cultures often clash for the same reasons that people do.

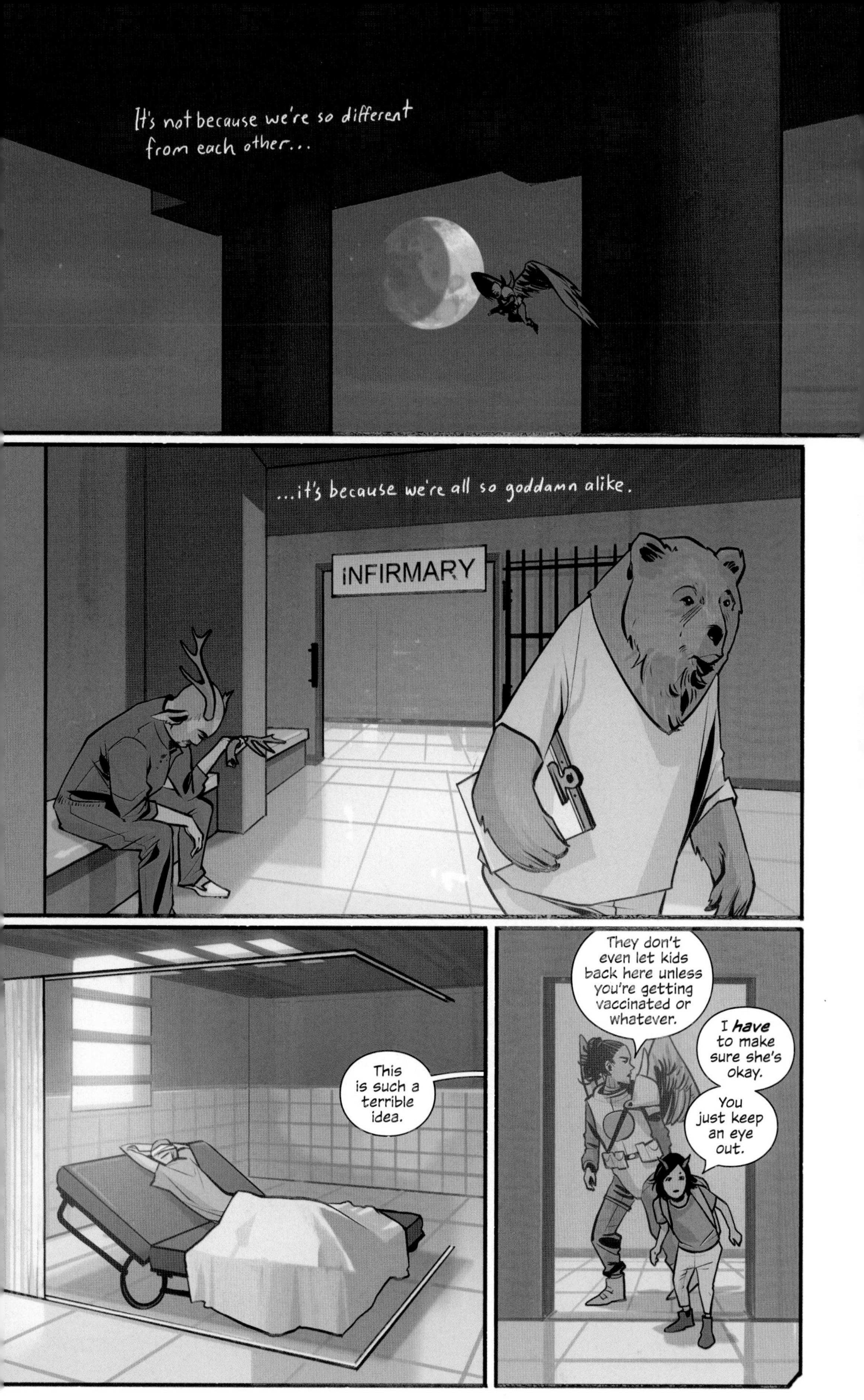
It's not because we're so different from each other...
...it's because we're all so goddamn alike.
INFIRMARY
This is such a terrible idea.
They don't even let kids back here unless you're getting vaccinated or whatever.
I **have** to make sure she's okay.
You just keep an eye out.

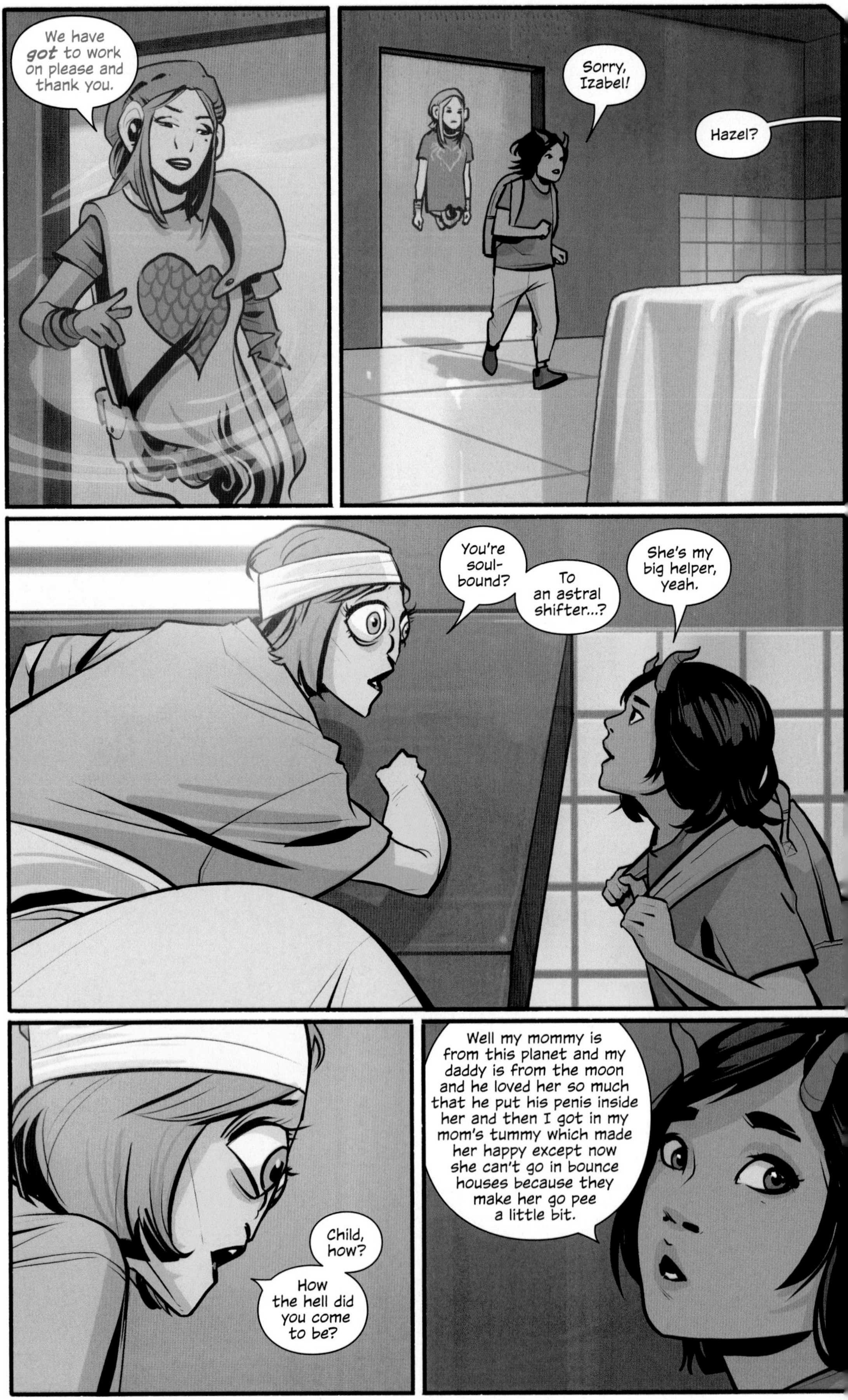

We have got to work on please and thank you.
Sorry, Izabel!
Hazel?
You're soul-bound?
To an astral shifter...?
She's my big helper, yeah.
Child, how?
How the hell did you come to be?
Well my mommy is from this planet and my daddy is from the moon and he loved her so much that he put his penis inside her and then I got in my mom's tummy which made her happy except now she can't go in bounce houses because they make her go pee a little bit.

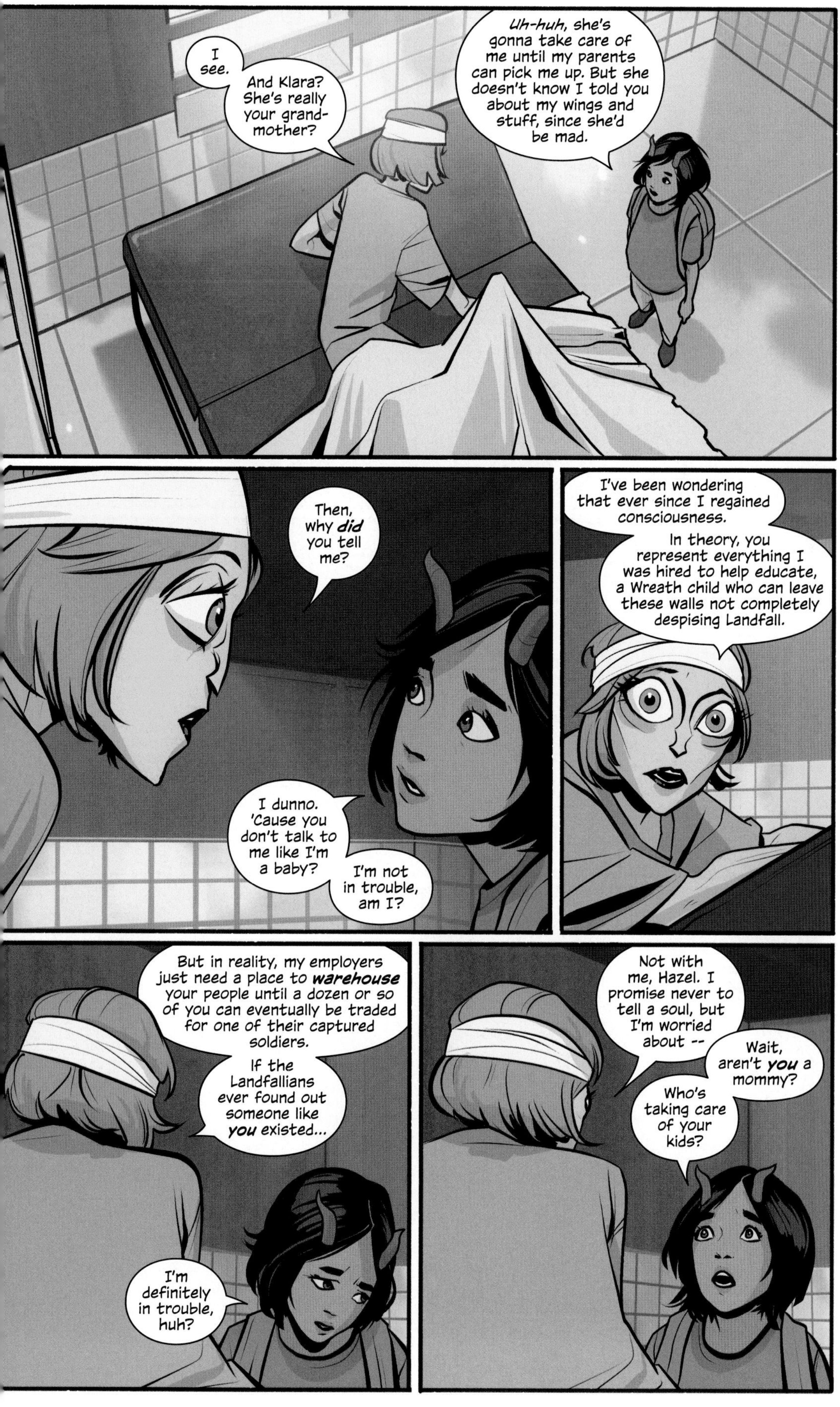
I see.
And Klara? She's really your grand-mother?
Uh-huh, she's gonna take care of me until my parents can pick me up. But she doesn't know I told you about my wings and stuff, since she'd be mad.
Then, why ***did*** you tell me?
I dunno. 'Cause you don't talk to me like I'm a baby?
I'm not in trouble, am I?
I've been wondering that ever since I regained consciousness.
In theory, you represent everything I was hired to help educate, a Wreath child who can leave these walls not completely despising Landfall.
But in reality, my employers just need a place to ***warehouse*** your people until a dozen or so of you can eventually be traded for one of their captured soldiers.
If the Landfallians ever found out someone like ***you*** existed...
I'm definitely in trouble, huh?
Not with me, Hazel. I promise never to tell a soul, but I'm worried about --
Wait, aren't ***you*** a mommy?
Who's taking care of your kids?

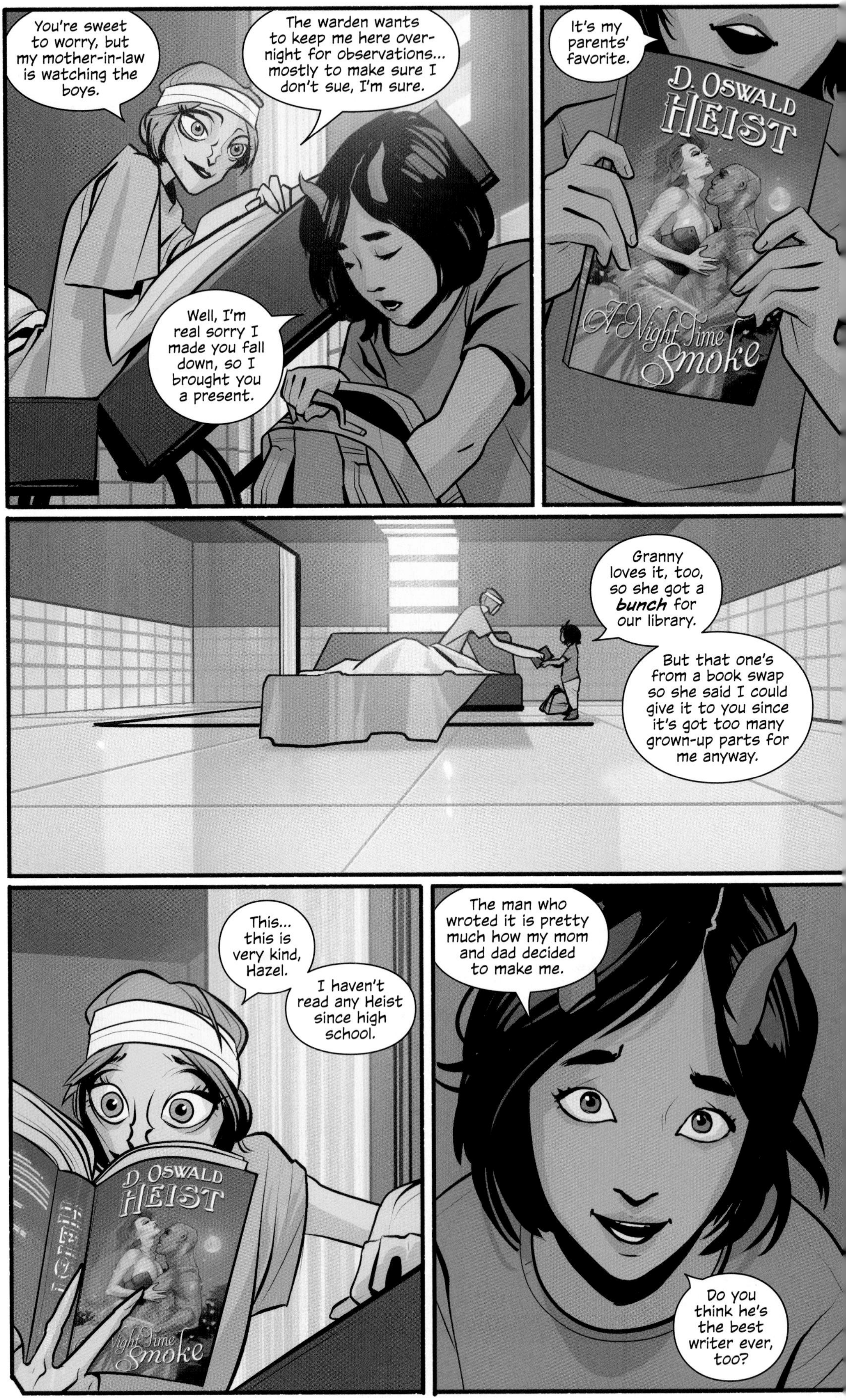
You're sweet to worry, but my mother-in-law is watching the boys.
The warden wants to keep me here over-night for observations... mostly to make sure I don't sue, I'm sure.
Well, I'm real sorry I made you fall down, so I brought you a present.
It's my parents' favorite.
D. OSWALD HEIST
A Night Time Smoke
Granny loves it, too, so she got a *bunch* for our library.
But that one's from a book swap so she said I could give it to you since it's got too many grown-up parts for me anyway.
This... this is very kind, Hazel.
I haven't read any Heist since high school.
D. OSWALD HEIST
Night Time Smoke
The man who wroted it is pretty much how my mom and dad decided to make me.
Do you think he's the best writer ever, too?

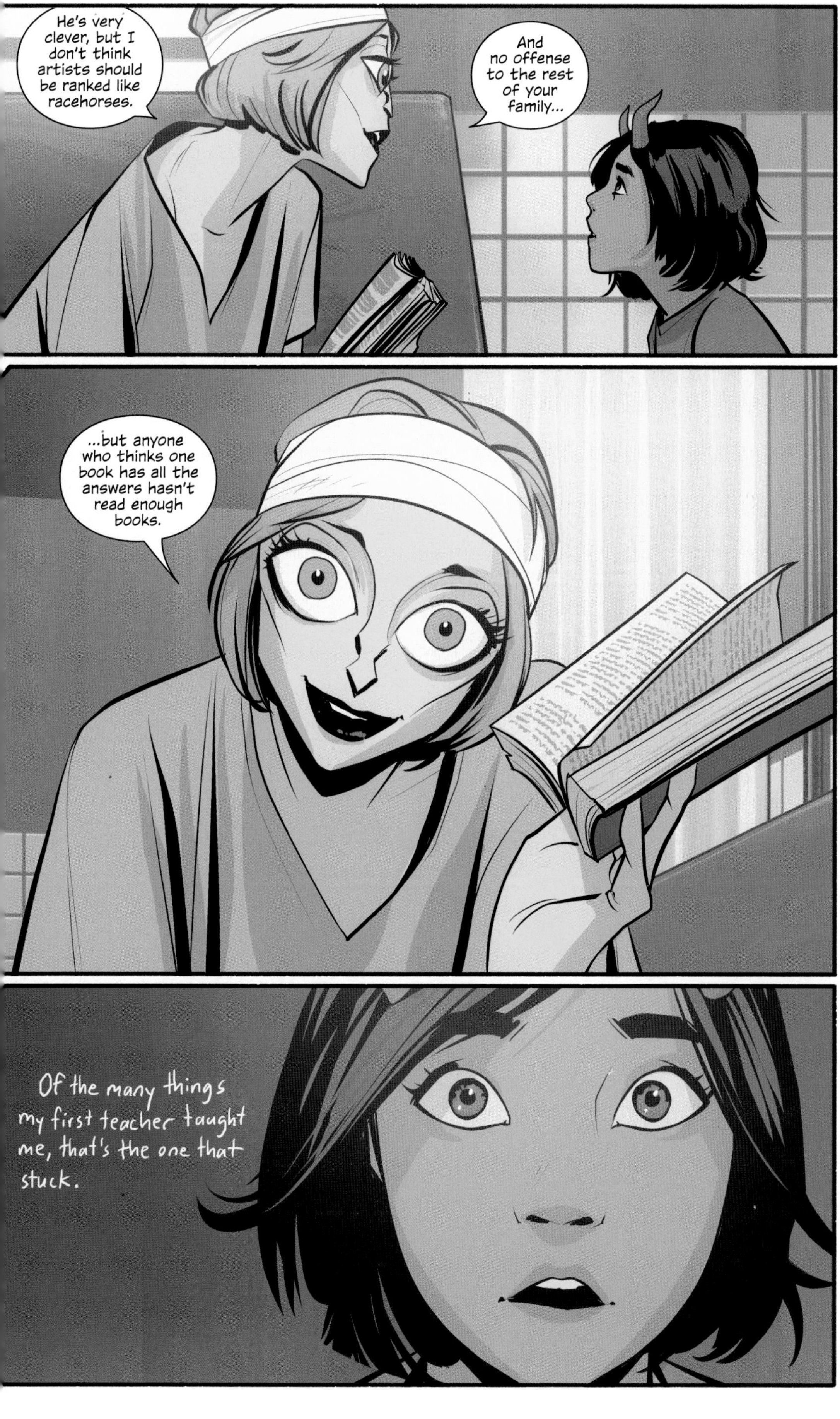
He's very clever, but I don't think artists should be ranked like racehorses.
And no offense to the rest of your family...
...but anyone who thinks one book has all the answers hasn't read enough books.
Of the many things my first teacher taught me, that's the one that stuck.

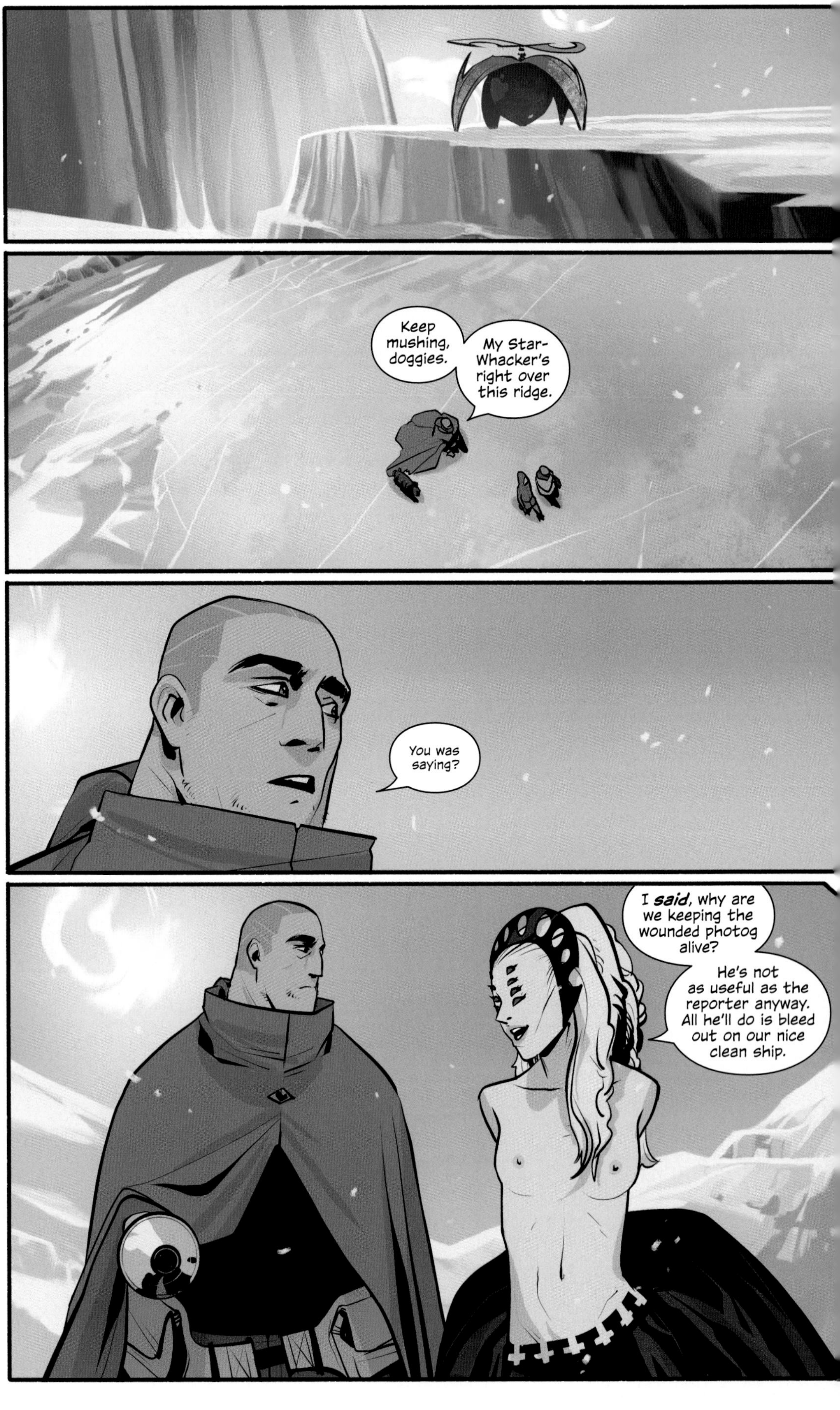
Keep mushing, doggies.
My Star-Whacker's right over this ridge.
You was saying?
I ***said***, why are we keeping the wounded photog alive?
He's not as useful as the reporter anyway. All he'll do is bleed out on our nice clean ship.

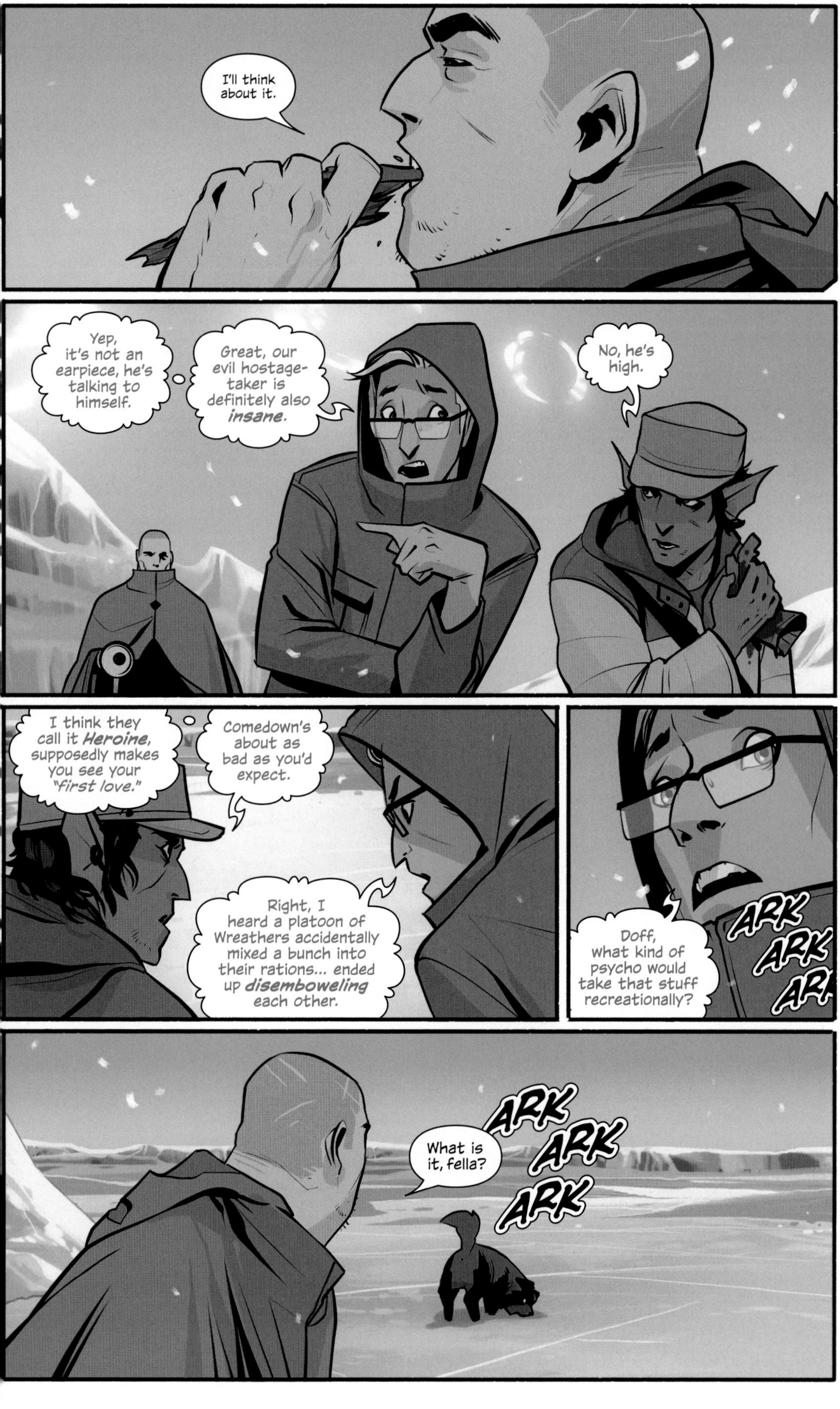
I'll think about it.
Yep, it's not an earpiece, he's talking to himself.
Great, our evil hostage-taker is definitely also *insane*.
No, he's high.
I think they call it *Heroine*, supposedly makes you see your *"first love."*
Comedown's about as bad as you'd expect.
Right, I heard a platoon of Wreathers accidentally mixed a bunch into their rations... ended up *disemboweling* each other.
Doff, what kind of psycho would take that stuff recreationally?
ARK ARK
What is it, fella?
ARK ARK ARK

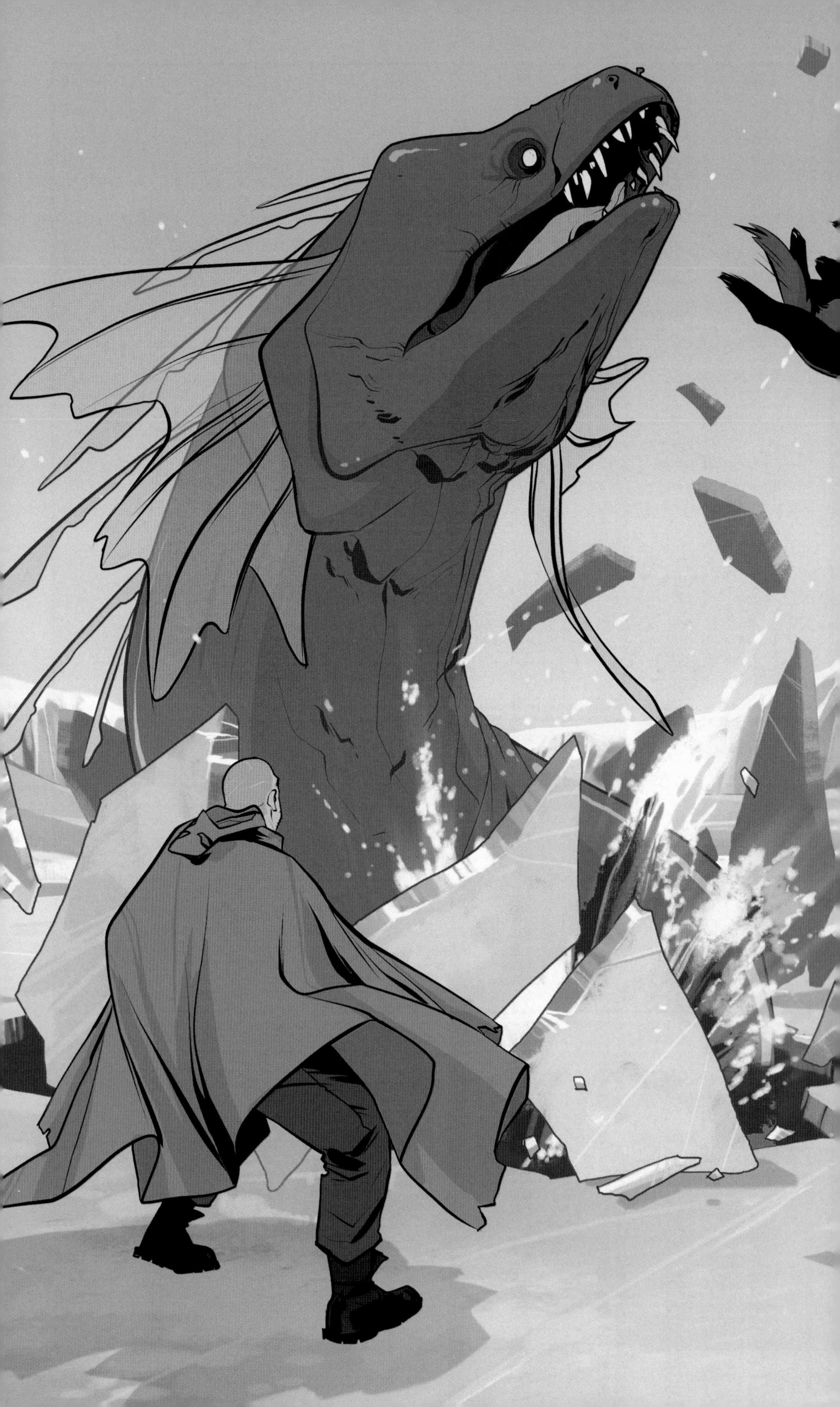

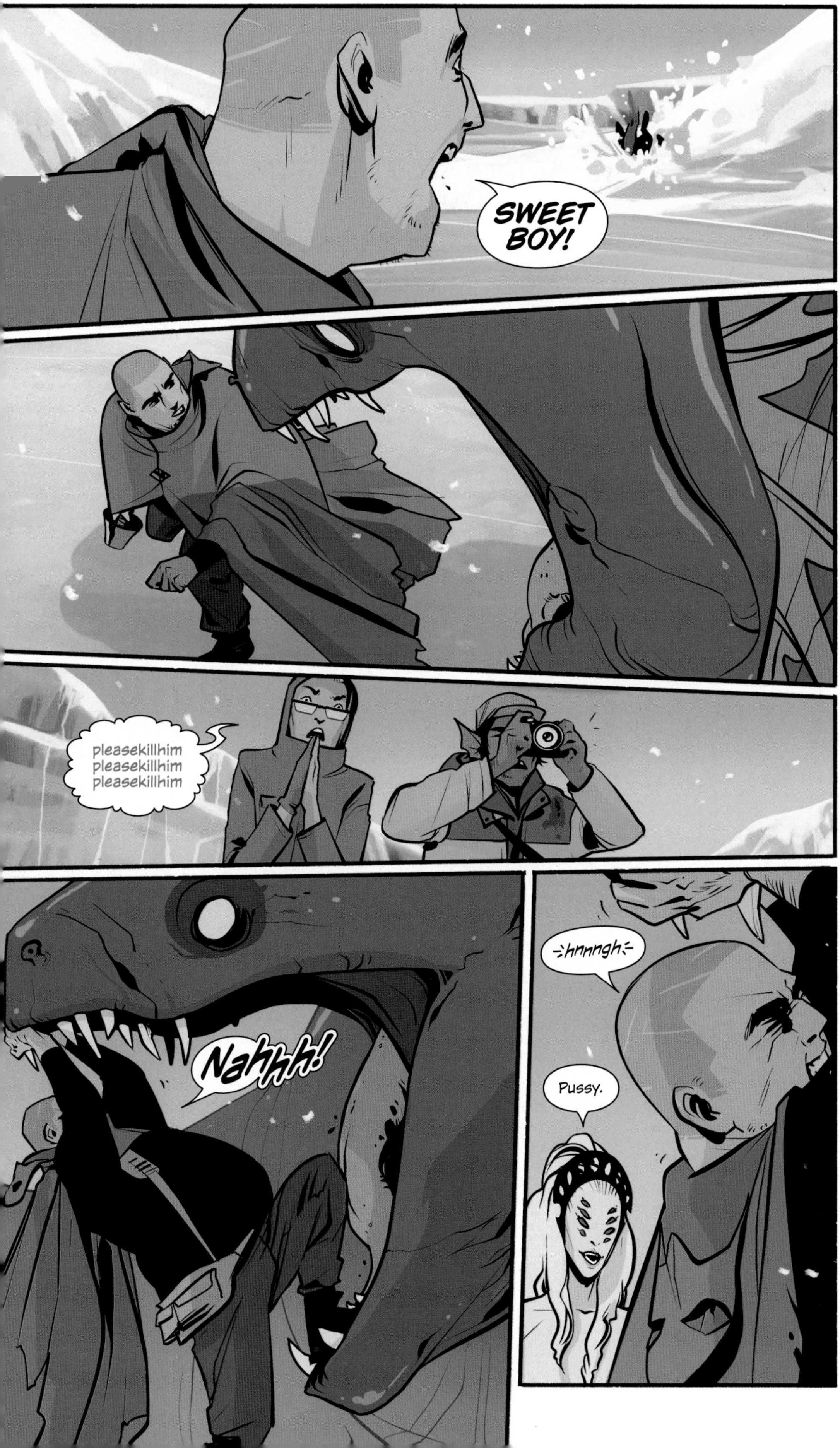
SWEET BOY!
pleasekillhim pleasekillhim pleasekillhim
Nahhh!
hnnngh
Pussy.

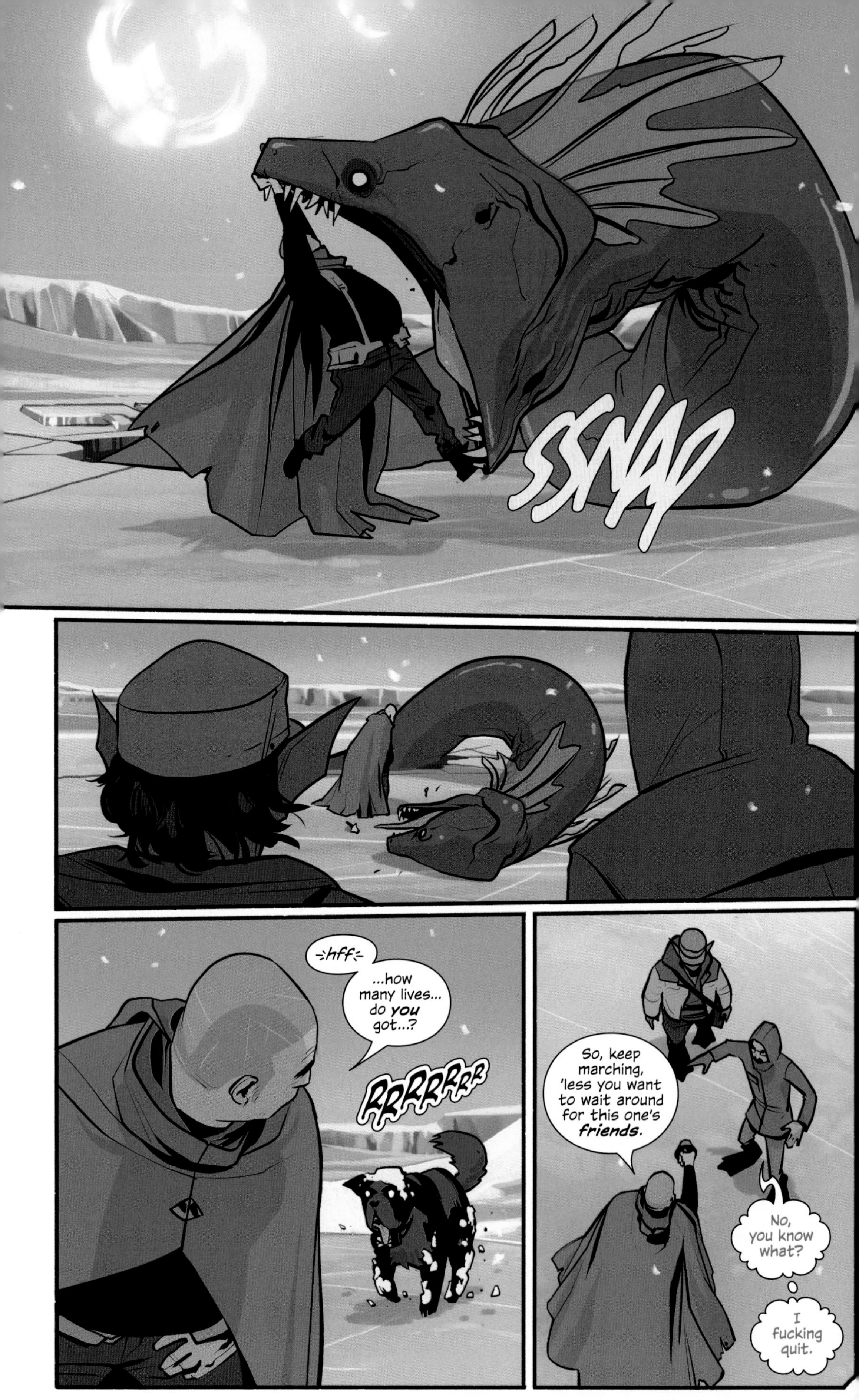
SSNAP
-hff-
...how many lives... do *you* got...?
RRRRRRR
So, keep marching, 'less you want to wait around for this one's *friends*.
No, you know what?
I fucking quit.

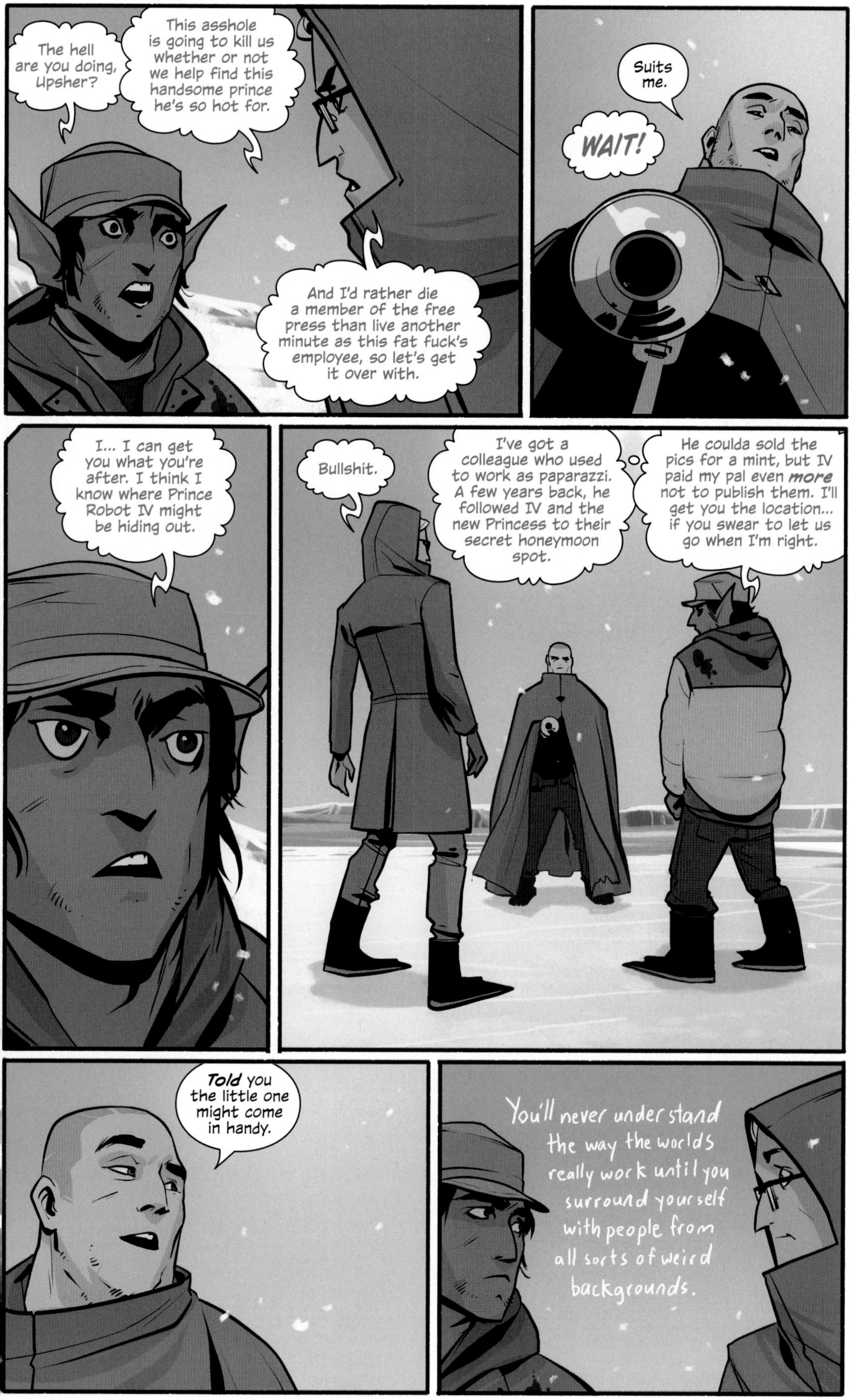

The hell are you doing, Upsher?
This asshole is going to kill us whether or not we help find this handsome prince he's so hot for.
And I'd rather die a member of the free press than live another minute as this fat fuck's employee, so let's get it over with.
Suits me.
WAIT!
I... I can get you what you're after. I think I know where Prince Robot IV might be hiding out.
Bullshit.
I've got a colleague who used to work as paparazzi. A few years back, he followed IV and the new Princess to their secret honeymoon spot.
He coulda sold the pics for a mint, but IV paid my pal even *more* not to publish them. I'll get you the location... if you swear to let us go when I'm right.
Told you the little one might come in handy.
You'll never understand the way the worlds really work until you surround yourself with people from all sorts of weird backgrounds.

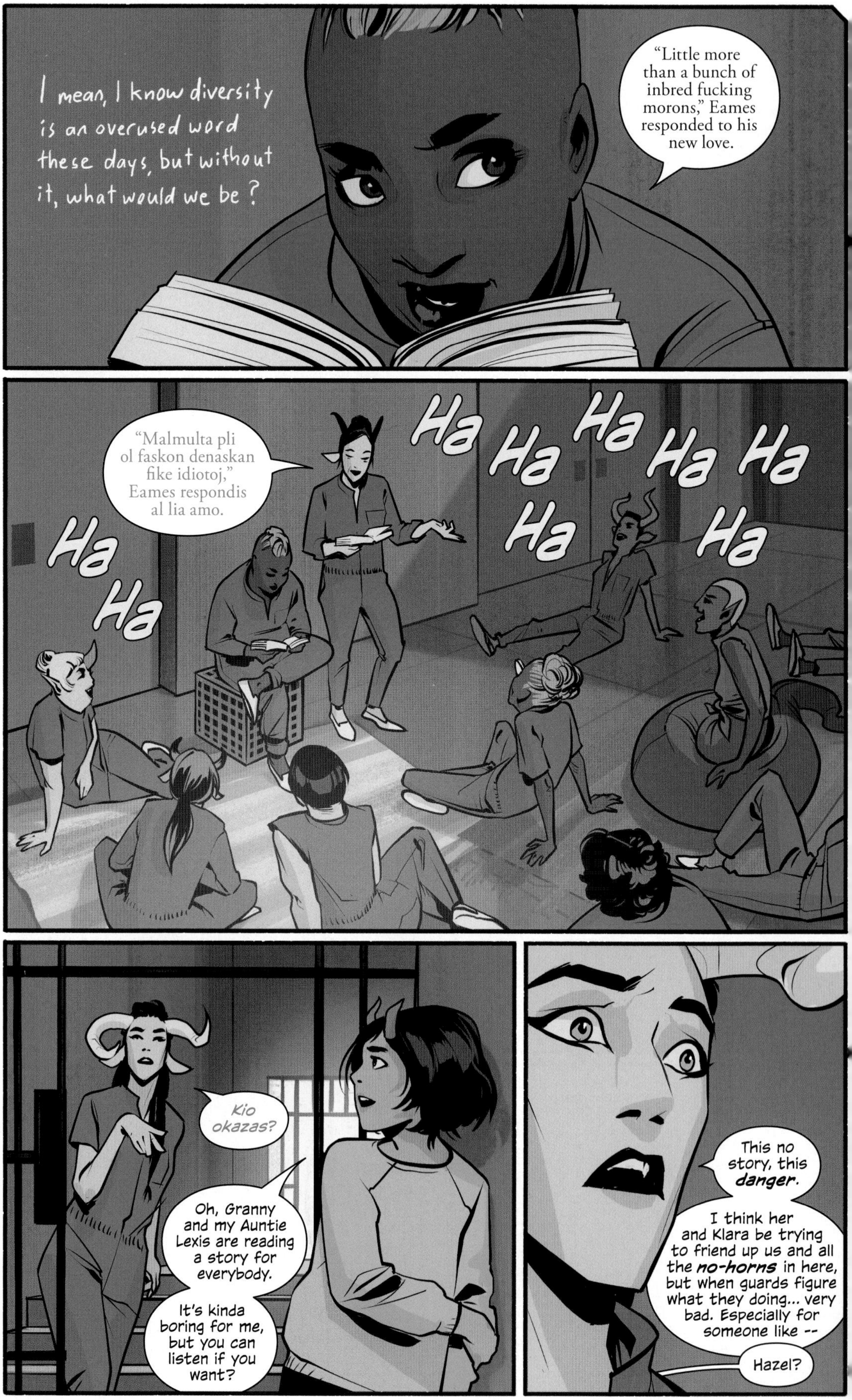
I mean, I know diversity is an overused word these days, but without it, what would we be?
"Little more than a bunch of inbred fucking morons," Eames responded to his new love.
"Malmulta pli ol faskon denaskan fike idiotoj," Eames respondis al lia amo.
Ha Ha Ha Ha Ha Ha Ha Ha
Ha Ha
Kio okazas?
Oh, Granny and my Auntie Lexis are reading a story for everybody.
It's kinda boring for me, but you can listen if you want?
This no story, this *danger*.
I think her and Klara be trying to friend up us and all the ***no-horns*** in here, but when guards figure what they doing... very bad. Especially for someone like --
Hazel?

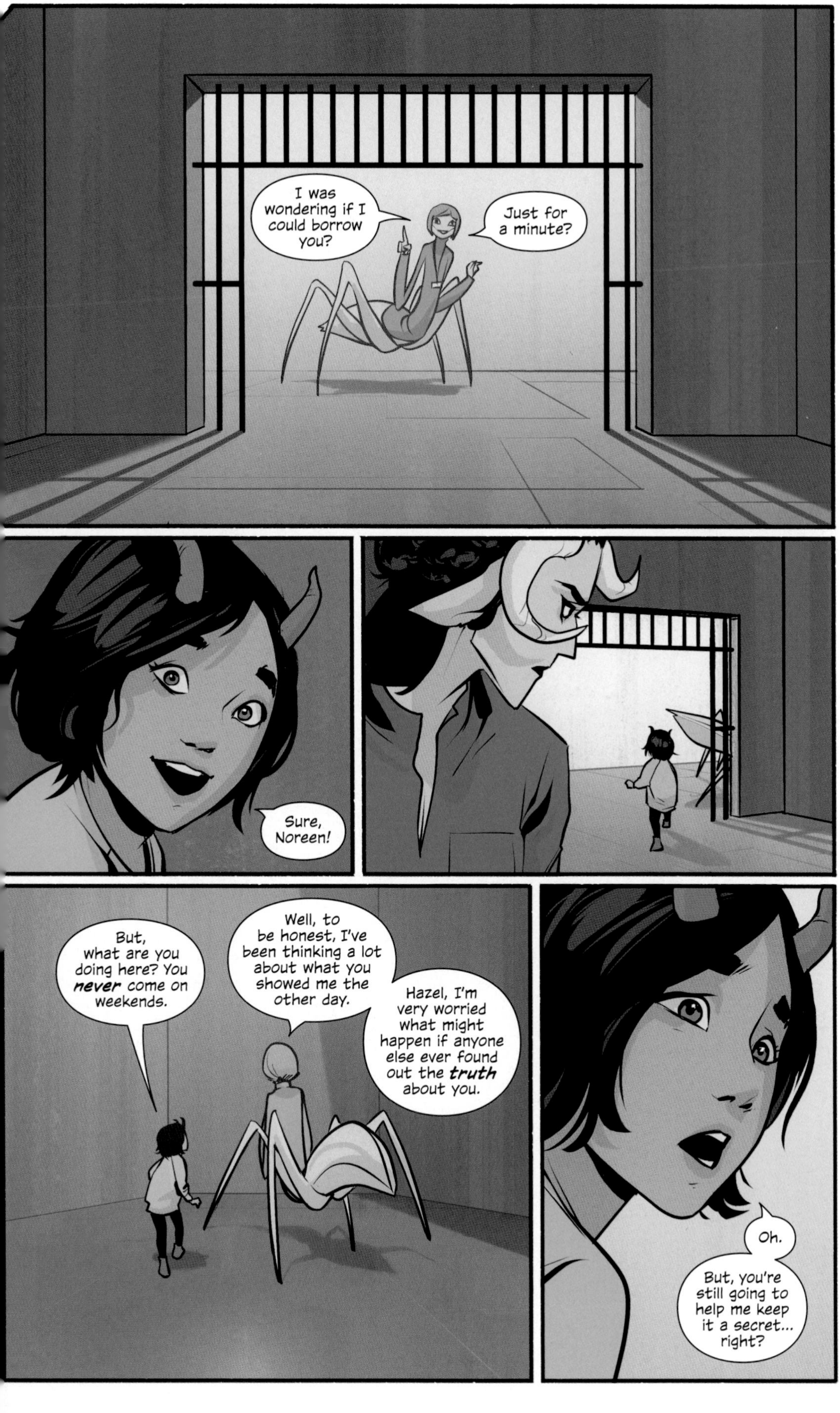
I was wondering if I could borrow you?
Just for a minute?
Sure, Noreen!
But, what are you doing here? You *never* come on weekends.
Well, to be honest, I've been thinking a lot about what you showed me the other day.
Hazel, I'm very worried what might happen if anyone else ever found out the *truth* about you.
Oh.
But, you're still going to help me keep it a secret... right?

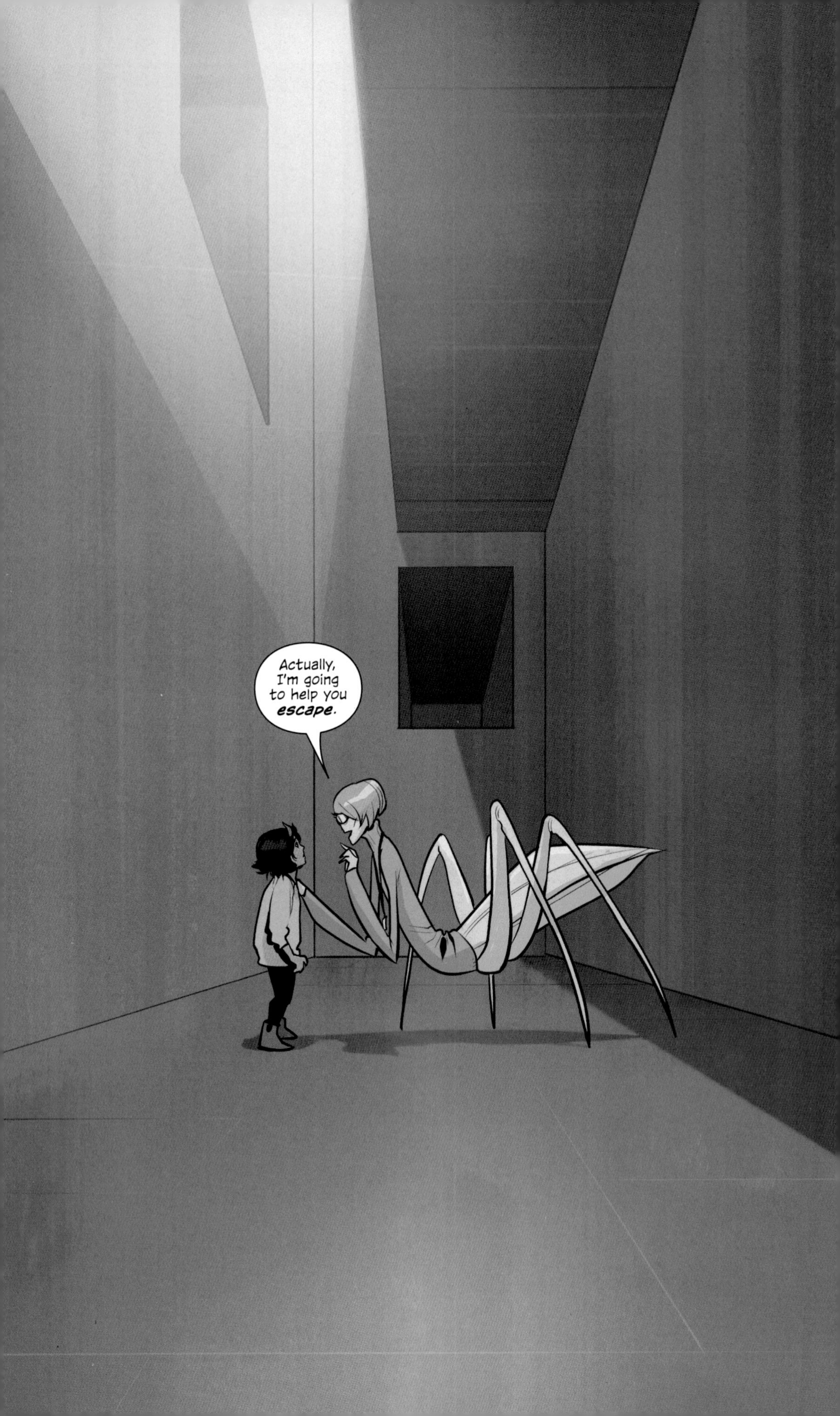
Actually, I'm going to help you *escape*.

end chapter thirty-four

CHAPTER
THIRTY-FIVE

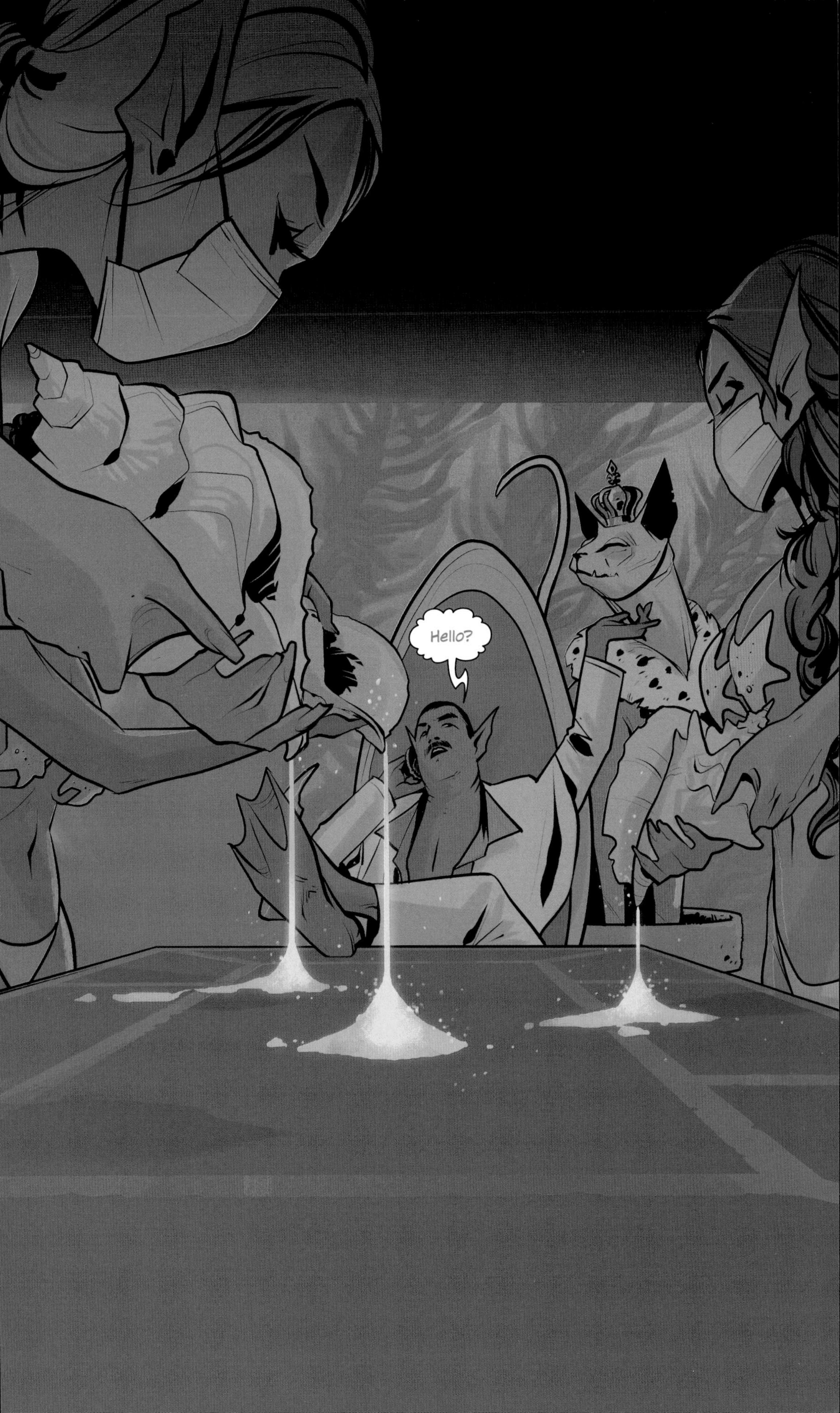
Hello?

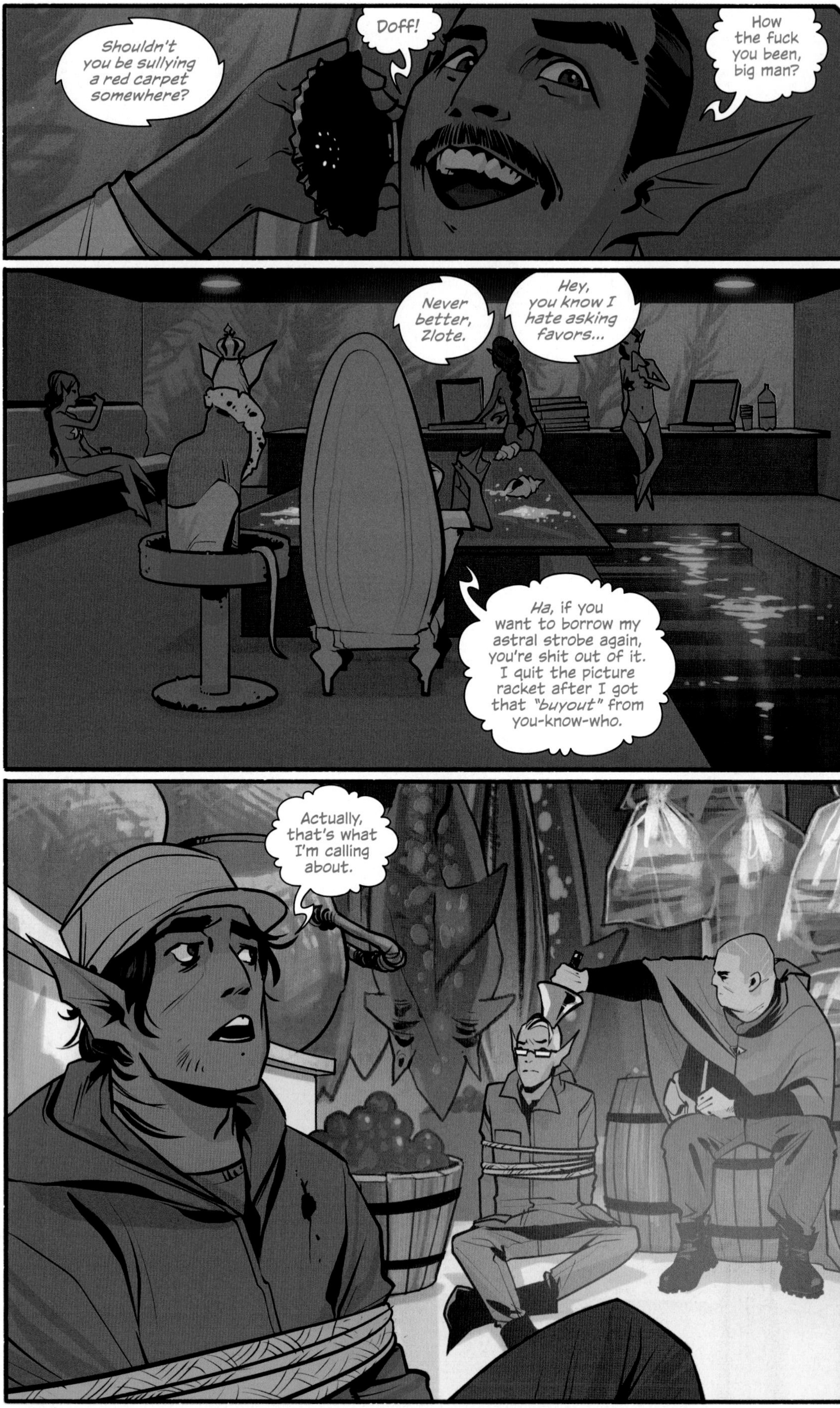
Shouldn't you be sullying a red carpet somewhere?
Doff!
How the fuck you been, big man?
Never better, Zlote.
Hey, you know I hate asking favors...
Ha, if you want to borrow my astral strobe again, you're shit out of it. I quit the picture racket after I got that *"buyout"* from you-know-who.
Actually, that's what I'm calling about.

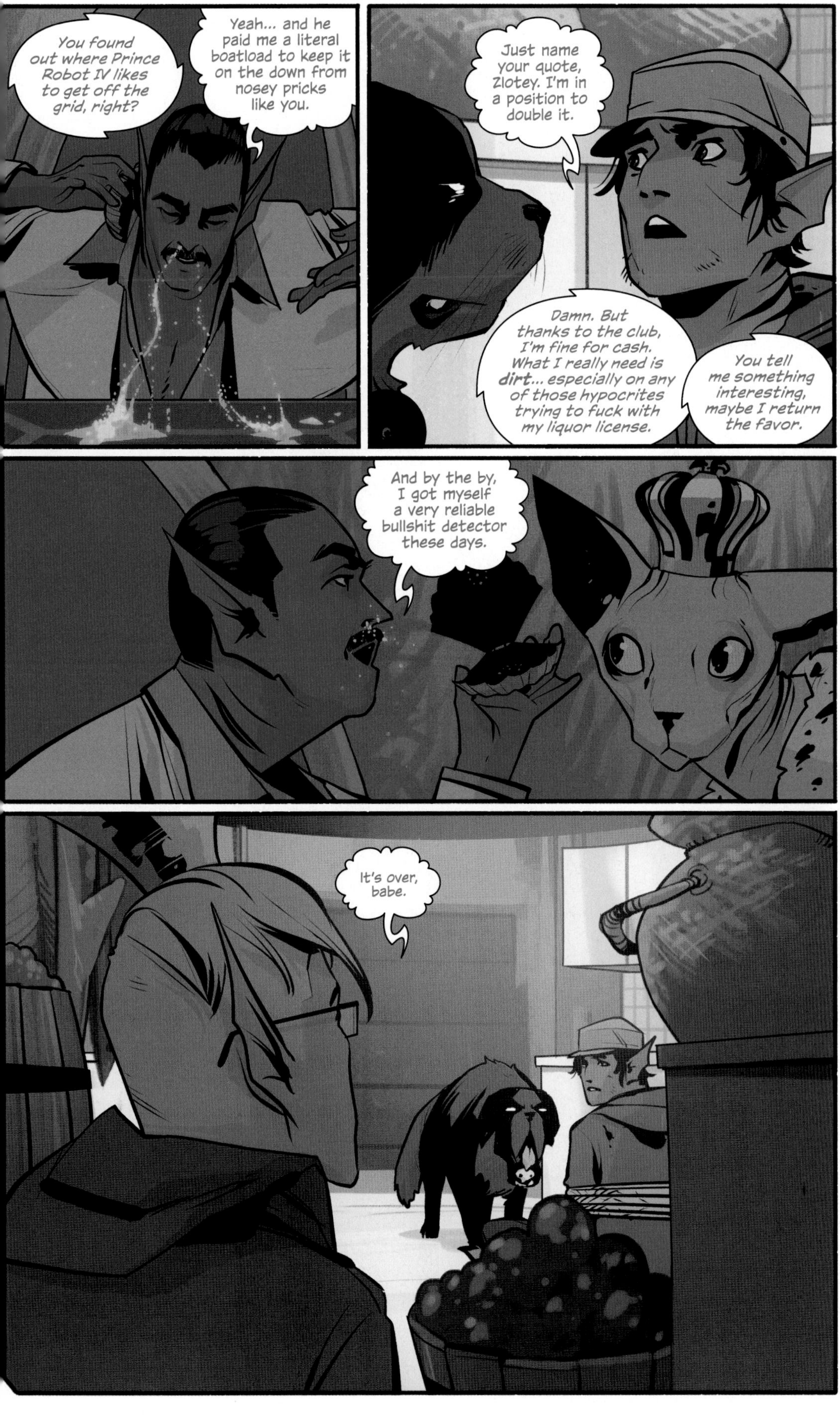
You found out where Prince Robot IV likes to get off the grid, right?
Yeah... and he paid me a literal boatload to keep it on the down from nosey pricks like you.
Just name your quote, Zlotey. I'm in a position to double it.
Damn. But thanks to the club, I'm fine for cash. What I really need is dirt... especially on any of those hypocrites trying to fuck with my liquor license.
You tell me something interesting, maybe I return the favor.
And by the by, I got myself a very reliable bullshit detector these days.
It's over, babe.

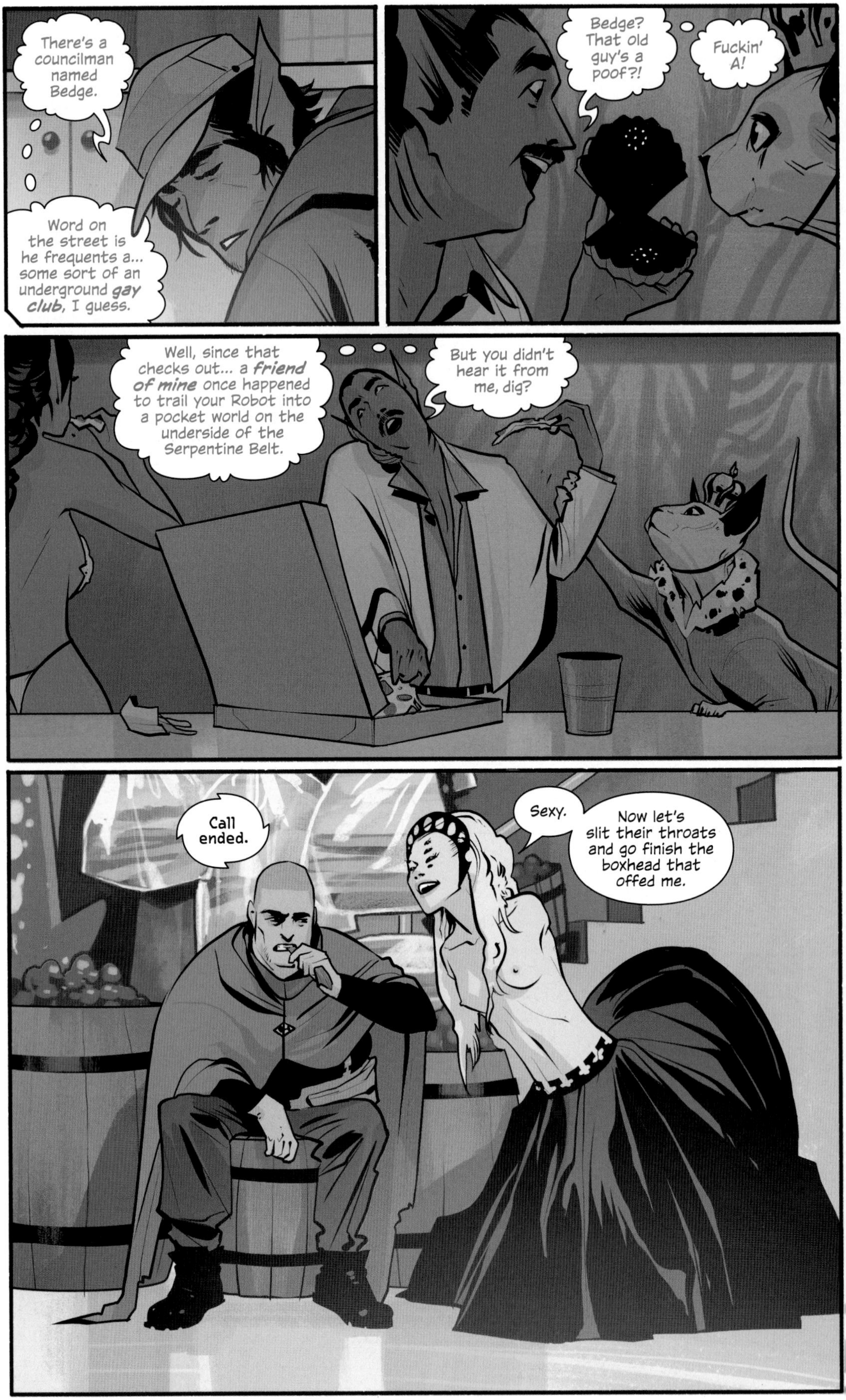
There's a councilman named Bedge.
Word on the street is he frequents a... some sort of an underground gay club, I guess.
Bedge? That old guy's a poof?!
Fuckin' A!
Well, since that checks out... a friend of mine once happened to trail your Robot into a pocket world on the underside of the Serpentine Belt.
But you didn't hear it from me, dig?
Call ended.
Sexy.
Now let's slit their throats and go finish the boxhead that offed me.

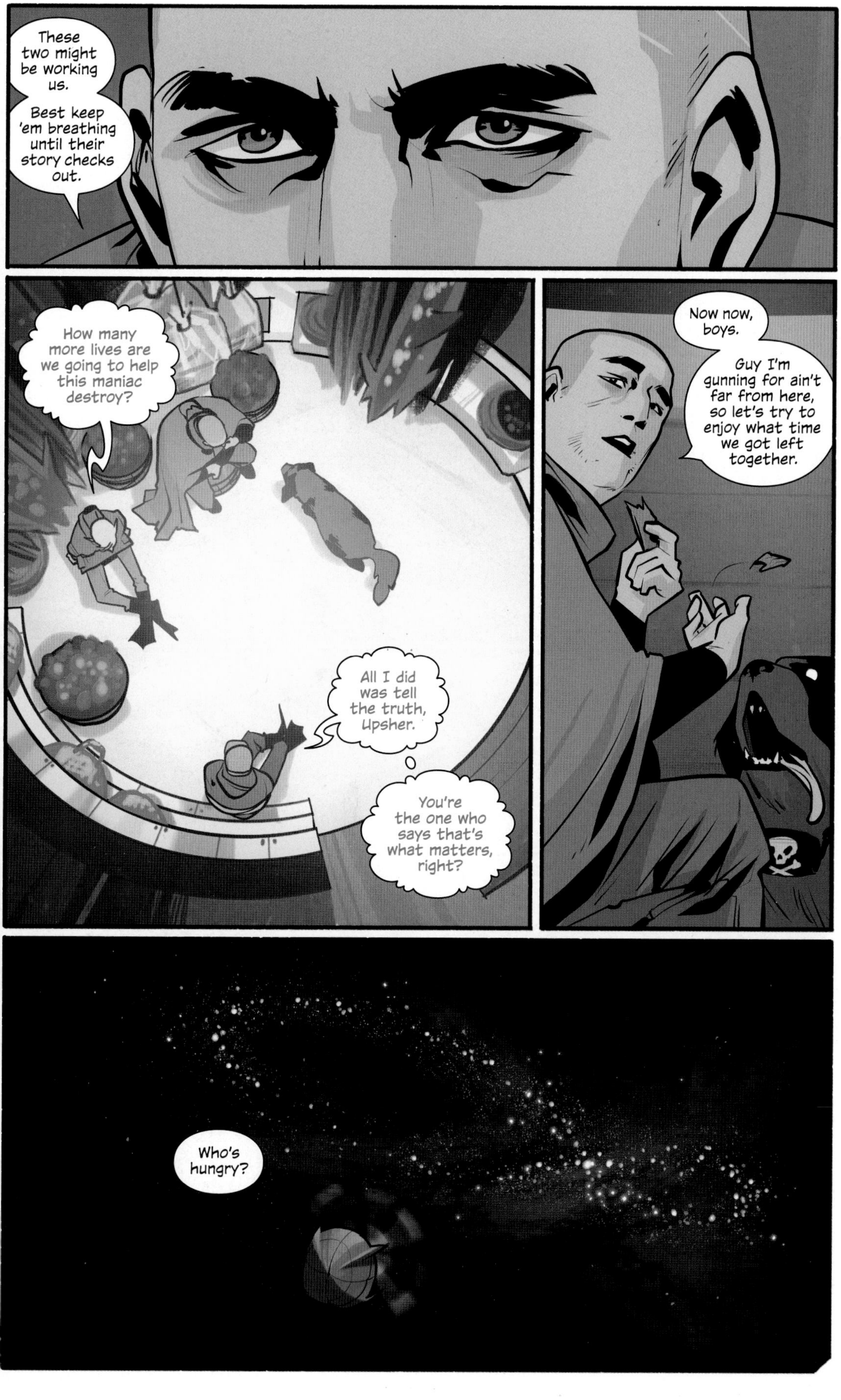
These two might be working us.
Best keep 'em breathing until their story checks out.
How many more lives are we going to help this maniac destroy?
All I did was tell the truth, Upsher.
You're the one who says that's what matters, right?
Now now, boys.
Guy I'm gunning for ain't far from here, so let's try to enjoy what time we got left together.
Who's hungry?

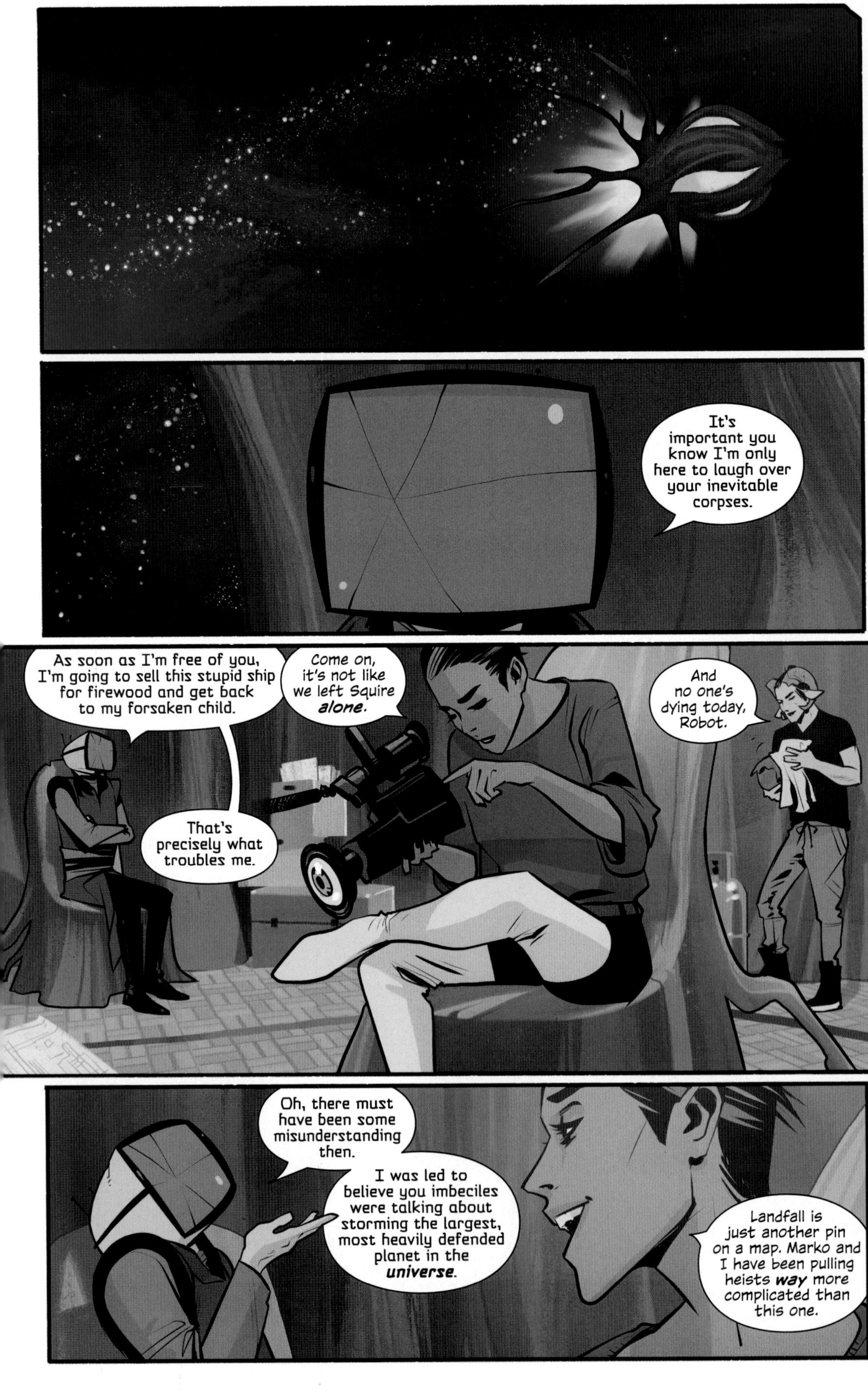
It's important you know I'm only here to laugh over your inevitable corpses.
As soon as I'm free of you, I'm going to sell this stupid ship for firewood and get back to my forsaken child.
Come on, it's not like we left Squire *alone*.
That's precisely what troubles me.
And no one's dying today, Robot.
Oh, there must have been some misunderstanding then.
I was led to believe you imbeciles were talking about storming the largest, most heavily defended planet in the ***universe***.
Landfall is just another pin on a map. Marko and I have been pulling heists ***way*** more complicated than this one.

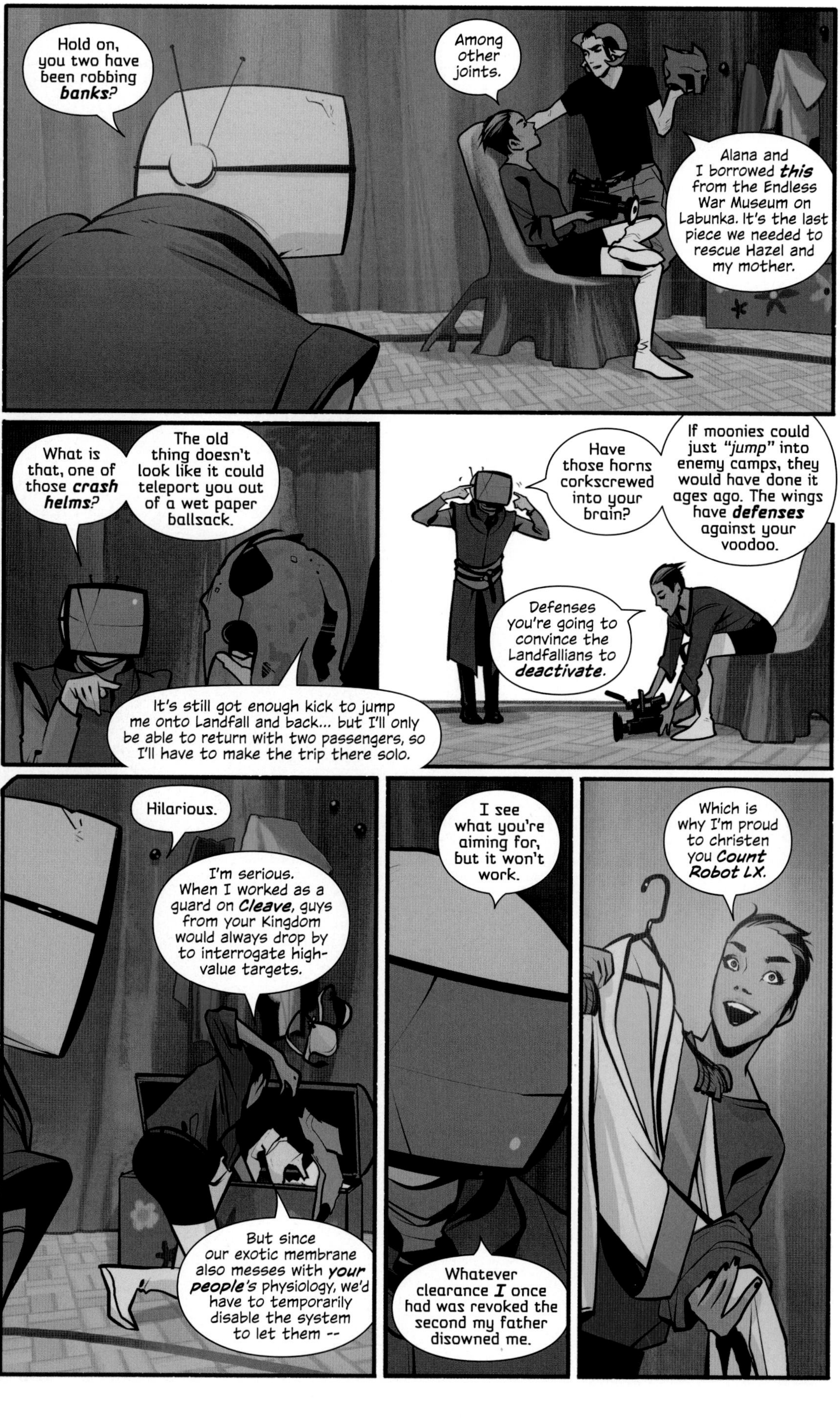
Hold on, you two have been robbing **banks**?
Among other joints.
Alana and I borrowed **this** from the Endless War Museum on Labunka. It's the last piece we needed to rescue Hazel and my mother.
What is that, one of those **crash helms**?
The old thing doesn't look like it could teleport you out of a wet paper ballsack.
It's still got enough kick to jump me onto Landfall and back... but I'll only be able to return with two passengers, so I'll have to make the trip there solo.
Have those horns corkscrewed into your brain?
If moonies could just "*jump*" into enemy camps, they would have done it ages ago. The wings have **defenses** against your voodoo.
Defenses you're going to convince the Landfallians to **deactivate**.
Hilarious.
I'm serious. When I worked as a guard on **Cleave**, guys from your Kingdom would always drop by to interrogate high-value targets.
But since our exotic membrane also messes with **your people**'s physiology, we'd have to temporarily disable the system to let them --
I see what you're aiming for, but it won't work.
Whatever clearance **I** once had was revoked the second my father disowned me.
Which is why I'm proud to christen you **Count Robot LX**.

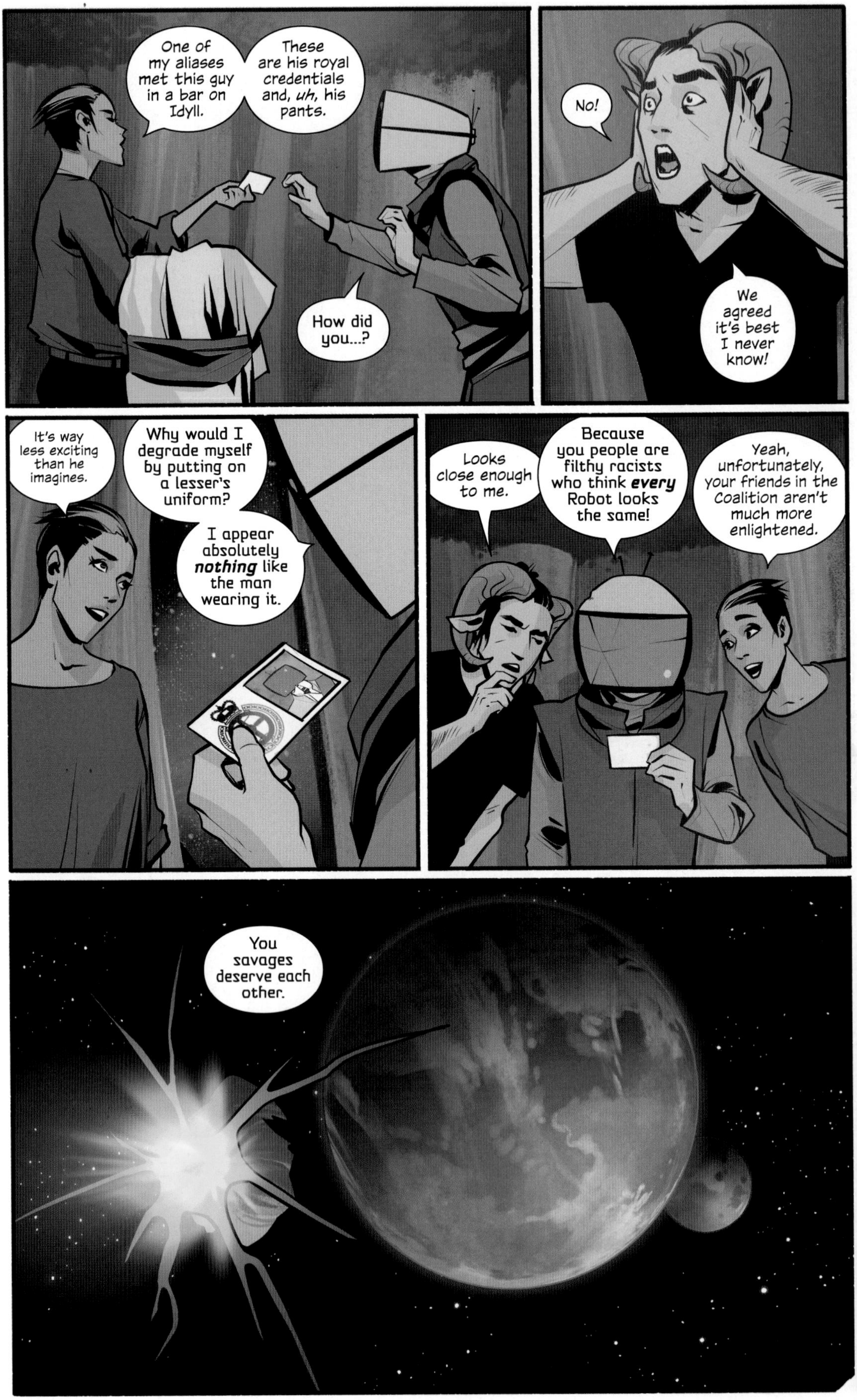
One of my aliases met this guy in a bar on Idyll.
These are his royal credentials and, *uh,* his pants.
How did you...?
No!
We agreed it's best I never know!
It's way less exciting than he imagines.
Why would I degrade myself by putting on a lesser's uniform?
I appear absolutely ***nothing*** like the man wearing it.
Looks close enough to me.
Because you people are filthy racists who think ***every*** Robot looks the same!
Yeah, unfortunately, your friends in the Coalition aren't much more enlightened.
You savages deserve each other.

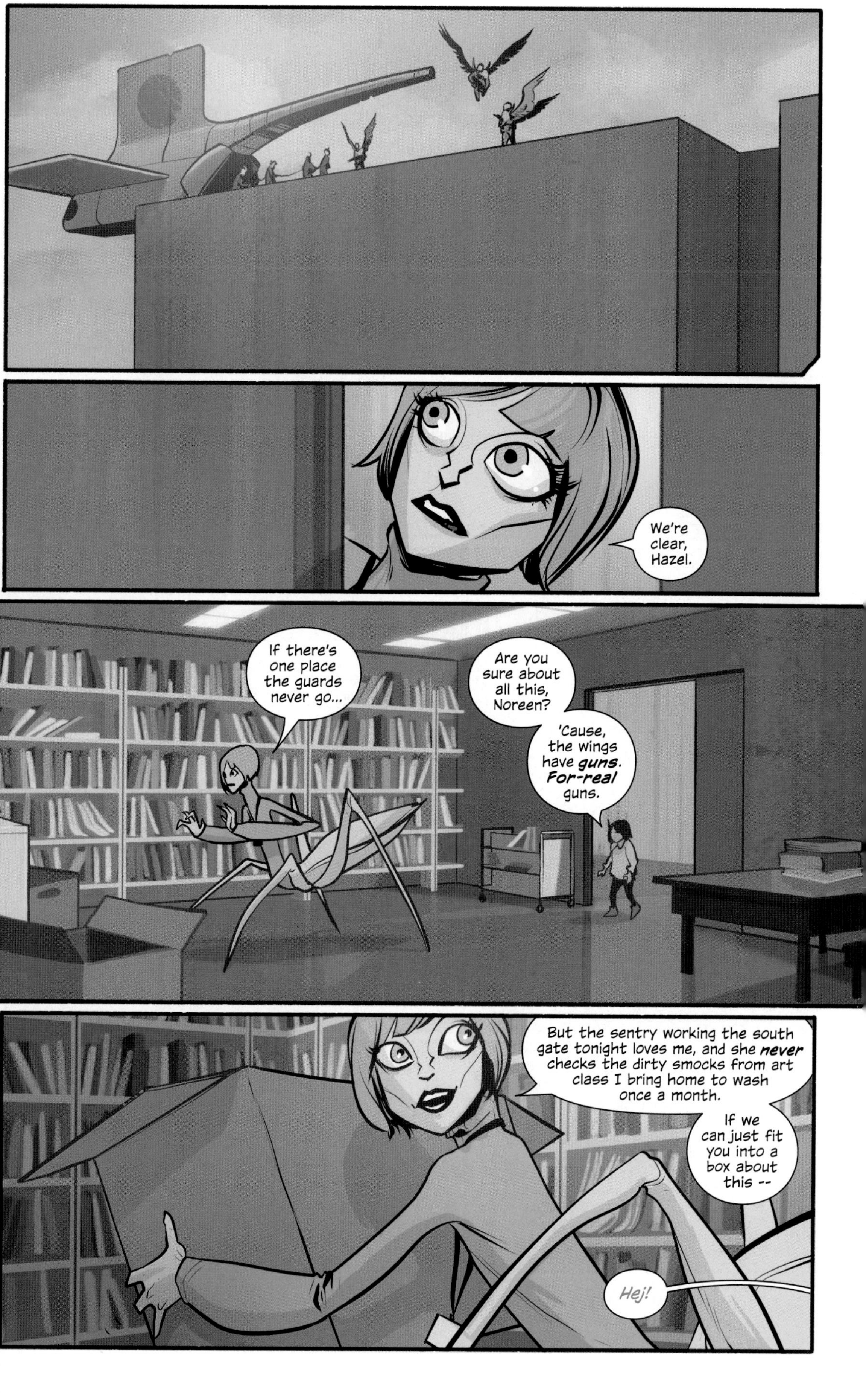
We're clear, Hazel.
If there's one place the guards never go...
Are you sure about all this, Noreen?
'Cause, the wings have *guns*. *For-real* guns.
But the sentry working the south gate tonight loves me, and she *never* checks the dirty smocks from art class I bring home to wash once a month.
If we can just fit you into a box about this --
Hej!

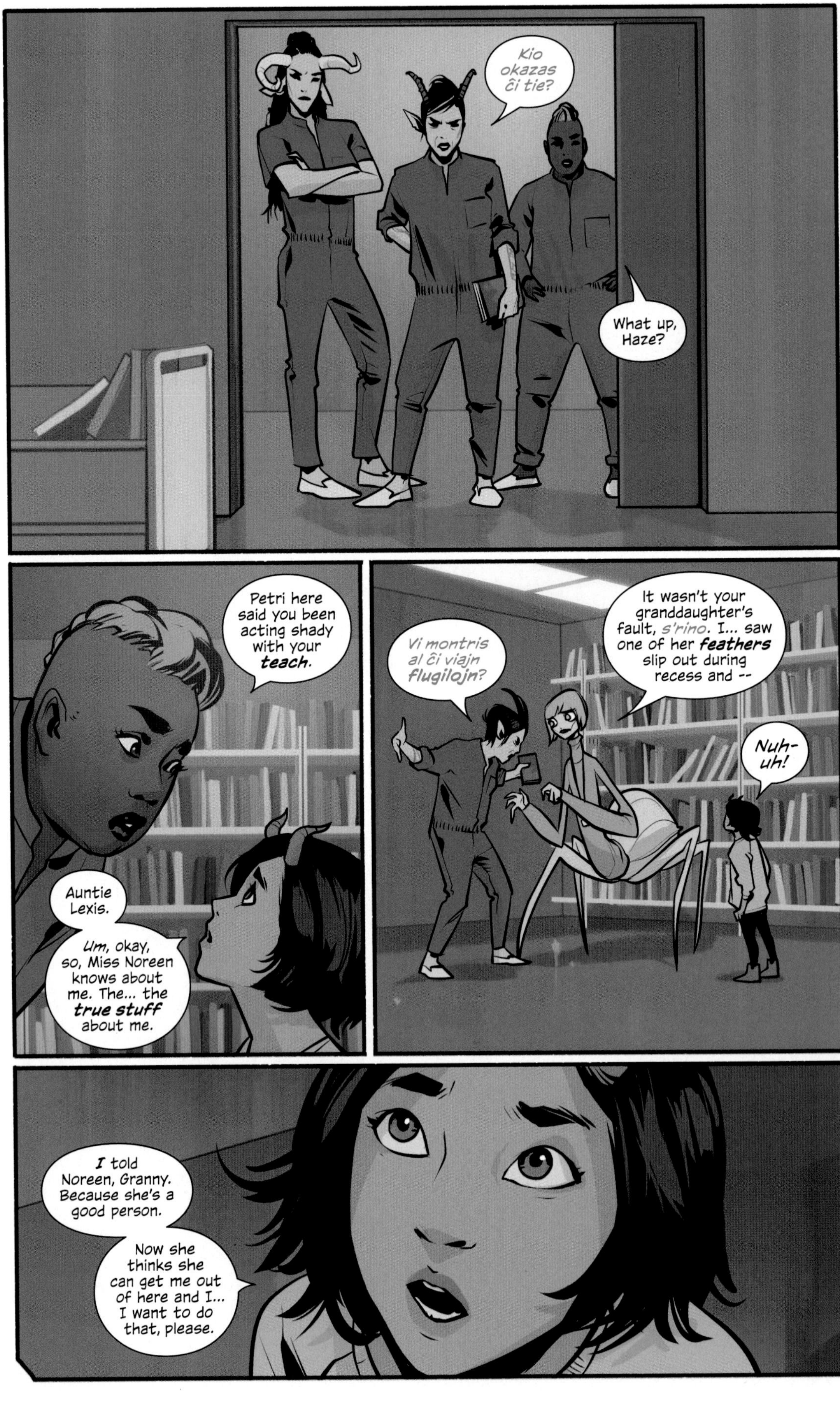

Kio okazas ĉi tie?
What up, Haze?
Petri here said you been acting shady with your teach.
Auntie Lexis.
Um, okay, so, Miss Noreen knows about me. The... the true stuff about me.
Vi montris al ĉi viajn flugilojn?
It wasn't your granddaughter's fault, s'rino. I... saw one of her feathers slip out during recess and --
Nuh-uh!
I told Noreen, Granny. Because she's a good person.
Now she thinks she can get me out of here and I... I want to do that, please.

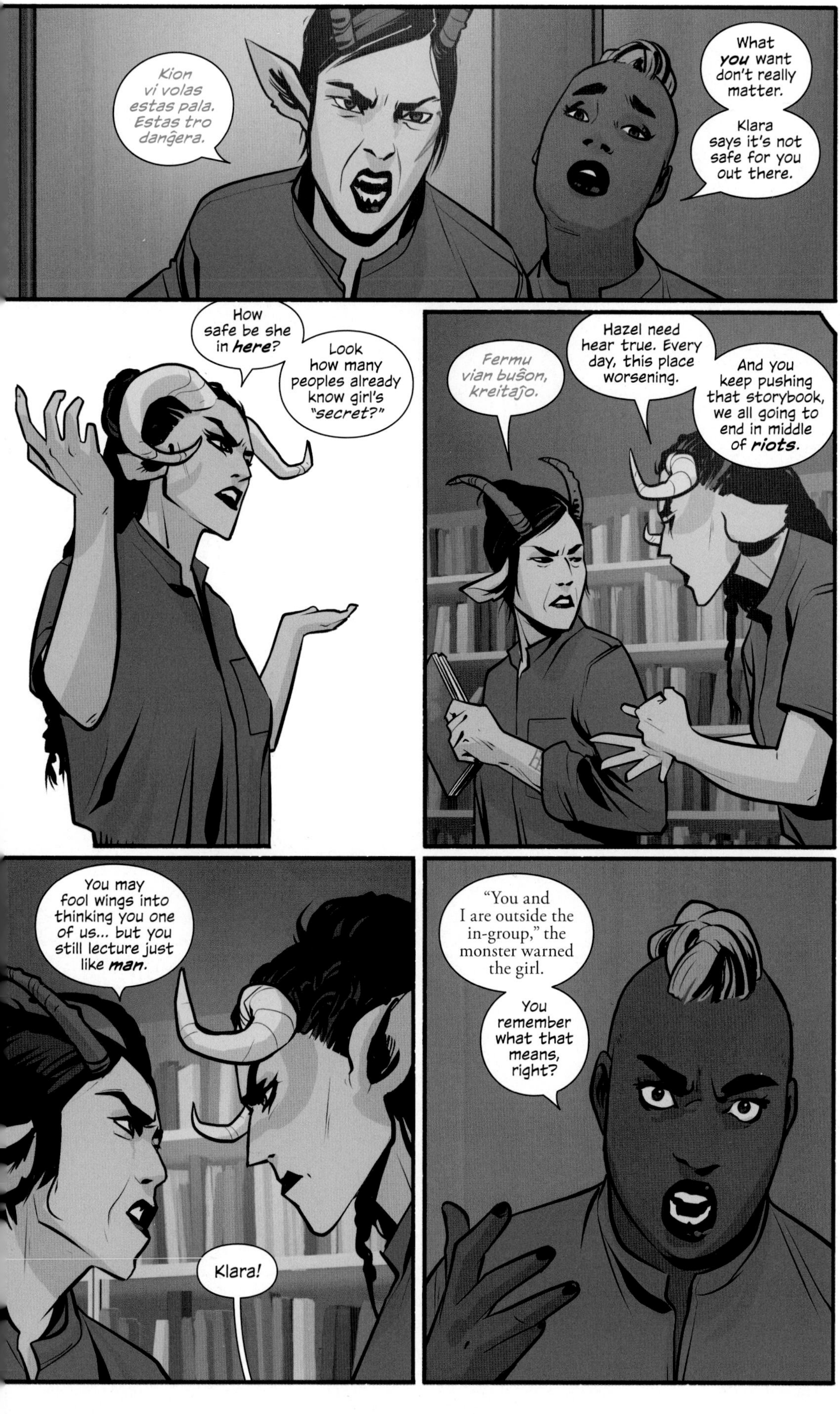

Kion vi volas estas pala. Estas tro danĝera.
What you want don't really matter.
Klara says it's not safe for you out there.
How safe be she in here?
Look how many peoples already know girl's "secret?"
Fermu vian buŝon, kreitaĵo.
Hazel need hear true. Every day, this place worsening.
And you keep pushing that storybook, we all going to end in middle of riots.
You may fool wings into thinking you one of us... but you still lecture just like man.
Klara!
"You and I are outside the in-group," the monster warned the girl.
You remember what that means, right?

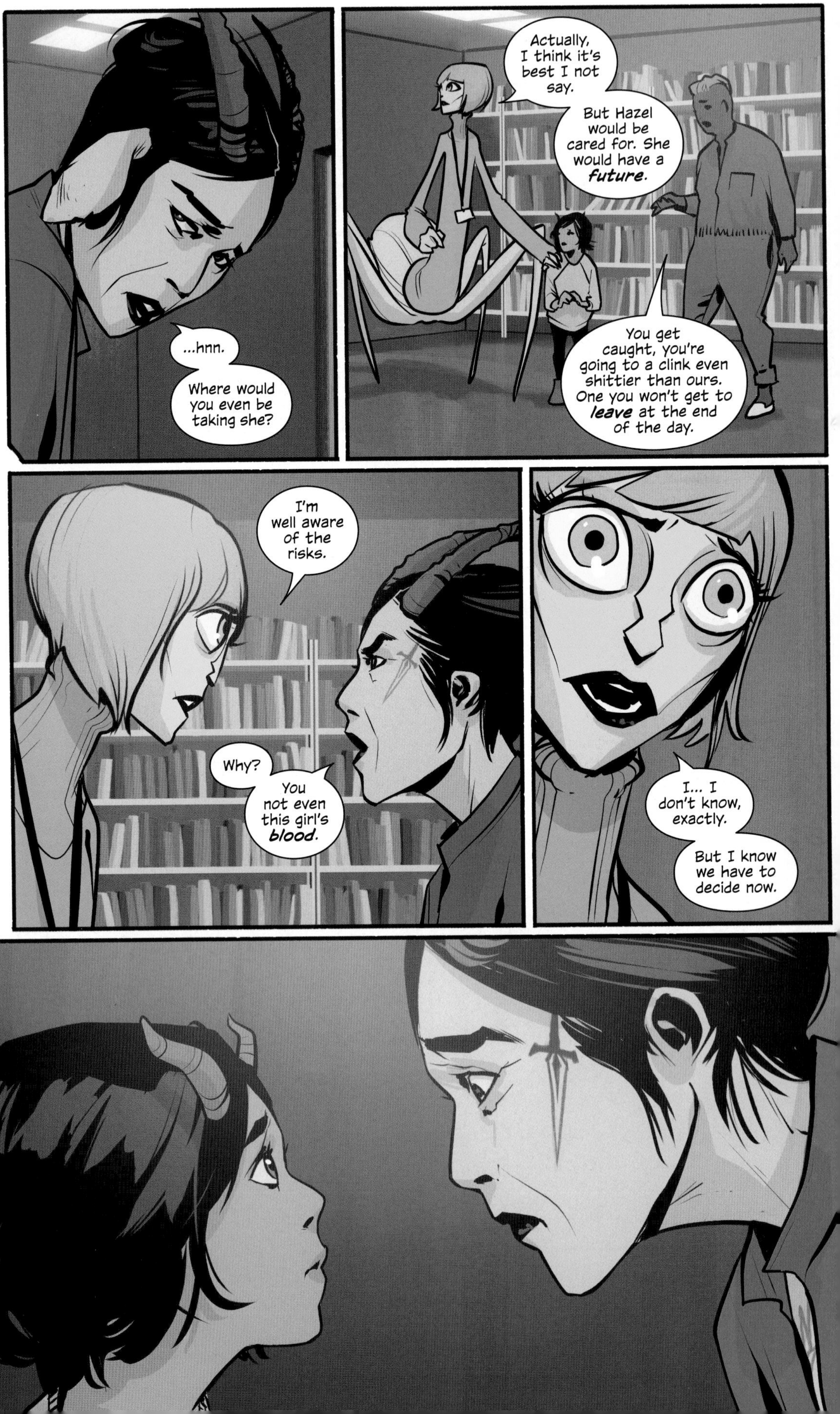

...hnn.
Where would you even be taking she?
Actually, I think it's best I not say.
But Hazel would be cared for. She would have a **future**.
You get caught, you're going to a clink even shittier than ours. One you won't get to **leave** at the end of the day.
I'm well aware of the risks.
Why?
You not even this girl's **blood**.
I... I don't know, exactly.
But I know we have to decide now.

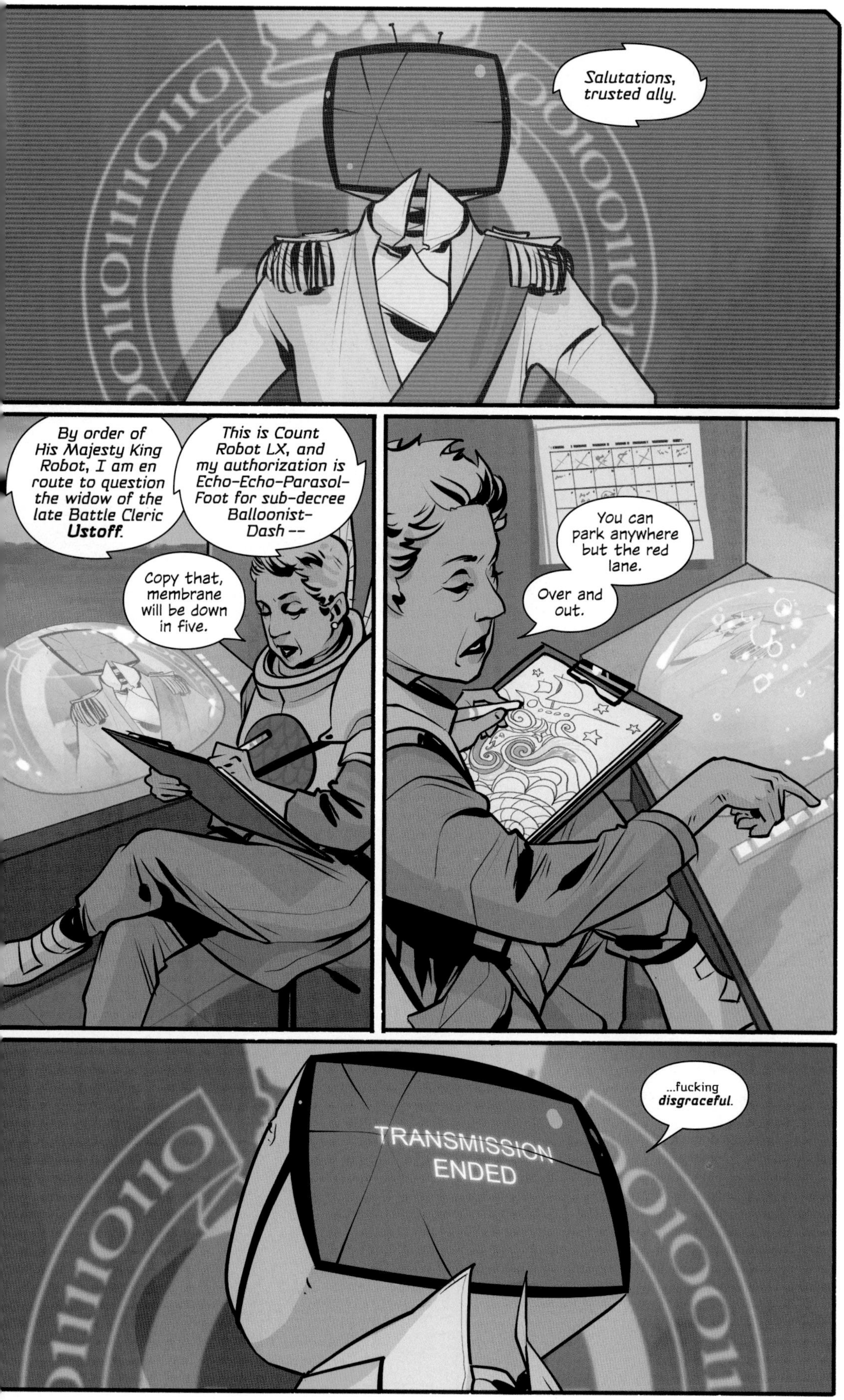
Salutations, trusted ally.
By order of His Majesty King Robot, I am en route to question the widow of the late Battle Cleric **Ustoff**.
This is Count Robot LX, and my authorization is Echo-Echo-Parasol-Foot for sub-decree Balloonist-Dash --
Copy that, membrane will be down in five.
You can park anywhere but the red lane.
Over and out.
TRANSMISSION ENDED
...fucking **disgraceful**.

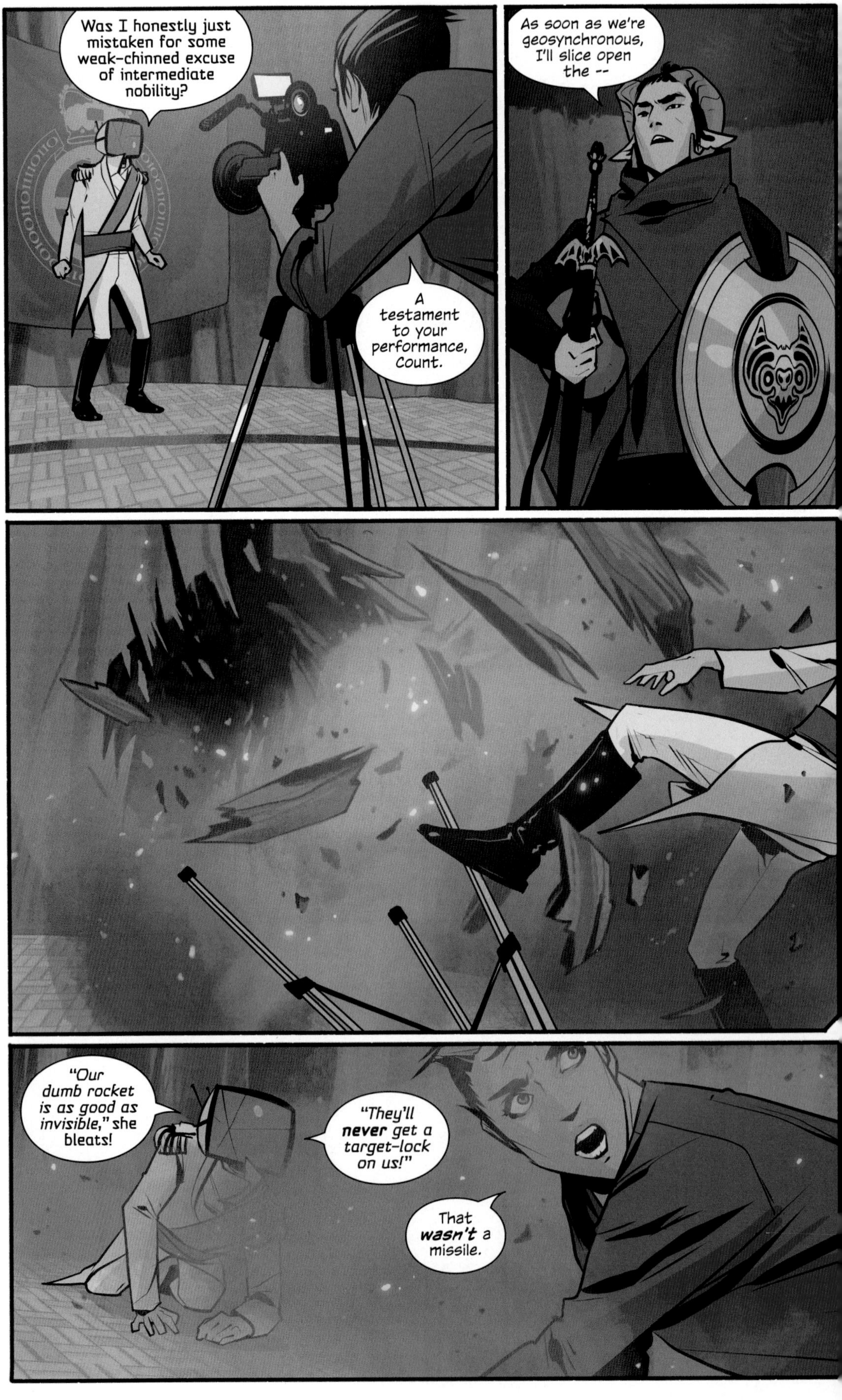
Was I honestly just mistaken for some weak-chinned excuse of intermediate nobility?
A testament to your performance, Count.
As soon as we're geosynchronous, I'll slice open the --
"Our dumb rocket is as good as invisible," she bleats!
"They'll **never** get a target-lock on us!"
That ***wasn't*** a missile.

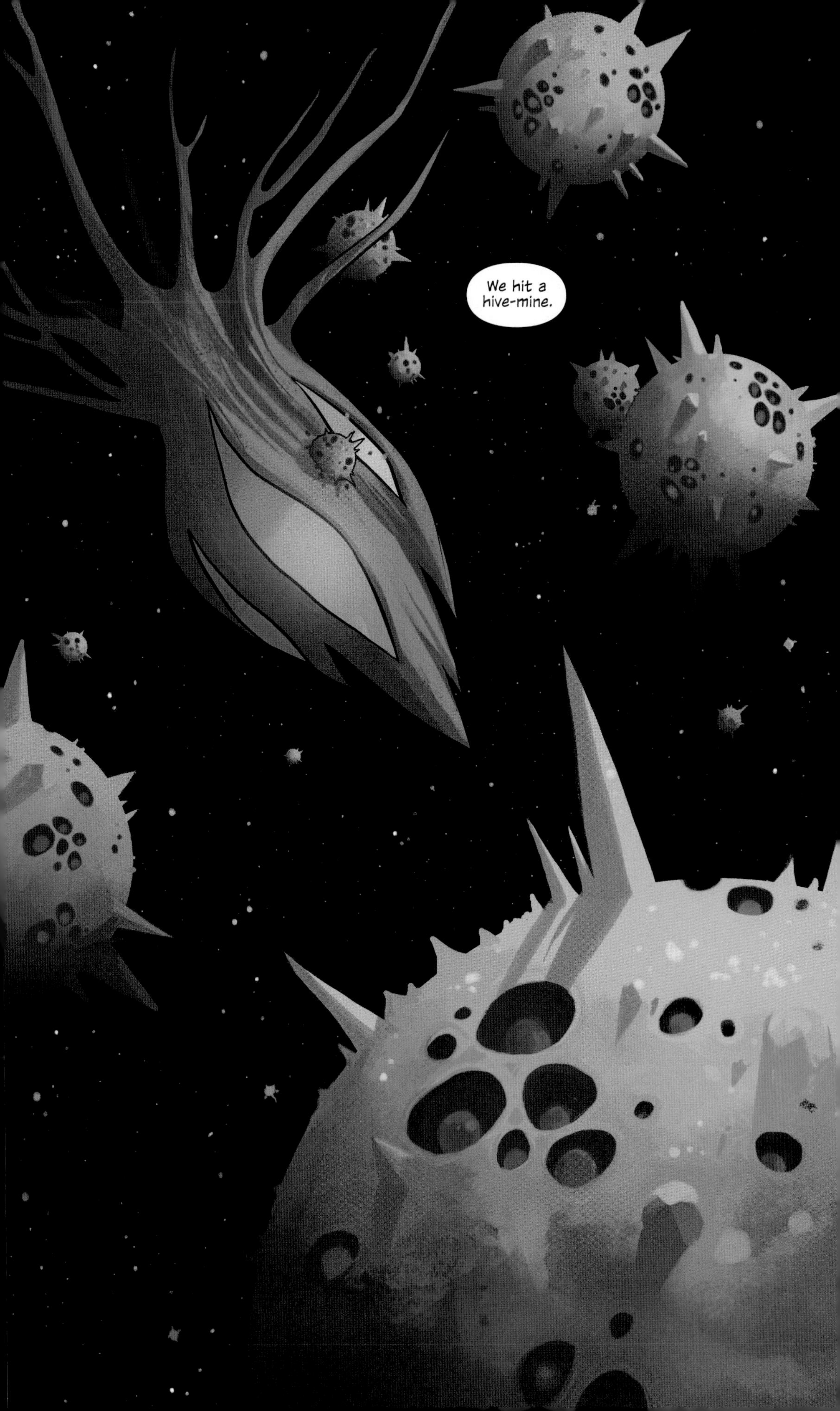
We hit a hive-mine.

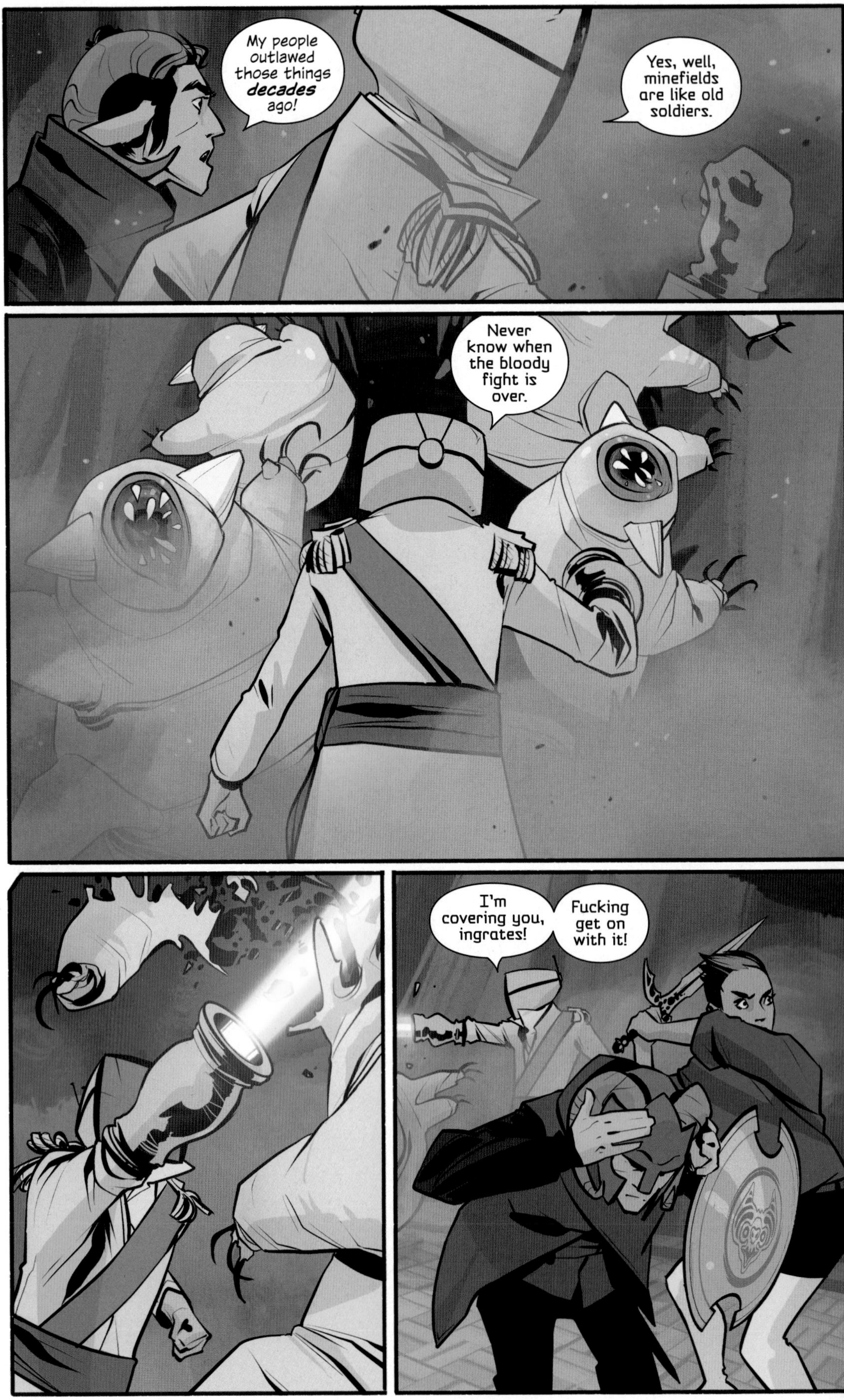
My people outlawed those things *decades* ago!
Yes, well, minefields are like old soldiers.
Never know when the bloody fight is over.
I'm covering you, ingrates!
Fucking get on with it!

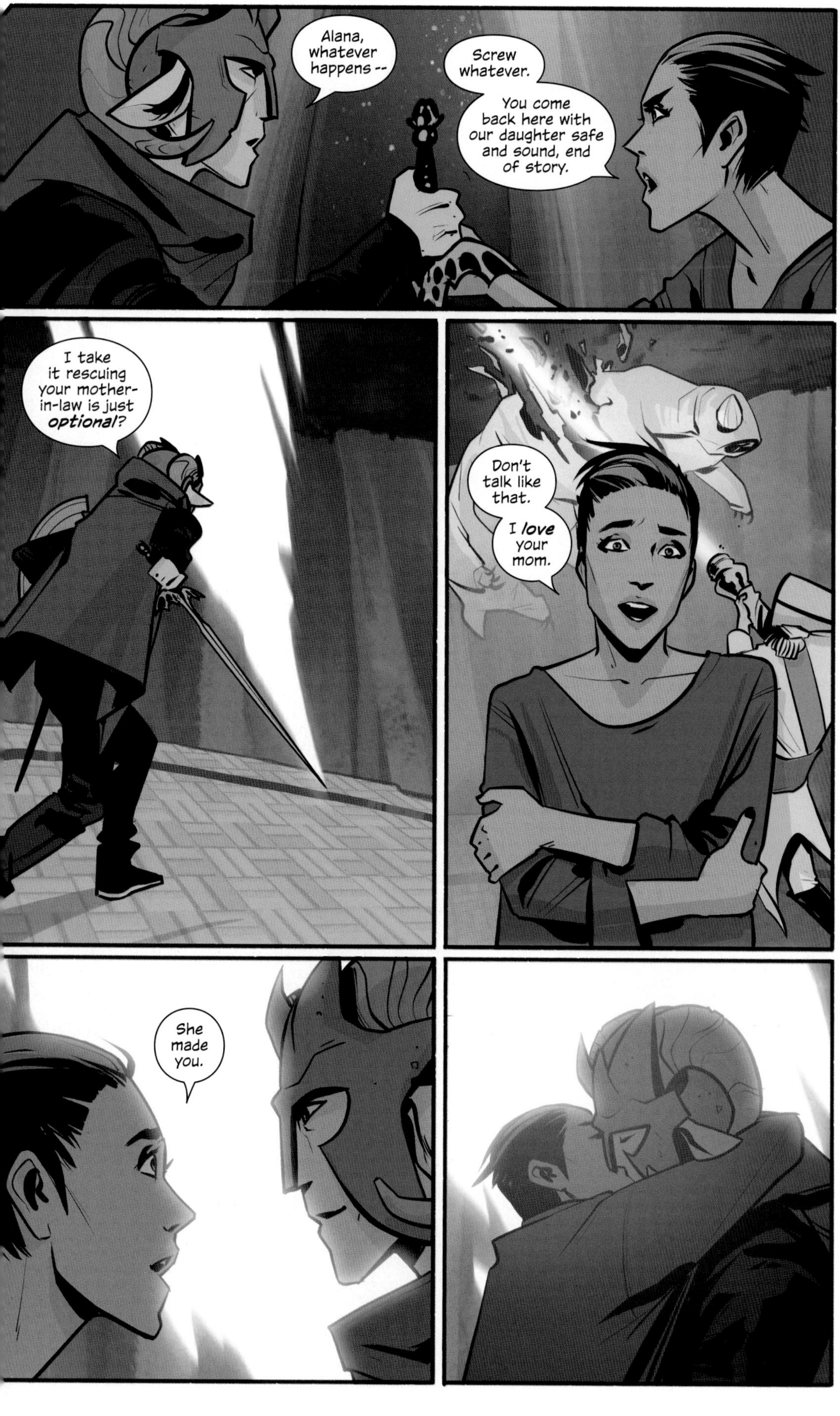
Alana, whatever happens --
Screw whatever.
You come back here with our daughter safe and sound, end of story.
I take it rescuing your mother-in-law is just *optional*?
Don't talk like that.
I *love* your mom.
She made you.

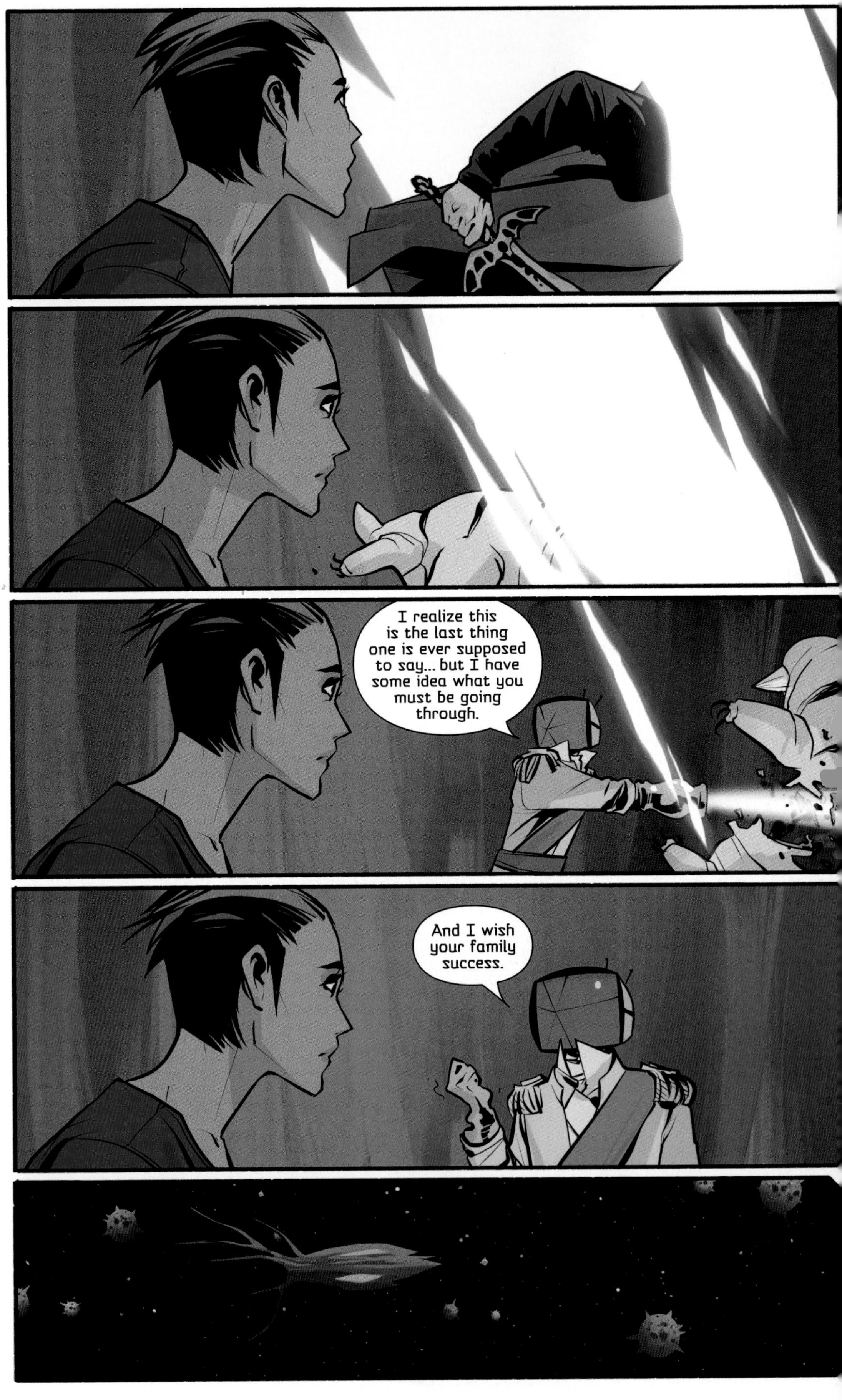
I realize this is the last thing one is ever supposed to say... but I have some idea what you must be going through.
And I wish your family success.

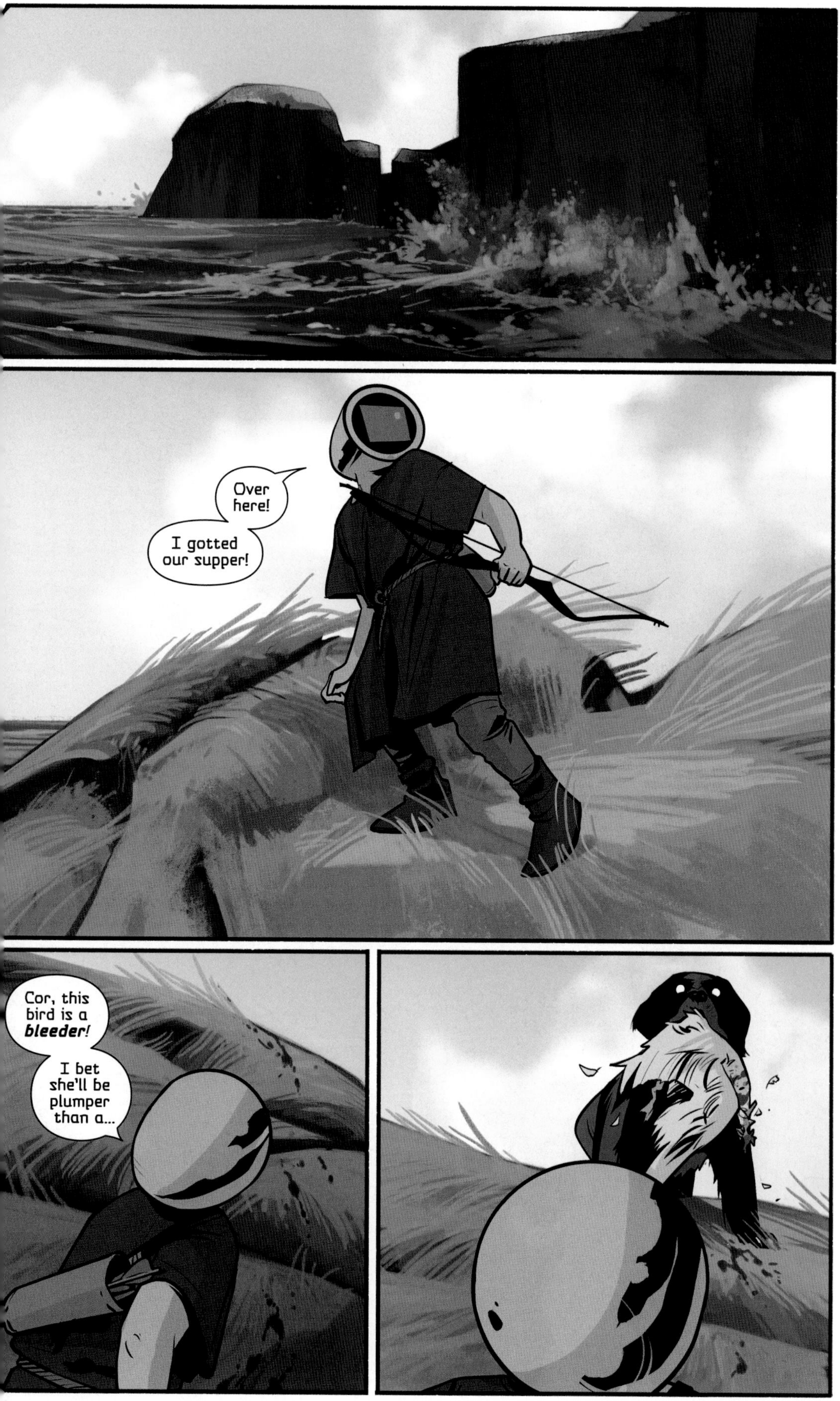

Over here!
I gotted our supper!
Cor, this bird is a *bleeder*!
I bet she'll be plumper than a...

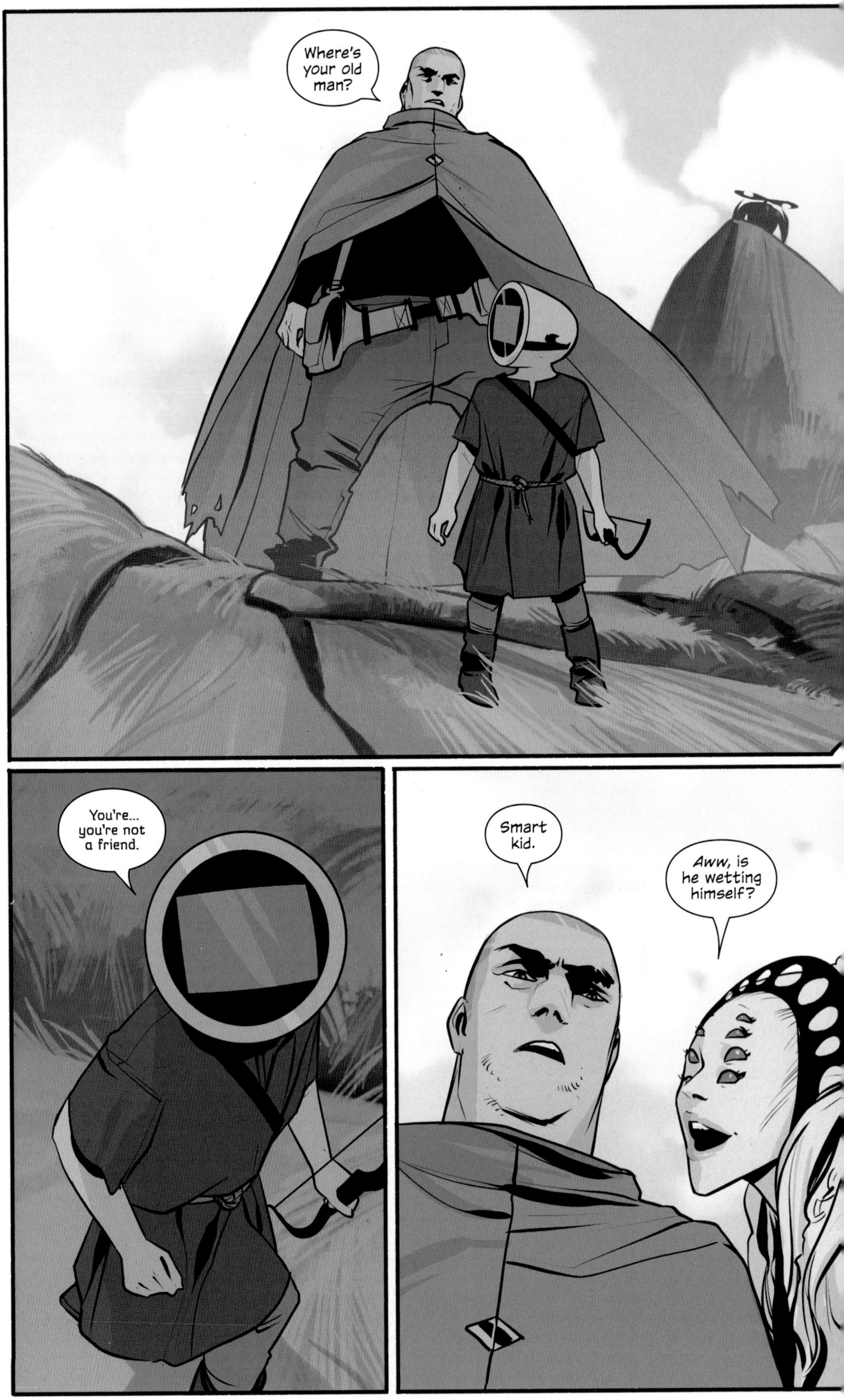
Where's your old man?
You're... you're not a friend.
Smart kid.
Aww, is he wetting himself?

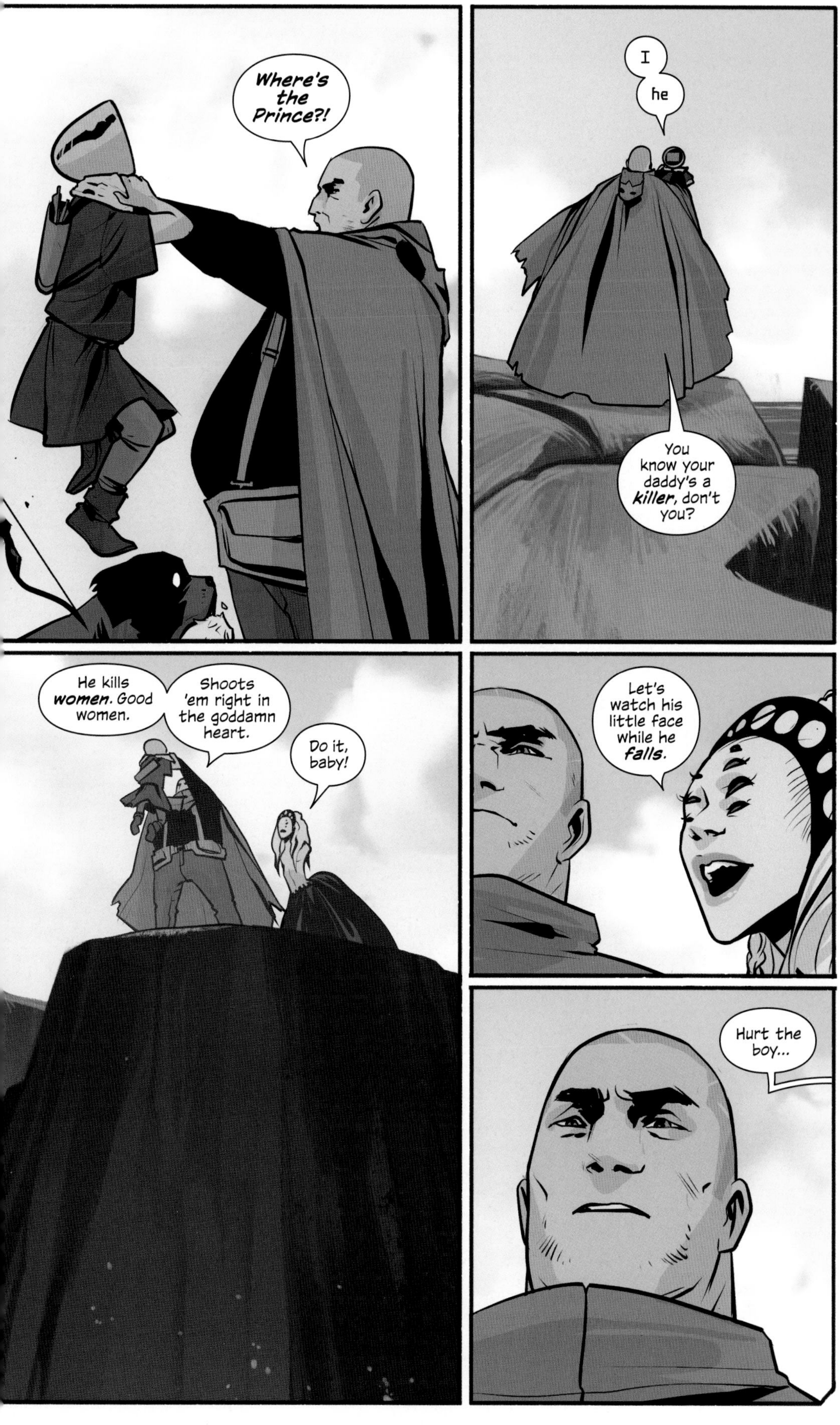
Where's the Prince?!
I
he
You know your daddy's a killer, don't you?
He kills women. Good women.
Shoots 'em right in the goddamn heart.
Do it, baby!
Let's watch his little face while he falls.
Hurt the boy...

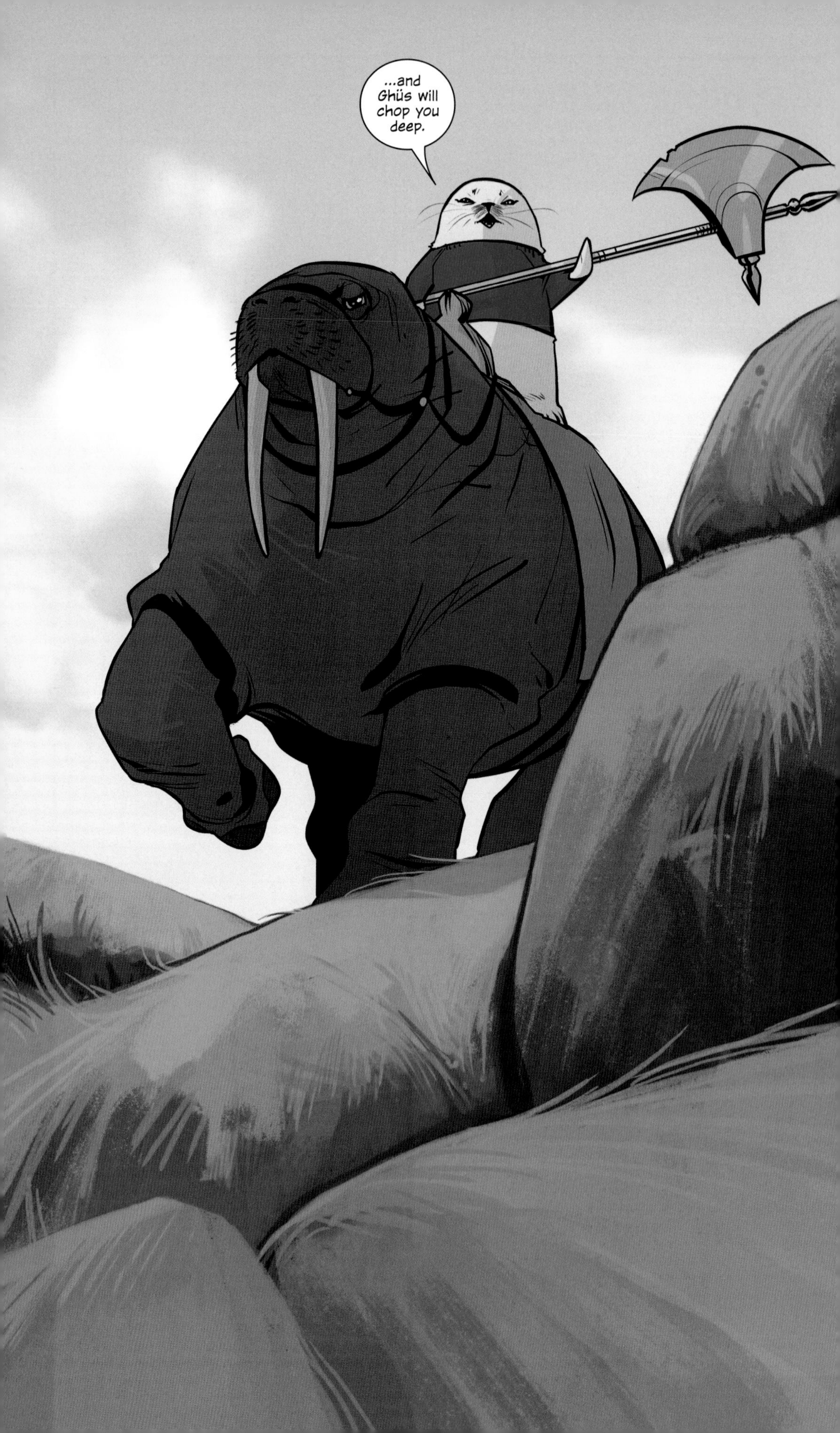
...and Ghüs will chop you deep.

end chapter thirty-five

CHAPTER
THIRTY-SIX

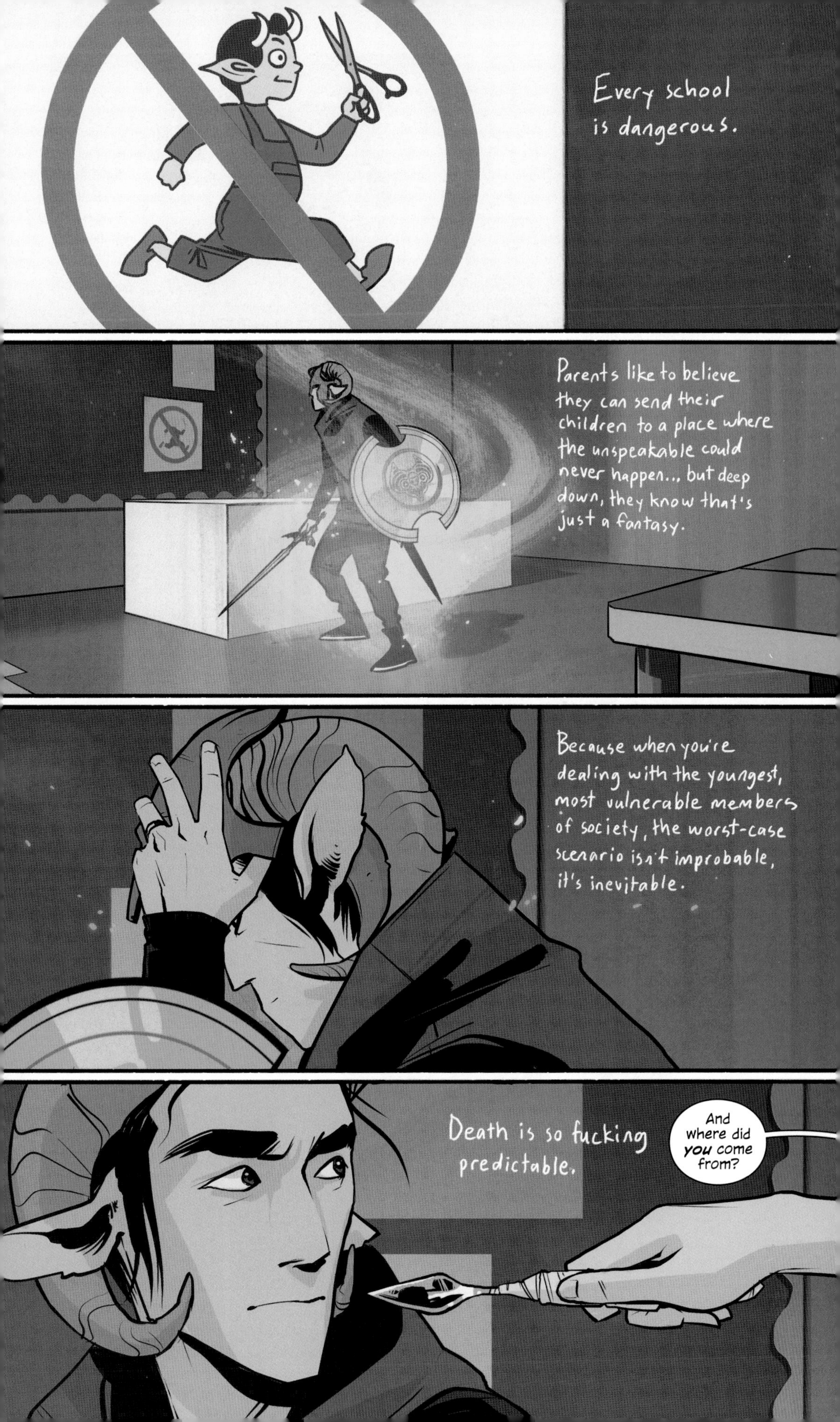
Every school is dangerous.
Parents like to believe they can send their children to a place where the unspeakable could never happen... but deep down, they know that's just a fantasy.
Because when you're dealing with the youngest, most vulnerable members of society, the worst-case scenario isn't improbable, it's inevitable.
Death is so fucking predictable.
And where did *you* come from?

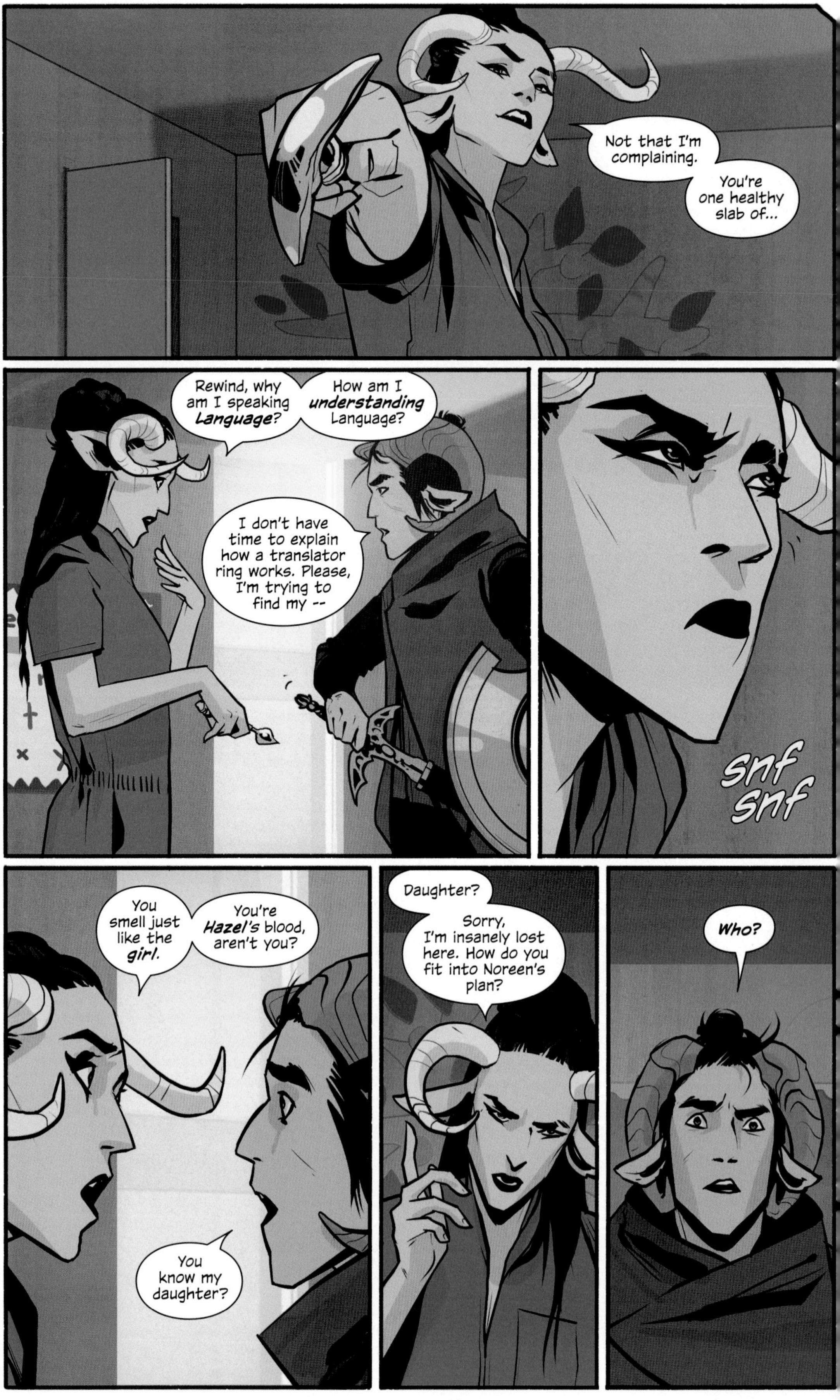
Not that I'm complaining.
You're one healthy slab of...
Rewind, why am I speaking *Language*?
How am I *understanding* Language?
I don't have time to explain how a translator ring works. Please, I'm trying to find my --
SNF SNF
You smell just like the *girl*.
You're *Hazel's* blood, aren't you?
You know my daughter?
Daughter?
Sorry, I'm insanely lost here. How do you fit into Noreen's plan?
Who?

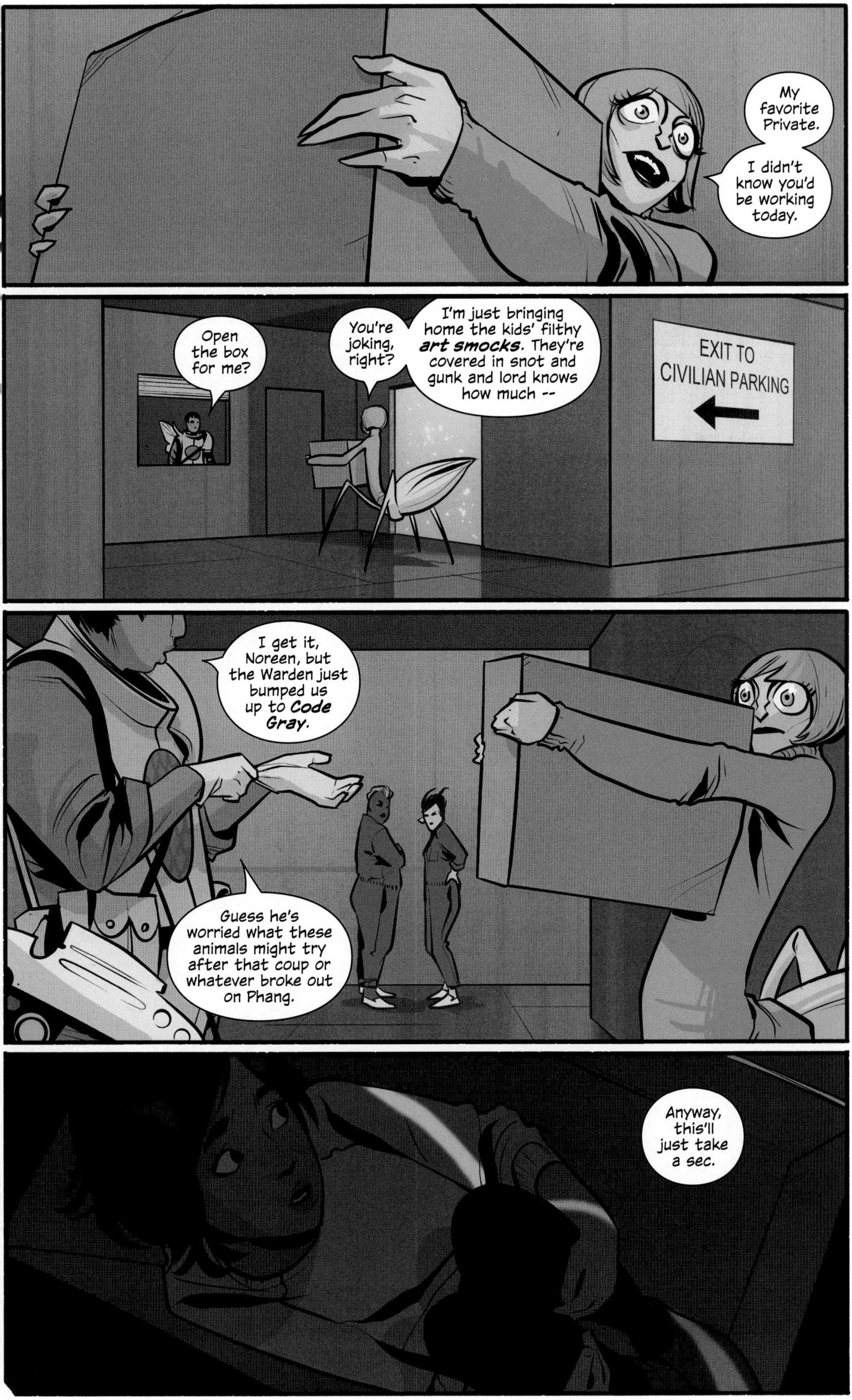
My favorite Private.
I didn't know you'd be working today.
Open the box for me?
You're joking, right?
I'm just bringing home the kids' filthy ***art smocks***. They're covered in snot and gunk and lord knows how much --
EXIT TO CIVILIAN PARKING
I get it, Noreen, but the Warden just bumped us up to ***Code Gray***.
Guess he's worried what these animals might try after that coup or whatever broke out on Phang.
Anyway, this'll just take a sec.

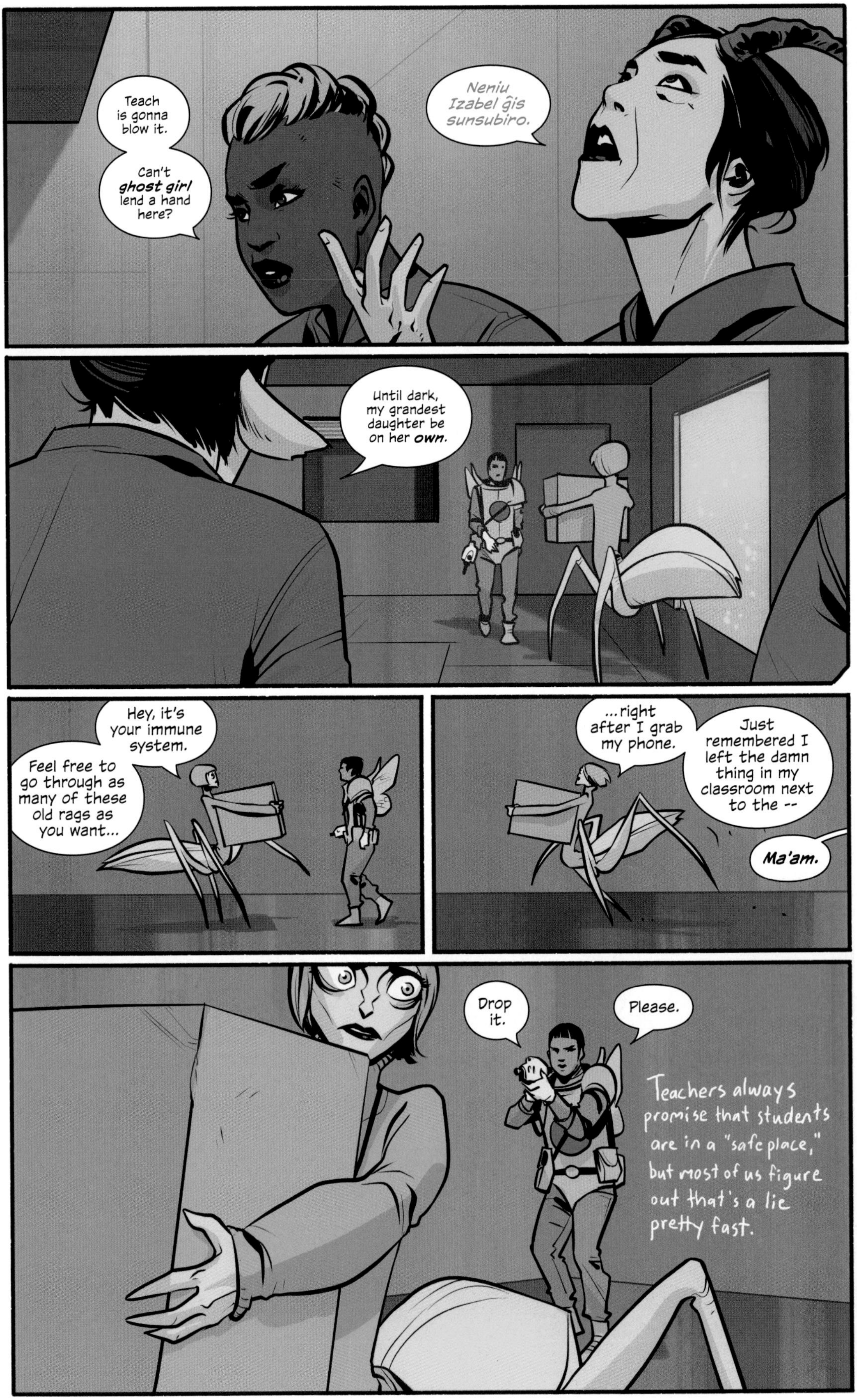
Teach is gonna blow it.
Can't **ghost girl** lend a hand here?
Neniu Izabel ĝis sunsubiro.
Until dark, my grandest daughter be on her **own**.
Hey, it's your immune system.
Feel free to go through as many of these old rags as you want...
...right after I grab my phone.
Just remembered I left the damn thing in my classroom next to the --
Ma'am.
Drop it.
Please.
Teachers always promise that students are in a "safe place," but most of us figure out that's a lie pretty fast.

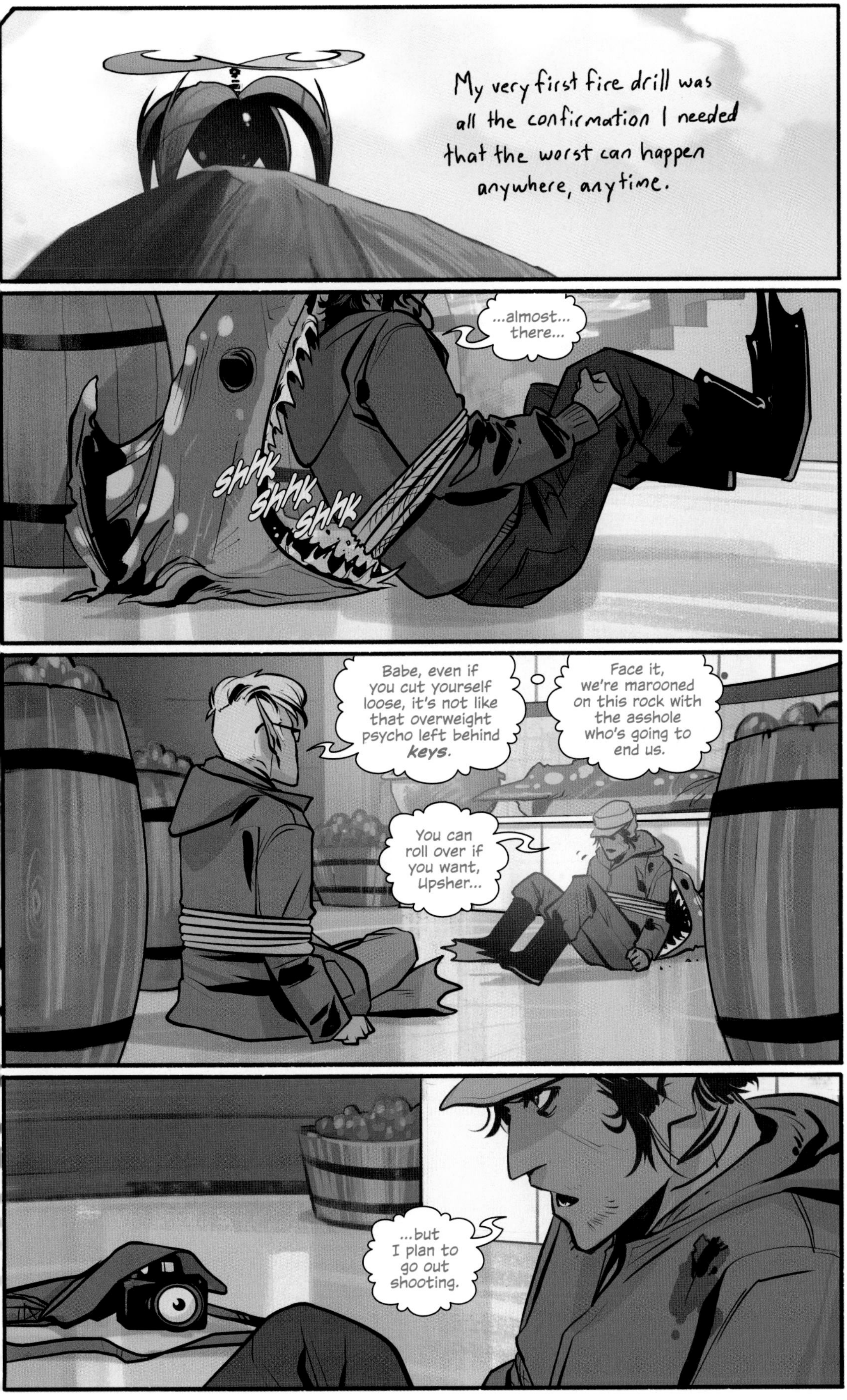
My very first fire drill was all the confirmation I needed that the worst can happen anywhere, anytime.
...almost... there...
SHHK SHHK SHHK
Babe, even if you cut yourself loose, it's not like that overweight psycho left behind *keys*.
Face it, we're marooned on this rock with the asshole who's going to end us.
You can roll over if you want, Upsher...
...but I plan to go out shooting.

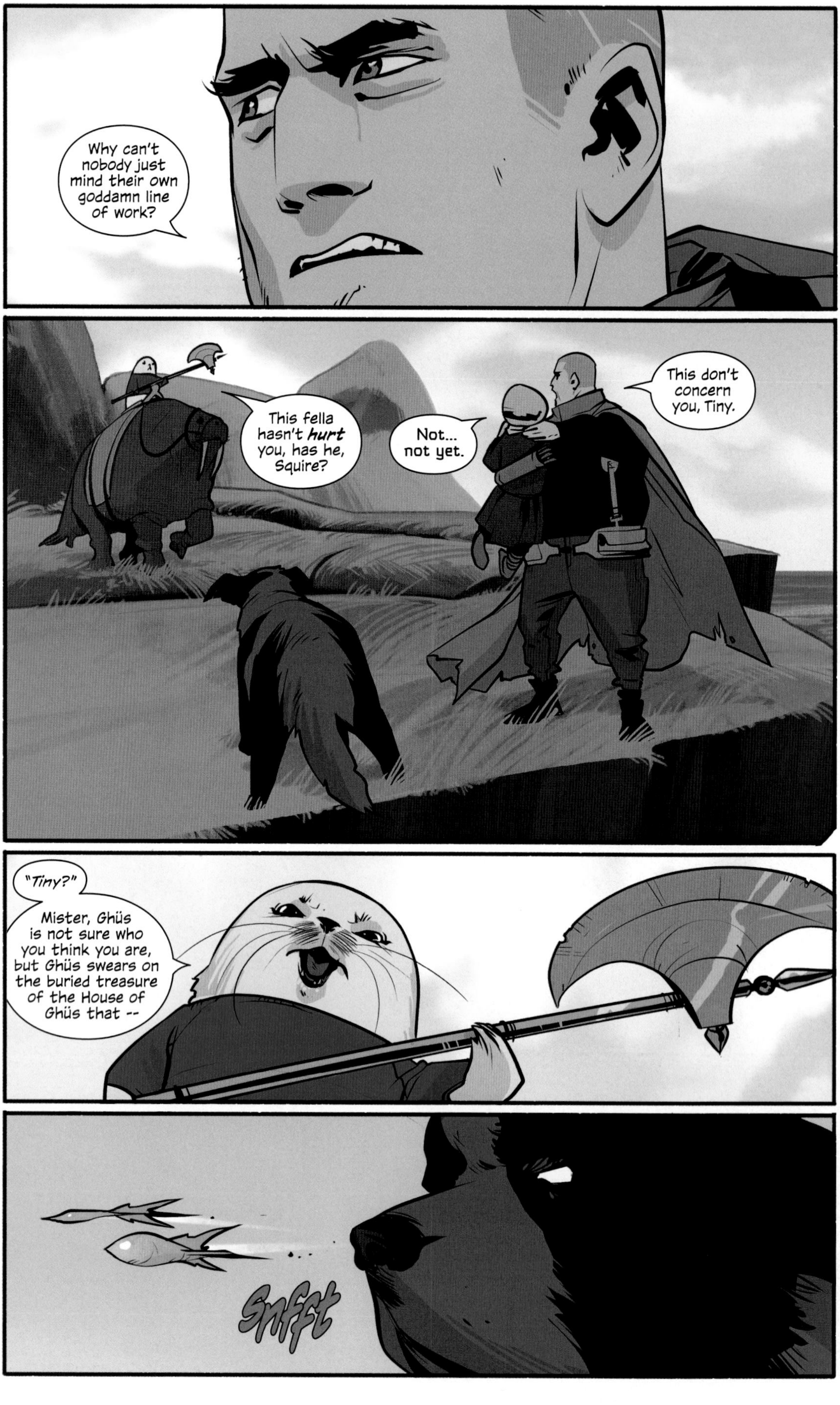
Why can't nobody just mind their own goddamn line of work?
This fella hasn't *hurt* you, has he, Squire?
Not... not yet.
This don't concern you, Tiny.
"Tiny?"
Mister, Ghüs is not sure who you think you are, but Ghüs swears on the buried treasure of the House of Ghüs that --
Snfft

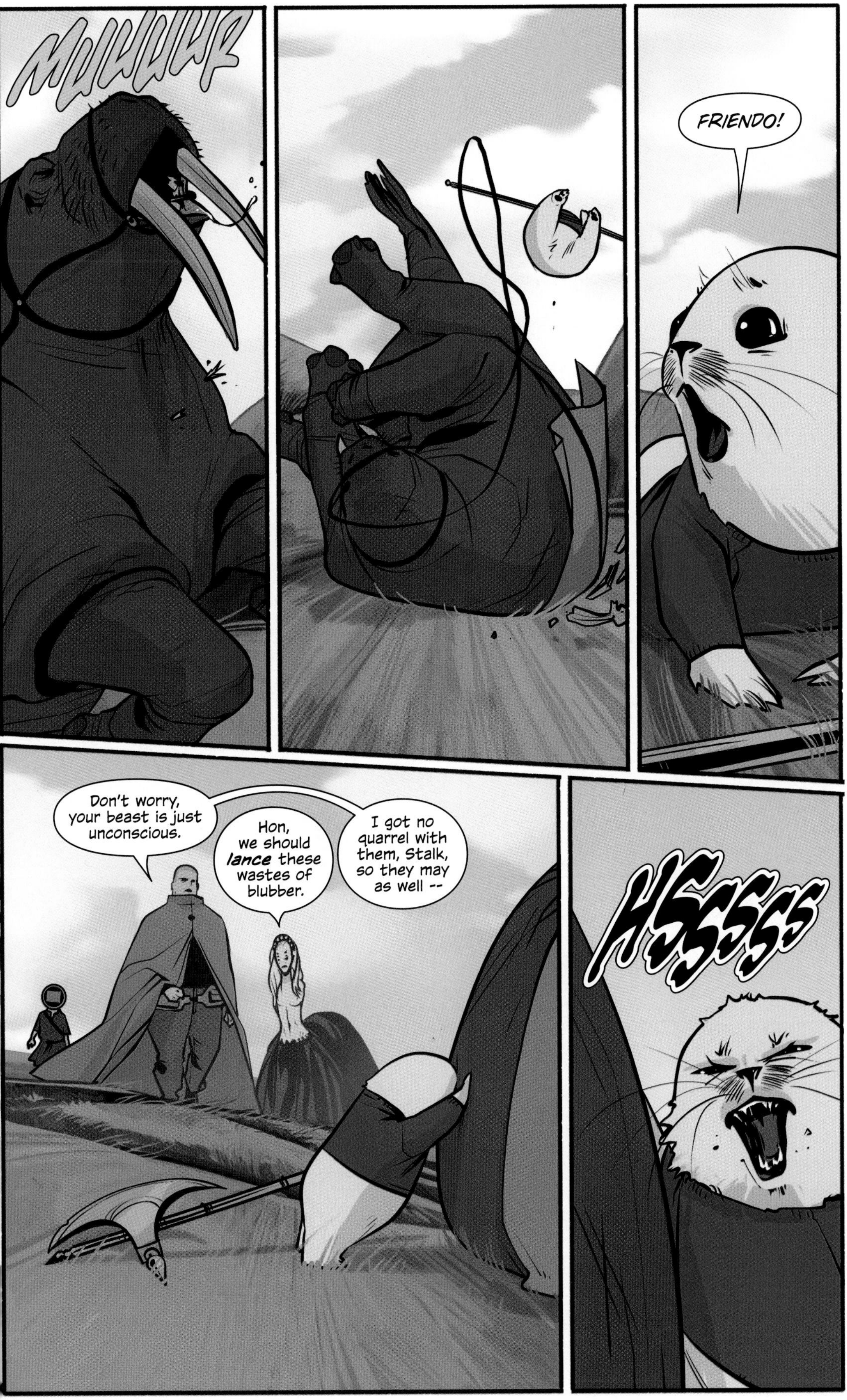
MWUUWP
FRIENDO!
Don't worry, your beast is just unconscious.
Hon, we should *lance* these wastes of blubber.
I got no quarrel with them, Stalk, so they may as well --
HSSSSS

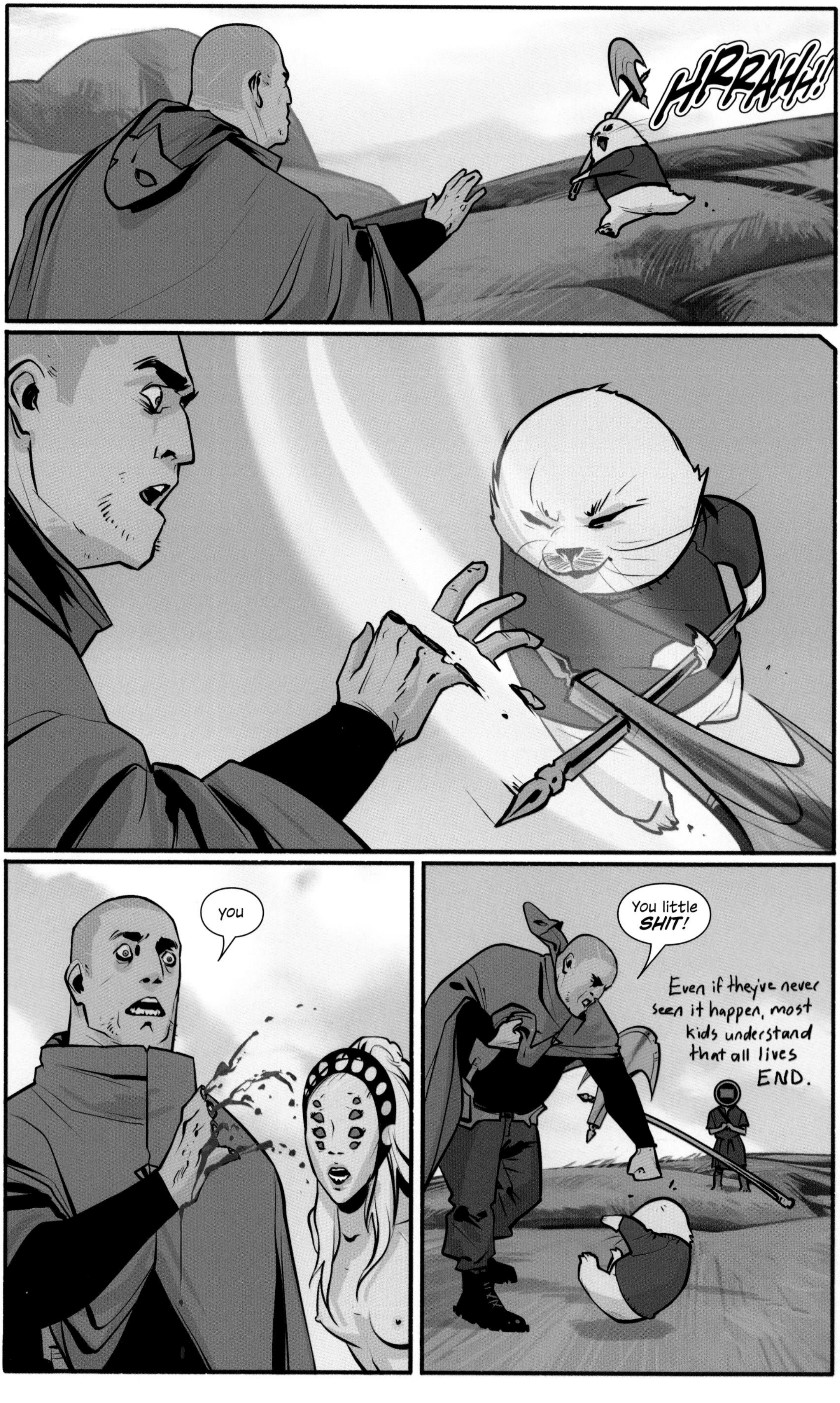
HRRAHH!
you
You little SHIT!
Even if they've never seen it happen, most kids understand that all lives END.

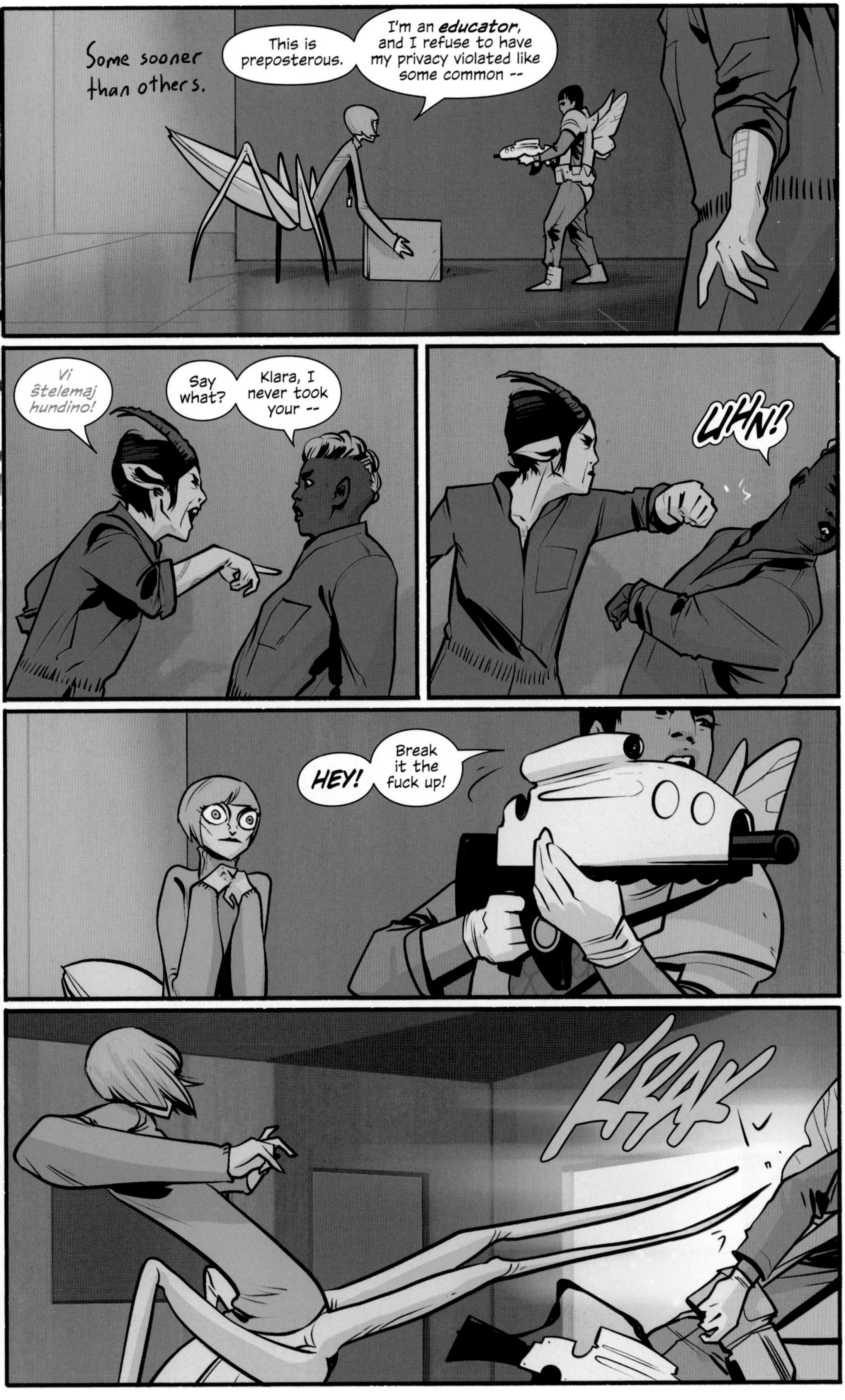
Some sooner than others.
This is preposterous.
I'm an ***educator***, and I refuse to have my privacy violated like some common --
Vi ŝtelemaj hundino!
Say what?
Klara, I never took your --
UHN!
HEY!
Break it the fuck up!
KRAK

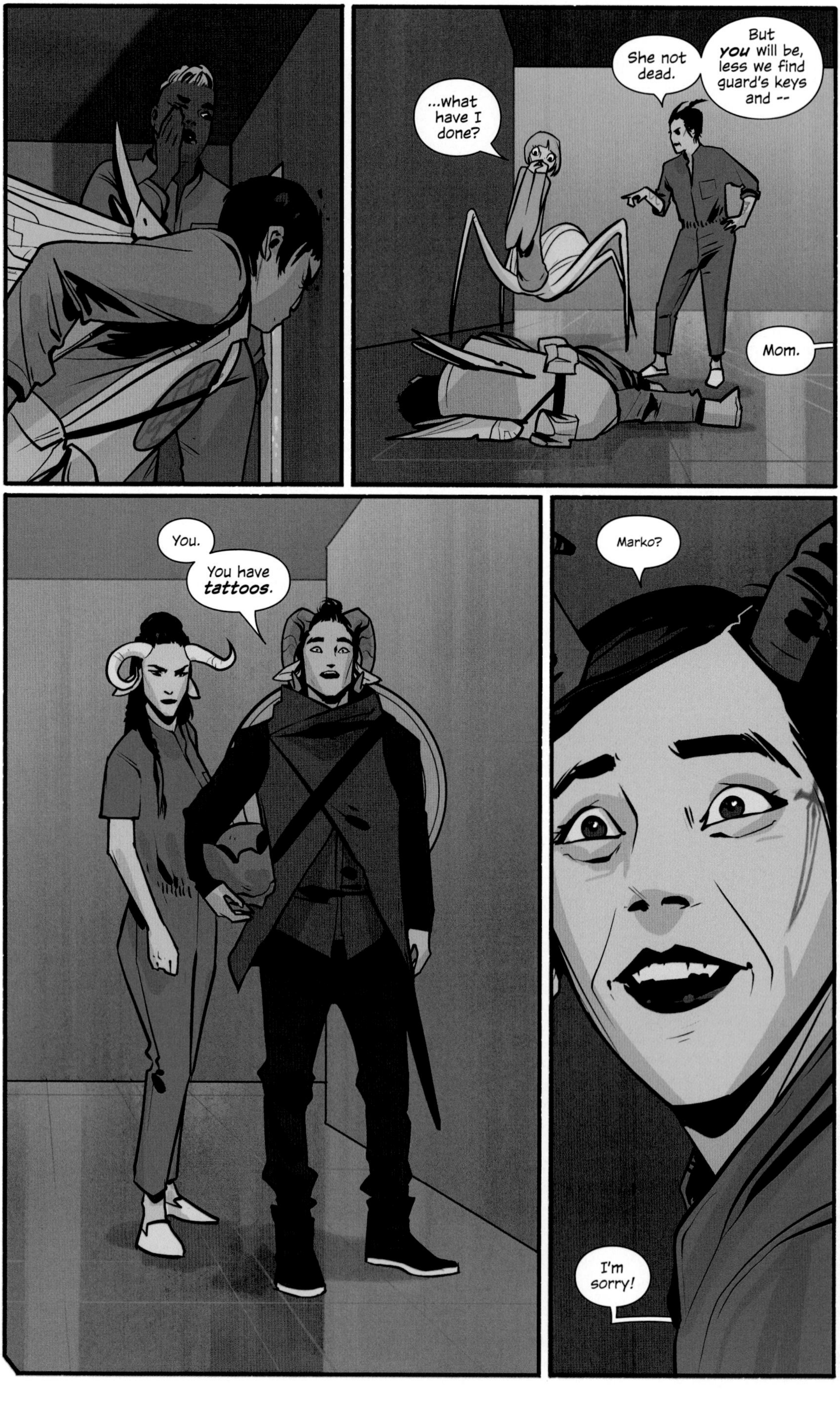
...what have I done?
She not dead.
But *you* will be, less we find guard's keys and --
Mom.
You.
You have ***tattoos***.
Marko?
I'm sorry!

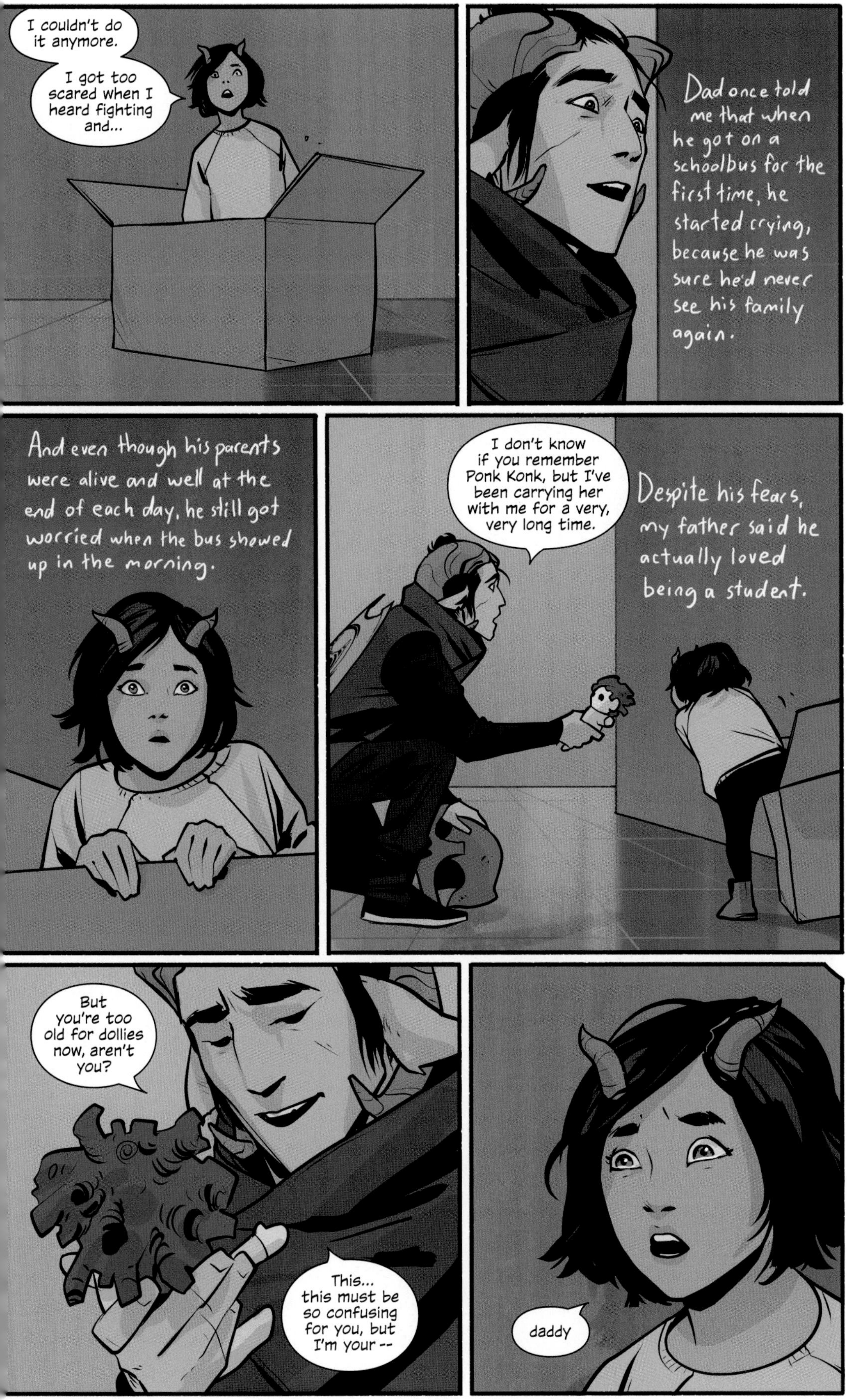
I couldn't do it anymore.
I got too scared when I heard fighting and...
Dad once told me that when he got on a schoolbus for the first time, he started crying, because he was sure he'd never see his family again.
And even though his parents were alive and well at the end of each day, he still got worried when the bus showed up in the morning.
I don't know if you remember Ponk Konk, but I've been carrying her with me for a very, very long time.
Despite his fears, my father said he actually loved being a student.
But you're too old for dollies now, aren't you?
This... this must be so confusing for you, but I'm your --
daddy

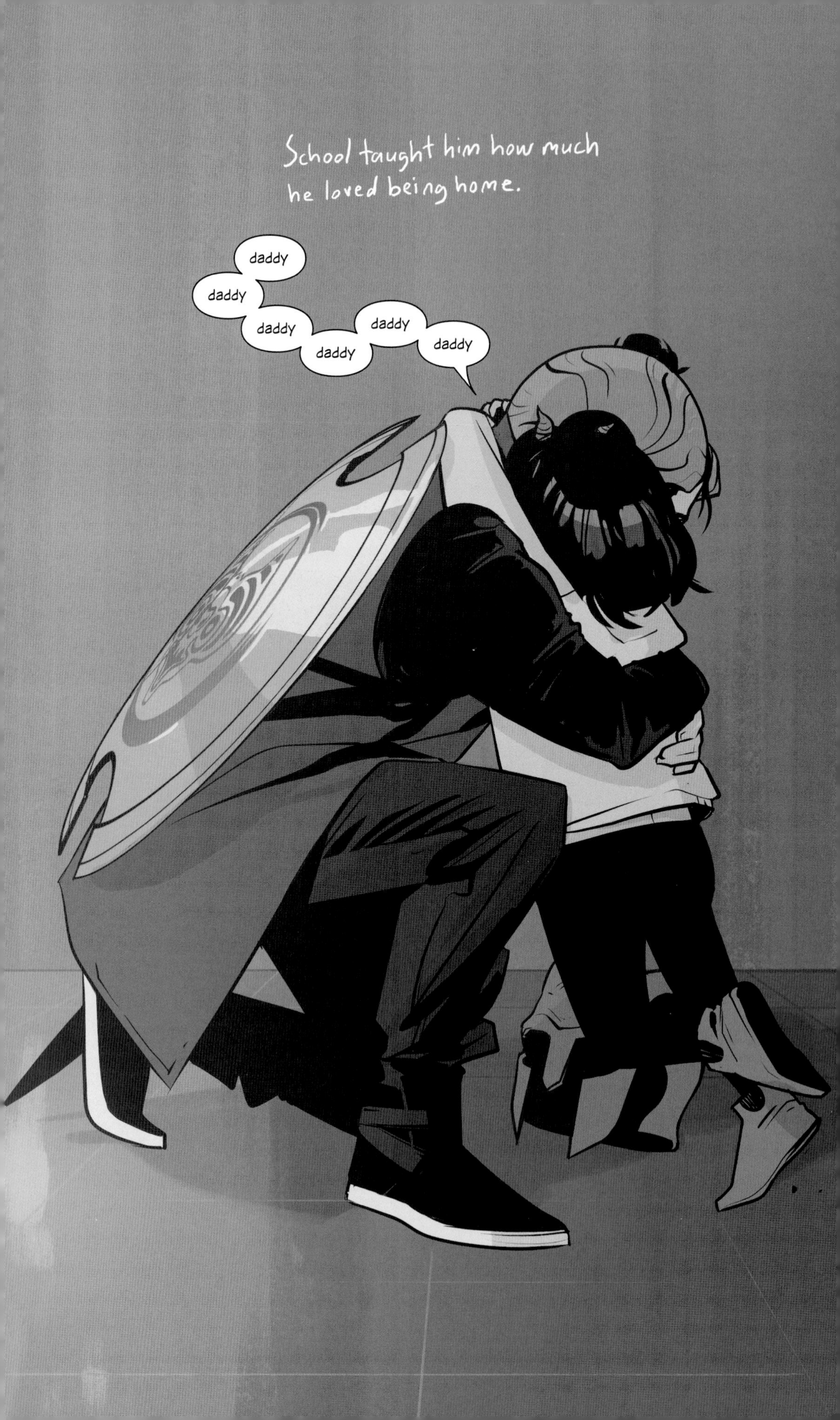

School taught him how much
he loved being home.
daddy
daddy
daddy
daddy
daddy
daddy

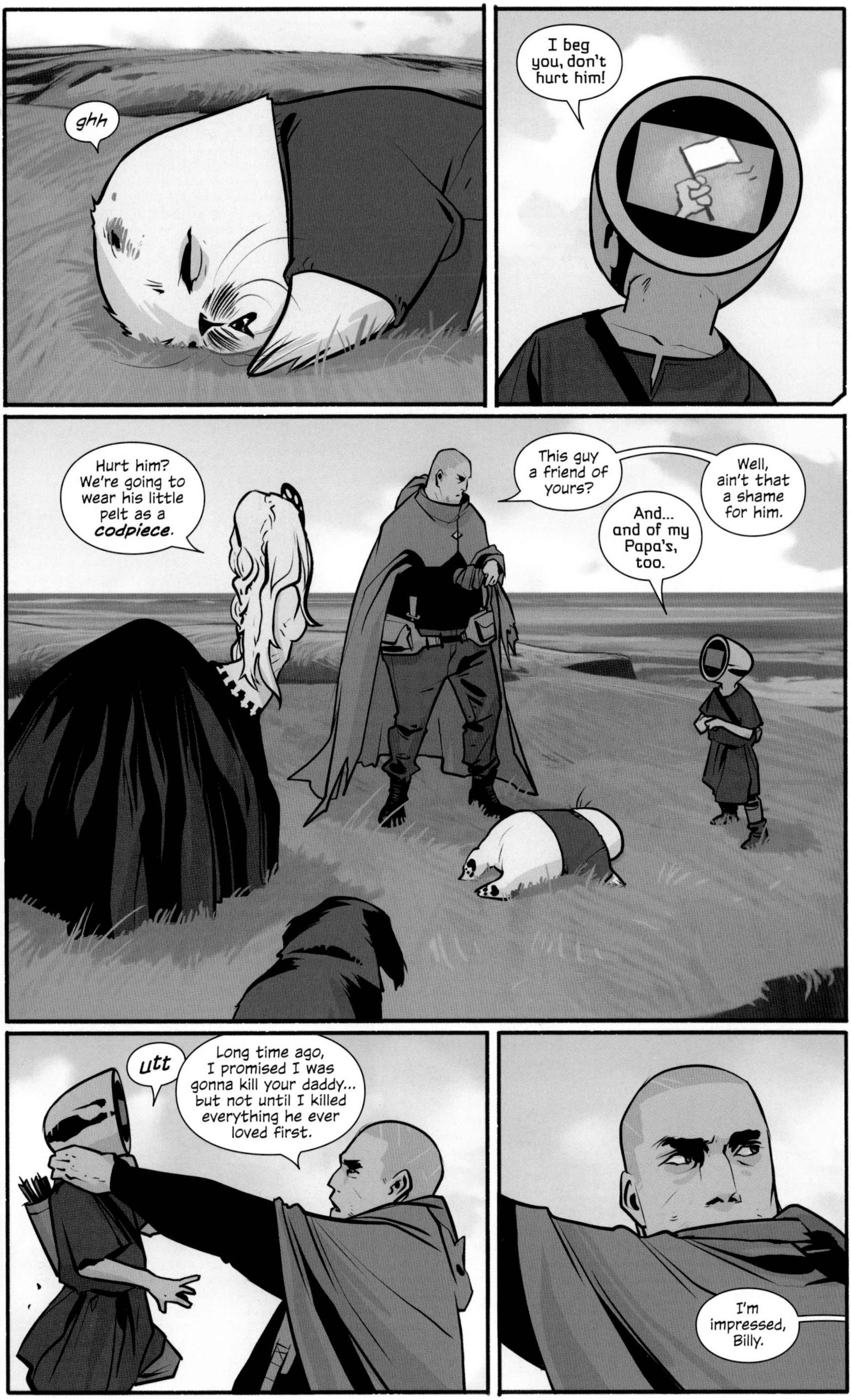
ghh
I beg you, don't hurt him!
Hurt him? We're going to wear his little pelt as a ***codpiece***.
This guy a friend of yours?
Well, ain't that a shame for him.
And... and of my Papa's, too.
utt
Long time ago, I promised I was gonna kill your daddy... but not until I killed everything he ever loved first.
I'm impressed, Billy.

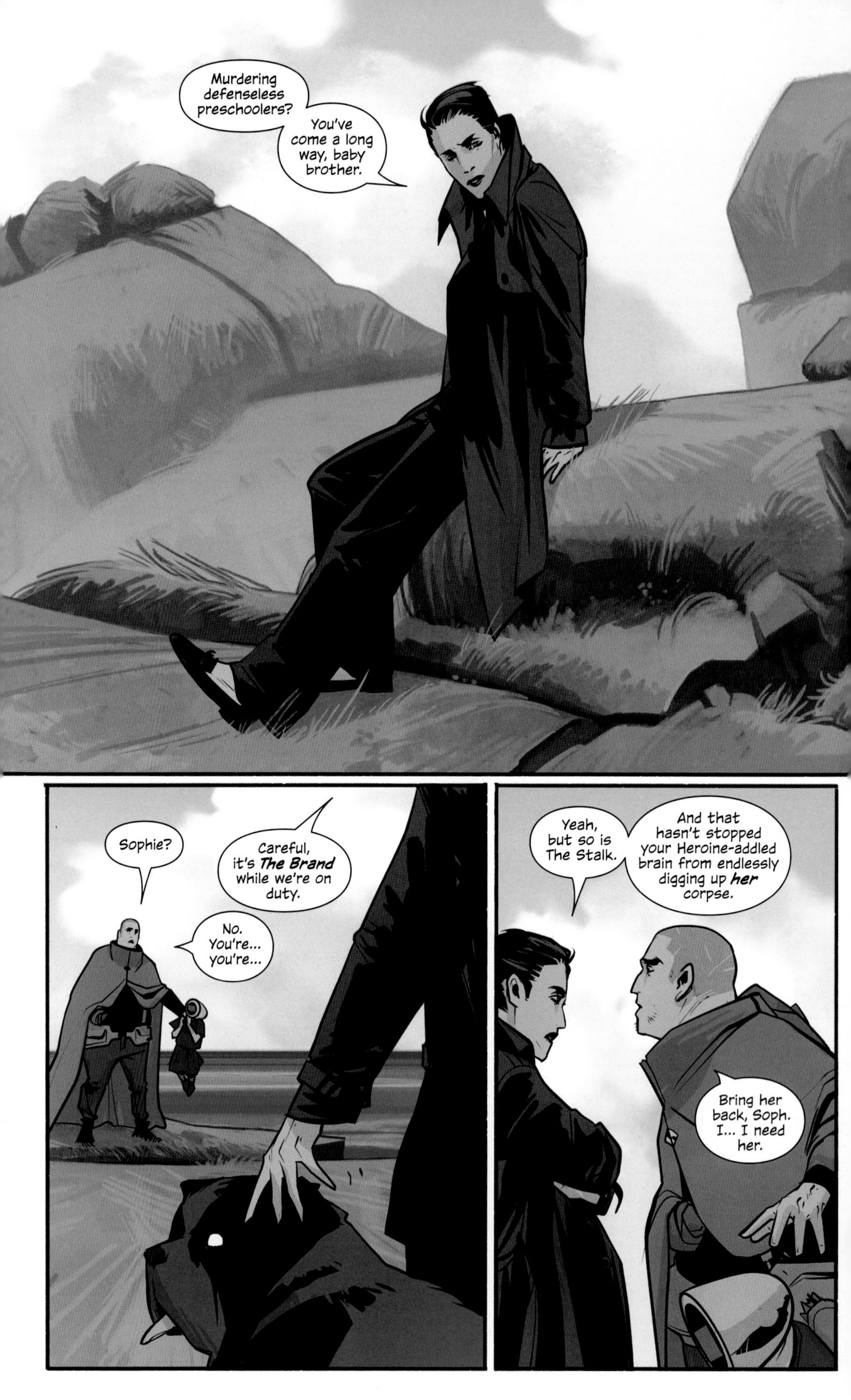

Murdering defenseless preschoolers?
You've come a long way, baby brother.
Sophie?
Careful, it's ***The Brand*** while we're on duty.
No. You're... you're...
Yeah, but so is The Stalk.
And that hasn't stopped your Heroine-addled brain from endlessly digging up ***her*** corpse.
Bring her back, Soph. I... I need her.

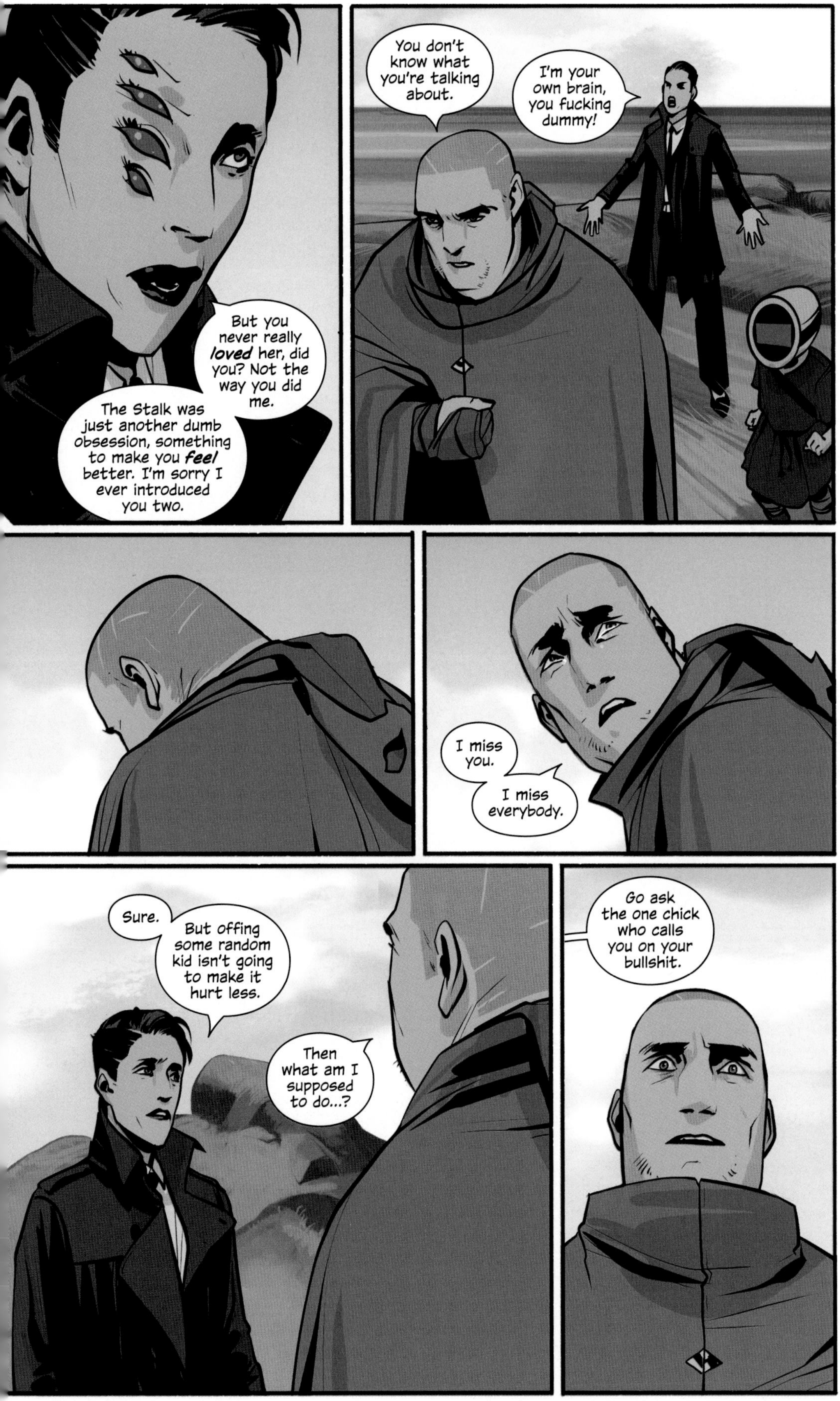
But you never really *loved* her, did you? Not the way you did me.
The Stalk was just another dumb obsession, something to make you *feel* better. I'm sorry I ever introduced you two.
You don't know what you're talking about.
I'm your own brain, you fucking dummy!
I miss you.
I miss everybody.
Sure.
But offing some random kid isn't going to make it hurt less.
Then what am I supposed to do...?
Go ask the one chick who calls you on your bullshit.

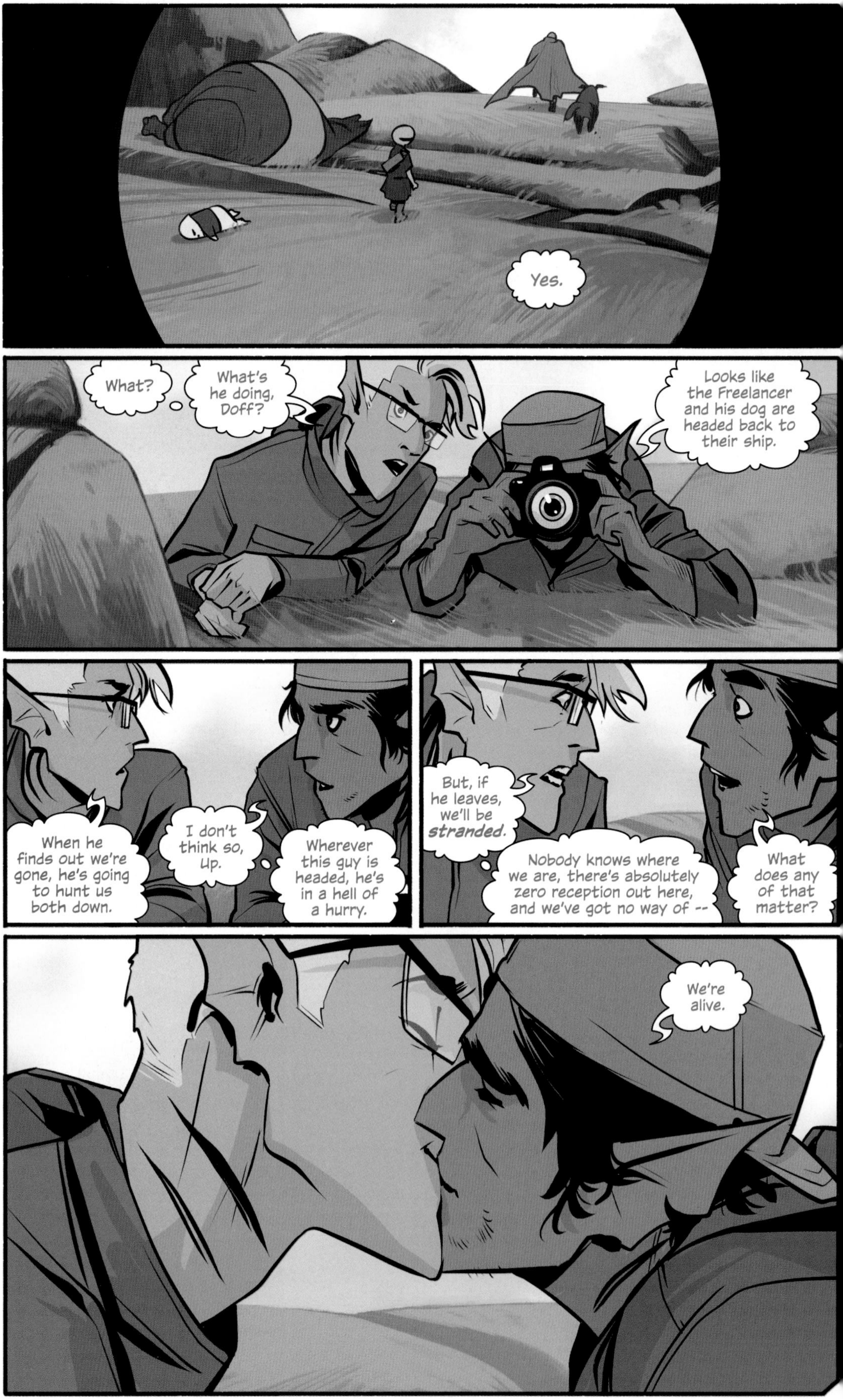
Yes.
What?
What's he doing, Doff?
Looks like the Freelancer and his dog are headed back to their ship.
When he finds out we're gone, he's going to hunt us both down.
I don't think so, Up.
Wherever this guy is headed, he's in a hell of a hurry.
But, if he leaves, we'll be *stranded*.
Nobody knows where we are, there's absolutely zero reception out here, and we've got no way of --
What does any of that matter?
We're alive.

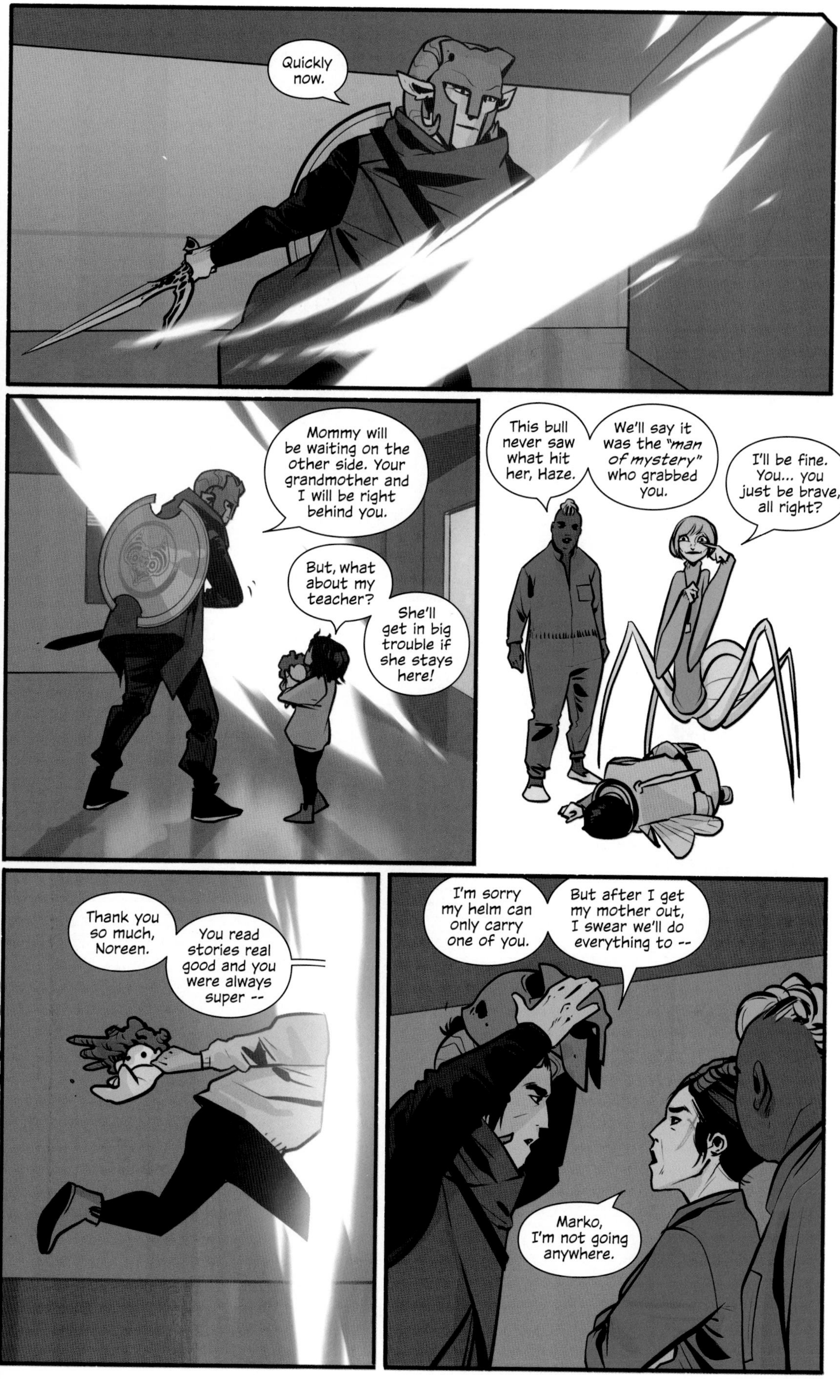

Quickly now.
Mommy will be waiting on the other side. Your grandmother and I will be right behind you.
But, what about my teacher?
She'll get in big trouble if she stays here!
This bull never saw what hit her, Haze.
We'll say it was the *"man of mystery"* who grabbed you.
I'll be fine. You... you just be brave, all right?
Thank you so much, Noreen.
You read stories real good and you were always super --
I'm sorry my helm can only carry one of you.
But after I get my mother out, I swear we'll do everything to --
Marko, I'm not going anywhere.

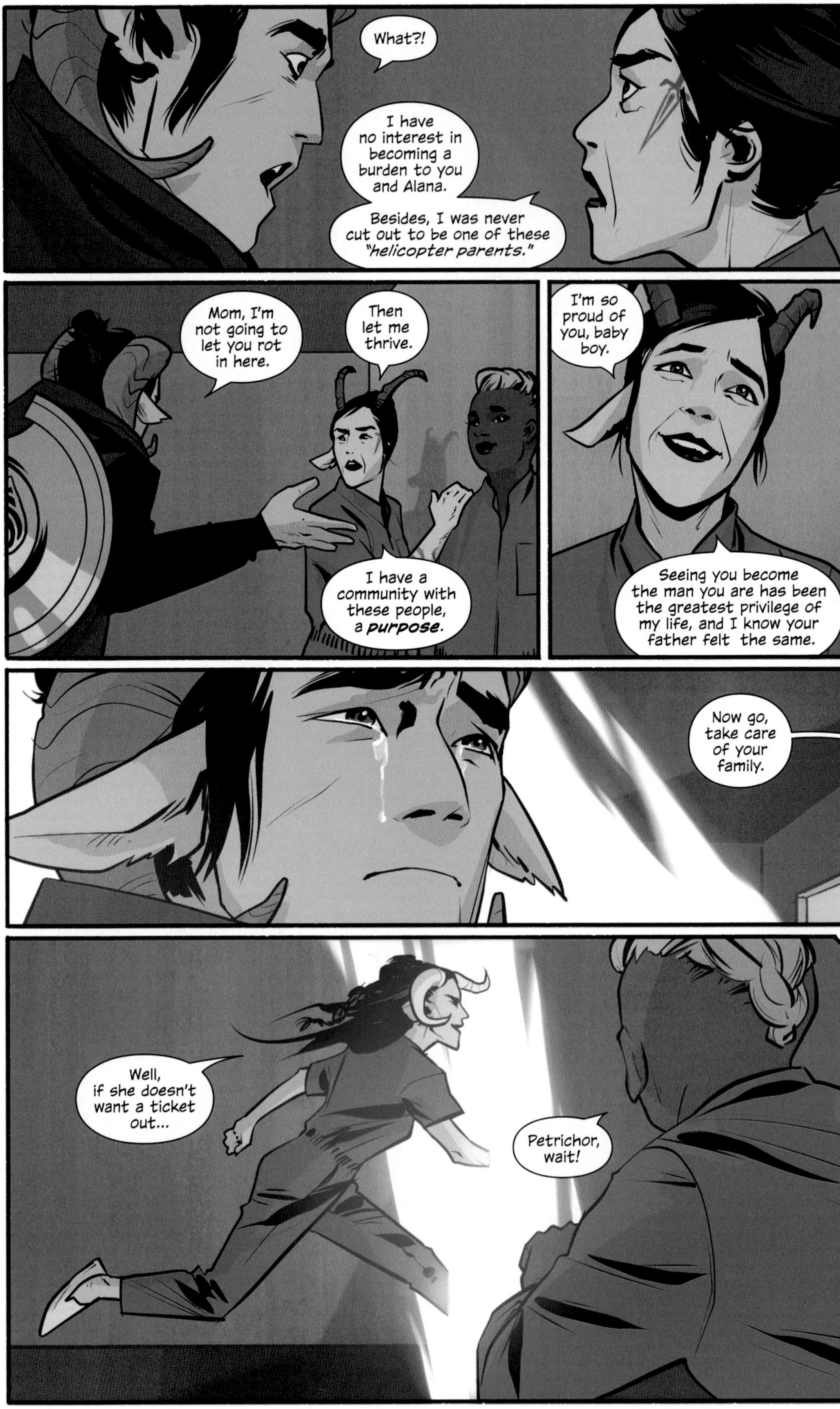
What?!
I have no interest in becoming a burden to you and Alana.
Besides, I was never cut out to be one of these *"helicopter parents."*
Mom, I'm not going to let you rot in here.
Then let me thrive.
I have a community with these people, a ***purpose***.
I'm so proud of you, baby boy.
Seeing you become the man you are has been the greatest privilege of my life, and I know your father felt the same.
Now go, take care of your family.
Well, if she doesn't want a ticket out...
Petrichor, wait!

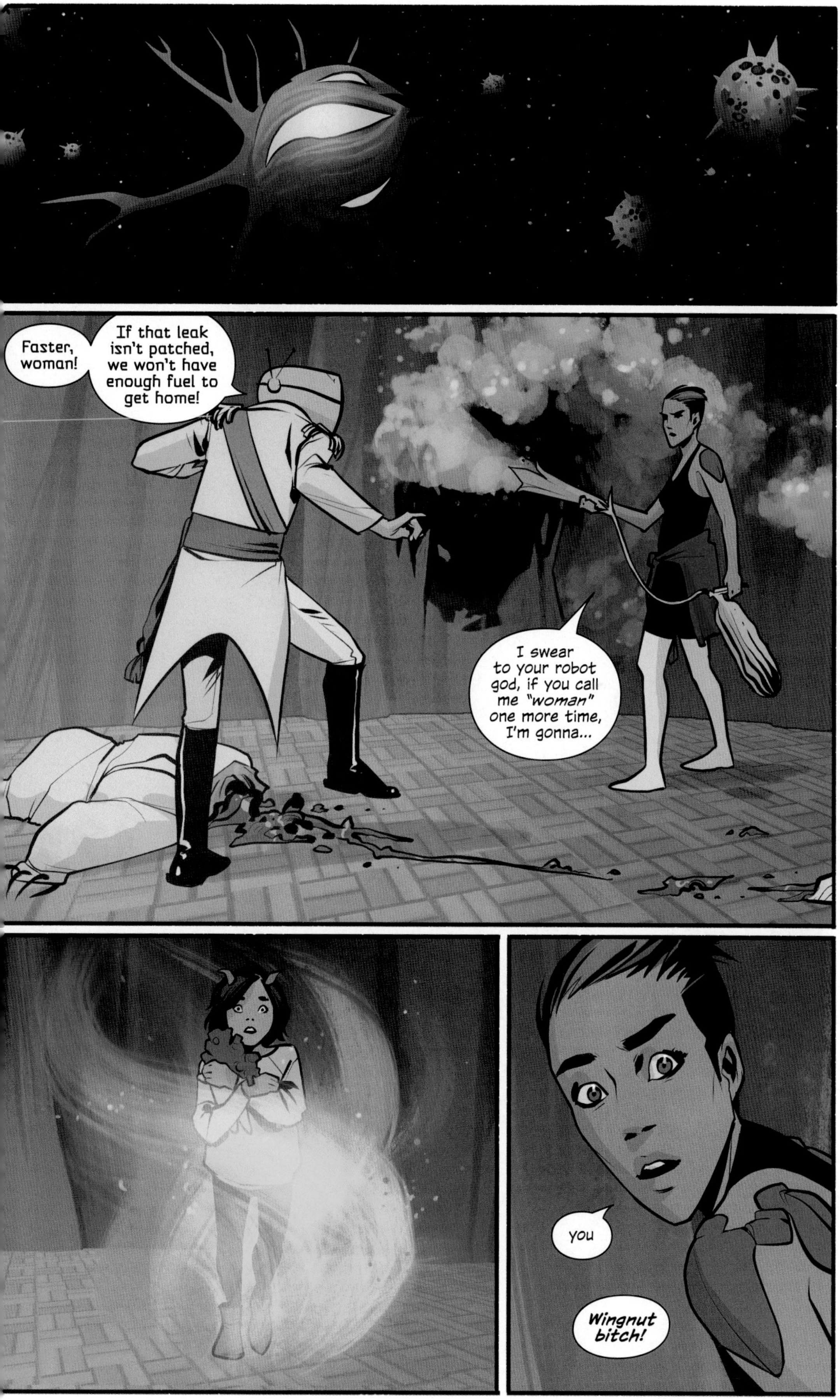
Faster, woman!
If that leak isn't patched, we won't have enough fuel to get home!
I swear to your robot god, if you call me "woman" one more time, I'm gonna...
you
Wingnut bitch!

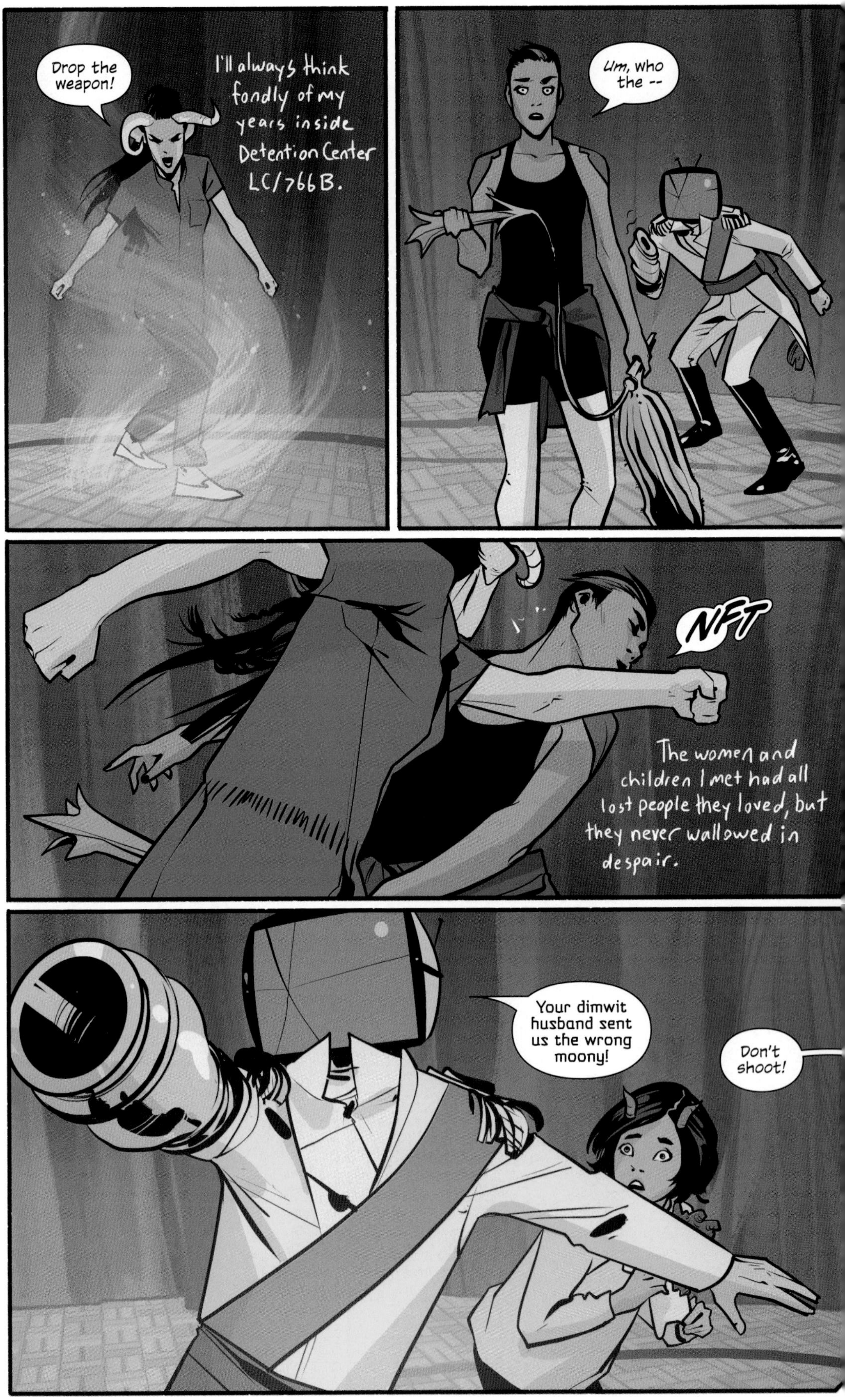
Drop the weapon!
I'll always think fondly of my years inside Detention Center LC/766B.
Um, who the --
NFT
The women and children I met had all lost people they loved, but they never wallowed in despair.
Your dimwit husband sent us the wrong moony!
Don't shoot!

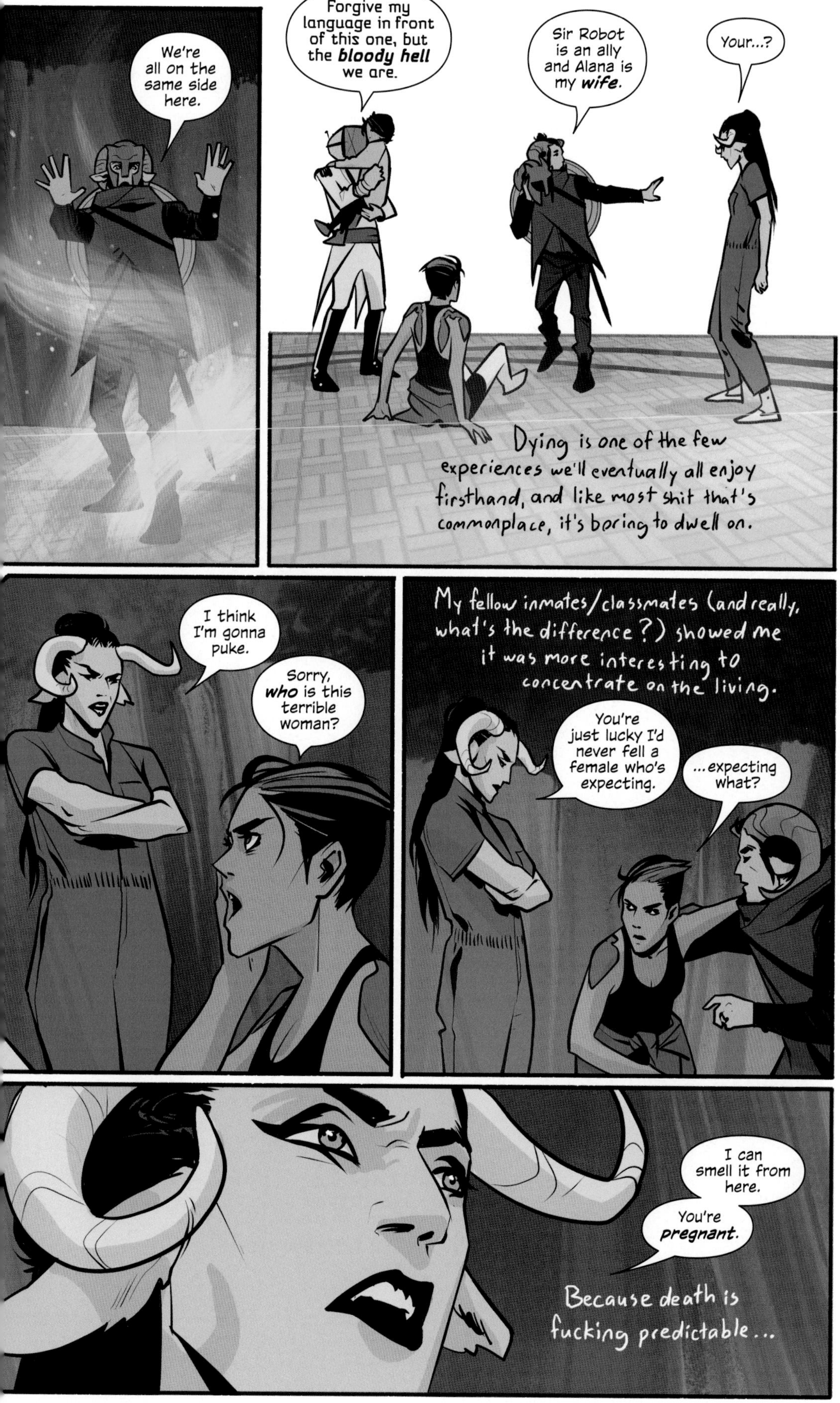

We're all on the same side here.
Forgive my language in front of this one, but the **bloody hell** we are.
Sir Robot is an ally and Alana is my **wife**.
Your...?
Dying is one of the few experiences we'll eventually all enjoy firsthand, and like most shit that's commonplace, it's boring to dwell on.
I think I'm gonna puke.
Sorry, **who** is this terrible woman?
My fellow inmates/classmates (and really, what's the difference?) showed me it was more interesting to concentrate on the living.
You're just lucky I'd never fell a female who's expecting.
...expecting what?
I can smell it from here.
You're **pregnant**.
Because death is fucking predictable...

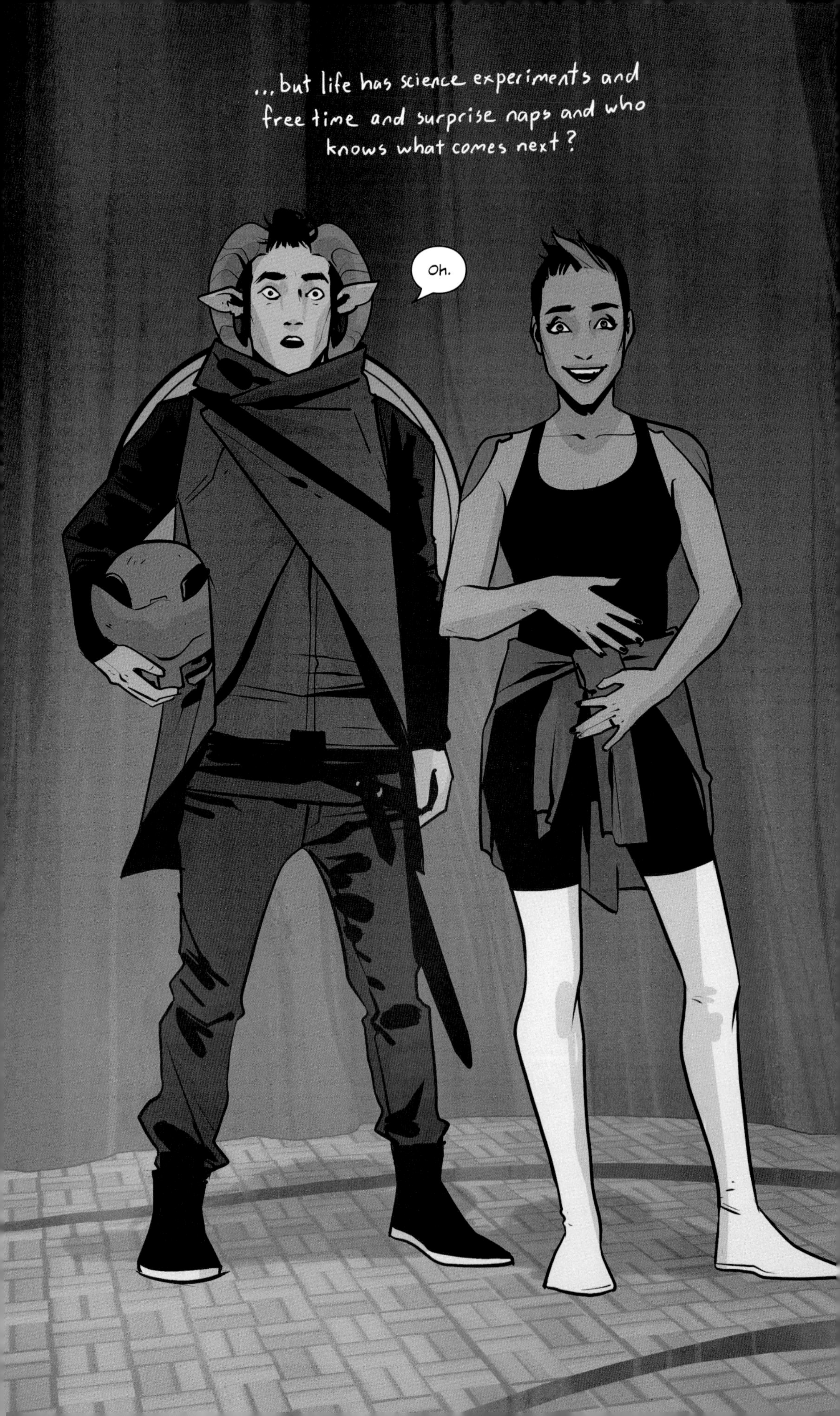
...but life has science experiments and free time and surprise naps and who knows what comes next?
Oh.

to be continued

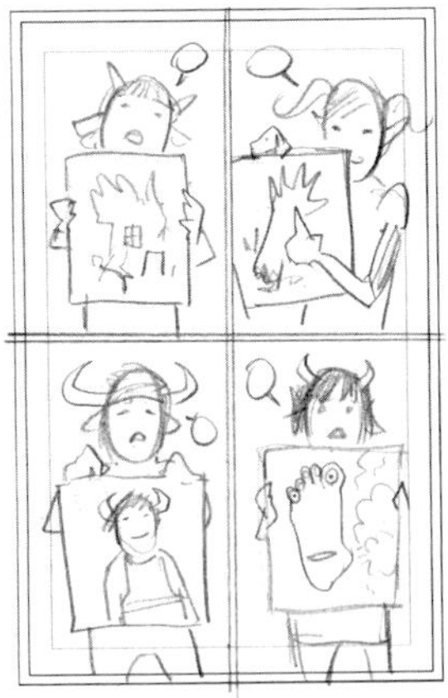
1

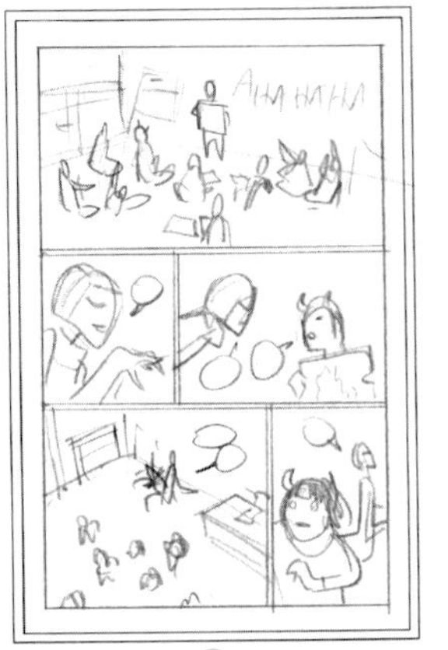
2

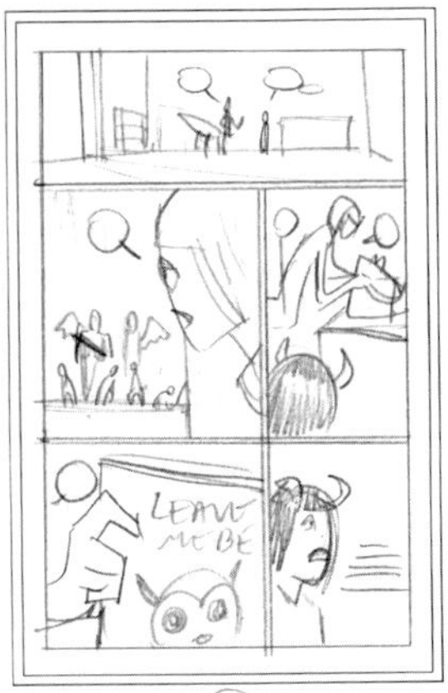
LEAVE ME BE
3

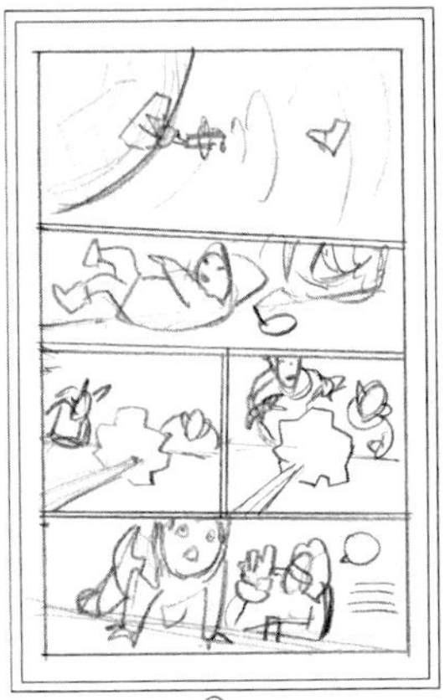
7

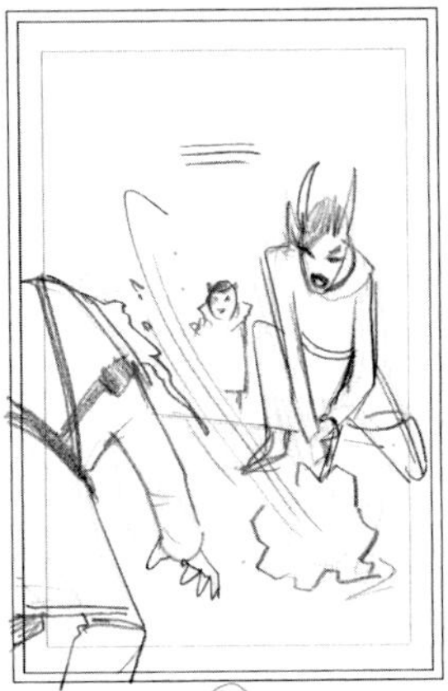
8

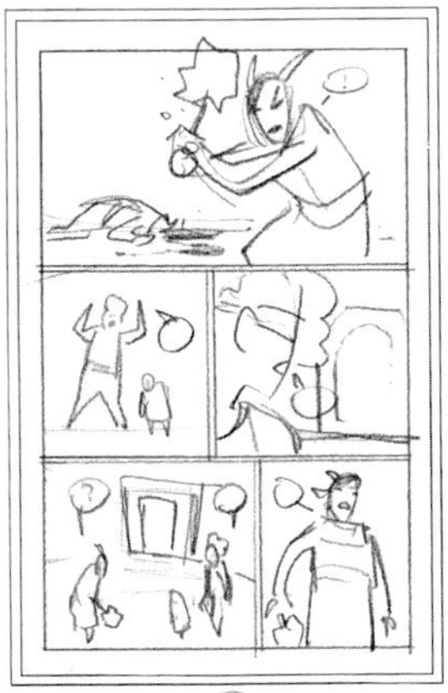
9

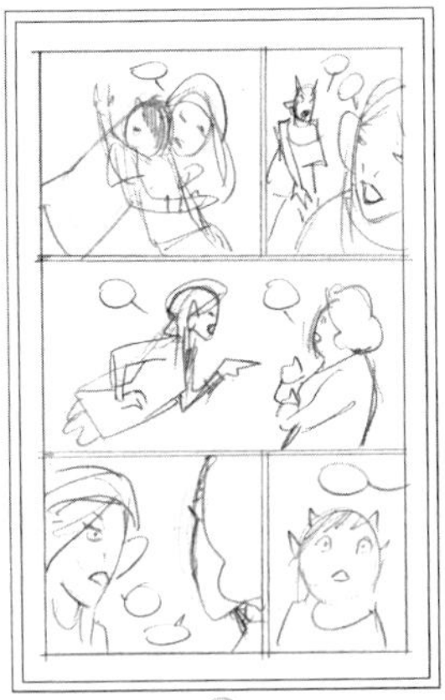
13

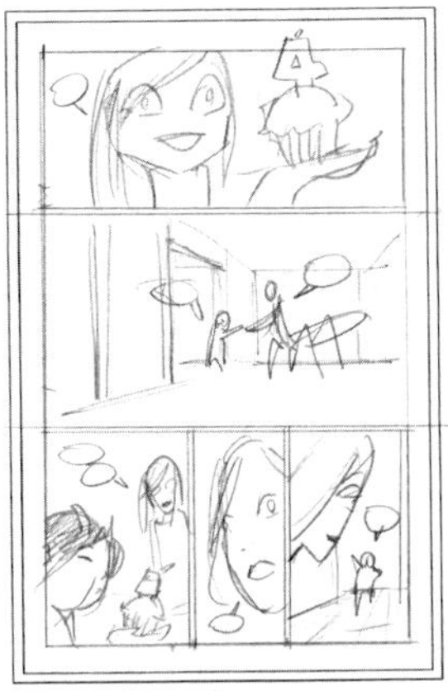
14

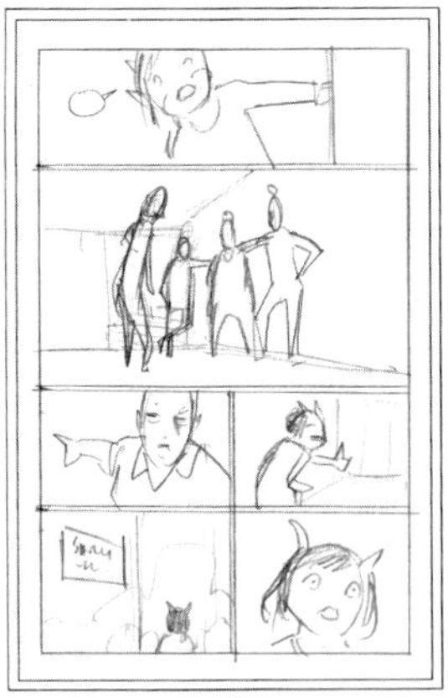
15

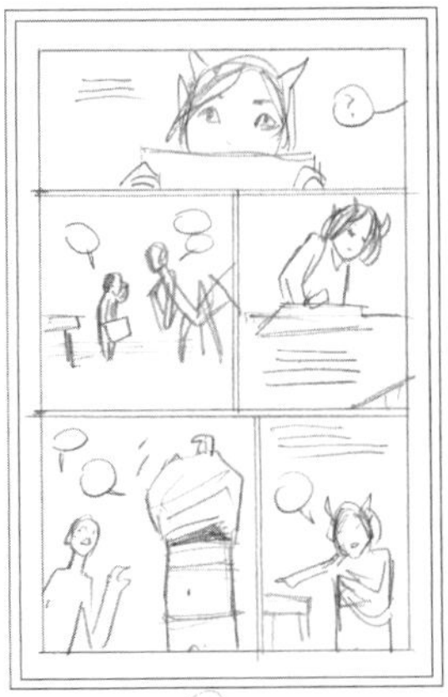
19

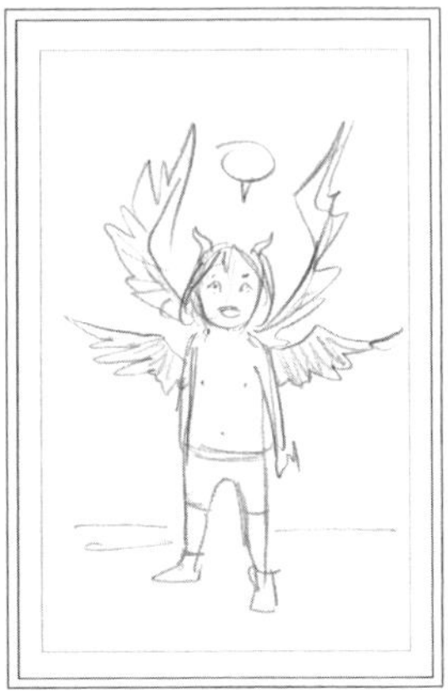
20

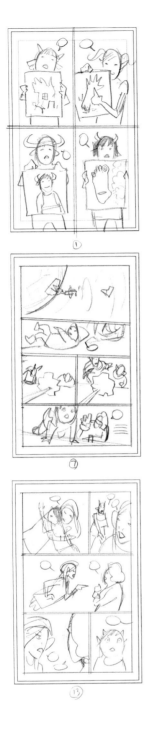

Fiona's thumbnail sketches...

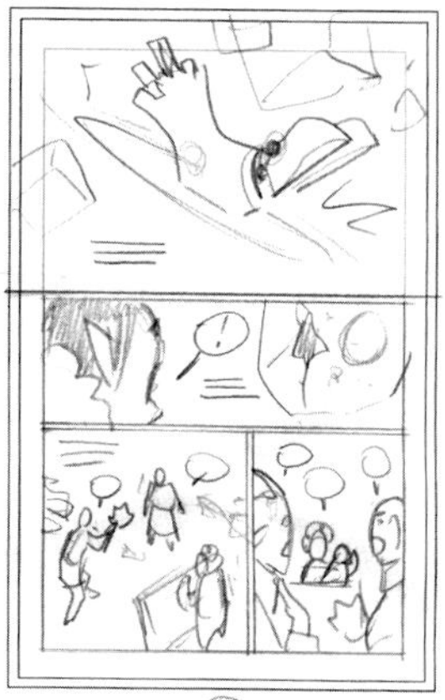

4

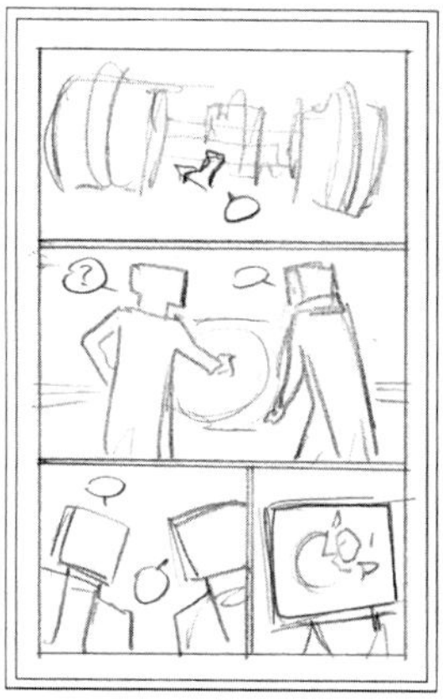

5

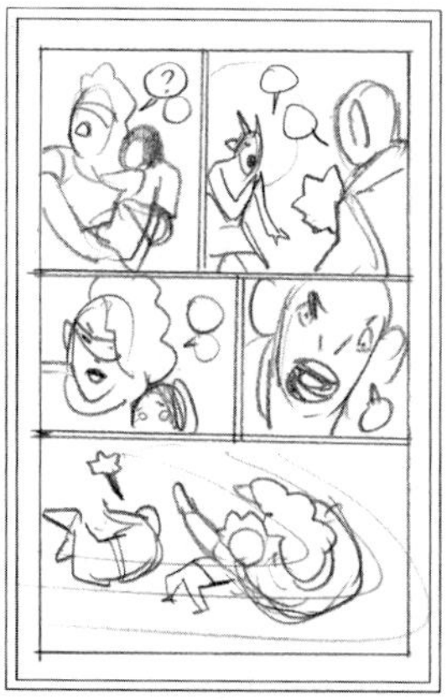

6

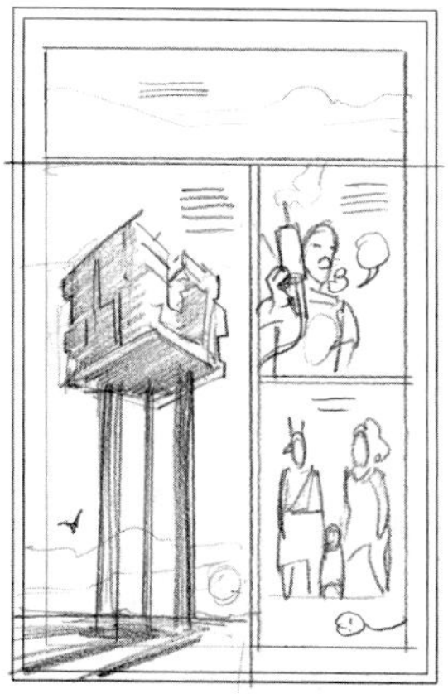

10

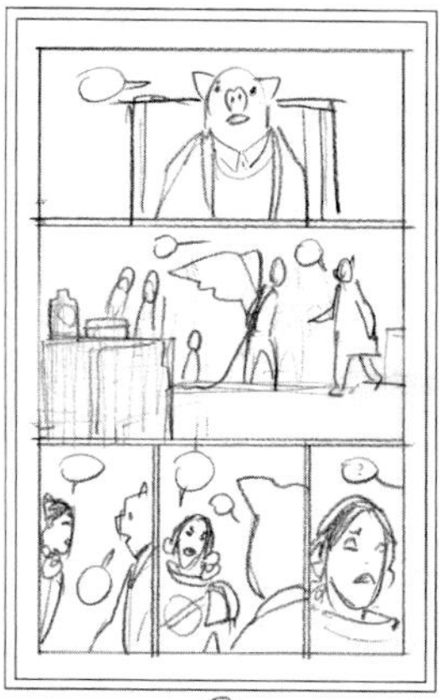

11

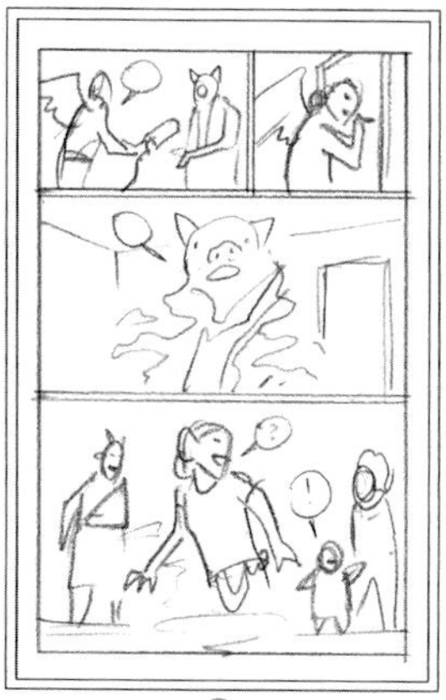

12

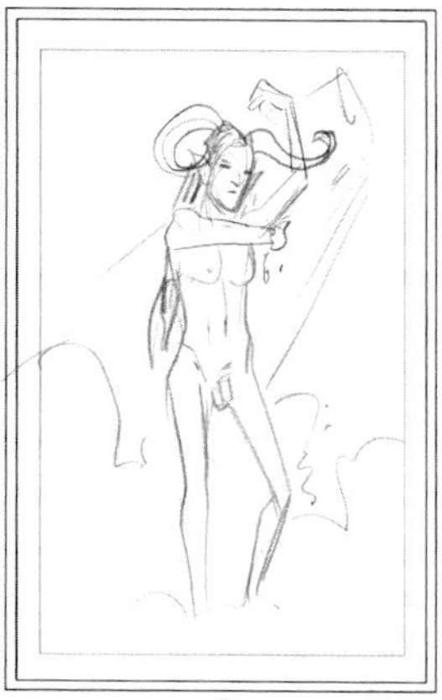

16

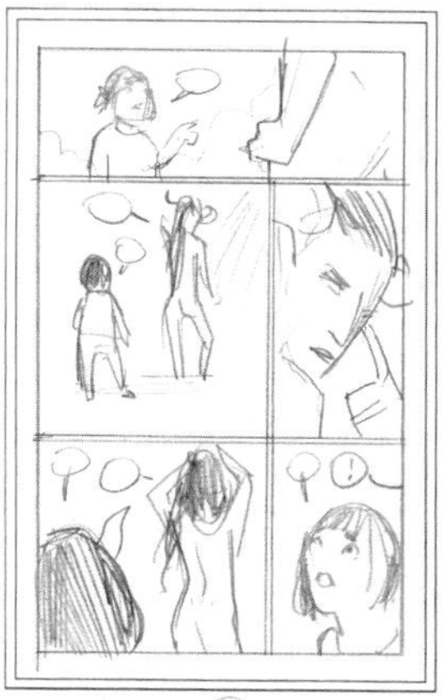

17

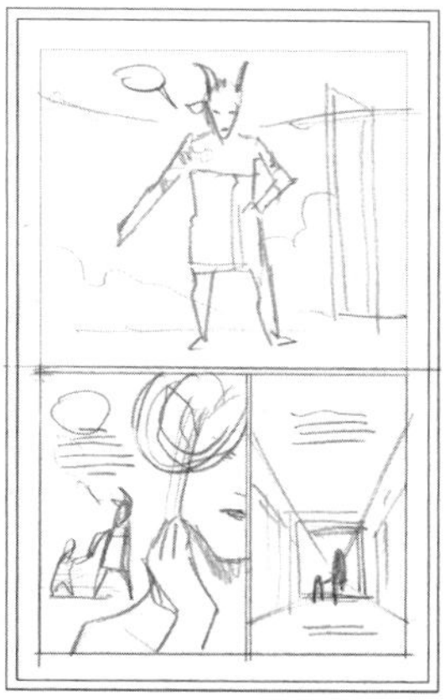

18

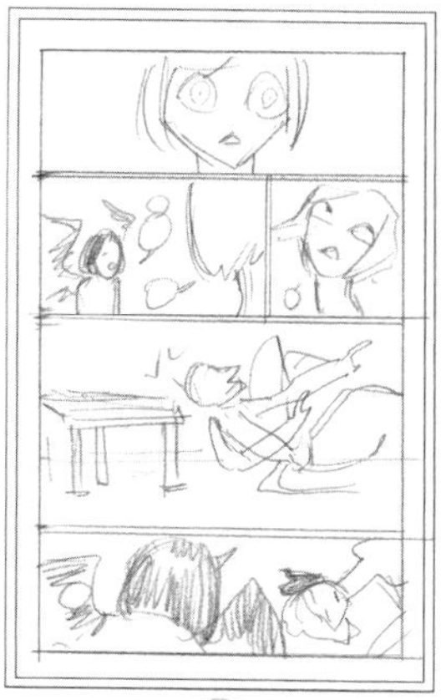

21

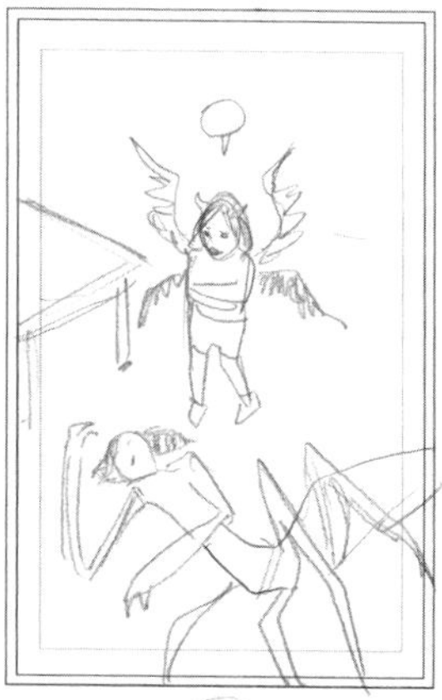

22

…for Chapter Thirty-One.

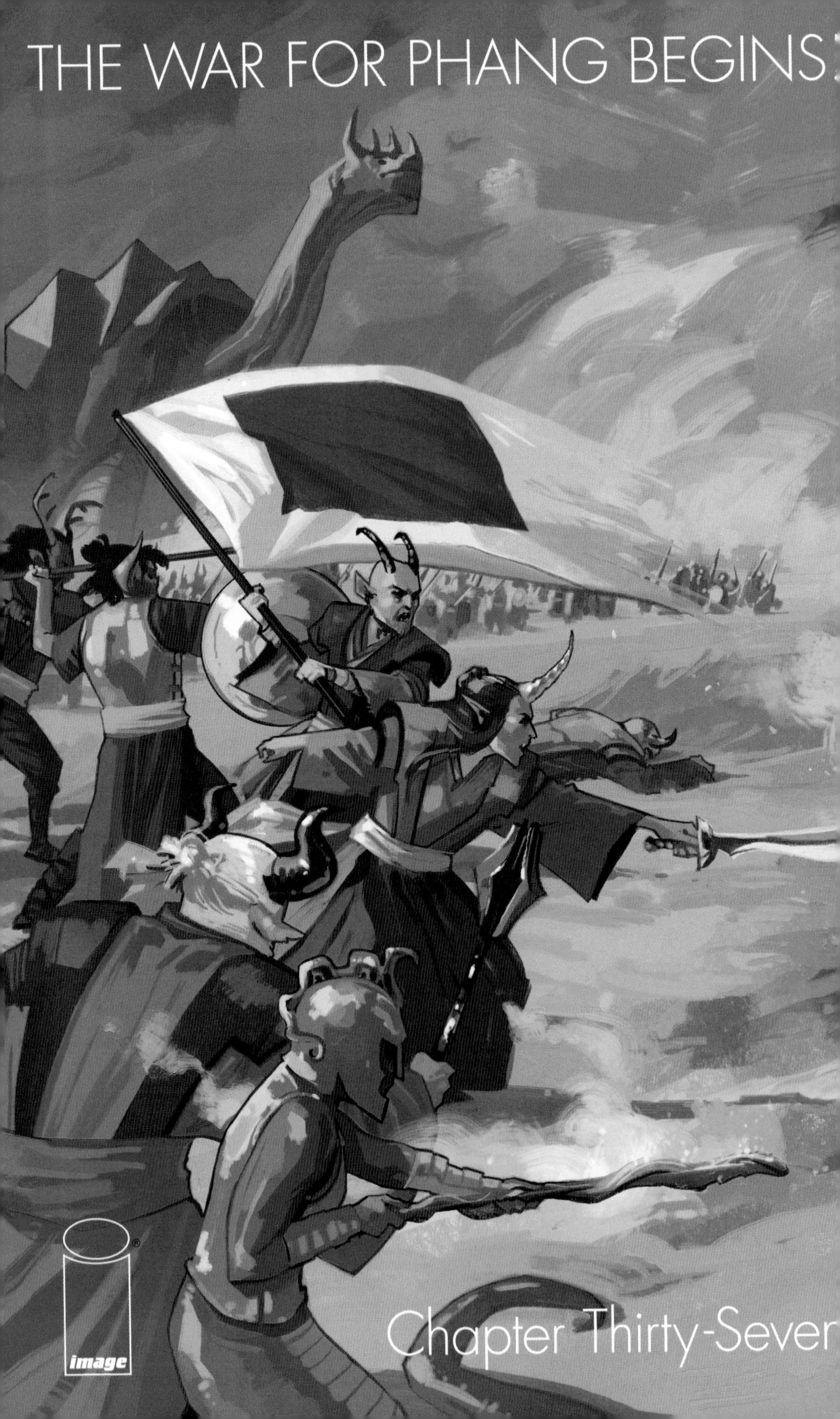
THE WAR FOR PHANG BEGINS!
Chapter Thirty-Seven
image

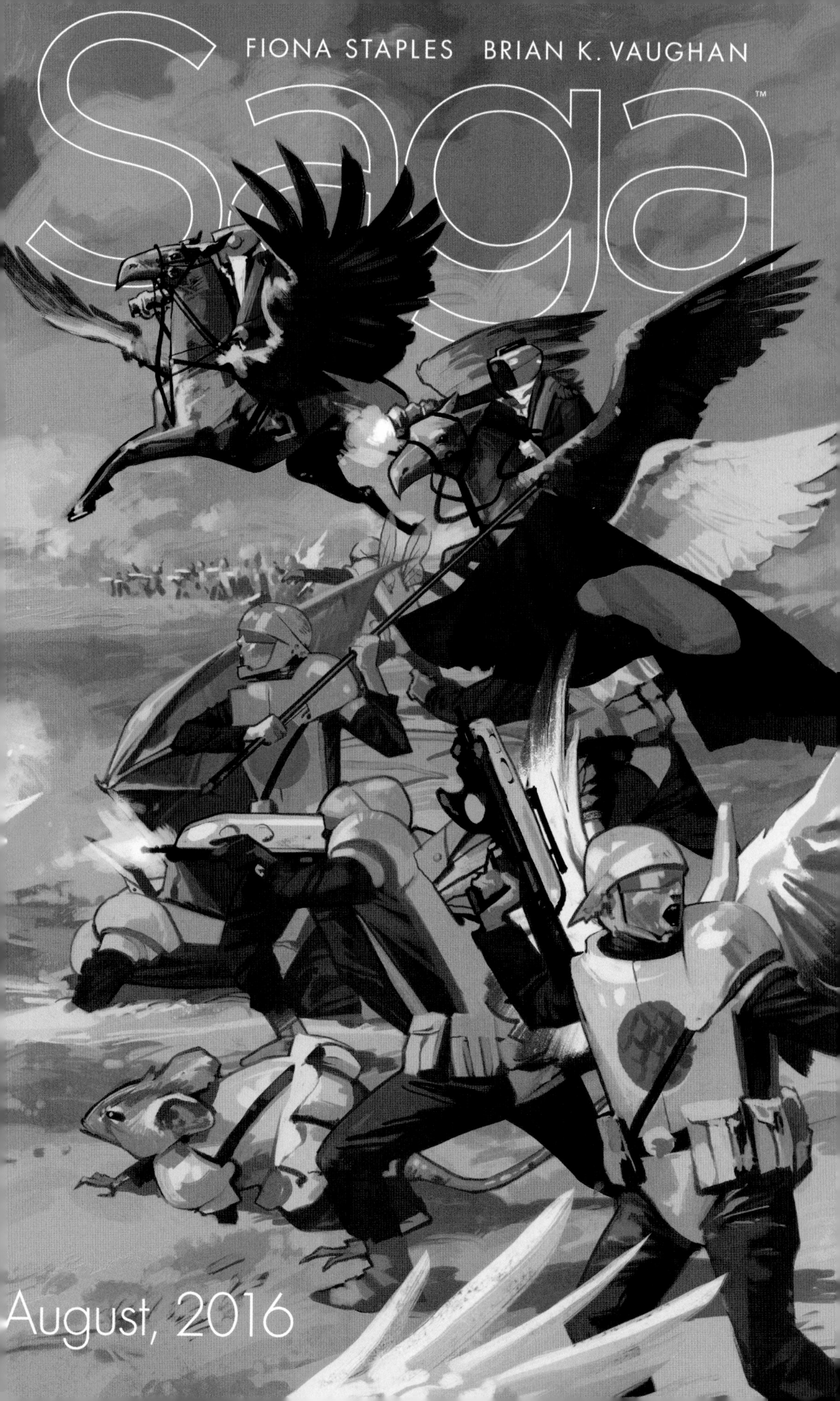
FIONA STAPLES BRIAN K. VAUGHAN
Saga™
August, 2016

ALSO AVAILABLE

BRIAN K. VAUGHAN FIONA STAPLES
Saga
VOLUME
ONE

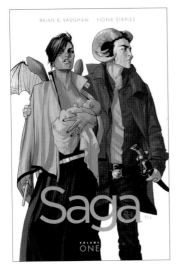

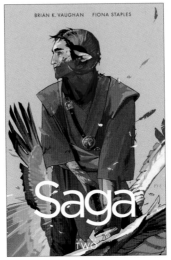

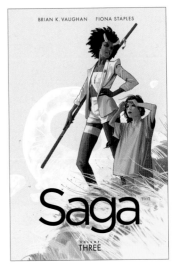

VOLUME ONE
collects chapters 1–6
160-page softcover
ISBN 978-1-60706-601-9
$9.99

BRIAN K. VAUGHAN FIONA STAPLES
Saga
VOLUME
TWO

VOLUME TWO
collects chapters 7–12
152-page softcover
ISBN 978-1-60706-692-7
$14.99

BRIAN K. VAUGHAN FIONA STAPLES
Saga
VOLUME
THREE

VOLUME THREE
collects chapters 13–18
152-page softcover
ISBN 978-1-60706-931-7
$14.99

BRIAN K. VAUGHAN FIONA STAPLES
Saga
VOLUME
FOUR

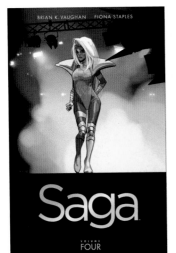

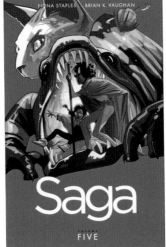

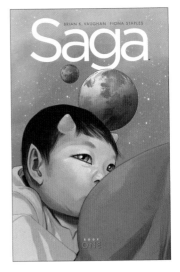

VOLUME FOUR
collects chapters 19–24
152-page softcover
ISBN 978-1-63215-077-6
$14.99

FIONA STAPLES BRIAN K. VAUGHAN
Saga
VOLUME
FIVE

VOLUME FIVE
collects chapters 25–30
152-page softcover
ISBN 978-1-63215-438-5
$14.99

BRIAN K. VAUGHAN FIONA STAPLES
Saga
BOOK
ONE

BOOK ONE
collects chapters 1–18
plus exclusive bonus material
504-page oversized hardcover
ISBN 978-1-63215-078-3
$49.99

imagecomics.com

"ONE OF THE MOST REMARKABLE AND INVENTIVE PIECES OF SCIENCE-FANTASY EVER TO EMERGE FROM THE COMIC MEDIUM." ALAN MOORE

"THE LAST GREAT BOOK I READ WAS CATCHING UP ON SAGA, THE GRAPHIC NOVEL SERIES. AN INCREDIBLE WORLD IN WHICH TO GET LOST." LIN-MANUEL MIRANDA

"STAPLES'S ART IS BOTH OPERATICALLY HUGE AND INTIMATE. A GRAPHIC NOVEL EVERY TWENTYSOMETHING WOMAN SHOULD READ." COSMOPOLITAN

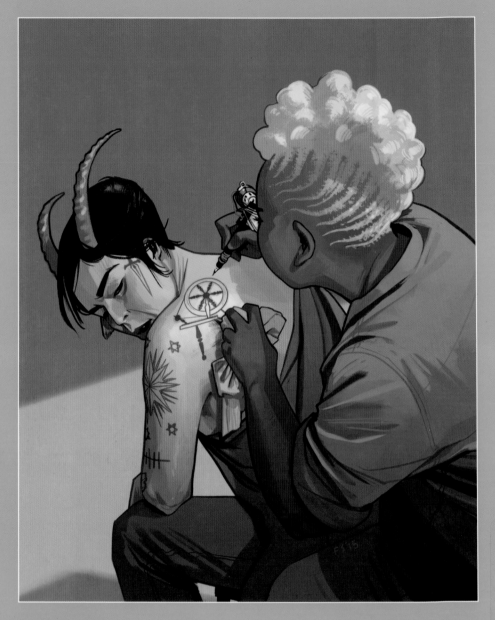

From the Eisner Award-winning duo of FIONA STAPLES (*Archie: Vol. One, North 40*) and BRIAN K. VAUGHAN (*Paper Girls, Barrier*), SAGA is the sweeping tale of one young family fighting to find their place in the universe. After a dramatic time jump, Hazel begins the most exciting adventure of her life: kindergarten. Meanwhile, her starcrossed family learns hard lessons of their own.

imagecomics.com

51499

9 781632 157119

$14.99
ISBN 978-1-63215-711-9
SCI-FI/FANTASY

RATED **M**/MATURE

FRANK MILLER LYNN VARLEY

THE DARK KNIGHT STRIKES AGAIN

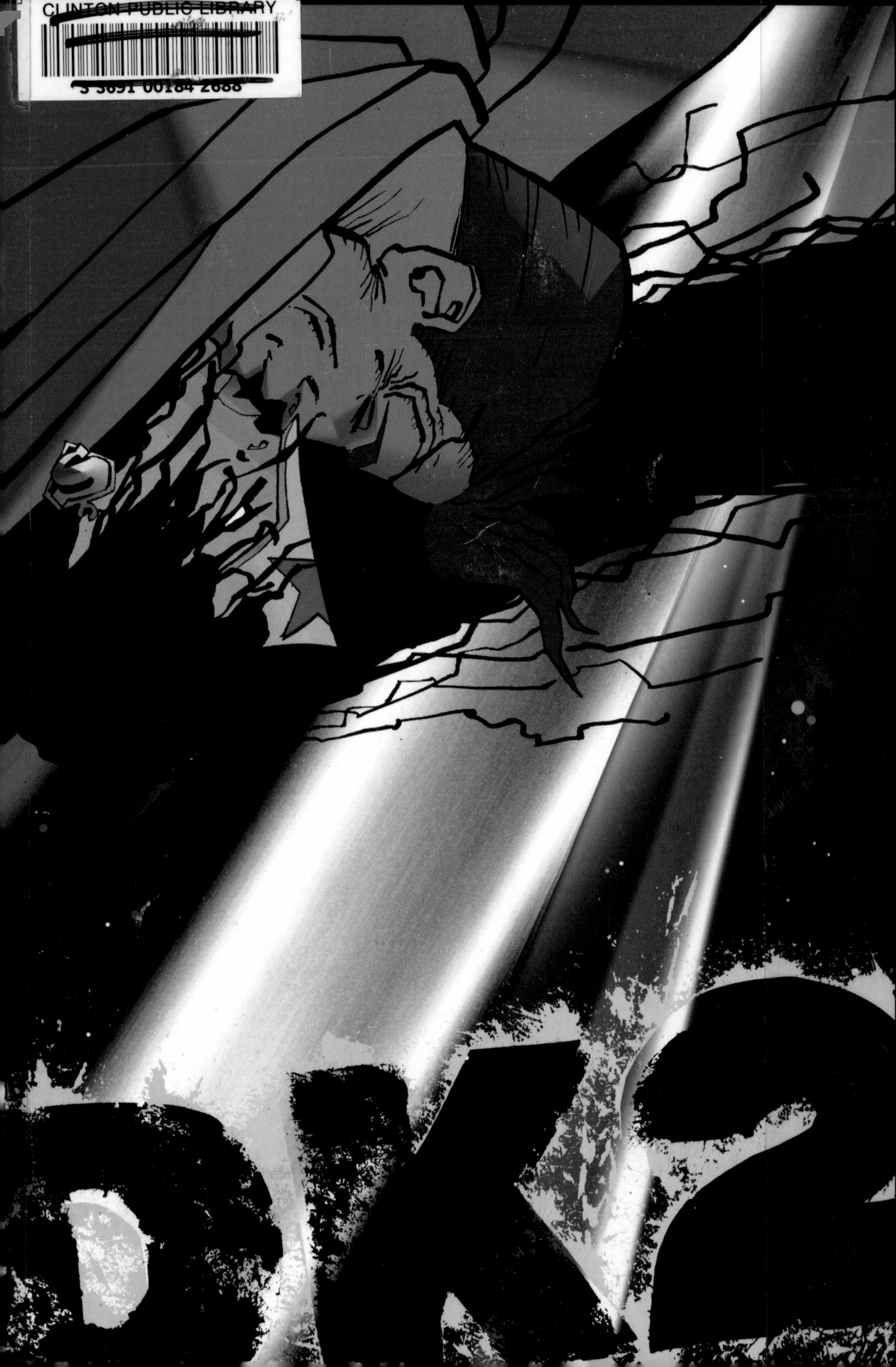

Written & Drawn by **Frank Miller**   Colors by **Lynn Varley**   Lettered by **Todd Klein**   Batman created by **Bob Kane**

The Dark Knight Strikes Again #2. Published by DC Comics. 1700 Broadway, New York, NY 10019. Copyright © 2002 DC Comics. All Rights Reserved. All characters featured in this issue, the distinctive likenesses thereof, and all related indicia are trademarks of DC Comics. The stories, characters and incidents mentioned in this magazine are entirely fictional. Printed on recyclable paper. Printed in Canada. DC Comics. A division of Warner Bros.-An AOL Time Warner Company

Cover Art by **Frank Miller**   Cover Color by **Lynn Varley**   Publication Design by **Louis Prandi**